THE
REMNANT

Also by Tim LaHaye
*   and Jerry B. Jenkins*
in Large Print:

Left Behind®
Tribulation Force
Nicolae
Soul Harvest
Apollyon
Assassins
The Indwelling
The Mark
Desecration

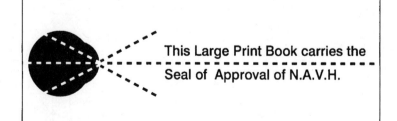

This Large Print Book carries the
Seal of Approval of N.A.V.H.

THE

ON THE BRINK OF ARMAGEDDON

REMNANT

Tim LaHaye

Jerry B. Jenkins

Thorndike Press • Waterville, Maine

Published in 2002 by arrangement with Tyndale House Publishers, Inc.

Thorndike Press Large Print Basic Series.

The tree indicium is a trademark of Thorndike Press.

The text of this Large Print edition is unabridged.
Other aspects of the book may vary from the original edition.

Set in 16 pt. Plantin by Elena Picard.

Printed in the United States on permanent paper.

Library of Congress Cataloging-in-Publication Data

LaHaye, Tim F.
   The remnant : on the brink of Armageddon /
Tim LaHaye, Jerry B. Jenkins.
      p. cm.
   ISBN 0-7862-4818-1 (lg. print : hc : alk. paper)
   1. Steele, Rayford (Fictitious character) — Fiction.
2. Rapture (Christian eschatology) — Fiction.
3. Armageddon — Fiction. 4. Large type books.
I. Jenkins, Jerry B. II. Title.
PS3562.A315 R46 2002b
813'.54—dc21   2002031979

To the memory of
Dr. Harry A. Ironside

Special thanks
to David Allen
for expert technical consultation

Forty-three Months into the Tribulation; One Month into the Great Tribulation

The Believers

Rayford Steele, mid-forties; former 747 captain for Pan-Continental; lost wife and son in the Rapture; former pilot for Global Community Potentate Nicolae Carpathia; original member of the Tribulation Force; international fugitive; undercover in Petra, disguised as an Egyptian

Cameron ("Buck") Williams, early thirties; former senior writer for *Global Weekly*; former publisher of *Global Community Weekly* for Carpathia; original member of the Trib Force; editor of cybermagazine *The Truth*; alias as GC officer Jack Jensen has been compromised; fugitive in exile, Strong Building, Chicago

Chloe Steele Williams, early twenties; former student, Stanford University; lost mother and brother in the Rapture; daughter of Rayford; wife of Buck; mother of fifteen-month-old Kenny Bruce; CEO of International Commodity Co-op, an underground network of believers; original Trib Force member; on undercover assignment in Greece, disguised as Global Community Peacekeeping senior officer

Tsion Ben-Judah, late forties; former rabbinical scholar and Israeli statesman; revealed belief in Jesus as the Messiah on international TV — wife and two teenagers subsequently murdered; escaped to U.S.; spiritual leader and teacher of the Trib Force; cyberaudience of more than a billion daily; visiting the Jewish remnant at Petra

Dr. Chaim Rosenzweig, late sixties; Nobel Prize–winning Israeli botanist and statesman; former *Global Weekly* Newsmaker of the Year; murderer of Carpathia; disguised as Micah, leading the Jewish remnant at Petra

Leah Rose, late thirties; former head nurse, Arthur Young Memorial Hospital, Palatine, Illinois; Strong Building, Chicago

Al B. (aka "Albie"), late forties; native of Al Basrah, north of Kuwait; pilot; former international black marketer; alias as GC Deputy Commander Marcus Elbaz has been compromised; Strong Building, Chicago

Mac McCullum, late fifties; pilot for Carpathia; presumed dead in plane crash; on assignment in Greece, disguised as a senior GC officer

Abdullah Smith, early thirties; former Jordanian fighter pilot; first officer, Phoenix 216; presumed dead in plane crash; on assignment at Petra, disguised as an Egyptian

Hannah Palemoon, late twenties; GC nurse; presumed dead in plane crash; on assignment in Greece, disguised as a New Delhian GC officer

Ming Toy, early twenties; widow; former guard at the Belgium Facility for Female Rehabilitation (Buffer); AWOL from the GC; Strong Building, Chicago

Chang Wong, seventeen; Ming Toy's brother; Trib Force's mole at Global Community Headquarters, New Babylon

Gustaf Zuckermandel Jr. (aka "Zeke" or "Z"), early twenties; document and appearance forger; lost father to guillotine; Strong Building, Chicago

Enoch Dumas, late twenties; Spanish-American shepherd of thirty-one members of The Place ministry in Chicago; recently relocated to the Strong Building

Steve Plank (aka Pinkerton Stephens), fiftyish; former editor of *Global Weekly*; former public relations director for Carpathia; assumed dead in wrath of the Lamb earthquake; undercover with GC Peacekeeping forces, Colorado

Georgiana Stavros, sixteen; escaped loyalty mark center in Ptolemaïs, Greece, with Albie's and Buck's help; captured by GC; whereabouts and well-being unknown

George Sebastian, mid-twenties; former San Diego–based U.S. Air Force combat helicopter pilot; captured by GC while on Trib Force assignment; held northeast of Ptolemaïs, Greece

The Enemies

Nicolae Jetty Carpathia, mid-thirties; former president of Romania; former secretary-general, United Nations; self-appointed Global Community potentate; assassinated in Jerusalem; resurrected at GC Palace complex, New Babylon

Leon Fortunato, early fifties; former supreme commander and Carpathia's right hand; now Most High Reverend Father of Carpathianism, proclaiming the potentate as the risen god; GC Palace, New Babylon

Viv Ivins, mid-sixties; lifelong friend of Carpathia; GC operative; GC Palace, New Babylon

Suhail Akbar, early forties; Carpathia's chief of Security and Intelligence; GC Palace, New Babylon

Prologue

From Desecration

Had Rayford not been petrified, he might have enjoyed that Tsion looked the same in the Jordan sun as he did around the Strong Building. It was Abdullah and Rayford who looked like Middle Easterners in their robes. Tsion looked more like a rumpled professor.

"Who is your pilot?" a GC guard asked.

Tsion nodded to Abdullah, and they were led to a chopper. Once in the air, Rayford called Chloe [in Greece]. "Where are you?" he said.

"We're on the road, Dad, but something's not right. Mac had to hot-wire this vehicle."

"Chang didn't tell the guy to leave the keys?"

"Apparently not. And of course you know

Mac. He's going to hop out and thumb a ride with some other GC while we drive merrily into town, trying to pass ourselves off as assignees from New Babylon to check on the Judah-ite raids."

"You ready?"

"Am I ready? Why didn't you make me stay in Chicago with my family? What kind of a father are you?"

He knew she was kidding, but he couldn't muster a chuckle. "Don't make me wish I had."

"Don't worry, Dad. We're not coming out of here without Sebastian."

When Abdullah came within sight of Petra, Chaim was in the high place with a quarter million people inside and another three-quarter million round about the place, waving to the helicopter. A large flat spot had been prepared, but the people covered their faces when the craft kicked up a cloud of dust. The shutting down of the engine and the dissipating of the dust were met with applause and a cheer as Tsion stepped out and waved shyly.

Chaim announced, "Dr. Tsion Ben-Judah, our teacher and mentor and man of God!"

Rayford and Abdullah climbed down unnoticed and sat on a nearby ledge. Tsion quieted the crowd and began: "My dear brothers and sisters in Christ, our Messiah and Savior and Lord. Allow me to first fulfill a promise made to friends and scatter here the ashes of a martyr for the faith."

He pulled from his pocket the tiny urn and removed the lid, shaking the contents into the wind. "She defeated him by the blood of the Lamb and by her testimony, for she did not love her life but laid it down for him."

Abdullah nudged Rayford and looked up. In the distance came a screaming pair of fighter-bombers. Within seconds the people noticed them too and began to murmur.

In New Babylon Chang hunched over his computer, watching what Carpathia saw transmitted from the cockpit of one of the bombers. Chang layered the audio from the plane with the bug in Carpathia's office. It became clear that Leon, Viv, Suhail, and Carpathia's secretary had gathered around the monitor in the potentate's office.

"Target locked, armed," one pilot said. The other repeated him.

"Here we go!" Nicolae said, his voice high-pitched. "Here we go!"

Tsion held out his hands. "Do not be distracted, beloved, for we rest in the sure promises of the God of Abraham, Isaac, and Jacob that we have been delivered to this place of refuge that cannot be penetrated by the enemy of his Son." He had to wait out the roar of the jets as they passed over them and banked in the distance.

"Yes!" Nicolae squealed. "Show yourselves; then launch upon your return!"

As the machines of war returned, Tsion said, "Please join me on your knees, heads bowed, hearts in tune with God, secure in his promise that the kingdom and dominion, and the greatness of the kingdom under the whole heaven, shall be given to the people of the saints of the Most High, whose kingdom is an everlasting kingdom, and all dominions shall serve and obey him."

Rayford knelt but kept his eyes on the bombers. As they screamed into range again, they simultaneously dropped payloads headed directly for the high place, epicenter of a million kneeling souls.

"Yessss!" Carpathia howled. "Yes! Yes! Yes! Yes!"

Rejoice, O Heavens! You citizens of heaven, rejoice! Be glad! But woe to you people of the world, for the devil has come down to you in great anger, knowing that he has little time.

Revelation 12:12, TLB

One

Rayford Steele had endured enough brushes with death to know that the cliché was more than true: Not only did your life flash before your mind's eye, but your senses were also on high alert. As he knelt awkwardly on the unforgiving red rock of the city of Petra in ancient Edom, he was aware of everything, remembered everything, thought of everything and everybody.

Despite the screaming Global Community fighter-bombers — larger than any he had ever seen or even read about — he heard his own concussing heart and wheezing lungs. New to the robe and sandals of an Egyptian, he tottered on sore knees and toes. Rayford could not bow his head, could not tear his eyes from the sky and the pair of warheads that seemed to grow larger as they fell.

Beside him his dear compatriot, Abdullah Smith, prostrated himself, burying his head in his hands. To Rayford, Smitty represented everyone he was responsible for — the entire Tribulation Force around the world. Some were in Chicago, some in Greece, some with him in Petra. One was in New Babylon. And as the Jordanian groaned and leaned into him, Rayford felt Abdullah shuddering.

Rayford was scared too. He wouldn't have denied it. Where was the faith that should have come from seeing God, so many times, deliver him from death? It wasn't that he doubted God. But something deep within — his survival instinct, he assumed — told him he was about to die.

For *most people,* doubt was long gone by now . . . there were *few* skeptics anymore. If someone were not a Christ follower by now, probably he had chosen to oppose God.

Rayford had no fear of death itself or of the afterlife. Providing heaven for his people was a small feat for the God who now manifested himself miraculously every day. It was the dying part Rayford dreaded. For while his God had protected him up to now and promised eternal life when death came, he had not spared Rayford injury and pain. What would it be like to fall victim to the warheads?

Quick, that was sure. Rayford knew enough about Nicolae Carpathia to know the man would not cut corners now. While one bomb could easily destroy the million people who — all but Rayford, it seemed — tucked their heads as close to between their legs as they were able, two bombs would vaporize them. Would the flashes blind him? Would he hear the explosions? feel the heat? be aware of his body disintegrating into bits?

Whatever happened, Carpathia would turn it into political capital. He might not televise the million unarmed souls, showing their backsides to the Global Community as the bombs hurtled in. But he would show the impact, the blasts, the fire, the smoke, the desolation. He would illustrate the futility of opposing the new world order.

Rayford's mind argued against his instincts. Dr. Ben-Judah believed they were safe, that this was a city of refuge, the place God had promised. And yet Rayford had lost a man here just days before. On the other hand, the ground attack by the GC had been miraculously thwarted at the last instant. Why couldn't Rayford rest in that, trust, believe, have confidence?

Because he knew warheads. And as these dropped, parachutes puffed from each, slowing them and allowing them to drop simultaneously straight down toward the assembled masses. Rayford's heart sank when he saw the black pole attached to the nose of each bomb. The GC had left nothing to chance. Just over four feet long, as soon as those standoff probes touched the ground they would trip the fuses, causing the bombs to explode above the surface.

Chloe Steele Williams was impressed with Hannah's driving. Unfamiliar vehicle, unfamiliar country — yet the Native American, who had been uncannily morphed into a New Delhi Indian, handled the appropriated GC Jeep as if it were her own. She was smoother and more self-confident than Mac McCullum had been, but of course he had spent the entire drive across the Greek countryside talking.

"I know this is all new to you gals," he had said, causing Chloe to catch Hannah's eye and wink. If anybody could get away with unconscious chauvinism, it was the weathered pilot and former military man, who referred to all the women in the Trib Force as "little ladies" but did not seem consciously condescending.

"I got to get to the airport," he told them, "which is thataway, and y'all have got to get into Ptolemaïs and find the Co-op." He pulled over and hopped out. "Whicha you two is drivin' again?"

Hannah climbed behind the wheel from the backseat, her starched white GC officer's uniform still crisp.

Mac shook his head. "You two look like a coupla Wacs, but 'course they don't call 'em that anymore." He looked up and down the road, and Chloe felt compelled to do the same. It was noon, the sun high and hot and directly overhead, no clouds. She saw no other vehicles and heard none. "Don't worry about me," Mac added. "Somebody'll be along and I'll catch a ride."

He lifted a canvas bag out of the back and slung it over his shoulder. Mac also carried a briefcase. Gustaf Zuckermandel Jr., whom they all knew as Zeke or Z, had thought of everything. The lumbering young man in Chicago had made himself into the best forger and disguiser in the world, and Chloe decided that the three of them alone were the epitomes of his handiwork. It was so strange to see Mac with no freckles or red hair. His face was dark now, his hair brown, and he wore glasses he didn't need. She only hoped Z's work with her dad and the others at Petra proved as effective.

Mac set down his bags and rested his forearms atop the driver's side door, bringing his face to within inches of Hannah's. "You kids got everything memorized and all?" Hannah looked at Chloe, fighting a smile. How many times had he asked that on the flight from the States and during the drive? They both nodded. "Lemme see your name tags again."

Hannah's was right in front of him. "Indira Jinnah from New Delhi," Mac read. Chloe leaned forward to where he could see hers. "And Chloe Irene from Montreal." He covered his own name tag. "And you're on the staff of who?"

"Senior Commander Howie Johnson of Winston-Salem," Chloe said. They'd been over it so many times. "You're now the ranking GC officer in Greece, and if anybody doubts it, they can check with the palace."

"Awright then," Mac said. "Got your side arms? This Kronos character, at least a relative of his, has some more firepower."

Chloe knew they needed more firepower, especially not knowing what they would encounter. But learning the Luger and the Uzi — which they knew the Greek underground could supply — had been more than enough to tax her before they left Chicago.

"I still say the Co-op people are going to

clam up when they see our uniforms," Hannah said.

"Show 'em your mark, sweetie," Mac said.

The radio under the dashboard crackled. "Attention GC Peacekeeping forces. Be advised, Security and Intelligence has launched an aerial attack on several million armed subversives of the Global Community in a mountain enclave discovered by ground forces about fifty miles southeast of Mizpe Ramon in the Negev Desert. The insurgents murdered countless GC ground troops and commandeered unknown numbers of tanks and armored carriers.

"Global Community Security and Intelligence Director Suhail Akbar has announced that two warheads have been dropped simultaneously, to be followed by a missile launched from Resurrection Airport in Amman, and that the expected result will be annihilation of the rebel headquarters and its entire personnel force. While there remain pockets of resistance around the world, Director Akbar believes this will effectively destroy 90 percent of the adherents of the traitorous Judah-ites, including Tsion Ben-Judah himself and his entire cabinet."

Chloe's hand flew to her mouth, and

Hannah grabbed her other hand. "Just pray, girls," Mac said. "We all but knew this was comin'. Either we have faith or we don't."

"That's easy to say from here," Chloe said. "We could lose four people, not to mention all the Israelis we promised to protect."

"I'm not takin' it lightly, Chloe. But we got a job to do here too, and this is no safer than a mountain under a bomb attack. You keep your wits about you, hear? Listen to me — we won't know what happened at Petra till we see it with our own eyes or hear it from our people. You heard the lies already, from the GC to their own forces! We know for sure there's only a million people in Petra and —"

"Only?!"

"Well, yeah, compared to several million like they said. And armed? No way! And did we kill GC forces — murder 'em, I mean? And what about commandeering those —"

"I know, Mac," Chloe said. "It's just —"

"You'd better practice callin' me by my GC name, Ms. Irene. And remember everything we went over in Chicago. You may have to fight, defend yourselves, even kill somebody."

"I'm ready," Hannah said, making Mac cock his head. Chloe was surprised too. She knew Hannah had warmed to this assignment, but she couldn't imagine Hannah wanted to kill anyone any more than she did. "The gloves are off," Hannah said, looking to Chloe and then back to Mac. "We've gone way past diplomacy. If it's kill or be killed, I'm killing somebody."

Chloe could only shake her head.

"I'm just saying," Hannah said, "this is war. You think they won't kill Sebastian? They very well already could have. And I'm not counting on finding this Stavros girl alive."

"Then why are we here?" Chloe said.

"Just in case," Hannah said, using the Indian lilt Abdullah had taught her in Chicago.

"Just in case is right," Mac said, hefting his bags again. "Our phones are secure. Keep the solar receptors exposed during the daytime —"

"C'mon, Mac," Chloe said. "Give us a little credit."

"Oh, I do," Mac said. "I give you more than a lot of credit. I'm impressed, tell you the truth. Comin' over here for somebody you've never met, well, at least you, Chloe. And Hannah, er, Indira, I don't guess you got to know George well enough to give a — to, uh, care that much about him personally."

Hannah shook her head.

"But here we are, aren't we?" Mac said. "Somebody was here workin' for us, and best we can figure out, he's in trouble. I don't know about you, but I'm not leavin' here without him."

Mac spun and stared at the horizon, causing Chloe and Hannah to do the same. A black dot grew as it moved their way. "Y'all run along now," Mac said. "And keep in touch."

Rayford's first inkling was that he was in hell. Had he been wrong? Had it all been for naught? Had he been killed and missed heaven in spite of it all?

He was unaware of separate explosions. The bombs had caused such a blinding flash that even with his eyes involuntarily pressed shut as tightly as his facial muscles would allow, the sheer brilliant whiteness seemed to fill Rayford's entire skull. It was as if the glare filled him and then shone from him, and he grimaced against the sound and heat that had to follow. Surely he would be blown into the others and finally obliterated.

The resounding *boom* sent a shock wave of its own, but Rayford did not topple, and he heard no rocks falling, no mountainous formations crashing. He instinctively thrust out his hands to steady himself, but that proved unnecessary. He heard ten thousand wails and moans and shrieks, but his own throat was constricted. Even with his eyes closed, he saw the whiteness replaced by orange and red and black, and now, oh, the stench of fire and metal and oil and rock! Rayford forced himself to open his eyes, and as the thunderous roar echoed throughout Petra he realized he was ablaze. He lifted his robed arms before his face, at least temporarily unaware of the searing heat. He knew his robe, then flesh, then bone would be consumed within seconds.

Rayford could not see far in the raging firestorm, but every huddled pilgrim around him was also ablaze. Abdullah rolled to one side and lay in a fetal position, his face and head still cocooned in his arms. White, yellow, orange, black roaring flames engulfed him as if he were a human wick for a demonic holocaust.

One by one the people around Rayford stood and raised their arms. Their hoods, their hair, their beards, faces, arms, hands, robes, clothes all roared with the conflagration as if the fire were fueled from beneath them. Rayford looked above their heads but could not see the cloudless sky. Even the sun was blotted out by the massive sea of raging flames and a pair of roiling mushroom clouds. The mountain, the city, the whole area was afire, and the fumes and plumes and licking flames rose thousands of feet into the air.

What must this look like to the world, Rayford wondered, and it struck him that the mass of Israelis were as dumbfounded as he. They staggered, eyeing each other, arms aloft, now embracing, smiling! Was this some bizarre nightmare? How could they be engulfed by the slaughtering force of the latest in mass-destruction technology yet still stand, squinting, with puzzled looks, still able to hear?

Rayford opened and closed his right fist, inches from his face, wondering at the hissing flarelike tongues of fire that leaped from each digit. Abdullah struggled to his feet and turned in a circle as if drunk, mimicking the others by raising his arms and looking skyward.

He turned to Rayford and they embraced, the fire from their bodies melding and contributing to the whole. Abdullah pulled back to look Rayford in the face. "We are in the fiery furnace!" the Jordanian exulted.

"Amen!" Rayford shouted. "We are a million Shadrachs, Meshachs, and Abednegos!"

Chang Wong joined the other techies in his department as their boss, Aurelio Figueroa, led them to a huge television monitor. It showed the live feed from the cockpit of one of the fighter-bombers as it circled high above Petra, broadcast around the world via the Global Community News Network. Later Chang would check his recording of the bug in Carpathia's office to monitor the reactions of Nicolae, his new secretary Krystall, Leon, Suhail, and Viv Ivins.

"Mission accomplished," the pilot reported, scanning the target and showing square miles raging in flames. "Suggest subsequent missile sequence abort. Unnecessary."

Chang clenched his teeth so tight his jaw ached. How could anyone survive that? The flames were thick, and the black smoke belched so high that the pilot had to avoid it to keep the picture clear.

"Negative," came the reply from GC Command. "Initiate launch sequence, Amman."

"That's overkill," the pilot muttered, "but it's your money. Returning to base."

"Repeat?" The voice sounded like Akbar himself.

"Roger that. Returning to base."

"That's another negative. Remain in position for visual feed."

"With a missile coming, sir?"

"Maintain sufficient clearance. Missile will find its target."

The second plane was cleared to return to New Babylon while the first, its camera continuing to show the world Petra burning in the noonday sun, circled southeast of the red rock city.

Chang wished he were in his room and able to communicate with Chicago. How could Dr. Ben-Judah have been so wrong about Petra? What would become of the Tribulation Force now? Who would rally what was left of the believers around the world? And where would Chang flee to when the time came?

It was four in the morning in Chicago, and Buck sat before the television. Leah and Albie joined him, Zeke having gone to collect Enoch. "Where's Ming?" Buck said.

"With the baby," Leah said.

"What do you make of this?" Albie said, staring at the screen.

Buck shook his head. "I just wish I were there."

"Me too," Albie said. "I feel like a coward, a traitor."

"We missed something," Buck said. "We all missed something." He kept trying to call Chloe, only imagining what she was going through. No answer.

"Do you believe this guy?" Leah said. "It's not enough to massacre a million people and destroy one of the most beautiful cities in the world. He's chasing it with a missile."

Buck thought Leah's voice sounded tight. And why not? She had to be thinking what he was thinking — that they had not only lost their leadership and seen a million people incinerated, but that everything they thought they knew was out the window.

"Get Ming, would you?" he said. "Tell her to let Kenny sleep."

Leah hurried out as Zeke and Enoch walked in. Zeke plopped onto the floor, but Enoch stood fidgeting. "I can't stay long, Buck," he said. "My people are pretty shaken."

Buck nodded. "Let's all get together at daybreak."

"And — ?" Enoch said.

"And I don't know what. Pray, I guess."

"We've been praying," Albie said. "It's time to reload."

Rayford could not keep from laughing.

Tears poured from him and huge guffaws rose from deep in his belly as the people in Petra began shouting and singing and dancing. They spontaneously formed huge, revolving circles, arms around each other's shoulders, hopping and kicking. Abdullah was glued to Rayford's side, giggling and shouting, "Praise the Lord!"

They remained in the midst of fire so thick and deep and high that they could see only each other and the flames. No sky, no sun, nothing in the distance. All they knew was that they were kindling for the largest fire in history, and yet they were unharmed.

"Will we wake up, Captain?" Abdullah shouted, cackling. "This is my weirdest dream ever!"

"We are awake, my friend," Rayford yelled back, though Abdullah's ear was inches from him. "I pinched myself!"

That made Abdullah laugh all the more, and as their circle spun and widened, Rayford wondered when the flame would die down and the world would find out that God had once again triumphed over the evil one.

An older couple directly across from him gazed at each other as the circle turned, their smiles huge and wonder-filled. "I'm on fire!" the woman shouted.

"I am too!" the man said, and hopped awkwardly, nearly pulling her and others down as he kept one foot in the air, showing her the fire engulfing his entire leg.

Rayford glanced past them, aware of something strange and wondering what could be stranger than this. Here and there within his range of vision, which extended only about thirty feet, was the occasional huddled bundle of clothes or a robe that evidenced a person still curled on the ground.

Rayford pulled away from Abdullah and a young man on his other side and made his way to one of those on the ground. He knelt and put a hand on the man's shoulder, trying to get him to rise or at least look up. The man wrenched away, wailing, quivering, crying out, "God, save me!"

"You're safe!" Rayford said. "Look! See! We are ablaze and yet we are unharmed! God is with us!"

The man shook his head and folded himself further within his arms and legs.

"Are you hurt?" Rayford said. "Do the flames burn you?"

"I am without God!" the man wailed.

"That can't be! You're safe! You're alive! Look around you!"

But the man would not be consoled, and Rayford found others, men and women, some teenagers, in the same wretched condition.

"People! People! People!" It was clearly the voice of Tsion Ben-Judah, and Rayford had the feeling it came from nearby, but he could not see the rabbi. "There will be time to rejoice and to celebrate and to praise and thank the God of Israel! For now, listen to me!"

The dancing and shouting and singing stopped, but much laughter continued. People still smiled and embraced and looked for the source of the voice. It was enough, they seemed to conclude, that they could hear him. The cries of the despairing continued as well.

"I do not know," Dr. Ben-Judah began, "when God will lift the curtain of fire and we will be able to see the clear sky again. I do not know when or if the world will know that we have been protected. For now it is enough that we know!"

The people cheered, but before they could begin singing and dancing again, Tsion continued.

"When the evil one and his counselors gather, they will see us on whose bodies the fire had no power; the hair of our heads was not singed, nor were our garments affected, and the smell of fire was not on us. They will interpret this in their own way, my brothers and sisters. Perchance they will not allow the rest of the world to even know it. But God will reveal himself in his own way and in his own time, as he always does.

"And he has a word for you today, friends. He says, 'Behold, I have refined you, but not as silver; I have tested you in the furnace of affliction. For my own sake, for my own sake, I will do it, for how should my name be profaned? I will not give my glory to another.

" 'Listen to me, O Israel,' says the Lord God of hosts, 'you are my called ones, you are my beloved, you I have chosen. I am he, I am the First, I am also the Last. Indeed, my hand has laid the foundation of the earth, and my right hand has stretched out the heavens. When I call to them, they stand up together.

" 'Assemble yourselves, and hear! Who among them has declared these things? The Lord loves him; he shall do his pleasure on Babylon. I, even I, have spoken.'

"Thus says the Lord, your Redeemer, the Holy One of Israel: I am the Lord your God, who leads you by the way you should go. Oh, that you had heeded my commandments! Then your peace would have been like a river, and your righteousness like the waves of the sea. Declare, proclaim this, utter to the end of the earth that the Lord has redeemed his servants and they did not thirst when He led them through the deserts. He caused the waters to flow from the rock for them; he also split the rock, and the waters gushed out."

As the Tribulation Force in Chicago watched, the fighter-bomber pilot acknowledged to GC Command that he had a visual on the missile originating from Amman. And from the right side of the screen came the thick, white plume trailing the winding projectile as it approached the flame and smoke rising from Petra.

The missile dived out of sight into the blackness, and seconds later yet another explosion erupted, blowing even wider the fire that seemed to own the mountainous region. But immediately following came a colossal geyser, shooting water a mile into the sky.

"I'm —," the pilot began, "I'm seeing — I don't know what I'm seeing. Water. Yes, water. Spraying. It's, uh, it's having some effect on the fire and smoke. Now clearing, the water still rising and drenching the area. It's as if the missile struck some spring that, uh — this is crazy, Command. I see — I can see . . . the flames dying now, smoke clearing. There are people *alive* down th—"

Buck leaped from his chair and knelt before the TV. His friends whooped and hollered. The TV feed died and GCNN was already into its apology for the technical difficulties. "Did you see that?" Buck shouted. "They survived! They survived!"

Chang's brows rose and his chin dropped. His coworkers swore and pointed and stared, groaning when the feed was interrupted. "That can't be! That looked like — no, there's not a chance! How long was that place burning? Two bombs and a missile? No!"

Chang hurried back to his computer to make sure he was still recording from Carpathia's office. He couldn't wait to hear the back-and-forth between Akbar and the pilot.

Rayford had reunited with Abdullah and was standing, listening to Tsion, when the earth opened with a resounding crash and a gush of water at least ten feet in diameter burst from the ground, rocketing so high that it was a full minute before it began to rain down upon them.

The flames and smoke cleared so quickly,

and the refreshing water felt so good, that Rayford noticed others doing what he was. They spread their palms toward heaven and turned their faces to the sky, letting it wash them. Soon Rayford realized he was about a hundred yards from Tsion and Chaim, who stood at the edge of the gigantic abyss from where the water had burst forth.

It appeared Tsion was again trying to gain the attention of the masses, but it was futile. They ran, they leaped, they embraced, singing, dancing, shaking hands, laughing, and soon hundreds of thousands were shouting their thanks to God.

Still, here and there, Rayford saw people grieving, crying out. Were these unbelievers? How could they have survived? Had God protected them in spite of themselves, just because they were here? Rayford couldn't make it make sense. Was it important to know who was protected and who was not and why? And would Tsion speak to that issue?

After several minutes, Chaim and Tsion were able to call the people to order. Somehow the miracle of Tsion making himself heard by a million people without amplification was multiplied in that they could hear him above the rushing sounds of the volcanic spewing water.

"I have agreed to stay at least a few days," Tsion announced. "To worship with you. To thank God together. To teach. To preach. Ah, look as the water subsides."

The noise began to diminish, and the top of the column of rushing water slowly came into view, now three hundred yards above them. Slowly but steadily the spring shrank, in height though not apparently in width. Soon it was just a hundred feet high, then fifty, then ten. Finally it settled into the small lake caused by the initial eruption and crater, and in the middle of the pool the spring bubbled as if it were boiling, a ten-foot-wide, one-foot-high gurgling that looked cool and soothing and seemed capable of adding to the already miraculous water supply.

"Some of you weep and are ashamed," Tsion said. "And rightly so. Over the next few days I will minister to you as well. For while you have not taken the mark of the evil one, neither have you taken your stand with the one true God. He has foreseen in his mercy to protect you, to give you yet one more chance to choose him.

"Many of you will do that, even this day, even before I begin my teaching on the unsearchable riches of Messiah and his love and forgiveness. Yet many of you will remain in your sin, risking the hardening of your heart so that you may never change your mind. But you will never be able to forget this day, this hour, this miracle, this unmistakable and irrefutable evidence that the God of Abraham, Isaac, and Jacob remains in control. You may choose your own way, but you will never be able to disagree that faith is the victory that overcomes the world."

Two

In Chicago Buck tried calling Chloe, then Rayford, then Chang. Nothing. He tossed his phone away, but couldn't sit. "Where's Ming?" he said. "She know any of this?"

"She's gone," Leah said.

"Downstairs? Tell her to let Enoch's people sleep and to get up here."

"My people won't be sleeping now," Enoch said.

"She's not downstairs," Leah said. "She left a note."

"What?"

"Her brother told her something about —"

"Where's Kenny?"

"Sleeping, Buck. He's fine. Now listen. Her brother told her something about her parents, and she's determined to get to them."

"Oh, man!" Zeke said.

"She say something to you, Z?" Buck said.

"Nah, but I shoulda seen it comin'. I just finished her stuff this morning. Cut her hair, all that. Her papers are the best I've ever done. Made a guy out of her, you know. I mean, not really, just made her look — well, you know."

Buck knew all right. Ming was tiny to begin with. She was anything but boyish, but Zeke had cut her hair, showed her how to carry herself as a man, clipped her nails, removed the color from her face. From his stash of clothes and alterations on her old GC uniform, he had turned her into a young, male GC Peacekeeper.

"What name?" Buck said.

"Her brother's," Z said. "Chang. Last name Chow. I didn't know she was gonna be out of here as soon as I got her ready."

"Not your fault. How long has she been gone? Maybe we can catch her."

"Buck!" Leah said. "She's an adult, a widow. If she wants to go to China, you can't stop her."

Buck shook his head. "How long do you think we're safe here with everybody running around the streets whenever they feel like it? Chang's already told us the palace is starting to suspect something. If Steve

Plank heard about it in Colorado, it won't be long before somebody comes snooping around."

"She probably didn't tell you what she was doing because she knew you'd try to talk her out of it."

"I might have tried to help. Find her a ride, something."

"Yeah, like you were going to arrange for a plane and a pilot."

Buck shot a double take at Leah's sarcasm. His father-in-law had groused that she was capable of it, but Buck hadn't been the brunt of it before. "This isn't helpful, Leah," he said.

"Helpful would have been to send Albie with her."

"I didn't know she was going!"

"Well, now you do."

"And I'm willing," Albie said. "But —"

"We can't spare you," Buck said. "Anyway, your cover's blown and we don't have a new one for you yet."

"I can take care of that inside twenty-four hours," Zeke said.

"No! Let's just hope she checks in and keeps us posted." Buck kicked a chair. "How in the world is she going to sound like a guy? She's got that soft, delicate voice."

"Not when she was barking orders at

the prison," Leah said.

"She'd better bark all the way to China, then," Buck said. "Imagine if she gets found out. They discover she's AWOL from Buffer, connect her with her brother, and bingo, he's history. And where does that leave us?"

Chloe hadn't known what to expect, but it wasn't that Ptolemaïs would look like it had been through a war. For so long, the GC had largely left Greece alone. Its being part of the United Carpathian States contributed, she was sure. Nicolae would not have wanted the publicity that came with exposing Judah-ites in his own region. But the network of believers had so flourished that eventually it was too big to hide. Once the first wave of strong-arm tactics swept through and resulted in many facing the guillotine rather than accepting Carpathia's mark of loyalty, the battle between the GC and the Christ-following underground escalated. The administration of the mark of loyalty had begun with prisoners and had not gone well. The leadership had been infiltrated. Two young prisoners had escaped. And once the worst of the guillotining task was over, things got sloppier.

One of the strongest branches of the International Commodity Co-op, Chloe's own brainchild, was headquartered in town. It had become the clandestine meeting place for believers. But the ambush had cost the church there not only Lukas "Laslos" Miklos, but also one of its most beloved senior members, Kronos, as well as the teenager Marcel Papadopoulos. And if the girl who claimed to be Georgiana Stavros was indeed an impostor named Elena, as Steve Plank had heard, then for all Chloe knew Georgiana was dead too.

Few people were on the street in the light of day, and many of them were GC. They saluted politely the Indian and the westerner in high-level officers' garb and smart white caps piped in blue braid. Albie had taught Hannah and Chloe a proper salute, which they soon realized was crisper and more dead-on than most of the real GC used. Indifference was their mask. No eye contact, no talking to each other loudly enough for anyone else to hear. A serious look, close to a scowl, made them look all business. They had places to go and people to see, and their demeanor discouraged cordiality and small talk.

From the GC Palace complex in New Babylon, Chang Wong, through carefully placed confidential memos from pseudo high-ranking palace Peacekeepers, had sparked a rumor in Greece that the brass were sending a top guy to start cleaning up the mess there.

Chloe believed that GC forces who looked at Hannah and her twice were not just lonely men. She assumed they assessed the uniforms and put two and two together. Some had to assume these two were with the new guy, whoever and wherever he was.

Hannah had affected the perfect walk, and Chloe — had she not been so on edge — would have been amused at "Indira." They hurried to a dingy storefront, where a cracked window had been crudely taped. A dusty TV sat on a shelf and pointed to the street, and a half-dozen or so GC knelt or squatted in front of the window watching it. One noticed Chloe's and Hannah's reflections in the window and cleared his throat. The others quickly stood and saluted.

"Just make way, gentlemen," Hannah said, again with her practiced accent.

It was all Chloe could do to compose herself when first she saw Petra burning, and eventually whatever it was that had caused GCNN to pull the plug on the coverage. The milling GC leaned forward and stared at the TV, then at each other. "What was that?" one said. "Survivors?"

Others laughed and punched him. "You're crazy, man."

"Back to work, gentlemen," Hannah said.

"Yes, sir, ma'am," one said, and the others laughed.

"You know the difference between a male and a female officer, son?" Chloe snapped.

"Yes, ma'am," he said, straightening.

"You think that was funny?"

"No, ma'am. I apologize."

"Where's the nearest pub?"

"Ma'am?"

"Hard of hearing, boy?"

"No, ma'am. Three blocks up and two over." He pointed.

"You on duty, Peacekeeper?"

"Yes, ma'am."

"Where are you supposed to be?"

"Squadron headquarters, ma'am."

"Carry on."

The women had left their phones off, having agreed with Mac that they would not use them until after their first contact with the underground or in case of an emergency. Chloe knew her father and her husband would be trying to reach her after what she had seen on TV, but that would have to wait.

A few minutes later a young man in a chair in front of the pub — Chloe guessed him in his early twenties — glanced at them from behind his *Global Community Weekly*. Chloe wondered if the young man would believe her husband used to publish that very magazine. The boy appeared to casually shift position, pulling a corduroy cap lower over his eyes and resting his foot against a window at sidewalk level.

"Did you see what I saw?" Hannah said under her breath.

"Yep. Stick with the plan."

The women treated the lookout as if he were invisible and entered the pub. The shades were pulled and it took a minute to adjust to the darkness. The place carried the stench of stale alcohol and an indifference to plumbing.

A couple of GC at a table in the corner immediately slipped out a back door on the street side. Chloe and Hannah pretended not to notice. The proprietor greeted them apologetically in Greek.

"English?" Chloe suggested.

He shook his head.

A nearby man in a turban rose and said something quickly to Hannah in an Indian dialect. Chloe was stunned at how Hannah covered. She looked the man knowingly in the eye and winked at him, shaking her head slightly. This somehow satisfied him, and he sat.

The proprietor swept a hand toward a row of liquor bottles behind him. Chloe shook her head. "Coca-Cola?" she said.

"Coca-Cola!" he said, smiling, and reached below the counter. Instinctively, Chloe rested her elbow on the handle of the Luger at her side, and she noticed Hannah casually place her hand on the leather strap snapped over the grip of her nine-millimeter Glock.

The man behind the counter kept his eyes on them even when reaching, and now he smiled, bringing into view one ancient glass bottle of Coke. He held up one finger, pointing at the bottle and pushing two glasses across the counter. Chloe lay two Nicks in front of him and carried the stuff to a table.

After a sip, the lukewarm liquid biting at her dry throat, Chloe turned in her chair and quickly surveyed the room. People who had been gawking turned away. "English?" she said. "Anyone?"

A chair scraped and a heavyset man wearing several layers of clothing, his face moist from perspiration, approached with shy, small steps. He saluted politely, though he was clearly not GC. "Leedle Englees," he said.

"You speak English?" Chloe said. "You understand me?"

He made a tiny space between his thumb and index finger.

"A little?" she said.

He nodded. "Leedle."

"Downstairs," Chloe tried. "Where's downstairs?"

The man furrowed his brow, wrinkling the small *216* tattooed on his forehead. "Dounce?" he said.

She pointed down. "Downstairs. Basement. Cellar?"

He held up a meaty hand and shook his head. "Clean," he said. "Wash. Launder."

"A laundry?" she said, and felt Hannah's gaze. This was it.

He nodded.

"Thank you," she said.

"Tank ye," he said, but stood there, thick fingers entwined. Chloe dug half a Nick from her pocket and held it out to him. He took it with a bow and headed for the bar.

"Wonder what they know?" Hannah said quietly. "Rest of the place seems to be waiting for us to make a move."

"Uh-huh," Chloe said. "Let's just sit awhile, then mosey out. The laundry is a front, but people must actually take clothes there."

Hannah shrugged. "Do they have to come through here to get there? I have to think place."

The women sipped their Cokes and glanced at their watches. No one but the two GC had left since they arrived, and no one had entered either. The young man from the chair walked lazily back and forth in front of the door twice. At least two passersby saw the women in uniform and apparently chose not to enter.

Chloe and Hannah stood and wandered out, looking for another entrance that could lead downstairs. "English?" Chloe asked the young man out front. He shrugged, staring at her. "Is there another entrance to this place?"

He shook his head.

"Not around back? Not through the alley?"

He shook his head again.

"I heard there was a laundry here," she said. "I need some cleaning done."

He stared at her. "I see no laundry." His accent was Greek.

"We don't carry it around," she said. "How do I get downstairs to the laundry?"

"Past the toilet," he said, his voice husky. "Back door, this side." He nodded toward the exit the GC had used. He tilted his chair back until it bumped the wall. "But they're closed."

"In the middle of the day? Why?"

He shrugged, pulling his cap lower and turning back to his magazine.

"Oh, well," Chloe said, sighing. Hannah followed her to the corner and out of sight. "I give him thirty seconds," she said.

After a beat, Hannah peeked around the corner. "You're right, as usual," she said. "Gone."

The women hurried back to the pub, went in the back door, past the washroom, and down rickety wood steps. A thin, middle-aged woman wearing a bulky gray sweater and a bandanna that covered her hair and much of her face stood terrified in the light from the window.

"Laundry?" Chloe said.

The woman nodded, a fist pressed under her neck.

"We can bring laundry here?"

She nodded again. Through the edge of a thick curtain hanging in a doorway behind the woman, Chloe spotted the young man. His eyes were wide. She pointed at him and beckoned with a finger.

"No!" the woman said desperately, backing against the wall.

The young man ventured out, a weapon showing under his shirt.

"Uzi?" Chloe said.

"Yes, and I'll use it," he said.

"Take off your cap," Chloe said.

"I'll shoot you dead first," he said, reaching for his weapon.

The woman moaned. "Costas, no."

As he brought the ugly weapon into view, Chloe and Hannah reached not for their guns but for their caps. Revealing their foreheads, they whispered in unison, "Jesus is risen."

The boy closed his eyes and exhaled loudly. The woman slid down the wall to the floor. "He is risen indeed," she managed.

"I almost killed you," Costas said. He turned to the woman. "Are you all right, Mama?"

His mother had buried her face in her hands. "You come disguised as GC?" she said, her English labored. "What are you doing here?"

"I am Chloe Williams. This is my friend, Han—"

"You are not!" the woman said, wiping her face and struggling to her feet. She rushed to Chloe and embraced her fiercely. "I am Pappas. I go by Mrs. P."

"This is my friend Hannah Palemoon."

"You are in the Co-op too?" Mrs. P. said. Hannah shook her head.

"You are from India?"

"No. America."

"You disguised in disguise?"

Hannah smiled and nodded and looked to Costas. "Are we safe?"

"We should move," he said, leading them through the curtain to a huge concrete-walled storeroom full of supplies from all over the world. "The Co-op works as well here as anywhere," he said. "But we are suffering. Only a few of us are left."

"The people upstairs don't bother you?"

"We give them things. They ask no questions. They have their own secrets. Someday, when it serves them, they will turn us in."

"Head of the Co-op in my place," Mrs. P. whispered, her hand over her heart. "No one will ever believe."

"You can't stay long," Costas said. "How can we help you?"

Two young GC Peacekeepers flashed an obscene gesture at Mac as they flew past in a small van; then Mac noticed the look on one's face when the uniform must have registered in his mind. The vehicle skidded off the asphalt and threw gravel as it backed toward him. "We waved!" the passenger hollered as the van stopped. He jumped out. "We waved at you, sir! Did you see us?"

"I did, and I thank you very much." The

driver tumbled out as well, and Mac returned their salutes. "My support staff had an errand headin' the other way, and I have business at the airport."

"We can drop you. Do you need us to drop you? We'll drop you."

"I appreciate it," Mac said, as he shoved his bags ahead of him and climbed in back. "What's goin' on in Petra?"

"We got 'em, sir," the driver said, turning up the radio. Mac rested his forehead in his hand as if trying to listen carefully. He prayed desperately for his comrades. "Smoked 'em all. There'll be nothing left to bury."

"Let me hear it, boys," Mac said, and the two fell silent. Just before the connection was lost, Mac heard enough from the pilot to encourage him. "Well, that is good news, isn't it?" he said.

The passenger turned. "Sure enough. I don't know what to make of that last bit, but we got 'em, we sure did."

At the airport Mac could hardly believe the disarray. What was left of the GC force there looked undisciplined and lackadaisical. That could work only to his advantage. "I need wheels," he told the only Peacekeeper who rose and saluted him in the main hangar. "I need the key to those wheels, I want to store my stuff, and I want to see a Rooster Tail, if it's here."

"Oh, it's here, sir, and we've been expecting you. I'll take your stuff."

"Did I say I wanted you to take my stuff?"

"No, sir, you plain as day said you wanted to store it yourself." He ran to a desk where he dug keys out of a huge cardboard box. "The Rooster Tail's in Hangar 6. The car's the first one on the end. I can bring it to you."

"You do that."

"Oh, almost forgot. I've got to put your code into the computer and —"

"Not before you bring the car, you don't."

"Well, that's true enough." And he ran off.

Mac was aware of others staring at him, sitting straighter, looking busy. But nothing seemed to be going on, no planes coming or going.

"Gonna get us some help here, Commander?" someone called from across the room.

Mac glared at him. "Excuse me, officer?"

"I said, are you —"

"I heard what you said! Now get your seat out of that chair and address me properly!"

The man rose quickly and caught his foot on a wheel of the chair, stumbling before he righted himself and approached. Mac leveled his eyes at him. The man stopped and saluted. Mac ignored it. "You make it a practice to holler at your senior officers across the room?"

"I wasn't thinking, sir."

"You had a question."

"Just wondering if we were going to get some support here, sir. You see how short-handed we are."

Mac looked from one side of the hangar to the other and out onto the runway. "You're overstaffed and underworked, and you know it."

"Yes, sir."

"Am I wrong?"

"No, sir. It's just that, well, we used to —"

"As you were."

The man saluted again and backed away. The younger officer skidded Mac's car to a stop in front of the hangar and opened the trunk. "You want some assistance with that high-speed Transatlantic, sir?"

"I need nothing but a toolbox and to be left to it. What'd you people find in it?"

"Nothing, sir."

"You're not serious."

"We were instructed to leave it for the brass. That would be you, I guess."

Mac pressed his lips together. Was there

nothing Chang Wong could not accomplish with a few keystrokes? "Give me a toolbox and tell me who's handling the Judah-ite roundup."

"Sir?"

Mac cocked his head and squinted at the kid. "You tellin' me we had one of the most successful busts of the underground right under you people's noses out here, and nobody knows a thing about it?"

"Oh, that, no. Yeah, we knew. We know. I just, I mean, what are you asking?"

"Who's handling it? They took an operative alive and I want to see him. I'm under orders to see him."

"Well, I wouldn't know where they were holding him, sir. I mean, I —"

"I didn't expect you to know where they're holding him! Did I ask you that?"

"No, sir. Sorry."

"I expect whoever's handling the operation for us locally will know that. You follow?"

"Of course."

"So who is?"

"Guy with a funny name, sir. You'd have to check at headquarters in Ptolemaïs."

"Happens to be Nelson Stefanich. You in touch with him?"

"Yes, sir."

"Can you make sure he's expectin' me?"

"Yes, sir."

"Tell 'im I expect all the cooperation and information I need as soon as I get there."

"Yes, sir. Now could I get you to give me your six-digit security code for the —"

"Zero-nine-one-zero-zero-one," Mac rattled off, then took the toolbox and drove to the hangar where George Sebastian's plane had been quarantined. He knew where George hid his arsenal, and within seconds he had removed panels in the cargo hold and lifted a directed energy weapon and a fifty-caliber rifle with bipod into the trunk of the car. He could tell from the safety tab George had positioned on the cargo door that the GC had searched the hold. Clearly, they had not discovered the secret panels.

Mac rushed back to the main hangar. "Clean as a whistle," he told the young man, handing the toolbox out the window. "Ptolemaïs know I'm comin'?"

"Expecting you, sir."

George Sebastian pretended to still be asleep. For the last several minutes he had been awake, hearing urgent staticky messages coming to his captors and their earnest, desperate replies, so quiet he could not make out the details.

He lay on his right side, his huge frame pressing into the packed dirt floor. He was cold, stiff, and ravenous. His right arm was asleep from the elbow to the tips of his fingers. He was handcuffed behind his back. George's head and face throbbed, and he tasted blood.

He heard soft snoring behind him. Oh, if only his hands were free. He would position himself to get blood flowing into that right arm again, would move silently into position. And if the sleeping guard was the only one with him, he could pounce, disarm the man, and silence him in a second. George turned painfully, his whole body aching and desperate for food and water. He rubbed his cheek against the soil enough to push the blindfold away from his eye — just enough to get a peek. Sure enough, the guard sat there asleep, one arm dangling, his high-powered weapon in his lap. Strange. Maybe he was wrong, but George thought he had figured out the hierarchy of this crew. The big man, who tried to cover a French accent, was not the leader. He talked a lot, but it was the other one — the Greek man George had not injured — who seemed to hold the cards. Yet, unless he was unusually cunning and was trying to fake George into trying something, he was the one who now slept just a few feet from his prisoner.

George's right arm tingled, but with his left hand he maneuvered enough to feel the handcuffs. Tight and strong. He had broken out of conventional cuffs before, but not ones applied this securely. He heard the door open at the top of the stairs, and the young woman — he'd heard them call her Elena, though she had originally posed as Georgiana — said, "I say give him one last chance, then do what we have to do."

The big man, George's double, clomped down the stairs with his handgun out. Elena followed, unarmed, but called back up the stairs, "Come now, Socrates!"

They've got a dog?

Elena's yell woke the leader, and he stood, clearing his throat and wiping his eyes.

"Anything?" the big man asked him.

"Nah. Hasn't moved."

"Still alive, isn't he?"

"Breathing."

The big man spoke into the ear of the just roused one.

"Really?" the smaller man said. "What time?"

"Nobody knows yet, but today or to-night."

The leader swore.

George hoped the moved blindfold didn't

show. The big man put a heavy boot on his left shoulder and rolled him roughly onto his back. "Wake up, big boy," he said, and the leader added, "Last chance."

George wanted to say, "For what? Uncuff me and take this blindfold off, you coward, and I'll kill you unarmed." But he was determined to remain silent. No satisfaction for these amateurs.

Heavy, awkward steps resounded from upstairs, and the guard with the injured knee slowly made his way down. The big man handed his side arm to Elena and straddled George. He dug his hands under George's arms, bent his knees, and lifted, grunting as he propped George up against the far wall. George let his chin drop to his chest.

"All right," the leader said, "Plato, over there, and Socrates, over here." George thought he was hearing things. He had been one of the few scholarship football players at San Diego State who'd read Greek history, but his mediocre performance on the exams had nudged him toward the military. His mind had to be playing tricks on him. So it was Plato and Socrates who stood six feet from him on each side, their weapons trained on his head? It was the hunger, he decided.

"He tries anything, kill him, but be careful of me."

The leader — George could only imagine his name — knelt in front of him and yanked off the blindfold. George blinked and squinted but kept staring at the floor. Now the man pressed the barrel of his handgun into George's forehead and lifted his face. "Look into my eyes and see how serious I am." George was tempted to spit at him.

"You have been brave, a model prisoner of war. But you have lost. You are down to your last chance. I am willing to waste no more time or energy on you. The only way for you to leave here and see your wife and child again is to tell us what we need to know. Otherwise, I will kill you with a point-blank round through your brain. You have ten seconds to tell me where the Judah-ite safe house is."

George could think of no reason to disbelieve the man. He was weak, wasted, at the end of himself, but he had succeeded. He had given away nothing, and he would not now. No way he would be allowed to go free even if he gave up Chicago. There was one option, but he didn't trust himself to choose it. He could make up a story — a long, rambling, nuance-filled tale anyone might believe. It could include a poisonous gas in the cockpit of his plane that would be triggered by someone trying to fly it who didn't first enter the proper code into the security system.

That might keep the GC from absconding with the Rooster Tail. It might even leave it available for the Trib Force if anyone came to try to spring him. But he was sure Captain Steele and the rest assumed him dead by now, and why not? And if he tried fashioning a story to delay his execution, in his present state he wouldn't be able to keep it straight — and he couldn't risk letting something slip that might be true.

George let his forehead rest on the muzzle of the gun and kept his mouth shut. He did not want to flinch, to grimace, to shudder. He merely clenched his teeth in anticipation of the shot that would deliver him to heaven.

Three

"We were with the group that had the leaders," Costas Pappas explained. "The pastor and his wife. The Mikloses. Old man Kronos. His cousin is still with us. You know who all these people are?"

"We know everything," Chloe said. "But how can you know so much and still survive?"

"Marcel told us the plan the night it happened," Mrs. Pappas said. "The girl was supposed to have been seen by people in the underground who knew her, but it was just a rumor. Everything seemed to add up. Help from the Tribulation Force, a military man, an operative from America, on his way back from the operation in Israel."

"But how did you learn what had happened? What did you do when Mr. Miklos and Mr. Kronos did not check back in?"

"We went looking," Costas said, his lips quivering. Chloe had thought him a bumbling lookout, then an angry young man. But he had to be brave, she decided, to live as he did. This softness touched her. "We knew the plan. We never found the stones at the side of the road. They had either been run over or brushed away. But those animals left that car right where it stopped, not far from there, in plain sight."

"But surely they were watching it," Hannah said, "lying in wait for you."

"We were sure of that," the boy said. "We drove past quickly, trying to appear as if we were not even looking. But we know K's car. It was just a few meters off the road — the lights gone dim, the engine off, a door open. We were desperate to search it, to find out what happened, but we didn't want to be stupid."

"And so . . . ?"

"We waited. We had to. There was no way to know when they would tire of waiting for someone to come, but after a few days, we could not stand not knowing anymore. Kronos's cousin lent us a four-wheel-drive truck, and from topography maps we plotted a way to get to the car from the fields rather than the road. We did it after midnight, slowly making our way from tiny trails through thick woods to the open, rocky plain. Cousin Kronos drove, and two others and I walked ahead in dark clothes to be sure no one saw or heard. It had to be three in the morning before we had brought the truck as close as we dared. We could not see Kronos's car yet, but we knew where it was. When we crawled over a rise where we thought it would come into view, we saw nothing.

"There is no longer money for streetlights, and the battery in the car had long since died. There was no moon and we didn't dare use our flashlights, so nothing illuminated the car. If the GC were waiting to ambush us, they would not have thought of our coming the hard way, especially that far. We were almost upon the car when we finally saw it in the darkness. We listened and watched and even fanned out to see if we could hear any GC. Then we felt in the car and found the bodies. Maybe we were foolish, but we dared shine our lights, just seconds at a time, our bodies hiding most of the light."

Costas quivered at the memory and broke down. He struggled to be understood. "All three of them," he managed. "Shot. Marcel in the face. Back of his head gone. We had to work to pull him from under the dashboard. K took one in the neck from behind. Probably cut his spinal cord. Laslos in the forehead."

"No sign of the American?"

Costas shook his head. "We dragged the bodies, one by one, all the way back to the truck. They stank and were stiff. It was awful. My friend, who was studying criminology before all of this, determined that whoever shot them was probably in the car with them. We also found Marcel's bag, one we had given him. It was under Laslos's body, covered with his blood. It still had a change of clothes and food in it. We do not know what happened to the American."

Chloe told him and his mother what Steve Plank had reported, that the GC boasted the successful thwart of an escape attempt. "There was an impostor for the girl and for our man. Something went wrong and all this resulted."

"The American is alive?" Mrs. P. said.

Chloe nodded. "Being held somewhere. They're probably trying to break him for information, but he's well trained. We're more worried he will get himself killed for not cooperating."

"You must think the GC is stupid," Costas said.

"Sorry?" Chloe said.

"You come here disguised as GC and you think they will just take you to him."

"It's risky, we know."

"It's suicide," Costas said.

"What would you do, son?" Chloe said, realizing that if Costas was younger than she, it wasn't by much.

He shrugged. "The same, I suppose, but I can't imagine it working."

"We have a man inside the palace in New Babylon, or we wouldn't dream of trying this," Chloe said. She began to outline the preparations and Mac's plans.

"Ah, excuse me," Hannah said. "A minute, please?"

Chloe glanced at her, then followed Hannah to a corner.

"Chloe, do they need to know this?"

"We can trust them! They're Co-op."

"But what if they are caught and forced to talk? Don't burden them with all this."

"Think of what they've been through, Hannah. They'll never cave."

"Well, if they do, it's more than just your funeral, you know."

They returned to Mrs. Pappas and her son.

"This works?" Costas said. "The GC falls for this?"

71

"Not for long," Chloe admitted, sneaking a peek at Hannah. "But with the right setup on the main database in New Babylon, we have bluffed ourselves into some remarkable places."

"We just met you," Mrs. Pappas said. "And we will bury you soon."

"We are people of faith," Hannah said, dropping her accent. "And we know you are too. We must also be people of action. We know the odds and we accept them. We don't know what else to do. Would you leave a comrade to a certain death?"

Costas was still emotional. He shrugged. "I don't know. I don't see that you have a choice, but you have a better chance going in with artillery than with disguises. I just can't see it working."

"But we don't know where our man is!" Chloe said. "How do we find that out without infiltrating?"

"What about your man in Colorado? He seems to know so much."

"He can tell us only what he overhears. If he asks for more details than seem appropriate, he'll soon be found out too."

"How does he get along in the GC without the mark?"

Chloe explained Steve's new identity and facial reconstruction, aware of Hannah's loud sigh and slight shaking of her head. "His forehead is plastic. The mark of loyalty would have to be applied under that, and no one can stand looking at him with his skull exposed."

"Please," Hannah said under her breath.

"I want to come with you when you go for your man," Costas said.

"Can't allow it," Chloe said. "We have our papers, our uniforms, and we're covered, for now, on the computer. It would take days to do the same for you."

"I could get a GC uniform, and you could cover for me. I —"

"No," Chloe said. "We appreciate it, but it's not going to happen. We have a plan, and we will follow it, succeed or fail."

"You need more firepower?"

"We do. It would have looked suspicious, bringing in heavy weapons that are not GC issue. Mr. McCullum is trying to get something, either from our man's plane or his car."

"Where is the car?"

"According to Plank, Sebastian's captors also have his car, which he talked his way into at the airport."

"And they wouldn't have searched it for weapons?"

"We don't know and we haven't heard."

Costas motioned the women to follow him to a corner where a large wood trunk was buried under piles of blankets. It was full of Uzis. "Don't ask," he said. His mother provided a large laundry bag into which Costas placed three cloth-wrapped weapons and several clips of ammunition. "Now, you'd better go."

George Sebastian had been told that you never hear the shot that kills you, but how could that ever be proved? He fought to remain composed, not wanting to give his captors the satisfaction of even tensing before the death blast. He held his breath way past what he believed were his final ten seconds, and then could not contain a shiver as he exhaled.

"All right," the leader said, "get him presentable, and fast. Food and water first, then the shower. And do something about this lip. Think of a story for that. We didn't do it."

George opened his eyes and blinked.

"You're still in trouble, California, but none of us is getting fried because of you. I'm taking the cuffs off, but you've got two weapons aimed at you, and all we need is a reason."

When his hands were free, George rubbed

them together, making Plato flinch. George was tempted to scare him with a feigned swing or even a shout.

"Do something about his wrists," the leader told Elena. "Let's go, we've got to move."

They shoved George up the stairs and gave him two sandwiches stuffed with what tasted like summer sausage. The bread slices were nearly two inches thick and dry. He had to press them hard together over the meat to fit them into his mouth. His split lip stretched and bled as he chewed. He sucked eagerly from a bottle of warm, stale water.

George wanted to sit back and take a few deep breaths, but this was clearly not supposed to be a leisurely lunch. He gagged and coughed, but he made sure to force down all the food. His best chance to escape or do some damage would be when he was unbound and they were moving him. He didn't want to invest the mental energy guessing what it was all about, but he felt relieved to be alive and to have accomplished his one objective so far — silence.

When he finished, George quickly scooped bread crumbs from the table and pushed them into his mouth. He chased them with the last few drops of water, tipping the bottle all the way up. Elena snatched it from him and pointed toward a tiny room where he would just barely fit into a shower.

"Clothes there," she said, pointing to the floor. "You probably can't fit through the window anyway, but someone will be outside and armed."

She left and shut the door, and though he knew she and probably the others could hear what he was doing, he looked under a cot and found only dust. He yanked open three drawers of a spindly wooden dresser. Empty. There was nothing else in the room except a window he guessed faced west. He pulled back a paperlike shade, and Socrates leveled his weapon at him.

"Get going!" Elena called from outside the door.

He shed his clothes and edged into the shower. He turned on the left faucet first and was blasted with icy water. He stepped back out and reached in, trying the other. Also cold. He turned both on and let them run a minute. He tried angling the showerhead away from him, but it was rusted into place.

"The tap water is not drinkable!" he heard from outside. He wanted to ask if there was soap or a towel, but he would not speak. Gritting his teeth, George forced himself under the spray. His body jerked and shook, but he let the frigid water flood him from his short hair to his whole body. He vigorously rubbed everywhere for as long as he could stand it, and just as he was turning off the water, he heard the room door shut. He peeked out. Where his clothes had been lay a pile of clean stuff, clearly belonging to Plato, his supposed look-alike. *Great. He doesn't appear nearly as tall.*

A single hand towel lay on the bed. George made it work and threw on the clothes. A nondescript undershirt protected him from a prickly brown sweater. Military-issue underwear was tight. Gray wool socks started to warm him, and khaki pants with a canvas belt were tight around the middle and rode three inches above his ankles. The GC-issue boots were snug but okay.

George pushed the door open, and Elena motioned that he should follow her back to the table where he had eaten. Plato stood watching, weapon in hand, but George wondered how valued the girl was. He could have had her in a headlock before the others noticed, and he could have killed her before they fired.

She awkwardly dabbed at his lip with ointment and massaged his hands and wrists. He studied her face for any sign of weakness. The blood he had seen on her when he thought she was his underground contact was obviously not her own. She was a killer.

Elena pressed a bulge over his eyebrow that smarted, but George would not recoil. If he couldn't stand a little pain, how would he fight his way out of this? It seemed incongruous that she could find ice in that place, but she wrapped some in a cloth and held it against his swollen forehead. She did the same to a knot on the back of his head. Why couldn't she have spared a cube or two for his drinking water?

The food, whatever it was, lay heavy and troubling in his stomach, but he also felt a surge of energy from it. Part of him wanted to do some damage, to show these yokels what an American captive was capable of. Oh, he could do more than clam up. He had already broken one guard's knee, if he had to guess. And all during her administering to his wounds, George had sat close enough to Elena to have blinded her with a two-fingered shot to the eyes, broken her jaw with a punch to the chin, or crushed her to death by flipping the table onto her and dropping his whole body atop it.

Little would have been gained, of course, as he would have been shot. He fantasized about ignoring her and charging Plato, disarming him, butting him with the weapon, shooting Elena, and taking his chances with the two camped outside. That had better odds, but still not good ones.

They were making him presentable and moving him. Why? Someone above them must have wanted to try eliciting information. And they wanted to be sure he was being treated right. George was apparently as close as they had come to anyone connected with the Judah-ites, and that was why he was still alive.

He relished the idea of performing for GC brass. His silence would infuriate them. Better, from his perspective — the higher up you went, the less prepared they were for creative escape attempts. At some point these people would realize he was not going to help them. There would be no information volunteered or beat from him. Finally, at long last, he would be expendable. They would either use him as an object lesson, claiming he *had* ratted out the enemy, or they would execute him. Or both.

George's goal formed slowly in his mind. He wanted to stay alert, to be aware of every nuance. He wanted to know when the GC finally lost patience and realized he was a hopeless, lost cause. Because when they had finally had enough and his end had come, he wanted to be sure to take one or two with him into eternity. He knew from their marks they wouldn't be going where he was. But they'd get to their destination sooner than they thought.

George had to fight a smile as they led him to a Jeep. He was cuffed again, but not until after he had been fitted with a large pair of gloves. *How thoughtful,* he decided. *Protect my tender wrists.*

By the time Mac rendezvoused with Chloe and Hannah at a clearing in the woods north of Ptolemaïs, all had been in touch with the rest of the Trib Force. "I can't wait to see how New Babylon spins Petra," Hannah said. "How can anyone remain an unbeliever now?"

"Who knows when Daddy and Abdullah will be able to leave?" Chloe said. "For all we know, Tsion will want to stay there, if they have the technology to let him continue cyberteaching around the world. I have to think the GC will kill anybody who leaves."

Mac told Chloe and Hannah that squadron headquarters in Ptolemaïs was expecting him, but that he wanted to downplay everything.

"How so?" Chloe said. "Sounds like your way has been paved."

"Yeah, but if I go in there, buttons shining, it's like I'm on display, tryin' to impress. I could give off the smell of a rat without even trying. Plus, if that headquarters is anything like the rest of this place, I'm gonna look suspicious if I don't start rippin' on anybody who's supposed to be in charge."

"Tell us about it," Hannah said. "I hated working at the palace, but the organization and decorum made this place look sick."

"If I was really a senior commander, I'd be pushin' paper to New Babylon for a week about this place. I had hoped to just rush in there, get what I needed, and get going. I wasn't even going to ask 'em for any support, 'cause I oughtn't need it. Now I'm of a mind not to even show up."

"What?"

"Myself, I mean."

"Us, then?"

"One of you."

"I'll go," Hannah said.

"Now, wait a minute," Chloe said. "I —"

"Frankly, I'm leaning toward Chloe myself, Hannah. I don't expect any suspicion, but if worse came to worst and they checked your iris or your handprint, you know you're on file in the palace."

"As a dead woman."

"Well, yeah, but then how would you explain an Indian lady havin' the exact ID marks of a dead Native American?"

"As long as it's not that you don't think I can pull it off."

"You kiddin'? Half the time I look at you and forget who you are. But Chang has entered Chloe's readings under her new name, so even if they got feisty and made a member of my executive staff prove her identity, she'd sail through."

"What do you want me to do, Mac?" Chloe said.

"I want you to be bored."

"Bored?"

"And irritated. You got grunt duty. While the fat-cat boss you came with and his other personnel are takin' a nap at a nice place — where is none of anybody's business — you got assigned to go get the info he needs. Any red tape, any holdup at all, and you're ticked off. Can you work that up?"

"What do you think?"

"Your approach is that this is bottom-end stuff — just give me the info and let me be on my way. Make sure the hostage takers know we're comin' so they don't get spooked, but they'd better have their man ready. The boss is none too pleased that they haven't gleaned anything from him yet, so make way for somebody who knows what he's doing."

"Gotcha."

"That flyboy friend of Abdullah's believes if everything goes well, we can take Sebastian — in cuffs, of course — right back to his own plane and fly out of here tonight."

"Does local have any idea you're planning to take the prisoner?"

"No, and by the time they find out, we oughta be out of here."

"Not going to be easy," Hannah said. "Even if they buy everything up to where we visit him."

"It never is, Indira," Mac said, smiling. "The key, though, is not trying to convince them of anything. You sting somebody by getting them to come your way. Follow?"

"Not sure."

"For instance, if I hinted to you that Rayford or Tsion wanted you to do something you didn't want to do, like head straight back to Chicago right now, your first reaction would be negative. You wouldn't want to do it, you'd refuse, and I'd say, okay then, I can't tell you the rest of it. You'd say what's that, and I'd say, no, you made your decision so you don't need to know. Now I don't know for sure about you, but if I was in your shoes, I'd be all over me trying to find out what the whole story was and whether I made the right decision."

"You bet I would, and I'd wear you down too. You know I would."

"You probably would. But see, you'd be comin' my way then. It wouldn't be me trying to convince you of something. It would be you trying to drag it out of me. I tell you whatever I need to, to get you to do what I wanted in the first place, and you don't realize until later, when you realize I manipulated you, that you were stung and it seemed like your idea."

"Other words," Hannah said, "you're going to somehow make these people beg you to take Sebastian off their hands."

"You got it."

"And they're going to think you're doing them a favor."

"Exactly."

"This I've got to see."

"You will."

"And where am I while Chloe's doing her thing at headquarters?"

"Waiting in the Jeep, eyes and ears open. The impression is, yeah, there are two of you, but it takes only one to pick up directions for the boss."

"And where will you be?" Chloe said.

"On the phone to Chang and then to the kid at the airport. I want that Rooster Tail gassed up and ready to go."

"You going to tell him we'll have a prisoner with us?"

"I'll play that by ear. If we don't find a weapon in George's car, I've got one for him and one for me anyway. You've got your side arms."

"Think we'll need them?"

"At least for show. There's nothing suspicious about a superior officer bringing armed staff with him on a visit like this."

Chang hurried as casually as he could to his quarters during his afternoon break and flew across his keyboard, trying to track his sister. She was better at this than he expected. He wished only that she had let him in on it so he could have helped pave the way. Maybe if she arrived somewhere and discovered he had precleared her for transport on assignment, she would know he was watching.

Peacekeeper Chow was already in the system. Apparently "he" had gotten out of Chicago and found himself a ride to Long Grove, Illinois. Chang was glad his sister had avoided Kankakee and the old

Glenview Naval Air Station. Though short-staffed like everywhere else, they had been burned by Judah-ites for the last time and were impossible to hoodwink. But Chang had never before seen anything on his system that mentioned even an airstrip in Long Grove.

He finally found an executive runway that had recently been reopened for limited commercial routes. With his break time running out, Chang contacted the tower there as a high-ranking official in the GC aviation administration, "requesting routine confirmation of a Peacekeeper from international sector 30 catching a ride on a commercial cargo plane bound for Pawleys Island, South Carolina."

Chang couldn't wait for the response and hurried back to his desk. There it became clear that Suhail Akbar himself was interrogating the first pilot to return from Petra. Chang could only assume that the second was also bound for Suhail's private conference room. With a few keystrokes, he activated the bug in that office to record, and later he would download it from the central system.

Chloe appreciated that Hannah seemed sensitive enough to leave her to her thoughts on the drive back in to Ptolemaïs. "You're okay with my doing this, right?"

"Makes perfect sense," Hannah said. "If I was going to get checked, this would be the place."

Chloe tried to slow her pulse by breathing deeply and trying to doze. It didn't work, but she knew her life depended on what Mac referred to as her ability to play bored. Irritated was all right, if it came to that. But bored would play truest.

Squadron headquarters was on the top three floors of a four-story building with an abandoned first floor that appeared to have been some sort of business.

One of the men Chloe and Hannah had encountered on the street sat in the dark near the elevator at ground level, smoking and reading by the sliver of light from the street. He stood when he saw her and saluted. "Elevator's broke, ma'am," he said. "You want the stairs there behind you."

"As you were. This your assignment?"

"Yes, ma'am. Somebody's got to tell people or they'd wait all day for that thing."

"No one thought of a sign?"

"Yeah, but the commanding officer wants the personal touch."

She nodded. "He's the one I'm here to see. Could you tell him that I'm —"

The young man held up both hands. "I have no way to tell him, ma'am. There's a receptionist up there."

"Thought you people were understaffed."

He shrugged. "Doing what I'm told, ma'am."

The stairs led to a dingy, tiled room with about half the fluorescent lights working. No one was at the receptionist's desk, but another Peacekeeper began to rise from the end of a tired couch. Chloe stopped him with a wave. "What's your role here, son?"

"GC Morale Monitor, ma'am. And telling people the receptionist is not here."

"I can see that."

"Well, telling them she will be right back."

"How soon is 'right back'?"

He looked at his watch. "Supposed to have been ten minutes ago, so should be any minute now."

"Couldn't you just as easily inform Commander Stefanich that Ms. Irene is here from Senior Commander Johnson's staff?"

"Well, I could, ma'am, but I was instructed to —"

"Just do it. I'll take the heat."

"Yes, ma'am. Ms. who from what?"

"Never mind, I'll find him," Chloe said, reaching for the door.

"Oh, I can't let you do that, ma'am. Now,

88

please. I'm sorry I forgot your information."

"Is your hand on your gun, Monitor?" she said.

"No, ma'am, well, yes, ma'am, it is, but not on purpose. I —"

"Read my name badge, son, and get that memorized. Now all you have to know is *Senior Commander* Johnson."

"Got it. One moment."

Chloe shook her head. It was a wonder the GC accomplished anything. The door had barely shut when it opened again and the Morale Monitor gestured her in with a nod. He pointed to a glassed-in office in a corner of the floor where the commander sat at his desk, a female underling stationed outside. "I have to get through her too?" Chloe said.

"Yes, ma'am. That is the commander's secretary."

Most of the other desks were empty, and the lights here were intermittent too. It seemed all this commander had were enough people to keep him buffered. Chloe strode toward the older woman in uniform. The woman smiled expectantly, but Chloe swept past her. "Irene, Johnson's staff, to see Stefanich."

The woman had no time even to protest. Nelson Stefanich looked startled and began to rise.

"Hi, sorry, sir, but Senior Commander Johnson doesn't have time for me to work my way through all your layers. You have some information for him?"

"Of course, but —"

Chloe whipped out her leather bifold and produced her GC ID card. "What do you need?"

"Well, I'd like to visit with Commander Johnson." Stefanich sounded eastern European, she guessed Polish.

"He sends his regrets. The GC brass would like this handled with dispatch, and we understood you were prepared to —"

"Sit down, Ms. Irene, please."

"I really —"

"Please, I insist."

Chloe sat.

"I had hoped to bring your commander up to speed on the ones we chose for this assignment. We are very proud of their —"

"Excuse me, sir, but we understand zero information has been extracted from the rebel operative."

"That's just a matter of time. He is highly trained military, and we have been patient to this point."

"Might I suggest that if your assignees were at the level you say they are, Commander Johnson would not have had to come all this way?"

"Perhaps. But I am happy with what they have accomplished thus far and plan to recommend them for —"

"Do whatever you like, sir, but please send me back to my boss with what he needs to make contact."

Stefanich made a show of pulling a file from his desk drawer, but he did not hand it to Chloe. "Are you not aware of what happened today? This prisoner became immediately less valuable with the success of the attack."

"I understood the results of that are not conclusive. If they were, wouldn't it be broadcast internationally?"

"There were technical difficulties. You will learn that millions of traitors are dead, including their leadership."

"We still don't know where their headquarters are," Chloe said, "or how much of the leadership might be left."

"We have them narrowed to the Carpathian States. Even the rebel would not refute that."

"Sir, are you refusing a senior commander access to your prisoner?"

"No, I'm —"

"Because if you are, I will be the first to fall under his displeasure. But you will be next." She rose. "I'm already late, but showing up empty-handed, well, I don't mind telling you, that is going to fall on you."

"Here you are," he said, offering the file.

Chloe was moving toward the door. "You can put in for commendations for the locals you hired, but you won't be in a position to award them if —"

"Here, no, please," he said, smiling apologetically.

Chloe stopped and looked at him with suspicion. "A folder? I don't want a folder. All I need to give the commander are directions to the prisoner."

"That's what this is! Now, here!"

Chloe stood with her hand on the doorknob, shaking her head. "And your people expect us."

"Of course!"

She stood with her lips pressed together, squinting at Stefanich. She had come this far; she wasn't going to return to him. "Let's have it, then."

He sat reaching, offering the file. She stared him down. Finally he sighed and rose and approached her. Chloe snatched the folder and left.

Four

Chang sat fidgeting at his desk, pretending to work, unable to concentrate. He was supposed to be coordinating flights and convoys of equipment, food, and supplies from production plants to the neediest areas. He had devised a way to make it appear his instructions were logical and complete, even efficient. But the actual transmissions caused no end of delays. Because of a glitch he had introduced into the system, shipments were held for days at remote locations, then delivered to the wrong places. Often the wrong place for the GC meant the right place for the Co-op or the Trib Force.

Chang had received a commendation for his work, somehow covering his tracks and avoiding having the problems traced to him. Something was niggling at the back of his mind now, though. Something didn't make sense.

Ming had left a note informing the Chicago Tribulation Force that she was on her way to see her parents in China. If that was true, why would she go east? It only made sense for her to find a flight to the West Coast. True, the major California cities were rubble and the big airports gone, but there were still many places to fly out of.

Chang considered feigning illness and taking the rest of the afternoon off, but he couldn't risk bringing attention to himself. Too many Trib Forcers were in precarious positions. He needed to be in place for them without suspicion. He watched the clock.

Buck sat with Kenny on his lap and chatted with Zeke and Leah. It was just after eight in the morning, and Leah was riffling through stacks of messages and reports from Co-op people all over the world. Amazingly, the thing was largely working, even with the tragedy of the seas. The sheer audacity of people without the mark of loyalty transporting in their own vehicles gigantic shipments of goods to one another, no money changing hands, boggled the mind.

"Do you know what you have in that wife of yours, Buck?" Leah said.

Buck hadn't learned how to read Leah yet. He wanted to take that as a straight-out compliment, praise for Chloe. But did he detect a challenge? Was Leah implying he was insensitive, that he *didn't* know what he had in Chloe? "Yes, I think I do," he said.

"I don't think he does, Kenny. Do you? Do you think he does?"

"Does!" Kenny said.

"Do you?"

The baby giggled.

"Do you know what you've got in that mommy of yours, sweetheart? She's a genius. She —"

But Kenny heard "mommy" and began to squirm and repeat, "Mama. Mama."

"Thank you, Leah," Buck said.

"I'm sorry," she said, and sounded as if she meant it.

If she hadn't, Buck was prepared to add, "Brilliant. Real smart." That was the effect Leah had on him. She appeared to be trying to distract Kenny by changing the subject, but she should have tried with something that would interest him, not Buck.

"I'm serious," she said. "You know what I've learned here? Chloe knows how many one-thousand-ton or larger oceangoing vessels there were in the world before the seas turned to blood."

"You don't say."

"Say!" Kenny said.

"I do say," Leah said. "Can you guess?"

"I don't know," Buck said. "Thousands, I suppose."

"Can I guess?" Zeke said.

"Z!" Kenny shouted.

"I'm guessin' more'n thirty thousand."

"Ships that big?" Buck said. "Sounds high."

"He's right on the money," Leah said. "What, did Chloe tell you or something? How'd you know that?"

Z couldn't hide a grin. "Yeah, she told me. But that's a pretty good memory, right?"

Buck turned it over in his mind. "What happens to all those ships?" he said.

"Ruined," Leah said. "Dead in the water. Well, dead in the blood anyway."

"And if God lifts the judgment? The blood turns back to salt water, then what?"

She shook her head. "No idea. I can't imagine what it would take to clean a ship of blood throughout its works."

"And the dead fish," Z said.

"Fish!"

"Who could stand the smell? You don't see it on the news, but people who live on the coasts are trying to move. If nothing changes, the smell will only get worse, and the disease and all that. Ugh!"

"Ugh!"

Buck let Kenny run off. "I can't imagine how Carpathia deals with this. You can't spin it, can't gloss over it. Thousands are dying every day, and think of the crews marooned. They'll eventually all die. Hey, Leah, I did a piece a few years back on the surprising dependence Panama had on its shipping industry. What does this do to a country like that?"

She flipped through some sheets. "They're the only country with more ships than Greece," she said. "It's got to bankrupt them."

The mention of Greece made Buck check his watch. "Late afternoon there," he said. "If the plan is working, they ought to be ready to move in when it gets dark."

"Why are they waiting?"

Buck shrugged. "Mac thinks it gives them an advantage. He doesn't know what's going to unfold, but if they have to shoot their way out or try to escape somehow, he figures they're a leg up in the darkness."

Leah sat staring, as if she wasn't listening.

"Something on your mind?" Buck said.

"I was expecting a call or an e-mail by

now. Chloe told me a businessman had something he wanted to ship to Petra. Cheap housing modules of some kind."

"Yeah?"

"Wealthy guy, made a killing in low-cost housing, then became a believer. He's really into the timing. Totally buys into Tsion's charts and graphs, figures the Glorious Appearing exactly seven years from the original agreement between Carpathia and Israel."

"Don't you?"

"Sure. If Tsion told me today was yesterday, I'd believe it." It was clear she had lost her train of thought. "I miss him, Buck. I pray for him constantly."

"We all do."

"Not like I do."

"Yeah, I know."

"What?"

"I know."

"You do?"

" 'Course," Buck said. "Just thinking about him makes you forget what you were talking about."

She looked embarrassed. "That's not true!"

"Prove it."

"We were, uh, talking about ships. Panama and Greece."

"We were onto modular housing, Leah."

"We were, weren't we?"

"We were. Now who is this guy and what do we need to hear from him?"

Leah stood and looked out a pinhole in the black paint that covered the windows. "Not sure," she said. "He's from right here in Illinois. Something Grove. Says we've got less than three and a half years left, and he'd like us to help him figure a way to get his inventory to Petra. Says they could build the houses themselves in no time. You think he survived, don't you, Buck?"

"Survived what?"

"The bombing."

"This guy was in Petra?"

"Tsion!"

"Oh, pardon me. We're back to him. Well, I'm just as concerned about my father-in-law, and Chaim, and Abdullah, but yes, I do."

"Do what?"

"Think they survived."

"We won't be able to tell from the news, will we?"

"No. But Chang should know. He knows all."

Chang had skipped lunch, so when his day was over he went back to his quarters by way of the central mess and filled a bag with food. There was so much he wanted to listen to, but top priority was tracking his sister. He didn't know if his parents were on the move or already in hiding, but they would be vulnerable regardless, without the mark of loyalty. He had sent them contact information on an underground church in their province, but he had never heard back whether they had or would try to make a connection.

How would Ming find them if he didn't even know where they were? And how long would it take her to get to China, heading east out of the United North American States?

The mood was somber in the palace complex. Everyone seemed in a hurry to get to their quarters. It had been a strange day. Who had not seen the attack on the rebels, and was anyone snowed by the so-called technical difficulties that suddenly swept the coverage from the air, just when the pilot clearly said he thought he saw people alive below?

Chang casually glanced up and down the corridor, quickly entered his quarters, and locked the door. He ran his computer through a quick program that checked his room for bugs. It showed his systems, installed by David Hassid and left for his use and safekeeping, still secure and running normally.

Chang wolfed down fruit and crackers, then checked his e-mail. There was his confirmation, addressed to the bogus name he used as an operative of the Global Community aviation administration. "Passenger, GC Peacekeeper Chang Chow from sector 30, riding with pilot Lionel Whalum, Long Grove, Illinois. Flight plan nonstop to Pawleys Island, South Carolina. Round trip for Whalum. Mr. Chow's papers in order, destination San Diego, California. Note: Whalum did not bear the mark of loyalty, but Mr. Chow asserted that he would see to it when they arrived in South Carolina."

Chang fired off a thanks, then searched the database for flights from Pawleys Island to San Diego. A flier scheduled for that route the next day rang a bell in Chang's mind. It was a Co-op pilot. So Ming was using Co-op people to get herself to China. Was Whalum Co-op too? He ran a search against Chloe's records. Nothing. If he was Co-op, he hadn't been used yet, or at least she hadn't logged him. Maybe he used another name, or maybe Chloe was behind in entering her records.

Chang checked the international GC database, and while the search engine looked for Whalum, he finished eating. He came back to the computer to find a photo of and an entire page on Lionel Whalum of Long Grove, Illinois. The man was black, of African descent. He and his wife and three kids had moved from Chicago to the suburbs when his business became successful. He had won many civic and business awards. His loyalty to the Global Community was listed as "unknown, but not suspicious."

Chang switched to another database and copied information for a loyalty oath administration center at Statesville in Illinois. Switching back to Whalum's records, he changed the loyalty designation to "confirmed," documented by the GC squadron in Statesville on the date Whalum had received his mark. If he *was* Co-op, that would take the heat off. And it ought to tip off Ming that Chang was watching out for her.

A tone sounded on Chang's computer and scrolling type informed him, and all other GC personnel, of "the unfortunate loss of both pilots involved in the attack on rebel forces today. Due to pilot error, their payloads missed the target by more than a mile, and the insurgents fired missiles that destroyed both planes. The Global Community expresses its sympathy to the families of these heroes and martyrs to the cause of world peace."

Chang quickly flipped to the hangar manifests and found that both multimillion-Nick aircraft were back and accounted for. The morgue listed both pilots as "deceased — remains delivered from crash sites in the Negev." Their personnel records had already been flagged in red with the date of their deaths.

He called up the recording from Akbar's office around the time the first flier would have returned. There was clear conversation with Akbar's secretary and the pilot being escorted to the conference room. A few minutes later came the pleasantries, the invite to sit again. Then Suhail. "Good effort out there today, man."

"Thank you, sir," came the answer with a British accent. "Perfect execution. Felt good."

"I'm sorry. You're unaware then that your mission failed?"

"Sir?"

"That the outcome was negative?"

"I don't follow, Director. Both incendiaries were bull's-eyes, and the entire area was consumed, as ordered. When I turned for home, the missile had been launched, and according to what I heard —"

"You seriously don't know that you missed your target."

"Sir, if the coordinates were correct, we did not miss."

"There were no casualties, young man."

"Impossible. I saw people there before we launched, and I saw nothing but fire for several minutes before I left."

"The effort was there, as I said. Unfortunately, human error resulted in utter failure."

"I don't . . . I'm not . . . I'm . . . at a loss, sir."

"You will be demoted, and the party line is that you don't know how such a significant oversight could have occurred."

"Begging your pardon, sir, but I am not convinced it occurred!"

"I'm telling you it occurred, and that is what you will tell anyone who wants to know."

"I will not! Either you prove to me we missed our target or I will maintain to everyone I know that this mission went off without a hitch."

"You will see in due time reconnaissance photos that show no loss of life in Petra."

"You've seen these?"

"Of course I have."

"And you have no doubt as to their veracity?"

"None, son."

There was a long pause. The young man's voice sounded pitiful. "If there is one survivor on that mountain, it's a miracle. You know what we dropped there. You ordered it yourself! It can't be explained away, and I won't take the heat for it."

"You already have. You and your compatriot will be reassigned, and you know how to respond to —"

"I will not testify to something I don't believe, sir."

"Come, come, mister. I see the 2 on your hand and the image of our leader. You're a loyal citizen. You contribute to the cause, you —"

"Would the potentate want me to say I made a mistake when I didn't?"

"But you did."

"I did not."

"His Excellency is most disappointed in you, son."

"I'm not doing it, Director Akbar."

"Excuse me?"

"I won't play along. I take great pride in my work. I didn't question the order. I believed these people were dangerous and a threat to the Global Community. I did what

105

I was instructed to do, and I did it right. No one can tell me we missed the primary target or that our 82s didn't waste that whole area and all those people. If you have evidence that proves concretely that they survived, then I'm going to call it what it is. I'll accept no demotion and I won't parrot a party line. If those people are still alive, they're superior to us. If they are still alive, they win. We can't compete with that."

"You realize you leave me no choice."

"Sir?"

"We cannot have personnel shirk responsibility for their own errors."

"You will not be able to silence me."

Akbar laughed and was interrupted by the intercom. "Primary pilot is waiting, sir."

"Send him in."

As soon as Chang heard the sound of the door, the Brit started in. "Tell him, Uri. Tell him we didn't screw up."

"What?"

And the conversation began anew, Akbar blaming the failure on the pilots, the Brit protesting, Uri silent for the moment. "Excuse me a moment, gentlemen," Suhail said. The door opened and closed.

"Kerry," Uri said, "listen to me. He's right. The —"

"He's *not* right! I saw what I saw and I will never —"

"Shh! Listen! You and I both know we launched perfectly. But I was there after you had gone. You heard my transmission. Those people survived the Blues and the Lance, lived through it all."

"Impossible!"

"Impossible but true."

"A miracle."

"Obviously."

"Then we must live with it, Uri. We must make the GC and the world face it. They are a more than formidable enemy, and unless we admit that, we'll never have a chance to defeat them."

"I agree. You heard me try to say it."

"They took you off the air! Now they want to make us the scapegoats. Demote us. Make us admit failure."

"Not me," Uri said.

"That's my man," the Brit said.

They traded encouragement.

"Be strong."

"Don't give in."

"Let's stick together."

Chang checked Akbar's phone.

Suhail had called the medical wing and asked for Dr. Consuela Conchita. Only the day before Chang had read the staff bulletin announcing her promotion to surgeon general of the Global Community. "Connie," Akbar said, "I need two heavy doses of sedative, the quick stuff. My conference room, ASAP. I'll have security here, in case the patients resist. And bring gurneys from the morgue."

"The morgue?"

"I want them cremated."

"You're asking for *lethal* doses?"

"No, no. I just want them out before they leave here, under sheets. The cremation will do the rest, will it not?"

"Kill them? Of course it will. You're asking that we execute two people?"

"This is from the top floor, Consuela."

A pause. "I understand."

Chang grimaced as he listened to the recording of Akbar trying to convince the fliers that he had asked for injections to help calm them. Both began scuffling and shouting, and Chang could tell they were held down and given the shots. And now they were gone. Anyone who had seen either of them land in New Babylon and make their way from the hangar to the palace and to Akbar's office would never admit it or mention it. They had been shot down by the enemy, and that was that.

Chang checked on the planes again. Already their serial numbers had been changed. And the original numbers were marked as lost in action. Somehow the total number of operative GC fighter-bombers in New Babylon did not change.

The story that had scrolled across Chang's screen would broadcast around the world that night. No doubt Carpathia himself would express abject personal sorrow over the losses.

Chang checked the records in Greece and found that Nelson Stefanich had forwarded location coordinates to "Howie Johnson's" team. It was a couple of hours yet till nightfall, when Mac planned to pay the visit. Chang had time to confirm Mac's instructions to the crew at the Ptolemaïs airport to refuel the Rooster Tail and entered into the computer that Senior Commander Johnson had been cleared at the highest levels to fly it to New Babylon.

That done, Chang found Stefanich's cell phone number and called it in to Mac. "Got everything else you need?" Chang said.

"Well, I'd still like to know the disposition of the Stavros kid."

"Nothing on that here, sir. Do you hold out any hope?"

"Always, Chang. But that's just me."

"Ask Stefanich."

"Oh, I will. Hey, Chang?"

"Sir?"

"Who's better than you?"

"Thank you, sir."

Finally, Chang was able to check his other recordings from throughout the day. He located the one emanating from Carpathia's office and backed up to several minutes before Nicolae, his secretary Krystall, Leon Fortunato, Suhail Akbar, and Viv Ivins sat watching the feed from the cockpit of the initial fighter-bomber. Suhail had just told the potentate he had arranged for him to watch live, and Carpathia had expressed excited anticipation. Chang sped through several minutes of setup and of Nicolae welcoming the various ones into the room.

Then, pay dirt. Akbar informed Carpathia that the fighter-bombers were set for takeoff from Amman, and that he could bring that up on the monitor, "if you wish."

"If I wish? Please!"

"Palace to Amman Command," Suhail said.

"Amman. Go ahead, Palace."

"Initiate visual coverage of takeoff."

"Roger that."

Several seconds of silence. Then Carpathia. "Suhail, these are fighter-bombers? Is it an optical illusion? They look *huge*."

"Oh, they are, Eminence. They have been in service only a few weeks. Notice how high they sit off the ground. The gear is the tallest of any fighter ever. It has to be to allow room for the payload."

"That is the bomb, underneath?"

"Yes, sir."

"Talk about huge. It looks massive!"

"Way too big to be carried internally, sir. It's four and a half feet in diameter and eleven feet long. The thing weighs fifteen thousand pounds."

"You do not say!"

"Oh, yes, sir. It's carried on what we call an underbelly centerline station."

"And what is it, Suhail? What are we serving the enemy today?"

"The Americans used to call these Big Blue 82s. They are concussion bombs. Eighty percent of their weight is made up of a gel consisting of polystyrene, ammonium nitrate, and powdered aluminum."

"Is it as powerful as it is large?"

"Excellency," Suhail said, "nothing but a nuclear weapon would be more so. These are designed to detonate just a few feet off the ground and generate a thousand pounds of pressure per square inch. It should kill everything — even the little creatures below the ground — in an area as large as two

111

thousand acres. The mushroom cloud alone will rise more than a mile. And we're dropping two."

"Plus a missile."

"Yes, sir."

"Fire?"

"Oh, Your Highness, that's the best part. Each concussion bomb creates a fireball six thousand feet in diameter."

Chang recoiled at a loud hiss, and he imagined a nearly overcome Carpathia inhaling deeply through his nose and exhaling through clenched teeth.

Later, when the pilots let loose their payloads, Nicolae said, "Suhail! How quickly can we get this on television?"

"I'm sure it's just a matter of a few switches, Excel—"

"Do it! Do it now!"

Someone left the room.

The recording was interrupted only with occasional outbursts from Carpathia. "Ahh! Look! Ohh! Perfect! On target! Both of them. The best revenge is success."

"Absolutely."

"And victory."

"Yes, sir."

"Total and complete," Nicolae said.

Several grunted.

A loud sigh ended in a hum. It reminded

Chang of a lion he had seen at the zoo in Beijing. It had just gorged itself on several pounds of raw beef, roared, yawned and stretched, settled its wide chin on its paws, and sighed like that, followed by a low rumbling from deep inside.

For several minutes they watched, and occasionally someone congratulated Nicolae. "Finally, Your Lordship." That was Viv Ivins. Carpathia did not respond, making Chang wonder if she was still in his doghouse.

To all the other compliments he merely said, "Thank you. Thank you."

The suggestion from the primary pilot to abort the missile launch was immediately rejected by Suhail. "Yes," Nicolae said in the background. "Very good, Director Akbar. The final dart."

When the pilot sounded insubordinate, Suhail immediately countered. Then silence, finally broken by Carpathia. "Was I hearing things, or did he dare cross you?"

"He came right to the edge, Excellency."

"Reprimand him!" Leon squawked.

"I do not believe he meant for me to hear it. He is watching in person what we are seeing on a screen. Of course it sounds like overkill to him."

"But still . . . ," Leon said.

Someone shushed him.

When the missile hit and the pilot began his halting, disbelieving commentary, Chang heard a chair roll back as if someone had stood suddenly.

"What?!" That was Nicolae.

"Impossible!" Fortunato.

"Cut the feed!" Carpathia said, and Akbar repeated it, loud.

Footsteps away from the table and, Chang assumed, toward the monitor. The door opening. The sounds of people leaving, evidently everyone but Nicolae and Suhail.

"Two of our largest incendiary bombs?" Carpathia whispered. "You said one was more than enough."

"It should have been."

"We saw the flames, watched them burn, for how long?"

"Long enough."

Several minutes of relative silence, during which Chang believed he heard Carpathia panting. And when the potentate finally spoke, he sounded desperate and short of breath. "Listen to me, Suhail."

"Yes, sir."

"Are you listening?"

"I am, sir."

"Deal with those pilots. They missed.

They failed. Their eyes deceived them. Do not allow this victory to go to the Judah-ites. Do not."

"I hear you, sir."

"Then contact the other nine regional potentates, personally, on my behalf. Tell them the Judah-ites have raised arms against us and have dealt a severe blow. We shall retaliate. I told them this only recently."

"You did, sir."

"But the time is now; the budget is limitless. I will sanction, condone, support, and reward the death of any Jew anywhere in the world. I want this done as a top priority, by any means. Imprison them. Torture them. Humiliate them. Shame them. Blaspheme their god. Plunder everything they own. Nothing is more important to the potentate. Do you understand?"

"I do."

"Go quickly. Do it now."

"Yes, sir."

"And Suhail?"

"Sir?"

"Send Reverend Fortunato in."

In seconds, Leon came bustling. "Oh, Highness, I don't know what to say. I can't understand it. What went —"

"My dear Most High Reverend Fortunato. Kiss my hand."

"How may I serve you, Potentate? I kneel before you."

"Be still and hear me. Are you still my most trusted devotee — ?"

"Oh, yes, Supre—"

"Shh — my Reverend Father of Carpathianism?"

"I am, sincerely."

"Leon, do you love me?"

"You know I do."

"Do you cherish me?"

"With all my —"

"Do you worship me?"

"Oh, my beloved —"

"Stand up, Leon, and hear me. My enemies mock me. They perform miracles. They poison my people, call sores down on them from heaven, turn the seas into blood. And now! And now they survive bombs and fire! But I too have power. You know this. It is available to you, Leon. I have seen you use it. I have seen you call down lightning that slays those who would oppose me.

"Leon, I want to fight fire with fire. I want Jesuses. Do you hear me?"

"Sir?"

"I want messiahs."

"Messiahs?"

"I want saviors in my name."

"Tell me more, Excellency."

"Find them — thousands of them. Train them, raise them up, imbue them with the power with which I have blessed you. I want them healing the sick, turning water to blood and blood to water. I want them performing miracles in my name, drawing the undecided, yea, even the enemy away from his god and to me."

"I will do it, Excellency."

"Will you?"

"I will if you will empower me."

"Kneel before me again, Leon."

"Lay your hands on me, risen one."

"I confer upon you all the power vested in me from above and below the earth! I give you power to do great and mighty and wonderful and terrifying things, acts so splendiferous and phantasmagorical that no man can see them and not be persuaded that I am his god."

Leon sobbed. "Thank you, lord. Thank you, Excellency."

"Go, Leon," Carpathia said. "Go quickly and do it now."

Five

George felt pretty good, considering. How long had it been since they had put him in the backseat of the Jeep? He was opposite the driver's side with Elena in front of him, Plato beside him. The leader slid in behind the wheel and told Plato to blindfold George again. George liked the fact that he was again sitting on his hands, giving him an excuse to bounce and tumble into Plato. If he timed it right, maybe he could even bang heads with him.

The leader backed up the Jeep and stopped, idling. "Where is he?" he asked, testy.

"There, by the road."

"What is he doing there?" A loud sigh. "Socrates! Come here!" George heard the hobbling footsteps. "Are you finished with the car?"

"Hidden, Aristotle."

"Give me the keys."

"Why? What if I need it?"

"That will ruin everything! Give them to me."

George heard the jangling as Aristotle took the car keys. "Think, man!" he said. "This way, no matter what happens, you have no keys to surrender. And stay away from the road! You have no reason to be outside. Just wait in there." Aristotle lowered his voice, as if thinking a blind Sebastian couldn't hear either. "Remember, the closer you come to the edge, the more believable you are."

"You know I can do it."

"You know I do! You can still produce tears at will? Take it right to the brink. It has to look like you tried everything before you crumbled. Now, I am sorry you are hurt, but this is just as important as what we are doing."

Chloe could see why her father so admired Mac. He was earthy and plain, but he was also meticulous. He had spread the pages of the local GC's Sebastian file on the dashboard of his borrowed car. In the woods north of Ptolemaïs, with the other vehicle — the hot-wired Jeep — hidden deeper in the underbrush, they studied the record. Chloe leaned in from the passenger's side; Hannah peeked over their shoulders from the backseat. All three wore GC-issue camouflage, their faces streaked with grease.

"They were thinkin' when they got this gal that looks like the Stavros girl."

"Georgiana," Hannah said.

"Right. This one's real name is Elena, last initial *A*. Hmm, the only one whose actual name is given. Guess they don't feel any need to protect her. Then a couple of no-account locals, both of which it looks like tried to get out of Peacekeeping duty but wound up on this vigilante squad. Oh, get a load of these monikers."

"One of them's the leader, Mac," Hannah said, pointing.

Mac shook his head. "Aristotle. Other one's Socrates. Real creative. Given this, shouldn't Elena be Helen? Of Troy, get it? And the big guy, the one that's supposed to pass for George. Plato? Oh, for the love of all things sacred! Well, whatever you gotta do to keep track of each other. He's French. Brought in just for this. Sebastian would be insulted. This guy's heavy, but he's under six-two. He's no George."

Mac kept glancing at his watch, and as night fell, they kept reading, memorizing.

They finally had to resort to the dome light and three tiny flashlights. "The original plan wasn't half bad," Chloe said. "Only somebody didn't cooperate."

"I don't know the boy or the other old guy, the driver," Mac said. "But from what I know of Miklos, my money's on him. Anyway, somebody smelled a rat. They were supposed to pick up the girl eight kilometers north of the airport, then have Plato, pretending to be Sebastian, show up just down the road."

"But Sebastian was expecting to hook up with them closer to the airport," Hannah said.

"They must've wanted to be sure the deal was done before he came looking," Mac said. "They're pretty proud of this change of plans. Looks like they originally wanted to take 'em all in, including George, and then threaten to kill the others if George wouldn't talk. Then, even if he did, they were gonna execute 'em together if they wouldn't take the mark."

Chloe had turned the page slightly. "Did we know this?" she said.

"What's that?" Mac said.

"The shootings, all three of them, were done by the girl."

Chloe had that tingling sensation inside

as the zero hour drew near. Mac had studied the coordinates and determined they were about forty minutes from where George was being held. At 2130 hours he called Stefanich on his private cell phone with the number provided by Chang.

Early in the afternoon in Chicago, Buck and Enoch called their people together. "Quick update," Buck said. "Chang has a trace on Ming, and it appears she's probably on her way to San Diego. Then on to China. Problem is, he doesn't know where their parents are, so she couldn't either — far as we know."

"How'd she get to San Diego?" Albie said.

"The long way. Guess she got a ride with some private pilot out of Long Grove to South Carolina, then was able to —"

"Whoa!" Leah said. "Hold on! Long Grove?"

"Yeah. Then she —"

"Buck! Was the pilot this Whalum guy?"

"I don't know. The point is, she —"

"The point is, if it *is* him, he's the guy who wants to ship housing modules to Petra."

That stopped Buck. "I don't get it."

"She might be going to Petra."

"She'll never make it. Security's too tight."

"Tell me about it."

"Maybe she just caught a ride with a guy who's going on to Petra, but she isn't."

"That's worth praying about," Leah said.

"That's why we're here."

"So Ming used a Co-op contact . . ."

"Can we move on here, Leah?"

"Sure, but we haven't even checked him out yet. Don't know if he's legit. And here I thought when Ming was reading through all these records that she was just helping out."

Buck cocked his head at Leah. "Weren't you the one who said Ming was an adult and free to do what she wants?"

Mac was surprised when the phone rang four times. GC policy was that command officers always be available to the brass.

"This is Nelson Stefanich," he heard finally, "and the only reason I'm answering a call from a hidden number is because of a current operation, so state your business."

"Well, Nelly diggin'-a-ditch Stefanich, how in the world are ya?"

"Who — ?"

"Sorry I missed ya today. Howie Johnson, here."

"Yes, sir, Commander. Have we met?"

"Naw, but I hear such good things about ya, I feel like I know ya, know what I mean?"

"Thank you, sir."

" 'Preciate the info you gave my aide today."

"No problem."

"We're 'bout ready to roll here, Nels, and I just wanted to give you a heads-up so you can let your guy Aristotle know we're on our way. I'm assumin' your phone's secure."

"Of course, Commander."

"Good, good. Now I don't want them gettin' spooked. They should be expecting us and not start shootin' the minute they hear us. We want to protect them too, so we won't be drivin' right to their door. We'll approach on foot and when we're within range I'll give out two loud whistles. They should respond with one, and we'll know it's safe to come on ahead."

"Got it. You whistle twice; they whistle once."

"And they understand that as soon as I'm on the scene, I am the ranking officer."

"Oh, yes, sir. Absolutely."

"Pretty creative, the code names, by the way."

" 'Thank you. I —"

"Listen, we keep forgettin' to ask about the original target, a G. Stavros, female, escapee from the pen there. What's the dispo on her?"

"Well, you know she was the source of much of what we know about the Judah-ite underground here, sir."

"So she's a valuable commodity."

"Yes, she was."

"Past tense?"

"Affirmative. Deceased."

"That so?"

"Yes, sir. Still refused the mark, even after providing a lot of information."

"Guillotine?"

"Actually, no, sir."

"You understand the blade is protocol, don't you, Commander Stefanich?"

"Under normal circumstances, yes, sir."

"And the difference here was . . . ?"

"She, ah, well, she began giving us false information."

"Such as?"

"Well, we never did get a straight answer on the location of the underground now. She was one of them caught in the raids of their original meeting places, so we know when she came back she had to know at least one of the new locations."

"Makes sense. Wouldn't give it up, eh?"

"No, sir. In fact, after the third wild-goose chase, that was when she was . . ."

"Executed?"

"Yes, sir."

"How?"

"Firing squad."

"It took a squad to shoot a teenage girl?"

"*Squad* is a euphemism we use, sir."

"I'm listening."

"Anyone past a certain level is authorized to attack enemy personnel with extreme prejudice."

"Shoot them dead?"

"Exactly."

"And then whoever did it shares the credit with the rest of the team? The squad?"

"Right."

"You shot her, didn't you, Commander?"

"Yes, sir, I did."

"Well, that showed remarkable, almost indescribable, fortitude there, Nelson."

"Thank you, sir."

"I know you did it on behalf of and with the deep gratitude of the Global Community, starting right at the top."

"Thank you very much."

"Don't thank me, Commander Stefanich. The fact is that I wish I could personally reward you for that act —"

"Merely doing my duty, sir —"

"Pay you back, as it were, for that service to the cause."

"Well, I don't know what to say. That would be just —"

"All right, Nelly, time's a wastin' here. You inform the Greek philosophers and their lady friend that we'll drop by to see 'em in a bit, hear?"

"Will do. Uh, sir?"

"I'm here," Mac said.

"We're hoping you can help, of course, but you need to know we're pretty happy with this operation."

"Oh, I can see how you would be."

"Well, I may have read something into it, but I got the impression from your aide that you might want to express some impatience with the crew because the prisoner has not yet been forthcoming. We're planning to honor them for what they've accomplished."

"I hear you, Commander. I wouldn't worry about that. I think it's fair to say that we want to respond proactively to their actions as well."

"We'll want to give thanks also, of course, for the miracle at Petra today," Buck said. "That two experienced pilots could miss with such huge bombs at such close range, well, praise the Lord."

The others laughed. "Yes," Albie said, "and for the fact that somehow all the people caught fire anyway, well, talk about amazing."

"But seriously," Buck said, "God is acting

in ways beyond description, and we never want to take for granted his power and sovereignty, his care for us, his protection of our loved ones."

And with that, several kneeling at the safe house began spontaneously to pray and praise the Lord. Enoch led in prayer for the safety of "our new friends, our brother and sisters Mac, Chloe, and Hannah, as they undertake a dangerous mission. Protect them, go before them, send angels to guard them, and may they bring our brother from California out safely so we can all thank him and rejoice with them."

Chloe was grateful when Mac turned in his seat and held out an open palm to her and to Hannah. They both grabbed hold, and he prayed. It wasn't long, and it wasn't eloquent. But it was Mac, and he sounded as if he knew who he was talking to. And that settled Chloe. A little. Temporarily.

When Mac pulled to within what he said should be a half mile from their destination, Chloe was glad for the chance to get out of the vehicle. The ground was uneven but not bad, and she knew a short hike would be good for her nerves. They all turned off their cell phones and carried them in their left rear pockets. Tiny walkie-talkies were set to a unique frequency, set on Low, and carried in the right rear pockets.

Chloe took the safety off the ancient Luger on her right hip, and Hannah un-snapped the leather strap over the grip of her Glock. The three of them strapped loaded Uzis on their right shoulders so they hung near their rib cages.

Mac tossed Chloe the DEW from the trunk, and she angled it over her left shoulder. He handed Hannah a small, heavy canvas bag with extra clips for the Uzi and several rounds for the fifty-caliber rifle, which Mac wrestled vertical, the feet of the bipod pointing away from him. He supported the four-foot-long, thirty-five-pound weapon by cradling the butt in his right palm and wrapping his left hand around the stock.

"Good thing I'm in reasonable shape for one of my vintage," he said. "Pushin' sixty, and I can still outrun either one of ya if the course is long enough."

"Not carrying that thing," Hannah said, and Chloe noticed the quaver in her voice. It was comforting to know she was not the only one scared to death.

"Don't bet on it," Mac said, deftly reaching up with his left foot and slamming the trunk. He held out his compass toward

Hannah's flashlight and started off. "Follow me, ladies."

Mac's boots crunched a steady pace, and Chloe soon found herself perspiring and breathing heavily. But she felt good, and Hannah appeared able to keep up too. The work did not, however, take Chloe's mind off the danger. The bluffs had worked well so far. Maybe too well. If this were going to be easy, they wouldn't be so heavily armed.

Chang tracked Ming to San Diego and noticed she would not be flying out of there until early evening, West Coast time. He called her cell phone.

"Hello, Chang," she said.

"Where are you?"

"Is this a test? Do you think I'm going to try to convince you I'm at the safe house in Chicago?"

"You have to know I've talked to them."

"Of course. And I can tell from the benefits to my pilots that it didn't take you long to track me."

"But where are you specifically, Ming, and what are you doing?"

She sighed. "I am in a tiny charter terminal south of San Diego. My papers and my look are working perfectly. No one asks to see my mark because I am in uniform, and when the pilots see my believer's mark, they become very protective."

"You don't tell them who you are, do you?"

"Yes, Chang. I am a fool. No! Of course not. Why burden them with something that could bring them trouble? They cannot be held responsible for what they do not know. This is the perfect cover. They are helping the Global Community by transporting an employee. They know secretly I'm a believer, but they don't know I'm a woman, or former GC, or AWOL."

"Ming, you know Father and Mother are not at home."

"I assumed."

"Then how will you find them?"

"I will ask around, in my official capacity. Maybe I will arrest them."

"You have not thought this through."

"I have, Chang. More than you know. They have to contact you somehow before I get there. You can tell them I am coming and we can set a meeting place."

"Why didn't we try to arrange this before you left?"

"Because you would have refused. You think you know so much. Well, you *do*. But you don't know everything, or you would know that I cannot sit in a safe house while my parents flee for their lives. Do we know they are true believers, or have we just talked them out of taking the mark of loyalty? I must know. I must get them together with believers. I know I cannot save their lives or even my own. But I have to do something."

Chang was moved. So she *had* thought it through. Maybe not every detail. Maybe not strategy. But who could?

"You must let me know where you are as soon as you get there," he said.

"You love me, don't you, Chang?"

"Of course."

"We never tell each other. We never have."

"I know," he said. "But we know we do."

"You cannot say it."

"Yes, I can," he said, "but even thinking about it makes me emotional, and I must not allow that. Not right now."

"You, emotional? Impossible."

"Don't say that, Ming. If you say that, you don't know me."

"I'm sorry, Chang. I was teasing you."

"Well the truth is, sister, I do love you." Chang immediately teared up, and he felt a lump in his throat. "I love you with all my heart, and I worry about you and pray for you."

"Thank you, Chang. Don't now. It's all right. I didn't want to make you uncomfortable. And anyway, I know. I know, okay? I love you too and pray for you often. You *do* need to stay rational and practical, so don't worry about me."

"How can I not?"

"Because I go with God. He will protect me. And if he decides my time is up, it won't be that long before I see you again anyway."

"Don't say that!"

"Come, come, Chang. It's all right. You know it's true. There are no guarantees anymore, except we know where we are going. I will call you from China. I will be hoping for good news about Father and Mother."

After about ten minutes' walking, Chloe moved aside and let Hannah fall in behind Mac. Hannah gave her a long look in the low light, as if to ask if she were all right. "It's okay," Chloe said. "I'll be right behind you." She'd had a little trouble staying with Mac, but she decided if she was behind Hannah she'd be more motivated. If Hannah could stay with Mac, she could too.

And she was right. Chloe didn't want to give either of them the idea she was petering out. In fact, she didn't believe she was. They were on a gravel road now, and she had a rhythm going and her breathing was steady and deep. She was sweating through her clothes, but Mac and Hannah had to be doing the same.

Finally Mac held up his right hand briefly before having to get it under the fifty-caliber again. He slowed and stopped, moving to the side of the road and turning to face the women. "Everybody okay?"

They both nodded.

"Anybody need a breather?"

Though panting, both shook their heads.

"Almost there," he said, and they started uphill. Just over a rise Mac knelt and lay the fifty-caliber on the ground. He made a *V* with his fingers under his eyes, then pointed through a clearing to a small, wood shack. A faint light shone through the sliver between a shade and one window in the front. He took the directed energy weapon from Chloe and leaned it against a tree.

Mac motioned that they should follow him around back. Chloe was surprised how wide he made the arc, staying in the shadows and somehow walking so quietly she could barely hear his boots on the soil. When her Uzi brushed the handle of the Luger, it made a muted scraping sound and she held her breath. Mac stopped and half turned. Chloe had to resist the urge to raise her hand in acknowledgment and apology. She set herself again, and they crept around the back, where trees blotted any light from the stars and the shack was totally dark.

Mac squatted about forty feet behind the place. "I don't like it," he whispered. "Only one vehicle, and that looks like mine, so it's likely the one Sebastian got from the GC pool at the airport. And does that place look like it's got five people in it? I mean, I know they're hiding out, but . . ."

"You lost me already," Hannah said between gulps of air. "I don't see *any* vehicles."

Mac put a hand on her shoulder and turned her toward the side of the shack, where a small white car sat mostly hidden in underbrush. Hannah nodded. Chloe hadn't seen it either. "Maybe your eyes aren't adjusted to the light yet," Mac said, as if he meant it. Chloe nearly laughed aloud. They had all been traipsing around in the dark.

Mac slipped the Uzi off his shoulder and lay it on the ground. He pulled what looked like a utility tool from a vest pocket. "I know this is gonna sound like a cowboy movie," he said, "but cover me."

Before Chloe could ask where he was going, he moved quickly to the car and went to work on the trunk lock. Every time he made a sound loud enough for the women to hear, he stopped dead and remained motionless a few seconds. Eventually came the thump of the lock giving way, and the trunk lid sprung free. Mac kept a hand atop it so it wouldn't fly open.

He snaked his other hand in as far as he could, then finally had to let the lid rise another half inch or so. That triggered the trunk light, so he lowered the lid again. He set the tool on the back bumper, reached in, and held the lid down with his left hand, feeling around inside with his right. Once he found what he was looking for he quickly pulled his hand out, grabbed the tool, reached back in, let the trunk up enough to give himself room to maneuver, and — as the light came on — ground the tool into the bulb, breaking it and dousing the light.

Now he let the lid open all the way, silently, and felt around inside the trunk. From where she waited, it looked to Chloe as if the whole top half of his body was inside.

Suddenly he stopped and backed out, quietly shutting the trunk and hurrying back. "Just as I thought," he said. "Check it out."

"A twelve-gauge," Hannah said. "Learned to use one when I was a kid."

"These GIs love their shotguns," Mac said. "Leaves a DEW and a Fifty in the plane, brings his double-barrel on the job. And brilliant as this hostage team is supposed to be, they don't even search his car."

"We going in?" Hannah said.

"Yeah, but I still don't like it. Half of 'em take off when they found out we were comin', or what?"

He clearly wasn't expecting an answer. Mac handed the shotgun to Hannah. "Makes a lot of racket when you cock it, so do it when I whistle."

He picked up the Uzi, and they followed him back around to the front and the darkest area they could find, about twenty feet left of the door. Mac nodded to Hannah and whispered, "On three." He counted with his fingers and whistled shrilly twice while Hannah expertly, and noisily, cocked the shotgun.

From inside the shack came hurried movement, heavy steps, one louder than the other, like someone limping. The door squeaked open a couple of inches and someone whistled. Or tried to. It was mostly air. Then came the second try.

"All right!" Mac shouted, so loud Chloe jumped. "You know who it is, so show yourself and let us in."

The door opened in and struck the man or his weapon as he tried to get out of the way. "Right this way," he said with a heavy accent.

Mac marched straight toward the door, and Chloe noticed he had a finger on the Uzi trigger. "Senior Commander Howie Johnson comin' through with officers Irene and Jinnah. Stand aside, Peacekeeper."

The man, clearly favoring one leg, hopped back against the wall, warily eyeing them and nodding a greeting.

"So which one are you?" Mac said. "Hercules? Constantinople? Who?"

"Socrates, sir."

"Well, sure ya are. Awright, where is everybody, particularly my prisoner?"

"Not here, sir."

Mac looked as if he were about to explode. He tilted his head back till his chin pointed at the ceiling. "Not here, sir," he mimicked. He brought his eyes down to Socrates. "That's all I git? Where are they?"

"They told me to tell you to read the fine print." That took a second to register with Chloe, and from Mac's look, with him too.

Mac dramatically moved past Socrates, flattening him against the wall again. He strode to the front door and kicked it shut so hard the window rattled and an echo came back from the trees. Mac turned on the man. "The fine print in what? You think I brought the Sebastian file with me into the woods?"

"I am only telling you what they —"

"Why don't you just tell me what the fine print says?"

"They gave me this duty because I slow them down. I was attacked by the prisoner and he injured me with a kick to the —"

"I asked you about the fine print, man! What'd I miss? What's the message?"

"That they have the right to move the prisoner at any time without informing the GC until —"

"Where are they, Peacekeeper? Where did they go?"

"They do not have to inform their superiors until they have reached their des—"

"Do you know where they are?"

"They thought they heard something long before it should have been you, so —"

"You understand English, Socrates. I know you do. Do — you — know — where — they — are?"

"I believe the reason they did not tell me was because —"

"You want me to believe they left you here alone to greet me and didn't tell you where they'd be?"

"Because if I didn't know, I could not tell the wrong person."

"I hope you're lying."

"Sir?"

"I hope you're lying, because then you can change your mind about telling me before you die."

"Commander, I do not know!"

"Officer Jinnah, show Socrates what a twelve-gauge does to the front door."

Chloe wondered if Mac was serious. Apparently Hannah did not. She lifted the shotgun toward the door with one hand, and as soon as the barrel was parallel to the floor, fired. It was as if a bomb had gone off. Chloe was deafened, but nothing was wrong with her eyes. A gaping hole appeared in the door, and the entire thing blew off its hinges and landed several feet from the shack.

"The next one goes in your face, Socrates."

"But, sir!" he cried. "I —"

"Then get on your squawk box and tell your people I want to know where my prisoner is, and I want to know now!"

"But they —"

"Kill him, Jinnah."

Hannah raised the shotgun as quickly and forthrightly as she had before, and Socrates immediately tumbled to the floor, tears streaming. "Wait! Wait!" He dug a walkie-talkie from his pocket, dropping his weapon in the process. "Socrates to Plato, come in, come in. Hello? Plato? I know you can hear me! Please! I need you!"

Mac shook his head as if he had no choice. "Jinnah?"

"No! Please! Wait! Elena! Elena, are you there? Come in now, please. I am not joking! Answer me! Aristotle! Aristotle, they will kill me! I know I was not supposed to call you, but I don't care! Please, please come in or I die!"

Nothing. His shoulders slumped and he bowed his head, weeping.

Mac knelt and put a hand on Socrates' arm. "They're not that far away, are they?"

He shook his head, sobbing.

"They're close by, aren't they?"

He nodded. "You might as well kill me, because I die either way."

"What are you saying?"

"They said not to contact them, no matter what. Don't tell, no matter what."

"But they didn't mean not to tell me, did they? Surely not. They meant if they were right about the sounds. If the wrong people showed up. They're not afraid of GC, are they?"

The man shrugged. "I don't know. Maybe I do not understand. But I am a dead man."

"Then what difference does it make if you tell me?"

Socrates seemed to think about it. He scooted back against the wall and wiped his eyes. He put his walkie-talkie back into his pocket. When he reached for his weapon, Mac said, "Just let that lie."

Socrates seemed to be trying to catch his breath.

"Were they close enough to hear the shot?" Mac said.

"No. Maybe."

"How close?"

"Five hundred meters east. There is a lean-to garage."

Mac sat in an ancient stuffed chair. "Then they heard you calling for them."

Socrates nodded.

"And they left you to die."

Six

The celebrating, singing, and dancing at Petra continued into the dark of night. People by the thousands filed into the new pool to submerge themselves and to drink directly from the wide spring in the middle. Manna covered the ground, and Rayford was nearly woozy from its refreshing taste.

"Eating directly from God's table," he told Abdullah, "was something I never expected in this lifetime."

Abdullah looked overwhelmed with joy. "How can this be, Captain? How dare we be so blessed?" The wording was lost on Rayford, but he knew what his friend meant.

A young woman, probably not yet twenty, approached. "Rayford Steele?" she said shyly.

Rayford stood. "Yes, dear."

"Two things, if I may," she said, speaking

very slowly and holding up two fingers. "You understand?"

"Yes, what is it?"

"Is it true you speak only English?"

"To my shame, yes. Well, a smattering of Spanish. Not enough to converse."

"Do not feel bad, sir. I speak only Hebrew."

"Well, your English is lovely too, young lady."

"You do not understand."

"I understand you perfectly. You speak English beautifully."

She laughed. "You do not understand."

Abdullah leaned in, chuckling. "And you are funny, young one. Speaking Arabic and yet talking about knowing only Hebrew. And Rayford, how is it you know Arabic?"

The girl threw back her head and laughed again. "We all speak in our own languages and understand each other perfectly."

"What?" Rayford said. "Wait!"

"Sir! I speak only Hebrew."

"And Arabic," Abdullah corrected.

"But no. I was forbidden to learn Arabic."

"I need to lie down," Abdullah said.

"You said there were two things," Rayford said.

"Yes," she said, holding up two fingers again. "Two."

Rayford put a hand over her fingers. "No need. I understand you."

She laughed. "The second thing," and now she spoke more quickly, "is that Drs. Rosenzweig and Ben-Judah request an audience with you."

"With *me?* I should request an audience with them! I'm sure they are very busy."

"They asked me to fetch you, sir."

Rayford followed her over piles of rock that had been blown to pieces by the bombs. Just inside a cave, by light from a torch lodged in the wall, Chaim and Tsion sat with several older men. Tsion introduced Rayford all around and said, "The one we have been telling you about."

The men nodded and smiled. "Praise the Lord, Rayford," Tsion said.

"Continually," Rayford said. "But forgive me if I am preoccupied."

Tsion nodded again. "I too await word from our compatriots in Greece, and yet even now, the Lord quiets me with his peace and confidence."

"He may be trying to communicate the same to me, brother," Rayford said, "but that one of them is my daughter may affect my faith."

Tsion nodded again and smiled. "Possible. But after what you survived here today, is it not fair to say that any breakdown in communication between you and the Lord has to be your fault?"

"Well, *that* goes without saying."

"Oh, by the way, I am speaking Hebrew, and you are —"

"I know, brother. I have been all through that with the young lady."

The others laughed and one said, "My daughter!"

"Lovely."

"Thank you!"

"Chaim and I have been talking with these brothers about plans," Tsion said. "We will be praying for the Tribulation Force members all over the world and are eager to see how God delivers them. But everyone needs accountability, and as Chaim and I are accountable to you, we —"

"Oh, Tsion, no! Surely we're way past that! You've been the spiritual leader of the Tribulation Force for some time, and of the worldwide church of Christ for almost as long."

"No, now, Rayford, hear me."

"Begging your pardon, sir, you always flattered me by deferring to me as the titular leader of the Trib Force, but please . . ."

"These men, Rayford, are a good start for us here. They are the core of a group of elders I hope will eventually arise to help Chaim with the daily decisions. But they are, naturally, new to the faith."

"As *I* am, Tsion. Surely you're not suggesting —"

"Excuse me, Rayford, but you forget. None of us is terribly mature in the faith. In years anyway. I am not going to insult your intelligence by implying that I will seek your counsel on the Scriptures, though I cannot deny I have learned from you. But God put you in a strategic place for me at a very dark time in my life. If you do not mind, I would like to run past you some thoughts regarding the immediate future and get your feedback."

"If you insist, but at least concede that it was not I who stood in the midst of a million people and saw God miraculously spare them from the fires of hell."

Tsion looked at him with a twinkle in his eye, then turned to the other men. They laughed uproariously.

Chaim pointed at Rayford and chortled. "Was it not you? Then my eyes fail me!" He turned to Ben-Judah. "Tsion! Did I not see this very man standing in the midst of us, and could he have not seen what God did?"

"Well, okay," Rayford said. "Point taken. But *I* was not the reason the enemy attacked, Tsion. You and Chaim were. And I was not preaching, not praying, not standing there full of faith when the bombs fell. Truth be told, my faith is stronger in the aftermath than it was in the fire."

Tsion fell serious and ran a hand through his beard, studying Rayford. "You would make a good Israeli," he said.

Rayford shrugged. "Zeke was going for the Egyptian look, but whatever."

"No, I mean you argue like my countrymen. We could debate all night. And even when you are wrong, still you argue!"

That brought more laughter from the others.

"All right, Tsion. I don't know why you would want to hold yourself accountable to one you find it so easy to ridicule —"

"All in good fun, my dear brother. You know that."

"Of course. But anyway, I'm listening."

Mac pulled his phone from his pocket and turned it on. "What're they doin', Socrates, your pals? Checkin' us out?"

Socrates shrugged.

"C'mon, you won't hurt my feelings. They trying to make sure we're legit, that we're not gonna jump 'em, embarrass 'em, what?"

Mac punched in Chang's number.

"There are no cells out here, sir," Socrates said. "You won't get through to anyone."

"Well, I wouldn't if I had bad technology, would I? But what if I had a phone juiced by the sun and bounced by the satellites? Then I wouldn't care whether you've got cells in the woods here, would I?"

"But you won't be able to reach the commander unless —"

"This is Chang, Mac. You okay?"

"I'm fine, Supreme Commander, sir. Just checkin' in to see if my phone works all the way to New Babylon."

"Loud and clear, Mac. Talk to me. What's going on? You in trouble? What can I do?"

"Fine, sir. How's the weather there?"

Chang said, "I've got my screen open to the GPS, and I'm tracking you and, ah, Jinnah and Irene right to where you ought to be."

"Hang on, boss. Just a second."

Mac pretended to tuck the phone to his chest, but he held it lightly enough so Chang could hear. "What did you just say, Socrates? That I couldn't use my phone in the woods?"

"Yeah, well, obviously you can, with the satellite and all. But you couldn't talk to somebody unless they had the same thing is all I was saying."

"Who would I want to talk to here with my fancy phone who wouldn't have one?"

Socrates paled. "Well, like *I* don't have one."

"Who else?"

"My partners don't either. We have regular."

"Thought I was gonna call one of your partners, did you?"

"Well, no."

" 'Course not. Not unless their boss gave me their number, right?"

"Right."

"But even then, I couldn't call them out here, could I?"

"No. That's all I was saying."

"You were saying something else, weren't you, Socrates?"

"No. I was just talking."

"You thought I was calling Commander Stefanich, didn't you?"

"No, I —"

"Didn't you?"

"Yes."

"But you didn't think I could reach him." Socrates nodded miserably. "But how would you know that?"

"I was guessing."

"I can't get through to him in Ptolemaïs, in the middle of all the cells?"

"You probably can."

"But he's not there, is he?"

"How would I know?"

"Because he's here in the woods, isn't he?" Silence. "Isn't he, Socrates?"

He shrugged.

"So, how did he let you and your team know I was coming? Couldn't call you, could he?"

"I am so stupid."

"I'll grant you that, Socrates. Not livin' up to that name anyway, wouldn't you say?" Mac turned back to the phone. "Sorry to keep you, Chief."

"I'm way ahead of you, Mac. I can beam a signal to that phone of Stefanich's that will make the bells and whistles blow, even if I can't talk to him on it. He'll get a readout that Deputy Commander Konrad, who reports directly to Security and Intelligence Director Akbar, wants to talk with him immediately."

"Sounds good, Chief. I'll talk to you later. Things are going fine here."

"When he calls, I will use the voice modulator that can make me sound like an old German, and I'll tell him that Akbar himself is holding him personally responsible for giving Howie Johnson access to Sebastian."

"Perfect."

"And if he doesn't call, I'll have that on his phone's readout in time to help you out. Got you covered, Mac."

"Ain't that the truth, Commander!" Mac slapped the phone shut. "Lemme have that walkie-talkie, friend."

"You're going to get me killed."

"Who, me? Nah. You're a dead man anyway. Said so yourself."

"Are you going to kill me? Or let her?"

Mac shook his head. "I'll leave that to your partners. Look on the bright side. If they're as effective as you are, you'll be eatin' breakfast in the morning as usual."

Socrates stared at him.

"You eat breakfast, don't you, Socrates?"

The man nodded.

" 'Scuse me," Mac said, and pretended to mash the button on the walkie-talkie. "Now hear this, Plato, Aristotle, and Elena. I don't want to talk to any of you. I want Nelly Stefanich. Now, Nelly, I know you're close by, and I admire your creativity, goin' by the book and all. I'm not even insulted that you're checkin' up on me. I'll make ya a deal. When you get confirmation that me and mine are all we claim to be, I want you to personally bring Sebastian to me. You know where I am. And bring that team of philosophers out from under their rock so

152

I can see 'em. If you can get that done, Nelly, I promise not to take your command. Oh, and Nelson? That's an order, and you've got thirty minutes."

Mac turned and gave Chloe and Hannah a look. "Now, Socrates, you're free to go."

"What are you saying?"

"You heard me. Go on. Get out of here." Socrates struggled to his feet, then bent to pick up his weapon.

"That stays," Mac said.

"My radio then?" he said, reaching.

"Uh-uh. I'll keep that too."

"Where will I go?"

Mac shrugged. "That's up to you."

Socrates sat on the edge of a flimsy table and rubbed his knee. "I am a man with nowhere to go."

"You wanna be here when —"

The man stood quickly, teetering. "No. No. But it is so far to town. And with no protection or radio . . ."

"I can't help you, friend. You're part of an operation that didn't follow orders. You're lucky to be cut loose, considering the options. If you want to be here when the rest of your team —"

"Ach!" Socrates hobbled to the front door. Mac signaled Chloe with a nod to watch him. He gingerly stepped through the wood chips and splinters and made his way out.

"Follow him," Mac said, "till you're sure he's headed toward town. Hannah, check the perimeter. I'll clear this place and we'll meet by the weapons out front."

Rayford felt a fool, sitting in a cave, high on having personally lived through an Old Testament miracle, worrying about Chloe, and entertaining even the possibility that Tsion Ben-Judah himself should seek his opinion.

He knew he would be reunited with his daughter regardless, but was it wrong to wish her spared from a painful, violent death?

"You and Abdullah need to decide what you will do, Rayford," Tsion said. "You are welcome to stay, of course, but I do not know how practical it is to expect you to oversee the Tribulation Force from here. Our computer people tell me that David Hassid and Chang Wong have somehow already put in place here the basis for a mighty technological center, and that the bombs had no effect on the hardware or the software."

"Are you serious?" Rayford said. "The electromagnetic pulse from the missile alone should have fried everything."

"Everything is fine. Praise the Lord. So, you could conceivably keep track of everyone from here, but that is your call."

"Oh, I will be leaving," Rayford said. "I can't say when yet. I do worry about your returning to Chicago, Tsion."

"That is precisely what we have been discussing, Rayford. We do not know if it makes sense for any of us from there to attempt to return. Would not you and Abdullah be under as much scrutiny as I? Without another miracle, how could we return to the safe house without giving away its location?"

The thought of finding a new safe house, of moving, wearied Rayford. "We'll worry about that, Tsion. What are your plans? You could transmit your daily teachings from here."

Chaim interrupted. "That is my wish and that of the elders here. And I daresay the rest of the people."

"I do not know," Tsion said. "I will do as the Lord leads, but I believe Chaim is God's man here."

"My work is done, Tsion," Chaim said. "God did it in spite of my feeble efforts, and here we are. I shall hand off the baton to you, my former student."

"I remain your student, Doctor," Tsion said.

"Gentlemen," Rayford said, "the mutual admiration is inspiring but doesn't get us anywhere. This place needs leadership, organization, mediation. If you stay, Tsion, you should be protected from responsibilities that interfere with your teaching — here and to your Internet audience around the world."

The elders nodded.

"Perhaps among us," Chaim said, "we can ferret out young people with these gifts. I am willing to administer, coordinate a bit, but I am not a young man. This is a city, a country unto itself. We need a government. God provides food and water and clothes that will not wear out, but I believe he expects us to manage ourselves otherwise. We must organize and build — admittedly only for the short term, but still . . ."

"Maybe," Rayford said, "that very work is God's way of occupying your time here. Living together, getting along, functioning in harmony will be a full-time job. Imagine the boredom of a million people just sitting around waiting for the Glorious Appearing."

Tsion warmed to this. "Oh, that is why I believe we need to motivate people to help the rest of the world from here. We are not blind to the prophecies, to the machinations of the evil one. Trying to blow us up is only the beginning. He will think he can starve us out by cutting off our supply lines. He will not know or will not believe that God feeds us. But we know we are safe. What we must guard against are his schemes to lure the undecided away from this place, out to where they are vulnerable, not only emotionally and psychologically, but also physically. I am jealous to keep them here and to persuade them."

"I don't understand," Rayford said, "how anyone could remain undecided after today."

"It is beyond human comprehension," Tsion said, "but God foretold it. Now my dream for the faithful here is that they be useful in the cause of aiding our brothers and sisters around the world. Peter warns us to be sober and vigilant because our adversary walks about like a roaring lion, seeking whom he may devour. 'Resist him, steadfast in the faith, knowing that the same sufferings are experienced by your brotherhood in the world.'

"The evil one will grow angrier, more determined, more vicious, and many will die at his hand. What better, nobler task could the million strong here undertake than to aid your daughter's Commodity Co-op and equip the saints to thwart Antichrist?

"I envision thousands of technological experts creating a network of resources for believers, informing them of safe havens, putting them in touch with each other. We know we will lose many brothers and sisters, and yet we should offer what we can to keep the gospel going forth, even now."

Rayford sat back. "Can't argue with that. And it's not a bad idea, Tsion, this becoming your new base of operation. We will miss you, of course, but it makes no sense to risk losing you to the cause when all you need is right here."

"I have been thinking," Chaim said, "and, Rayford, feel free to correct me, as I am out of my element on this topic. But I wonder if the day of a safe house for the Tribulation Force is past. We know New Babylon is sniffing around and that it is only a matter of time before Chicago is exposed. Yes, perhaps we need a central location for the coordinating of the Co-op, but if I were you I would worry for my little one, being moved hither and yon. I leave the details to you and your compatriots. But I ask you, is it not true that anyone who is asked to remain at the safe house quickly gets the cottage fever?

"The young man there, Zeke, who so masterfully equips us to venture out, might find moving around a nuisance. And the matter of record keeping and computers is difficult. But perhaps the safe house of the future will be in a thousand places, not just one. Perhaps the time has come to make your home in the hiding places of the believers around the world."

Rayford feared Chaim was right, and it must have shown.

"I am not saying it will be easy," Chaim said, "but I urge you to take the initiative. Make the hard decision. Disband the safe house and disperse your people before they are found out, for then you could lose everyone at once. Surely you all know you have stayed in one place long past a reasonable hour."

"Oh, I know that, Chaim," Rayford said. "In reality, we have not been at the Strong Building very long. Too long, no doubt, but not even as long as we were at our previous location."

Tsion stood and stretched. "We need to leave this with you. God will lead you. I intended to seek your counsel, and now we have tried to counsel you."

"I appreciate it."

"But please, Rayford, counsel me. Let me

tell you what I believe God is impressing upon me, and see if it makes any sense to you. I know it will jar the sensibilities of many hearers, and yet I dare not casually disregard it. You see, because of what has happened since the Rapture of the church, I believe there is ample evidence of one part of God's nature and character. Clearly this is a time of judgment, even of wrath. We are in the middle of the last seven of the twenty-one judgments of God, and we even endured one he himself refers to in the Scriptures as the wrath of the Lamb.

"It would be easy for a preacher to illumine and drive home the truth of God's impatience, his judgment poured out on his enemies, his demand for justice for the blood of the prophets. But I have come to the conclusion that all this goes without saying. Yes, this is the last chance. Yes, everything has been telescoped into seven last years, and we are already well into the second half of that. God will do what God will do, but I am jealous to protect his reputation.

"Oh, I know he does not need me, does not require my assistance. I am humbled to the depths of my soul that he has seen fit to allow me *any* role in ministering to the nations. But a profound and seemingly contradictory message presses on my heart. I believe it is of God, but it is such a paradox, such a dichotomy, that I dare not run ahead of him without the counsel of and wisdom of my spiritual family."

Tsion massaged his temples and began to pace. "Gentlemen," he said, "walk with me."

"The crowds will press if you leave here," someone said.

"They will see we are engaged, I am sure," Tsion said. "Let us not make a spectacle. Surround me and let us move away from the masses."

The people still frolicked around the spring while others filled containers and gathered manna. Rayford joined the elders and Chaim and casually moved into a ravine and down a rocky slope.

When they were clear of others, Tsion talked as he walked. "I am not unaware that I have been bestowed a great privilege. I have a congregation here alone of a million souls. I have opportunity to teach the babies in the faith, offering them the milk of the Word. I also enjoy breaking the bread and carving the meat of the deeper things to the more mature. And I am blessed to preach the gospel, evangelizing, for even here, there are the undecided. We will not win all of them, a truth that astounds me, especially in the glow of an event such as we experienced just hours ago. But the point is, God daily refreshes me and allows me — expects me — to exercise all the gifts he has bestowed on a pastor-teacher."

When Tsion stopped, the rest stopped. He sat on a rock and they gathered around him. "It may sound strange to you all, because I have said many, many times that this is the worst seven-year period in the history of mankind, but in many ways I count it an almost limitless benefit to be alive right now. Technology has allowed me a congregation, if the figures can be believed, of more than a billion via the Internet. Someday in heaven I will ask God to let me get my finite brain around that figure. For now it is too much to take in. I cannot picture it, cannot tell you how many one-hundred-thousand-seat stadiums it would take to house them all. Well, of course I know that ten thousand such stadiums would equal a billion people, but does that help you picture it in your mind? Me neither.

"Now, let me tell you what weighs on me when I think of the responsibilities I have to such a congregation. I believe the time has come to stop talking about the judgment of God. There is no denying it. There is no pretending that his wrath is not being poured out. But I have come to the conclusion that the whole message of God throughout the ages is an anthem to his mercy.

"Most of you know that this comes from a man who saw his beloved wife and children murdered. Am I saying that the holiness of God is less important than the love of God? How could I when the Scriptures say that he is love, but that he is holy, holy, holy?

"I am merely saying that I will let God's justice and judgment and wrath speak for themselves, and I will spend the rest of my time here championing his mercy."

It seemed to Rayford that Tsion took the time to look into the eyes of everyone who had heard him. He could have gone on, defended himself and his novel opinion. But he simply finished by saying, "You have until noon tomorrow to correct me if you believe I am a wayward brother. Otherwise, my teaching begins, and you know my theme."

Buck was sympathetic to Albie. The diminutive Middle Easterner was wound tight, unable to sit still. "I can't live like this, Cameron," he said. "I'm going to spend this evening with Zeke and look through his files. Have you seen his inventory?"

"Of course."

"There has to be an identity in there for me. The GC thing probably won't work for me again, but I'll do anything. Anything but sit around here. You think he could make me tall and blond?"

Buck had to smile. One of two wasn't bad. "I might join you," he said. "Zeke's a master, and this sitting around is gonna kill me."

"But you write. You get to download all that stuff from Chang and get it out on the Net. I love your son, Cameron, but trading off baby-sitting, reading, looking out the window, and waiting for everybody to check in is going to drive me crazy."

"I know."

"Have you spent much time with Mac?" Albie said.

"Sure."

"Great man. Good mind. But we don't think the same. I can imagine all kinds of things he's doing in Greece right now that could get — oh, I'm sorry. I keep forgetting Chloe is right there with him."

"What? You think Mac won't look out for Chloe? She's probably looking out for him."

"I ought to be there is what I'm saying."

"Deputy Commander Konrad?"

"That is correct," Chang said, his voice electronically modulated, "and this had better be Nelson Stefanich."

"It is, sir, and —"

"Commander, I want to know what in the world is going on over there."

"Yes, sir, we —"

"I sent my senior commander all the way from New Babylon to talk directly with your prisoner."

"And that will happen, sir. I —"

"I don't appreciate him getting jerked around when you had fair warning and plenty of time to make arrangements."

"I know. We —"

"I'll expect a full report transmitted to my office by noon tomorrow."

"I'll definitely do that, sir, because it *is* explainable."

"Is Johnson meeting with Sebastian now?"

"Not quite yet —"

"Even as we speak? Because if not, I want to know why not."

"There was some mix-up with our local team, sir. They thought they heard —"

"I'll look for those details tomorrow, Commander, but meanwhile I'm going to assume you're effecting this meeting."

"Yes, sir."

"And not making Johnson come to you."

"Sir?"

"He's gone as far as I expect him to have to go. Anywhere he is, is a secure environment, so you have your people get the prisoner to him."

"Yes, sir. Deputy Commander, could I inform you of some good news?"

"There is no good news until I know Johnson has access to Sebastian."

"I just wanted you to know that we have located the central underground headquarters in Ptolemaïs and plan to raid it at midnight."

Seven

Chloe watched Socrates from inside the shack until he disappeared, limping down toward the road. Then she tiptoed out, went ninety degrees into the trees, hurried past the Fifty and the DEW, which her quarry had passed some forty feet to his left. She found it no chore to keep up with the lame Socrates.

Chloe held tight to the grip on the Uzi, pulling the strap taut to keep it away from her body and from clacking into the Luger. She turned sideways and mince-stepped the decline, carefully crossing the gravel road. Stopping on the other side, she heard movement in the underbrush, someone heading left, east, hurrying and not worrying about snapping twigs and thrashing through the thick stuff. Chloe squatted and regulated her breathing, gauging direction and distance to keep from following too close and giving herself away.

There was no need for her to step into the overgrowth. She could easily keep pace staying at the side of the road in the soft, silent dirt. The only danger was overtaking her prey and being seen. It had to be Socrates. When he came even with the shack again, though he was below the line of sight from the front door, he stopped, apparently to listen. Hearing nothing must have encouraged him, because now out he came, maybe fifty feet ahead of Chloe and also choosing to stay on the quieter surface next to the road.

Chloe stood stock-still in case he decided to turn around. She couldn't imagine being seen in the darkness, but who knew what kind of vision the limping, unarmed man might have? Some people could see or sense shapes in the darkness. Mac had proved that. And maybe this character knew the area, would notice a silhouette between trees that should have provided a clear shot to the stars.

Chloe waited until he went around a bend, then hurried to where she could again hear the labored footsteps. She peeled her eyes and saw — or at least imagined — that he was testing the knee, trying to walk more upright, more normal, and not succeeding. Occasionally she heard a grunt or a moan. He was in pain, and he certainly was taking the long way to town.

No, Socrates was going to lead her to George Sebastian. Chloe just knew it. Should she attempt a quiet transmission, let Mac know Hopalong was headed the wrong way? How much of a lead could he get if that took thirty seconds? Mac and Hannah could catch up with her quickly, and they could overtake him in no time.

But Mac was double-checking the shack, and Hannah was outside alone, making sure no ambush was afoot. Chloe would never forgive herself if a needless transmission gave someone an audible target. If Socrates led her right to this lean-to or whatever it was, unless she was seen, she couldn't be in any danger. If the other three were there — even if Stefanich was there — she'd still have plenty of time to call for the others.

Mac knelt in the cool dampness of the cramped cellar. The single bare bulb hanging from the ceiling revealed irregular shapes on the earthen floor. With his flashlight he tried to determine whether George had been mistreated. It was impossible to tell if those were flecks of blood among the footprints and indecipherable shapes. *It's where I would terrorize a hostage,* Mac decided.

He shined his light in every corner, flipped off the cellar switch, and was headed upstairs when his phone chirped. Eager to get outside to the rendezvous but hesitant to be on the phone in the open air, he paused on the stairs and flipped it open. Was it his imagination or had he heard a voice from out back? He assumed Hannah would have done her perimeter scan and would be waiting with Chloe by the tree in front.

Mac didn't dare say anything, so he just listened to the phone.

"Mac?"

It was Chang, but Mac didn't want to acknowledge. He pressed a button on the keypad.

"Mac? That you?"

He pressed the button longer.

"Okay, you can't talk, but neither can I until I can confirm it's you. One beep if the following is true; two if it's false: After the first book in the New Testament, the next four have exactly the same number of letters in their titles."

Now Mac for sure heard a voice from the back. Male. Chang's statement was true, but was it one for true and two for false or the other way around? He hesitated, listening while creeping to the top of the stairs.

"Mac would know this," Chang said. "One if true, two if —"

Mac pressed one quickly.

"Could have been a lucky guess," Chang said, and Mac closed his eyes. *Come on!*

"You have a contact in a very strategic location. Give me a beep for the number of letters in his sister's *maiden* name."

What? Chang would be so clever at a party. Okay, Chang's the contact. His sister is Ming Toy. Three. Wait! Maiden name. Same as Chang's. Wong. Four. Mac punched them quickly, now peeking out of the darkened shack toward the back. He could see nothing.

"Okay, Mac, right. Now listen. Talked to Stefanich as Konrad. He's going to make his guys bring Sebastian to you, so stay put but don't waste time. He claims they've found the underground headquarters and will raid it at midnight. I don't have any numbers on the Co-op people there. Do you? One if yes, two if no."

Mac pressed twice.

"I don't even know that they have phones. Can you send somebody to help? One if —"

Mac beeped once.

"Are you in immediate danger?"

Mac beeped twice.

"Okay, so you're somewhere where you can't talk. GPS shows you still where I talked to you last. Someone there with you?"

Twice.

"Outside?"

Once.

"See them?"

Twice.

"Okay, you hear them. Have you got personnel outside?"

Once.

"Both?"

Once.

"I'll let you go. You want me to stay on?"

Twice.

"Check in when you're clear. I want to know we're doing something for the Co-op there."

Mac put his phone away and crept outside. Half a dozen armed Peacekeepers milled about by the car.

"I say we take it. We've hiked for hours."

"No keys."

"So hot-wire it."

"Come on! Supposed to be only five hundred more meters."

The Peacekeepers headed east. Mac circled around to the front. *So Stefanich sent backup. Wonder if that's all of 'em?*

Neither Hannah nor Chloe was by the tree. Mac made a noise through his teeth, in case they were close by. Nothing. He knelt in the darkness. The Fifty was in place. The DEW was gone.

It felt to George as if Aristotle had turned left onto the road and driven east for about twenty minutes before pulling off to the side and waiting. He had once been able to keep track of the passage of time, but now he had to fight sleep. If he had to guess, George would have said they sat, not moving, for more than an hour. But neither would it have surprised him if it were actually twice that long.

Finally Aristotle said, "What do you think?"

"We could have gone long ago," Elena said. "The place clears out early, and there aren't that many people there anymore anyway."

"Plato?"

"Yes, go! We've got to get back up here before long."

It seemed to George that they eventually made their way out of the woods and off the gravel road to a main road and were heading south. Then they went east, and he had the sense, from ambiance and sound, that they were in a populated area, maybe town.

"Get him out of sight," Aristotle said a few minutes later.

Plato reached and grabbed George by the right shoulder and pulled him over to where his head now lay in the big man's lap.

Aristotle soon slowed and seemed to be parking.

"No, no!" Plato said. "Around back."

Once they finally stopped and parked, Elena said, "I'll see if we're clear." George felt a cramp in his lower back but could do nothing about it. She returned and got back in the Jeep, shutting the door. "About twenty minutes," she said.

"You got it?" Aristotle said. "Let me see it."

"And it goes where?"

"About a foot below the top of the right door."

"I never noticed before."

"Can I sit him up?" Plato said.

"Better wait."

Chloe stopped fifty feet in back of Socrates and guessed they were close to five hundred meters from the shack. He was bent over, hands on his thighs, breathing heavily. His pace had slowed the last hundred meters or so, and maybe he was trying to come up with an approach to his comrades that would gain him sympathy rather than hostility.

She was watching him carefully when she froze at the sound of footsteps on the gravel. Several. Not hurrying. Not sneaking. Just coming. She backed into the underbrush about ten feet off the road and knelt, the knees of her camouflage pants immediately soaked through and cold. She fought the temptation to hold her breath, fearing she would exhale right when whoever was behind her came by. Chloe knew it couldn't be Mac and Hannah. There were too many.

She was out of sight of Socrates now and hated not knowing whether he was off again. If he was, he would find his team without her knowing where. And here came half a dozen Peacekeepers, weapons in hand. They were in no hurry, chatting, a couple smoking. Chloe tried to make it make sense. They seemed to have an idea where they were going. Same spot? She could follow them, and maybe more easily because of the noise they made.

They were ten feet past her, and she would wait another thirty seconds before venturing out. Her walkie-talkie gave two quick, staticky squawks, startling her. The

Peacekeepers kept walking and talking, but she panicked. Though they hadn't heard the sounds, if someone started talking to her, they'd hear that.

She reached in her pocket to turn off the radio, but in feeling for the right knob turned it up. Frantic to shut it off, she lurched, lost her balance, and flopped onto her seat. "Johnson or Irene, come in, please."

Too loud!

Chloe leaped to her feet, yanked out the radio, squeezed the transmit button twice, shut it off, and set herself, readying the Uzi. The Peacekeepers had stopped and now crept her way.

Mac pulled out his radio and whispered, "Johnson here, Jinnah. What's your ten-twenty?"

"One hundred yards northeast of rendezvous point."

"You okay?"

"Ten-four. GC troops in the woods, sir."

"Irene with you?"

"Negative."

"The DEW?"

"Affirmative."

"On my way. How many?"

"Guessing two dozen, sir."

"Come back?"

"Minimum twenty-four."

"Roger. Be sure you're clear, cease radio transmission, and return to rendezvous ASAP."

"Roger."

So much for bluffing Stefanich. Either he wasn't buying or he's royally stupid.

"Johnson to Irene . . . Johnson to Irene . . . Johnson to Irene. Do you read?"

Mac looked at his watch, kicked the ground, pressed his lips together, and waited for Hannah.

Chloe stood in the bramble, finger on the trigger, feet spread in the mushy ground. The Peacekeepers stopped on the road, facing her position, close enough that she could hear their breathing. All six set their weapons at the same time. She could barely see them and assumed they could not see her. She held her breath and did not move.

"GC!" one called out. "Who goes there?"

Chloe entertained the hope that they would all six decide they hadn't really heard anything.

"Show yourself or we spray the area!"

"Friend!" she called out. "GC here too. Sister on assignment. Cool your jets."

"Armed?"

"Holding it over my head, Peacekeeper.

Ten-to-one I outrank you, so don't do anything rash."

A big flashlight made her squint. Holding the Uzi over her head, she said, "Turn that thing off! We're all here on the same assignment."

The light went off. "Hand over the weapon, ma'am, and we'll sort this out."

"No, we'll sort it out first. Now I'm tucking it under my arm to show my papers. Stand down now. So far you've been by the book and I can't fault you."

"Thank you. I'm going to need to turn the light onto your docs, ma'am."

"Hold on, I got a smaller beam. Going into the pocket."

With the weapon tucked and pointing her small flashlight at her papers, Chloe's heart drumrolled against her chest.

"Superior officer, guys," the leader said. "Salute."

"No need," Chloe said. "Good job. A little sloppy on the march, but at least you're on time."

"What were you doing in the bushes, ma'am?"

"Following orders. Now wait here for my CO and another officer, and we'll go together."

"That Uzi's not official issue, is it?"

"Something to look forward to."

"Really?"

"At my level it is."

"Wow."

"We still reasonably on schedule?" she said.

"About twenty minutes early, ma'am."

"Stand by, gentlemen." Chloe pulled out her radio and turned it on. "Officer Irene to Senior Commander Johnson."

"Johnson! Oh, man!"

"Senior Commander!"

Chloe turned to the Peacekeepers. "A little decorum, please."

"Johnson, go ahead."

"Sir, I've met up with six Peacekeepers who will join us on the assignment. Standing by for you approximately 480 meters east of your position."

"Six?"

"Ten-four."

"Everything copacetic, Irene?"

"Ten-four."

"For all I know, we could be surrounded," Mac told Hannah. "You sure you weren't seen?"

"Positive."

"What is going on?" He called Chang and filled him in. "What do you think Stefanich is up to?"

"I'm in his mainframe, Mac, and there's nothing there. Could be as bad as they're onto you, or he's still trying to cover."

"But what's he need all these people in the woods for? They mustering here for the midnight raid?"

"Seems out of the way."

"Sure does. Unless they're wrong about the location of the underground headquarters. We're not far from where the pastor hid out Rayford. You think they've finally discovered that?"

"You're a good thirty miles from there, Mac. I'll stay on it, but I don't know what to tell you."

Aristotle said, "All right, let's go."

Plato shoved George up. Someone opened his door, and it seemed Plato and Aristotle each took an arm and guided him, while Elena opened doors. They led him about fifteen feet, up three concrete steps, and inside. Then about twenty steps down a corridor that from the echoes seemed narrow. Finally into a larger room.

Aristotle let go of George and walked a few steps away. "Ach! I can't reach it. Plato?"

"Give me that."

George heard what sounded like metal

being slotted into metal, then a couple of loud clicks. Plato grunted. "What's the secret here?" he said.

"Let me get the other side," Aristotle said, and he was replaced at George's side by Elena. *If only I weren't cuffed,* George thought. That was when he would have taken his chances. Coldcock the girl, whip off the blindfold, race back down that corridor and outside, and hope for the best. But not with his hands behind his back. Any hesitation and she would shoot him, he was sure.

Plato and Aristotle grunted and Aristotle said, "Push him in, Elena. Come on, Plato and I have to get back."

Elena guided George forward, turned him sideways, and tried to force him through an opening apparently being held on each side by the men. He didn't fit. "Give me another couple of inches," she said, and they grunted louder. She pushed George through.

"Hold on now," Aristotle said. "I don't want him found cuffed and blindfolded."

Hands reached in and unlocked the cuffs. "Toss me the blindfold," Elena said.

George slipped it off and saw he was inside a dark elevator. Elena had a weapon pointed at him. Good thing for them,

George thought, because Plato and Aristotle were totally occupied holding the doors open. Elena took the blindfold, shoved it in a pocket, and pulled a bottle of water from another. She tossed it in and said, "Cheers," as the doors slammed shut.

George let the bottle bounce on the floor and tried to get his fingers between the doors. Just when he had found purchase he heard the key slide into its hole again and the throwing of the lock. He heard water sloshing and felt around in the dark for the bottle. He uprighted it and decided to save what was left for as long as he could.

With his arms spread, George could touch the walls on each side, and as he made a quarter turn, he realized the enclosure was square. It didn't surprise him that the buttons on a panel were not working, but he could tell from the pattern that he was in a four-story building. The ceiling was less than a foot above his head.

George felt for loose panels, missing screws, anything. Everything felt secure. A thin, plastic panel had to be the cover for the light. He removed that and felt a small, circular double fluorescent tube. Next to that was a mesh panel. He pushed up hard on the side until it gave way, then ripped it down. Now he could feel the fan blades, dusty, oily.

His body was already heating, and his breath was short. Were these people crazy? A malfunctioning elevator might make a perfect prison cell, but did they want him to suffocate? George shed his sweater and boots and socks and sat down, his back against the door. He found a boot and began swinging it backward over his shoulder against the door.

"Knock it off or I'll put you out of your misery," Elena called out. So they had left her alone to guard him. He wanted to tell her that if they didn't want a dead hostage to show to the brass, they'd better at least get the fan running. But he was committed not to speak. Not a word. And so he kept banging.

Chang had a bad feeling. Since the day he had been left as the only mole at the GC Palace, he had never felt so helpless. Was it possible Stefanich was playacting? They seemed to have him intimidated, eager to please. Even if he had checked on Mac, Chang had everything in place to make Howie Johnson look legit. He was certain Stefanich was embarrassed to find he had doubted this high-level Johnson character and should now be trying to cover that he had ever doubted him.

Chang was desperate to find out how vulnerable Mac and Chloe and Hannah were. Could they be walking into an ambush? Time was against him, but it might be wrong to just tell Mac to abort. Maybe they could hot-wire the car at the shack and get back to the airport, but Chang knew Mac wouldn't abandon Sebastian. What if he was already dead? If Mac had been exposed, there was no reason for the GC to keep him alive.

Chang slapped his forehead with both palms. *Think! If they're onto Mac, why are they? If you can find the connection, maybe you can figure out what they might do.*

Chang started a global search, asking David Hassid's superpowered engine to match anyone at high levels in the palace with the GC at Ptolemaïs. He even keyed in code breakers, in case the contact person feared someone within the palace was monitoring them. With the computer whirring away, darting through thousands of files in hundreds of locations, Chang fell to his knees.

"God, I have never asked you to override a piece of equipment. But you know a servant of yours designed this, and I want to serve you too. Help me think. Speed the process. Please let me protect these brothers and sisters. I know from what happened at Petra today that nothing is beyond you. We have lost so much to the enemy, and I know we will lose more before your ultimate victory. But don't let the Greek believers suffer more. Not tonight. Protect the Co-op. And help me get Mac and Chloe and Hannah and George out of there."

Mac liked a clear mission, a black-and-white assignment. This one was infiltrate, then storm the gates, free your man, and hit the road. Now there was the underground complication. He wouldn't leave Greece without his man, and now he couldn't leave without defending the believers.

The original plan didn't figure he and his people would be outnumbered. There were four hostage takers. Mac, his two team members, and George made four good guys. Those odds he could live with. But to walk Hannah down the road to Chloe and six GC, knowing there were at least two dozen more in the area, well, that didn't make sense.

"Hold up," he told Hannah. "You know how to hot-wire a car?"

"Do I admit it or not?"

"Just say so. Time is not on our side."

"Yes."

"Do it."

While she trotted to Sebastian's car, Mac radioed Chloe. "Johnson to Irene."

"Irene, go."

"Unforeseen delay here. Need your assistance."

"Ten-four. Should I bring help?"

"Negative. Let them go on. We'll catch up."

"You heard the boss, gentlemen," Chloe said. "We'll see you at the destination."

"We'd love to help the senior commander, ma'am."

"Thank you, no."

"Can we meet him later?"

"I'll see to it." And as she said it, Chloe was overwhelmed with a deep impression, and she had to express herself. "If you do me a favor."

"Anything, ma'am."

"Senior Commander Johnson's presence tonight is a surprise for Commander Stefanich. He's going to be compensated for some of his recent actions. So . . ."

"Don't let on he's coming?"

"Exactly."

"You got it, ma'am. And you know what? We didn't know Commander Stefanich was going to be here. Fact is, we don't know what we're doing here."

Chloe blanched. What if Stefanich wasn't there? "It's all part of the surprise, boys."

Chang knew God had protected him, probably more than he realized. But he had no reason to think God owed him anything or was obligated to act in this instance, just because Chang had asked. With zero confidence that his pleas had done any good, Chang wearily returned to his chair before the computer.

The screen was alive with red flashes. The search engine had reached secure files at the highest levels and was matching, comparing, translating languages, turning spoken word into written. A small box in the upper right-hand corner showed six matches already between some element of the GC operation in Ptolemaïs with top brass at the palace. Top.

Chang feared multitasking would slow the search, but he had to take the chance. Mac and the two women were in danger, outnumbered, without any idea what they faced.

He checked the first three matches and found they were routine interactions of Ptolemaïs administration reporting statistics to GC command. But the fourth was different. It was highest security interaction, a series of e-mails between TB and OT, plus more than one phone call, also between the same two, being reduced to typed transcription.

Chang keyed in, "Match logic?"

The response was immediate. "Meets broad, simple criteria: initials one letter removed from key personnel in GC Greece and GC Palace."

Chang squinted. That's what he had asked for: any connection based on standard search sequences and codes. TB was one letter away from SA. OT was one letter away from NS. Chang shot from his chair and stood hunched over the keyboard. He typed in, "Show interaction," and as the files cascaded onto the screen, he called Mac.

Mac heard the car running and footsteps jogging toward him from the north and the east. "Ladies?" he said.

"Yes."

"Yep."

His phone buzzed. "Stand by. Hey, Chang."

"Mac! I'll say this once and get back to you as fast as possible with details. Ready?"

"Go."

"Akbar and Stefanich have communicated personally several times today." *Click.*

"Busted," Mac said. "Listen up. No time for questions. Hannah, you're driving. Chloe, you're riding. Take the DEW, Uzi, and a side arm each, phones on, radios on. Get to the Co-op now. Clear 'em out, including anything they don't want found in a midnight raid. Then straight to the airport and wait out of sight for Sebastian and me, ready to hightail it to his plane. If we don't show, that means we're dead and you're on your own."

Mac bent and heaved the Fifty up against his chest. "Time to go to work, big boy," he said.

Hannah and Chloe ran around the shack to the idling car.

Eight

"Thank you, Lord," Chang said, still standing as his fingers danced on the keyboard. In seconds he had opened the transcripts of four phone conversations on a line so secure that Carpathia himself had once said even he didn't have access to it.

But David Hassid cracked it, Nicky. Access that.

Chang also had copies of e-mails that showed up on neither the palace nor the Ptolemaïs mainframe and were supposedly guaranteed to disappear from every record after they had been read. Hassid's master disk probably had the only copies in existence, including the correspondents'.

Though he was curious, Chang knew it was irrelevant how someone at Stefanich's level had personal access to the director of Security and Intelligence. The way they interacted evidenced some history, but if the box in the corner had not begun flashing again, Chang would not have wasted the time tracking it down until the crisis was over. He quickly clicked on the box to find "100 percent primary match, no decode necessary."

He opened the manifest and sped read: "Straight correlation from List A to List B: Suhail Akbar and Nelson Stefanich registered at Madrid Military School, overlapping tenures."

From the years listed, Chang calculated they had been there together as teenagers, more than twenty-five years before. *That would get a phone call returned.*

Chang was flying now, his eyes darting over the copy, looking for how the ruse fell apart.

Stefanich had asked whether Howie Johnson was "a fair man."

Akbar responded that the name didn't ring a bell.

Stefanich told him, "Senior Commander under Konrad."

"I'll look him up."

Akbar found him and reported, "Stellar record, but our paths have not crossed. Unusual for someone at that level, but it happens."

"Don't want to be a pest," Stefanich had followed, "but does Konrad vouch for him? Want to be sure before exposing him to prisoner."

"What prisoner? And who's Konrad?"

"The Judah-ite, George Sebastian."

"Still nothing out of him?"

"We'll break him or kill him."

"Break him. I know you can."

"You're not Konrad's immediate superior?"

"No. Do I need to look him up too?"

"You'd better. He's supposed to be your top guy, deputy commander, office on your floor."

"Send documentation."

Later, Akbar told Stefanich, "You're being duped. Johnson and Konrad are in the system, everything adds up, except they don't exist."

"Permission to reverse sting them?"

"With my best wishes. Bring them in, dead or alive, and I'll move you to the palace."

As the phone calls and e-mails progressed, the women's identities proved phony too. "The one from Montreal was in my office."

By early afternoon, Akbar had decided, "If Sebastian is worth all this, they're tied in tight with the underground. Announce a raid and see if they reveal location."

Chang called Mac. "The raid's phony. If you warn the believers, you could give them away."

"Call Chloe or Hannah. I'm occupied."

"Your location is a trap too, Mac."

"All right, listen, Chang. You saved our lives. But whatever you do, find Sebastian. I'll get him out or die tryin'."

Chloe answered her phone.

It was Chang. "Raid was a setup so you'd lead the GC to the underground. Abort."

"Hannah, you were right."

"What?"

"Hannah was right, Chang. She suspected we were being followed. I didn't notice a thing and thought she was paranoid."

"I told you!"

"Ditch them or lead them nowhere," Chang said. "From what I can tell, the GC has no clue where the Co-op is or that it's the meeting place. I gotta go. Mac is calling."

"Go, Mac."

"Question. If this is a trap, why wouldn't Peacekeepers have come back with Chloe and taken me then?"

"I don't follow."

Mac told him of her encounter with the half-dozen.

"You got me. I'm still reading the back-and-forth between Akbar and Stefanich. Possible not everybody knows."

"That could be."

"It's to your advantage."

"Confirm if you can."

"Will do."

Mac had moved east far enough to see the lean-to, if there was one. He saw nothing. Not even the GC Hannah or Chloe had seen. That meant the meeting place for the ground troops was at least a little farther on. If Chang was right, Sebastian wouldn't be within miles of there.

Brilliant military mind, Mac. Left yourself alone in the wilderness, way outnumbered.

Mac considered his options and few advantages. He was hard to see. He knew enough not to be lured to where Sebastian was purported to be. He had the Fifty. He was a long walk or a medium jog to the car, but the car had to already be under surveillance. It would be surrounded, so if he were stupid enough to try to get to it, he would be easily apprehended. "Lord," he said quietly, "I'm gonna thank you for keepin' me motivated to stay in shape, and I'm gonna ask you for more stamina than I've got. All I'm tryin' to do is get your man and my two partners out of here alive. Now I'm thankin' you as if you've already done it, 'cause I'm going to be busy here awhile. And if you've chosen not to, I figure you know best and I'll be seein' you real soon."

Mac made his way back toward the shack and stopped about a hundred yards above it. He removed his big, outer jacket, kept only three fifty-caliber shells and two clips for the Uzi, then wound the Uzi strap twice so the weapon was snug to his body.

He couldn't actually run carrying the Fifty, but he loped the best he could, staying high on the ridge and following the terrain, often as far as two hundred yards above the road. The air was cool on his arms and neck and face at first, but soon his body heat made him sweat. This, he knew, was only the beginning.

Mac's muscles ached and knotted and all but cried out, but he would not stop. He didn't even slow. He just kept moving, farther and farther west, trying to gauge the distance to where he had left the car. After traversing a rugged stretch with loose rocks that nearly made him fall several times, he finally decided to look for the vehicle.

Mac stretched out on the steep slant, facing down toward the road. He set the bipod, his arms shaking from effort and fatigue, popped open the telescopic sight, loosened the connection so he could scan with it rather than trying to move the heavy gun, and searched the road.

It seemed to take forever for his eye to adjust in the darkness. The gravel road was a ribbon of only slightly lighter gray against the blackness of the woods, but he knew what he was looking at. At the far right of his field of vision — far enough that he knew he would have to move the weapon nearly a hundred feet — he spotted something that picked up a hint of starlight. Only the white car would do that.

Mac gulped another minute's worth of the cool air, then forced himself up and over to where he could line the Fifty up with the car. He was nothing if not patient. While he tightened the sight and made several seat-of-the-pants calculations, he swore he saw movement on the north side of the road. If he was right, GC waited for him down there — and almost certainly on the other side of the road too.

He remembered from experience to tear cloth from his undershirt and stuff both ear canals. He set an extra round of ammunition next to the weapon, then dug himself footholds. It was a huge benefit to be pointing downhill, because the recoil could shove him up and back only so far. He had to remember to keep his knees bent.

Mac's plan was to fire two rounds into the car in as rapid a succession as possible, knowing that he would have to force himself to follow through, because no one who had shot this rascal once — and that included him — ever wanted to shoot it again, let alone right away.

He stretched out and settled in, leaving his finger off the trigger until he had drawn the butt of the rifle to his shoulder. He maneuvered it until it lay in a soft spot and not on bone, aware that the thing would still wreak havoc with his whole body.

Mac ran through the checklist. Steady. Relaxed. Pull firm to the shoulder. Trigger finger relaxed. Ears protected. Feet in holds. Elbows slightly bent. Knees flexed and ready to give. Barely visible crosshairs dead on the roof of the car, a tick left, allowing for wind. Distance just under two hundred yards. No matter what the thing does to me, reload and fire again, not worrying about accuracy the second time.

It warmed Mac as he silently counted himself down from three that he definitely saw movement through the lens. Unless someone was so spectacularly unfortunate as to step into his line of fire, no one would be hit, certainly not by the first round. By the second, even if he got it off inside a few beats, he expected the GC to be halfway back to the shack already.

When he got to one, Mac aborted. Better idea. Go for broke. Aim a little left, hope to hit the gas tank. Even if he missed, these guys had to think they were facing a tank or at least a bazooka. But if he got lucky, they'd think they were facing eternity.

He reset, just a smidge. Checklist. *Three, two, one, zero, oh, Mama!*

Mac thought he had been prepared. It was as if he had nothing in his ears. The sound was so massive it seemed to weigh on him. The woods had exploded, and yes, the erupting of that gas tank and the rebounding of that car on the gravel would have made a sound whether or not people had been there to hear it. The perverse nightmare of the sheer volume of it lay atop him longer than the orange ball rode his eyeballs.

The violence drove him back and onto his left side. As Mac struggled to gather his senses, he rolled back to his belly and slid back down into the same position. Fingers fluttering, he wrestled the extra round into the chamber, made sure the thing was generally facing away from him again, and forced himself against every instinct to pull the trigger again.

He should have run through the checklist again. One foot had not been secure. He was neither tight nor firm. The butt had been at least a half inch from his shoulder. The recoil sent it back seemingly at the speed of light and drove a ridge into the top of his shoulder he was sure would be there for weeks.

The sound was lessened only by the damage the first shot had done to his eardrums. His ears buzzed and rang, and he dumbly lifted his head to see trees falling, two on this side of the road, one on the other. His aim had been ten feet to the left of the now flattened and burning car, which prettily illuminated the carnage of machine and fauna — all wrought by two fairly simple pulls on a metal lever.

Mac wished only that he could have heard what had to be the frightened cries of the young Peacekeepers on the dead run. He awkwardly forced himself up on all fours like a spindly newborn colt and fought to keep from pitching down the hill.

When he was finally standing, arms outstretched for balance and to stop the woods from spinning, he waited. And waited. When his balance mechanism finally made the necessary adjustments, Mac caught his breath, shook his head, stretched each limb — even the one with the violated shoulder — and began to jog.

His intention was to jog what had taken him more than a half hour to drive. He would find his way back to where he and Chloe and Hannah had engaged in their sortie soiree that late afternoon that now seemed so long ago. There Mac would find the hidden Jeep,

hot-wire it, and set off on what he truly hoped was his last caper of the day. Surely by the time he got there, he would have heard from Chang where he might find George Sebastian.

And after all this, may God have mercy — or not — on anyone who dared stand between them and freedom.

Nine

Chloe didn't know the specifics of the directed energy weapon lying across the backseat, but she'd heard the effect it had on a target. And she was curious. She carefully lifted it into her lap, making Hannah alternate from watching the road to watching the DEW.

"Don't point that thing at me, Chloe."

"It's not even on!"

"That's like saying a gun isn't loaded. People get killed all the time with guns they swear aren't loaded."

"Looks pretty simple. You know the deal with these, right?"

"Yes," Hannah said. "Now, Chloe, please."

"Looks like you just turn it on, let it heat up or whatever it does, and fire away. It's nonlethal."

"Yeah, I know. But 130 degrees on soft tissue's going to make you wish you were dead."

"Bet I can get those guys to quit following us."

"Don't even think about it. You miss, they start shooting, and we're not going to help anybody."

"We're not helping anybody anyway," Chloe said. "We're sitting here with Uzis, side arms, a shotgun, and a DEW, and we've left Mac up there by himself with all those GC."

"And how long are these guys going to let us lead them all over town before they realize we're playing them?"

"We've got to shake 'em before we head for the airport, Hannah. They'll never let us in there."

"*Shake* them? Chloe, their ranks may be decimated, but they've got other personnel, more cars, radios. We're not going to shake them."

"I'm calling Chang."

"What for?"

"I want to know how many people know where we are."

"Why?"

"Hang on."

Running was much easier without the

cumbersome Fifty, but Mac had not run this far since . . . since when? Since never. No high school cross-country race was this far. This was longer than a marathon. With the slow but sure staccato of his steps, he repeated in his mind, "God, I'm yours. God, I'm yours. God, I'm yours."

If he was going to reach the Jeep, it would be only because God wanted him to. This was way past Mac's human capabilities.

Chang frantically read every tidbit of the communication between Akbar and Stefanich, hoping for something, anything, to help Mac. His secure phone chirped, and the readout told him who it was.

"You okay, Chloe?" he said.

"For now," she said. "Is there a way to know how many people are following us?"

"I can try to find out. What's your thinking?"

"If it's a bunch, we're dead. We'll run them around town and we could try to outrun them or shoot it out with them, but you know the odds there. If it's just one car, waiting to tell everybody else where the underground headquarters is, I have an idea."

"Hit me with the idea before I start trying to access the Ptolemaïs mainframe again."

"Why? If you don't like my idea, you don't look? Is that it?"

"Chloe, don't do this. Mac is in more imminent danger, and we have no idea where Sebastian is yet, so I have to prioritize."

"Sorry. I'll make it quick. If they're looking to us to lead them to the underground, we'll lead them to one. Only it won't be the real one. It'll be some other unfortunate citizens who'll get raided soon."

"I like it."

"That's a relief."

"No, I really do. And I think you two are small potatoes to them. Not that you're in the clear. Getting out of that airport tonight is going to be next to impossible, but they probably assume you have nowhere to go anyway and they can round you up when you try to leave. They want the locals."

"And we're going to lead them to 'em, only not really."

"Back to you as soon as I can."

"Stop the racket or I'll kill you!" Elena yelled.

George heard no one else. He kept pounding. How was she going to reach the lock? unlock it? open the doors?

She swore, and he heard movement. She was dragging something near the elevator.

He heard the key in the lock, then heard it turn over. It sounded like she had stepped down from the chair or whatever she had used to elevate herself. Now she was trying to open the doors. Not even Plato had been able to do it alone. George just sat there pounding.

"I'm trying to get to you!" she said. "But when I do, you're going to be sorry."

Thump!

Thump!

Thump!

"I'll shoot through the door!"

Thump!

Thump!

Thump!

"You'd better cut that out, and I'm not kidding!"

He could tell she was struggling with the doors. There was no way she could open them. If only he could get her to forget they were unlocked. He quit banging.

"That's better!"

He heard her step up again. The key was going into the lock.

Thump!

Thump!

Thump!

"No! I'm onto you! I'm locking it, and you can just thump all night!"

She locked it.

George stood and found the other boot. He put one on each hand. Now he leaned forward with his hands above his head, the boots pressing against the doors. He dragged them as he slowly slid to the floor and let them drop. George made sure his knee hit first, hard. Then his hip, then his side, then the boots, then his hands. He lay still.

"You finished playing around in there? . . . Huh? Are you? . . . You're going to get yourself shot! . . . You okay in there? . . . Hey!"

She swore again, and he heard her on the phone. ". . . was banging around in there. I threatened to shoot him and he quit, but now I think he's passed out . . . because it sounded like it . . . like he collapsed. You know there's no air in there. No ventilation. Where? I'll look."

She slapped the doors twice. "Hold on in there. I'll get you some air."

Chang found the tape of radio transmissions among local GC Peacekeepers in Ptolemaïs, but the quality was so poor, the conversion facility couldn't turn it into readable words. He downloaded it into his own computer and tried listening through earphones.

"Chloe," he reported, "I'm guessing, so

what you do with this is totally up to you. I believe there is only one car following you, and it's not official GC. They've farmed out your surveillance to two Morale Monitors. They're armed, of course, but all they're supposed to do is report who you warn about a raid."

"But you're guessing."

"I have to be honest, Chloe. I'm pretty sure that's what I heard."

"How sure are you?"

"Fifty-five percent."

She laughed.

"That's funny?"

"No. It's just that I was hoping for at least sixty. If I can get you to move to sixty, I'll buy this car today."

"Pardon?"

"Nothing. Could it be sixty-forty?"

"Max."

"We're going to give it a go."

Elena was still on the phone, but George had to press his ear flat against the elevator door to hear, and unless she was shouting, he could barely make it out.

"On the wall next to the elevator?" it seemed she was saying. "Yeah. Gray door. Got it. There's dozens of them in here, man. . . . Well, like furnace, air, water heater

— yeah, they sound like downstairs stuff. . . . How should I know? About twenty of them look like that stuff. Okay, twenty-one and further . . . okay, maybe this is first floor. . . . Alarm system, emergency lights, outside lights, stairwell lights, elevator. . . . Different one for vent, fan, or light? Doesn't look like it. . . . Yeah, all on one. . . . But I have to. He's going to suffocate in there. . . . No! Prop those open even an inch and I'd have to watch him every second.

"What if I turned it on but kept the doors locked? . . . Every floor? So I lock them on every floor. Then there's nowhere for him to go, right? . . . I'll call you."

George heard her leave the lobby and start up some stairs. He kept his ear against the door and could feel and hear her locking the outer elevator doors on the three floors above him. So she was going to flip on the circuit breaker for the elevator so the fan would run and he could get some ventilation. That wouldn't do. He had to somehow get her to open the doors.

She would be listening for the fan and for evidence of his being conscious. George reached up and felt the fan and the lights, pushing firmly around the sides. The panels were screwed on tight, but housings were hooked to wiring above the car, so those had to be the weakest panels in the ceiling. He pulled the gloves on and pushed hard. The metal was too tough and sharp in some places, even with the gloves on. Elena had to be nearly all the way back down.

George quickly slipped on the socks and boots, bent low, and stood on his hands, quietly walking up the sides of the car until the soles pressed against the ceiling. He toed around until he was sure he was pushing against light and fan, then stiffened his legs and pushed up from the floor with all his strength.

The fluorescents popped and fell; the fan blades bent and twisted and began to give way. His biceps shook and his chest ached, but he continued to push as if his life depended on it. He felt the panels tear away and the housing break away from the wires. The ceiling had to be a mess.

George tried to keep from gasping or making noise as he slowly brought his feet back down and lay panting on the floor, carefully brushing the debris into a corner. He heard Elena hurry past toward the circuit-breaker box and flip the breaker all the way off and then back on. The lights of the floor buttons on the panel came on, and he heard a hum in the ceiling where the light and fan should have been.

Trying to regulate his breathing, George turned himself around, laced up the boots and, catlike, moved into position.

"Getting any air in there?" Elena called out. She slapped the door. "Hey! Better?"

George got on all fours and crept backward until his feet were flat against the back wall. He reared up onto his knees until his seat was planted on his calves. Then he leaned forward and placed his palms on the floor, turned his face to the right, and lay his left cheek and ear flat on the floor. He fought to breathe deeply and slowly, preparing himself to hold his breath and appear dead.

Two more smacks on the door. "C'mon! That fan should be running. Is it? Give me a knock if you're getting any air!"

George lay there, crouched back against the wall, looking for all the world as if he had collapsed onto his face.

"All right! I'm unlocking these doors, but if you try anything, you're a dead man."

Now she was up on the chair. Metal into metal. The click. George was tempted to hit the Open Door button himself, but he knew she would be standing there with her weapon leveled at him. He blinked several times to moisten his eyes so he could lie there with them open, unblinking, hopefully able to see enough peripherally to know when to act.

"I'm opening the doors, so don't move! I'd rather the brass find you shot than dead by accident."

He heard her push the button, felt the car vibrate with the mechanism, and the doors began to separate. He wanted to drink in the cool, fresh air, but he dared not. In the faint light of the Exit signs and a light from down the hall, he saw her in his peripheral vision silhouetted before him, feet spread, both hands on the high-powered weapon.

She swore. She took a step closer. She took her left hand off the gun and reached for his carotid artery. As soon as her fingers touched his skin, he knew she would know he was alive. That touch would be his cue to spring.

"I'll do whatever you say, Chloe," Hannah said, "but I've got a priority higher than our getting out of here alive."

"Mac?"

"Of course."

"Me too. And George."

"I just can't imagine he's still alive, Chloe. What's in it for them to keep him around?"

"Don't think that way."

"Come on! We're not schoolkids anymore. Not thinking about it isn't going to change whether it's true."

"I'm just hoping they think they can still get something out of him."

"Well, I had limited contact with him, Chloe, but let me tell you something. He looked like the kind of a guy who was going to do what he was going to do, and nobody was going to make him do different. I'll bet he hasn't given them diddly."

"Pull over there."

"You're sure this will work?"

"Sure? I have to be sure?"

"Let's just not be too obvious."

"That's why you're stopping here and not at the front door, Hannah. When I head for the store, you stand outside the car, like you're watching for nosey nellies."

"Nosey nellies?"

"You know, GC or Morale Monitors nosing around."

"Nosey nellies?"

"I didn't know that was so obscure. I forgot you grew up on a reservation."

"Well, I *will* be looking for GC or MMs. So what do I do if they show up?"

"They won't. They just want to raid whoever we're warning."

"Or at least there's a 55 percent chance of that."

"Sixty."

"So a 40 percent chance they arrest us, or worse."

"You're carrying an Uzi. I've seen what you can do with a shotgun, and I can only imagine what you might do with a DEW."

"I'm just telling you, Chloe. If anybody comes, I'm jumping back in the car, honking the horn, and coming to get you."

"Well, I should hope so."

At the first sensation of skin on skin, George Sebastian called on all his years of training, football, and lifting. As he pushed off the floor with his palms and drove his heels into the back of the elevator, the massive quads and hamstrings in his thighs drove him up and into Elena, who had murdered her last believer.

George's 240 pounds slammed into her so fast and hard that as he wrapped his arms around her waist he felt the top of his head push her stomach against her spine. She projectile regurgitated over him into the elevator before her face banged off his back and her boots hit his knees.

He sailed four feet high and ten feet into the lobby with her body folded in two. When he landed, his chest pinned her legs, her torso whiplashed, and the back of her head was crushed flat on the marble floor. George pounced to his feet and ripped the weapon from her hand. He stuffed her phone and radio in his pockets, then grabbed her by the belt and slung her lifeless body into the elevator. He locked the doors and left the key on the chair she had used to reach the lock.

George laid a small rug from near the entry door over the gore where she had died and used the gloves to wipe up the blood trail to the elevator. He was about to charge out the back door to see if he could find a car to hot-wire when he heard keys in the entry door and looked up to see an old man smiling and waving at him.

The man wore a mismatched custodial uniform and carried two mops. As he entered, he said something in Greek.

"English?" George said, certain he was flushed and looked like an escaped hostage who had just killed his captor.

"I was wonder if elevator still to not work."

"Yes."

"Work?"

"No."

"Not to work."

"Right."

"Okay. Howdy, English, how are you?"

"Fine. Good-bye, sir."

"Bye-bye to you."

Chloe set her Uzi, gripping it with her right hand, and reached with her left to open the door. As soon as Hannah stopped the car in the shadows of an alley three blocks from Chloe's target, she stepped out and moved quickly.

Tempted to look back or to glance from right to left for GC Peacekeepers, Chloe kept her eyes on the storefront, where earlier that day she had watched the bombing of Petra on television. The place was dark, but in the back were at least two apartments with lights burning.

She banged loudly on the glass door with the heel of her hand. It would be customary for the locals to ignore such a knock, assuming a drunk was stumbling around at that hour of the night. So she persisted until she heard someone call out, "Closed!"

She banged and banged some more. Finally a light and a door, and a craggy man in a bathrobe and slippers ventured out. "What is it? Who are you?"

"GC!" she stage-whispered. "Open up. Just a moment, please."

He came, scowling, but would not open

the door. "What do you want?"

"I have an urgent message for you, sir, but I don't want to yell it aloud."

He shook his head and unlatched the door but would open it only a couple of inches. "What's so urgent?"

"I wanted to tip you off, sir, about a sweep through this neighborhood tonight, probably later."

"A what? A sweep?"

"A raid."

"Looking for what?" he said, pointing to his forehead and his *216*.

"For that," she said. "You are a loyal citizen, so we wanted to warn you early so you would not be alarmed."

"Well, you alarmed me!"

"I apologize. Good night."

He slammed and locked the door without a word, and Chloe hurried back to the car. "Well, that went well," she said. "Zap anybody?"

Hannah pulled away. "What?"

"With the ray gun."

"Is this how you cover your fear? Banter?"

"Must be. I'm numb all over."

"I saw no one, Chloe. I don't know what that means. Either they're very, very good, or we're paranoid."

"Probably both. We could hang around

216

and see if the GC come looking for the underground."

"I hope you're not serious."

"Of course not, but you have to admit it would be fun. Especially when they ask that old guy if he was tipped off about the raid."

"Where to now, Batgirl?"

"I feel like we're sitting ducks, Hannah. We can't call Mac unless we know he's somewhere he can talk. Chang will tell us what he can when he can. I say we look for somewhere we can wait without being seen, and watch for Mac and George."

"You're dreaming."

Rayford had been assigned a tent at Petra and was about to settle down for the night. He couldn't imagine sleeping after all he had experienced. As he studied the stars, he heard his phone, rolled up onto his side, and dug it out from his bag. He didn't recognize the calling number.

Rayford affected a Middle Eastern accent he was sure was awful. "This is Atef Naguib," he said.

"Ray?"

"Who is calling, please?"

"I memorized two numbers," the caller said. "Yours and Chang's. But this is not a secure phone, and I didn't want to expose him."

"Sebastian?" Rayford sat up. "They found you?"

"Who's *they?* I just busted loose. Is there a safe house around here? Somewhere I can crash until I figure a way out?"

Rayford was suddenly on his feet. He gushed the information about the Trib Force contingent in Greece and how Sebastian could get to the local Co-op. "I'll get to Chang and have him let the others know."

Ten

Mac lay in the dewy grass next to the Jeep, overcome with gratitude though aware that neither he nor his team was out of the woods yet. His overheated body arched and drew in the night air, and he thanked God over and over for having given him the strength to run this far.

He had barely been able to respond when Chang told him all that had gone on, but it quickly became obvious that of the four fugitives in Greece, Chloe and Hannah were now in the most immediate danger.

They had been followed, were in a GC vehicle, were in Ptolemaïs, and did not dare try to get to the Co-op, even on foot. They were heavily armed, but also inexperienced. George Sebastian had gone from most precarious to temporarily most secure, provided he had found the Co-op.

Mac painfully sat up and leaned back against the car. He had longed for and yet dreaded this operation. He had wanted to spring George, but the odds were so bad. When it had started, he thrilled to how easy it had seemed to snow the locals. Then it had gone haywire and fallen nearly hopeless. Now, little credit to Mac, the whole multifaceted effort had become straightforward again. Mac now had one job: reunite with the other three and get out of Dodge.

Chang was inconsolable over not discovering the connection between Akbar and Stefanich before the operation started. Mac tried to tell him that the whole Global Community hierarchy was so new and spread out that no one could have anticipated that those two would know each other. Chang had redeemed himself by breaking through the security and the ostensibly indecipherable codes. He and Mac now knew more about Stefanich's and the hostage takers' plans than they did. For one thing, Mac knew Sebastian was on the loose. Of Stefanich, Aristotle, Plato, Socrates, and Elena, the only one who knew that was dead.

Through his fast yet thorough examination of the interaction between Akbar and Stefanich, Chang discovered they had hatched the plan to draw Mac and Chloe and Hannah into the woods. There they would get them to move to where they would be far outnumbered by GC forces, most of whom had no idea what was going on. Even if the tables had turned and Mac and his people had gotten the drop on the Peacekeepers, few would have known enough to give away the double cross.

The GC expected Mac's people to lead them to the Judah-ite underground, then eventually be apprehended themselves. Johnson, Sebastian, Jinnah, and Irene would be reunited at local GC headquarters, then carted off to New Babylon as feathers in the cap of Stefanich, the newest palace member of Akbar's staff.

"Stefanich is beside himself looking for you," Chang had told Mac. "They were worried when they couldn't get through to Elena for a while, but they have reached her now and have been assured everything is fine at headquarters."

"What do you make of that, Chang?"

"I don't worry about it. Sebastian confirmed the Elena kill, and he has her phone. Who knows how he bluffed them? I wouldn't put anything past him. My worry is for Chloe and Hannah. The Morale Monitors lost them after the women led them to what the MMs thought was the Co-op. They won't know that was phony till they raid it. But Stefanich had so many of his people in the woods to help bring you three back, he was short on help in Ptolemaïs. That's all changed now. Everybody's on their way back."

The problem for Mac, he realized as he hot-wired the Jeep, was that he could call Chloe and Hannah, but he couldn't reach the Co-op or Sebastian except in person. He had an idea of how they might all escape, but the women had to stay safe in the meantime.

"How bizarre is that?" Chloe said. "We were probably walking distance from George when he came out the back door of GC headquarters. We could have driven him to the Co-op."

"And ruined it for everybody."

"Well, yeah, but I'm just saying. We've got to ditch this car and get where Mac can find us."

"The sooner the better," Hannah said. "I haven't noticed anyone for quite a while. Let's do it now."

"Let's at least get to the outskirts."

"Risky."

"Not as risky as parking in town and walking through the streets."

★ ★ ★

Mac hated the thought of having to walk even a few blocks, but he couldn't risk parking anywhere near the Co-op. He left the Jeep about a mile north and set off on foot. The trick would be to get in without getting shot, with those at the Co-op on the lookout for GC.

He thought about just waltzing into the pub above, but for all he knew Socrates had described him, and the whole town was watching for him. He was still in camouflage and armed with an Uzi — not your typical Ptolemaïst out for a nightcap.

Instead, Mac went by what Chloe and Hannah had told him of the place and stayed in the shadows, coming the far way around, slipping in the back door and into the tiny bathroom. The pub was full and noisy, and that was to his advantage. He locked the door, tried not to inhale deeply, and scrubbed the grease from his face. Mac didn't look much cleaner in the dingy mirror, and he was struck by the fatigue showing around his eyes. *Some night,* he thought, *and we've just started.*

Mac studied the pipes. They ran straight down through the floor, probably just a few feet from George and who knew how many local believers huddled in the back room of the laundry. He sat on the floor and used an Uzi clip to tap in Morse code on the pipe. "Seeking friend from S. D."

He repeated the message twice more.

Finally, return taps. Mac had nothing to write with, so he had to remember each letter. "Need assurance."

Mac responded: "Amazing Grace."

The reply: "More."

He tapped out: "Let's go home."

Back came: "Favorite angel?"

That was easy. And only a compatriot would know that. "Michael."

"Welcome. Hurry."

Mac turned out the light before he opened the door, saw no curious eyes, and hurried down the stairs. He heard a "Psst" from the back room and ducked through the curtain, only to look down the barrels of two Uzis in the dim light.

A young, dark-haired man appeared ready to shoot. "Let me see your hands."

Mac raised them, his own Uzi — supplied from that very room — dangling from his arm.

"Is that him?" the young man asked.

"Could be," George said.

"If it's not," Mac said, "how do I know you're Costas?"

Then he realized why George had to be

waffling and whipped off his glasses. "I used to work for Carpathia, man! The freckles had to go and the hair color had to change."

"That's him," George said, stepping forward to embrace Mac.

Several others — mostly men, all ages and all armed — emerged from under piles of clothing. Only three women were there — one middle-aged, one elderly, and one in her late teens. The first introduced herself as Costas's mother, Mrs. P. The older said, "My husband is K's cousin."

A thin, wiry man who looked to be in his late seventies said, "That would be me."

George pointed at the teenager. "This one answered Elena's phone a little while ago. Despite a very bad connection and a lot of static, she assured her partners I was still safely locked away."

"Nice to meet you," the girl said, adding the staticky sound as she spoke and causing the others to smile.

"Excellent work," Mac said. "Now, brothers and sisters, we have no time. There is a massive manhunt for me, and it won't be long before they find out Elena is dead and their prisoner gone. I have two compatriots on foot. K's cousin, are you also a Kronos?"

"I am, sir."

"Are you the one who lent your truck to the cause?"

He nodded solemnly.

"And is that truck available?"

"Two blocks from here."

"I want to buy it." Mac pulled a huge wad of Nicks from a pocket below his knee.

"No, no, not necessary."

"Actually it is, because by the end of the night, it will be well known to the GC and you will be unable to be seen in it again."

"I do not need the money."

"Does the Co-op? the underground?"

"Yes," Mrs. Pappas said, and she stepped forward to take it.

"Tell me about the truck. Four-wheel drive?"

"Yes. But not new, not fast. Five-speed manual transmission, very heavy and powerful."

"As soon as I connect with my other two team members, George and I will take the truck and pick them up. The GC expects us to head for the Ptolemaïs airport, but that's a suicide run. We have a plane at an abandoned strip eighty miles west of here. If we can head that way without attracting attention, that's where you'll find the truck tomorrow. If we draw a tail, pretend you never saw that truck."

"I want to come," Costas said.

"I'm sorry, no. Unless you are going all the way to America with us, there would be no way for you to help us and to also escape."

"But I —"

"We will accept all the ammunition you can spare. I would say if we leave now, our chances are only about fifty-fifty. Agree, George?"

"No, sir. I think that's optimistic. But I agree it's our only option and that we need to go now."

Mrs. P. held up a hand. "There is nothing wrong with working while someone is praying. Someone put extra ammunition clips in a bag while I pray.

"Our God, we thank you for our brothers and sisters in Christ and ask you to put around them a fiery ring of protection. Give them Godspeed, we pray, in the name of Jesus. Amen."

George took the bag and got the keys and directions to the truck, while Mac huddled in a corner and tried to bring up Hannah and Chloe on his walkie-talkie.

Chloe was on the phone to Chang when she heard Hannah take a radio message from Mac and give their location — off the road and behind underbrush north of the city.

"This is urgent," Chang was saying. "I don't have time to call everybody individually, so get this. All Ptolemaïs GC Peacekeepers and Morale Monitors are on high alert. They have abandoned the woods and are beginning a sweep of the entire town. We're talking hundreds of personnel and all working vehicles.

"They've found Elena's body, know they were the victims of an impostor on her phone, and are tracing that phone with GPS. If George has it, they'll know where he is, and if he ditches it, it needs to be far from the Co-op.

"The airport is crawling with GC, and though the Rooster Tail is sitting on the tarmac as if it's ready to go, it has been drained of fuel. If you can't get back to Mac's plane, the best I can offer is to try to get Abdullah's pilot friend to Larnaca on Cyprus tomorrow."

"Thanks, Chang," Chloe said. "Hannah tells me Mac and George are on their way. Forget Larnaca. We'd never get there. It sounds like the net is being drawn in all around us. Tell everyone we love them and that we're doing our best to get home."

★ ★ ★

Mac was driving toward the north road with George in the passenger's seat when he got the call from Chloe about Elena's phone. "That's easy," he said, stopping in the middle of the road. "Stick Elena's phone under the front tire, George," he said.

The truck flattened the phone.

As they reached the north road, Mac saw a sea of flashing blue lights in the distance. "We're toast," he said.

"They're not looking for this truck," George said. "Don't do anything suspicious."

"Like picking up two armed women?"

"Drive on. The women will see the GC and know we'll have to come back."

"When would we have time to do that?"

"What are you going to do, Mac?"

"They're setting up a roadblock. Stick the weapons and ammo under the seats and get a cap on. There's a better description of you than me out there. You can't hide big but you can cover blond."

Chloe and Hannah lay on their stomachs, watching the long line of GC cars, lights flashing. "There's the truck," Hannah said.

"Most of the GC are driving by them.

Guess they don't need all those for a road-block."

One GC car stopped on each side of the road, and a Peacekeeper held up a hand to stop the truck and wave through the rest of the squad cars.

"Hannah, if you can hear me, give me one click."

Chloe looked at her. "Was that George?"

Hannah nodded and clicked her walkie-talkie.

"All right, I've got Mac's radio on the seat here, and I'm staring straight ahead and pretending not to be talking, so I may be hard to hear. Listen carefully. If you have the DEW with you and can turn it on, give me a click."

Hannah turned on the weapon and gave another click.

"These guys are going to check us out. I'll leave the radio locked open. If it sounds like they're going to look closer, incapacitate both of them. Understand?"

Click.

"Here they come. Stand by. If one comes to my side of the truck, please use very careful aim."

Click.

Chang was exhausted and wished he could call it a night like most everyone else at the palace except Suhail Akbar and the literally indefatigable Carpathia himself, who did not require sleep anymore. Chang would not, however, be able to sleep anyway until Mac and Chloe and Hannah and George were safely in the air. He stayed at his computer, available to help. Meanwhile, he tapped into Carpathia's office.

"I really must stay on top of this Greece thing," Akbar was saying. "I'll return as soon as I can."

"Is it not something you can do from here, Suhail? The nights are so long, and there is much to learn from the daylight regions."

"Forgive me, Potentate, but we have had a serious breach of security. I am on a secure phone to Ptolemaïs and on a secure e-mail connection. The situation is about to be resolved, and I will hurry right back."

"And we can see how the morale effort is going in Region –6 and in Region 0?"

"Of course."

"There should be audio and video feeds where I see the last holdouts taking the loyalty mark, worshiping my image three times a day, or suffering the consequences. They are suffering, are they not?"

"I'm sure they are, Excellency. I don't know how you or I could have been clearer on that."

"And the Jews? There are many Jews in both those regions who might be enjoying the sunshine right now, but who do not know that this is their last chance to see it. Am I right?"

"You are always right, Highness. However, few people anywhere are truly enjoying anything with the seas as they are. I don't know how the planet can survive such a tragedy."

"This is the work of the Judah-ites, Suhail! They tell the Jews they are God's chosen. Well, they are my chosen ones now. And what I have chosen for them will taste bitter in their mouths. I want to see it, Suhail. I want to know my edicts are being carried out."

"I will see to it, my lord. By the time I return, someone will hook up the monitor to reporting stations in those regions so you may be brought up to date."

"This security breach, Suhail. It is here, inside the palace?"

"That's all we can conclude, sir. If such misleading, wholly false information can be planted on our main database from a remote location, we are much more vulnerable than we imagined. Bad as it is, we are most certain it is coming from inside, and that should not take long to trace."

"You remember, Suhail, what I have asked for in the way of treatment of the Jews, not to mention the Judah-ites. That would be retribution far too lenient for one under my own roof who would deceive me in such a way."

"I understand, sir."

"The perpetrator must be put to death before the eyes of the world."

"Of course."

"Suhail, have we not combed our entire personnel list?"

"We have."

"And are there any employees of the Global Community, here or anywhere in the world, who have yet to receive the mark?"

"Less than one thousandth of one percent, Excellency. Probably fewer than ten, and all loyalists with valid reasons, and all — to the best of our knowledge — with plans to rectify the situation immediately."

"But should they not be our primary suspects?"

"We have them closely watched, sir. And there is not one employee in the palace or in New Babylon without the mark."

After Suhail was finally able to excuse himself and get back to the situation in Ptolemaïs, Chang kept listening to Carpathia's office. Nicolae mumbled under his breath, but Chang could not make it out. Occasionally he heard banging, as if Carpathia was pounding on a table or desk. Finally he heard a clatter that sounded like Carpathia had kicked a wastebasket and stuff spilled out.

After a few moments, Chang heard a faint knock and Carpathia calling out, "Enter."

"Oh, excuse me there, Potentate, sir. I'm to get your monitor hooked up to the United North American States and the United South American States."

Carpathia ignored him until the man was on his way out. "Clean up this mess," he said.

Mac decided to take the initiative with the GC Peacekeeper in charge of the roadblock and not wait to be asked for his papers. George was slouched in the passenger seat.

"Wow, whatcha got goin' tonight there, Chief? I haven't seen this many of you guys on the streets since I started workin' road maintenance. All these guys are makin' it hard on our construction zones, but you gotta do what you gotta do. What're ya lookin' for, anyway? Something I can be watchin' for?"

"Confidential matter, sir. High-level manhunt. Long day for you guys, huh?"

"Tell me about it. We're hardly ever out this late. Had to come back around the long way from the airport. That part of this deal? That place is locked up tight. Went through the roadblock there too. They cleared us even though we don't have our papers on us, 'cause we had to work so late, asphalt and all. Goin' back to the work shed now."

"That's no excuse to not have your papers. Everybody is supposed to have their papers all the time."

"We know, and we both feel terrible about it. But we'll have 'em with us on the way home."

"They let you off down by the airport?"

"Yeah, nice guys. I mean, we aren't Peacekeepers, but we're all working for the people anyway, right?"

"That's not by the book."

"You know, I thought that very thing and really appreciated it that he wasn't one of those hard guys that gives the workingman a bad time."

"Well, I don't want to make your life miserable either, sir, so we can make this real easy. How about you two just show me your marks of loyalty, and you can move it along."

Chloe thought Mac had nearly talked his

way out of the situation. But if he was no threat, showing his mark would not have been a problem.

"Don't hesitate, Hannah," Chloe said.

"I wish that other guy would get out of his car."

From the walkie-talkie: "You just want to see our marks?"

"Yes, sir. Hand or forehead?"

"Mine's on the forehead here, under the cap. My partner's is, ah, where is yours, bud?"

"Hand," Sebastian said.

"Let's have a look," the Peacekeeper said.

"Where's yours, by the way?" Mac said. "You got the image of the potentate too?"

"Nah. Just the number. I'm kinda military that way."

Chloe glanced at Hannah, then back at the truck, where Mac slowly unlatched his seat belt and took off his cap. He leaned forward.

"I don't see anything."

"What? Look!"

From the walkie-talkie, George in a quiet singsong: "Now would be the perfect time."

The Peacekeeper spun in a circle, slammed back against the cab of the truck, and dropped, screaming. As he slowly started to rise, Mac said, "Say there, fella, what was that all about?"

"I don't know, I — ah, fire ants or something." He rubbed his back gingerly, now standing. He motioned to the officer in the other GC car, who quickly stepped out.

"What's the trouble?"

"Pain in my back, like I backed into a hot pipe or something. I think a blister's rising."

He leaned toward Mac again, then grabbed the back of his leg and howled, falling and writhing. The other officer drew his weapon. "What are you guys doing?"

"We're not doing anything!" Mac said. "What's his problem?"

The inside light of the truck came on, and George got out and went toward the front with his hands raised. He must have had the walkie-talkie in his pocket now, because Chloe could still hear him on Hannah's radio. "Can I help in any way?" he asked.

"Stay right where you are," the second Peacekeeper said, just before he flopped in the road, dropping his weapon and trying to cover his face.

Mac jumped out to help George. "Yank the radios in their cars," he said. "I'll get the ones on their uniforms."

By now the officers were delirious, glassy-eyed, and wailing. "Ladies," George radioed, "come help us with these cars."

Mac disarmed the officers and tossed their weapons into the bed of the truck. He took their radios and put them in the front seat. "Once you've got those car radios disconnected," he told George, "pop the trunks."

Chloe and Hannah came running. "Chloe," Mac said, "you two are going to give us an escort. Once I get this guy in the trunk of his car, I'll pull the truck in behind you. Hannah, you fall in behind once we get the other guy in his trunk."

The GC were whimpering. "You boys hush now," Mac said. "You're gonna hurt awhile, but you're not gonna die unless you make us shoot you. We're just going for a little ride."

With the GC ensconced in their respective trunks, Mac carefully turned the truck around and told George to give the women extra ammo from the bag they had gotten at the Co-op. With the truck and the two GC squad cars pointed west, one of the GC radios crackled. "North roadblock, acknowledge, please."

"North roadblock," Mac said, while only half mashing the transmit button.

"Repeat?"

"North roadblock here," he said, careful

to make sure he was heard, but not perfectly.

"Status?"

"Busy."

"Carry on."

George hopped back into the truck, and as Chloe pulled away and Mac followed, George said, "Looky here. I knew there was something about that old gal I really liked." In amongst the ammunition, Mrs. P. had had Co-op people pack bread, cheese, and fruit. "Chloe and Hannah took most of it," George said. "And I'm gonna take most of what's left unless you grab now."

Mac grabbed. And the unlikely convoy rolled west into the night toward their ride home. How long the ruse would hold was the mystery. For now, Mac enjoyed the food and the hope that they had beaten the odds.

Eleven

The report from Mac allowed Chang to breathe easier for the first time in hours. He checked back in to Carpathia's office, where Akbar was debriefing the big boss.

"We've had a setback, but there's no way this bunch can —"

"A setback?"

"Without going into all the details, sir, the hostage killed one of our people — a woman — and has escaped. We assume he's on the run with the three who —"

"He killed one of his captors?"

"Yes, Highness. We assume —"

"My kind of a man. Why cannot he be on our side?"

"We assume, sir, that he is reconnecting with the three who came for him, and we're hoping they will be foolish enough to try to get back to the airport. We have that sealed tight."

"Yes, well . . ." Carpathia sounded distracted, as if the rest of the story was not as interesting. "Suhail, how was damage control today?"

"Too early to tell, sir."

"Come, come, I count on you as one who does not try to simply appease me. They heard the pilot's report, and my telling them he was mistaken, that the bombs had missed their targets. Well, what are people saying?"

"I honestly don't know, Excellency. I have spent my entire day between your office and my own, trying to ride herd on this Greece thing."

"Let me tell you this, Suhail: The disc from the plane clearly shows direct hits and those traitors burning! Whatever is the magic that allows those people to survive simply cannot extend outside that area."

"Begging your pardon, but not that long ago we lost ground troops outside —"

"I know that, Suhail! Do you think I do not know that?"

"Apologies, Potentate."

"I want us to find the safe place surrounding that area, where we have not seen our weapons of war swallowed up by the earth, and from which we can stop all traffic in and out. They will need supplies, and we must see that they do not get them."

"Our armed forces have been so decimated, sir —"

"Are you telling me we have no pilots or planes that can cut off supplies to Petra?"

"No, sir. I'm sure we can do that. Ah, on another matter, sir, our ancient-text experts say that the next curse could be that the lakes and rivers of the world fall into the same predicament as the seas."

"*Freshwater* sources all turn to blood?"

"Yes, sir."

"Impossible! *Everyone* would die! Even our enemies."

"There are those who believe the Judahites will be protected, as they have been against our forces recently."

"Where will they get their water?"

"The same place they got their protection. Perhaps there is wisdom in negotiating with their leader to have the curses lifted."

"Never!"

"Not to be contrary, sir, but we cannot survive long with this devastation. And if the rivers and lakes do also turn —"

"You are not aware of everything, Suhail. I too have supernatural power."

"I have seen it, sir."

"You will see more. Reverend Fortunato

is prepared to match the wizardry of the Judah-ites blow for blow, and he has designates who can do this around the world."

"Well, that —"

"Now show me what I want to see, Suhail."

"North roadblock, this is Central."

"Roadblock," Mac said. "Go ahead, Central."

"Disposition of suspicious truck?"

"Repeat?"

"One of our squads reported that your first stop after they passed was a truck."

"Affirmative. Clean."

"Traveling west to east?"

"Affirmative."

"We traced a cell phone to the west side of the city and then east before losing it."

Mac looked at George. "What do they want to hear?"

"You know nothing about that."

Mac transmitted. "Can't help you there."

"Truck proceeded east?"

"Roger that."

"You reported lots of traffic."

"Ten-four."

"Busy?"

"Affirmative."

"Squads said they saw nothing but the

truck when they passed."

"Busy now."

"What's your ten-twenty, roadblock?"

Mac looked at George again. "They're onto us."

George pulled the weapons from beneath the seat and Rayford's walkie-talkie from his pocket. "Jinnah, Irene, be advised. We'll soon have company."

Mac clicked the GC radio button a few times. "Repeat," he said.

"Your ten-twenty, roadblock. What's your location?"

Chang froze. He had been nearly dozing, listening to Carpathia and Akbar's sparring while they watched reports from the United North American States and the United South American States. He had not kept up with the Ptolemaïs project.

The local GC had traced Elena's cell phone to the west side of the city, and it had remained in one location for more than an hour. Commander Nelson Stefanich and the survivors of the philosopher team were personally leading the raid on a pub in that area.

He phoned Mac.

"Talk fast, Chang. We may be in deep weeds here."

"How far west of the city are you?"

"Not sure. I've had this thing floored, but I don't think it goes faster'n fifty. They chasin' us?"

"Are you too far from the Co-op to help them?"

"Depends. What's up?"

"GC's raiding the pub right now. You know the next thing to go will be the Co-op."

"Any chance they got out?"

"Can't imagine. I couldn't warn them."

"I'm guessing we're less than thirty minutes from our plane. We'll go back if you think we can help."

"Hang on, a report's coming through. Judah-ite underground discovered beneath pub. Firefight. Sixteen GC dead, and another dozen injured. Building grenaded and torched. Several adjacent buildings destroyed. No enemy survivors."

While Mac filled in George, the GC continued to try to reach Mac on the radio, asking for some kind of a code. "We've blocked off both ends of the north road due to the raid, so wrap it up," they said. "Still need your all-clear code."

George looked devastated and tried to grab the GC radio from Mac. "I'll give 'em an all-clear code."

"Take it easy, friend."

"This was *my* fault, Mac! What was I thinking, hanging on to that phone?"

"I wish we could have gone back," Mac said. "I'd like to have taken out a few of them myself. But our brothers and sisters are in heaven, and it sounds like they put up some kind of a fight."

"That's it?" George said. "We're supposed to feel good because I got a bunch of people killed and now they're in heaven?"

"Need the all-clear code now," the radio said.

"I ought to tell them it's Psalm 94:1," Mac said.

"I know what I'd like to tell 'em. Have the women stop and we'll get those GC to tell us the code."

"They'd probably give away where we are."

"Not with the DEW starin' 'em in the face. Let me get it out of 'em, Mac. Please. I've got to do this."

"Chloe, pull it over," Mac said.

"Right now?"

"Right now."

"We okay?"

"Temporarily."

Mac's phone chirped. Chang. "Stefanich and Plato and a bunch of GC are looking for the truck and the two GC squads. They're heading west."

"Let's make this quick," Mac said, jumping out as Chloe emerged and Hannah pulled up behind.

"Pop that trunk, Chloe," George said, "and Hannah, let me have the DEW."

Chloe opened the trunk, and Mac shone a flashlight in on the nearly wasted Peacekeeper. George pulled him from the trunk with one hand, and he lay crying on the ground. "Blisters," he sobbed. "Careful, please. Or kill me."

"You'd like that, wouldn't you?" George said, wielding the DEW. "See this?"

The man opened one eye and nodded miserably.

"This is what cooks your flesh, and there's plenty more juice in it."

"Please, no."

George turned it on, and the thing whirred to life.

"Please!"

He aimed it at the man's ankle, and the man stiffened, whining. "Give me your all-clear code."

"What?"

"You heard me. Give me the all-clear or —"

"It's in the glove box! In my book!"

Chloe went to check. She brought back a small, black leather ring binder. "It's full of all kinds of notes," she said.

George took it and dropped it onto the man.

"We've got to get rolling," Mac said. "They're never going to buy the all-clear from us now anyway. They're on their way."

"These guys are deadweight," George said. "Maybe we can slow the others by leaving them here in the road."

The man was ripping through the pages. He gingerly held the notebook up to the light from the truck's headlamp. "It's one-one-six-four-eight!" he said.

George dragged him onto the road while Mac brought the other from the other car. The men lay writhing. "Just kill us," the second one pleaded.

"You don't know what you're asking," George said. "Bad as this is, trust me, you should prefer it."

"Leave one of the cars here," Mac said. "Block the road with it and the truck. It won't take the GC long to get around them, but any slowdown has to help."

Chloe maneuvered one car nose to nose with the truck across the highway; then they ripped out the distributor caps from both vehicles and took the keys.

"Last call for clear code," the radio said.

Mac hollered it into the mike. Then, "Chloe, you drive. And keep it to the floor. I'll ride shotgun. I don't expect them to catch us now, but everybody stay armed and ready."

George put the DEW in the trunk and climbed in the back with Hannah. The economy car was too small for the four of them and seemed to groan with the weight, but Chloe soon had the thing chugging along at over seventy miles an hour.

George said, "So, Mac, what's Psalm 94:1?"

Mac turned as far as he could in the seat. " 'O God,' " he said, " 'to whom vengeance belongs, shine forth!' "

The GC radio came to life again. "We need an immediate ten-twenty. Personnel on the north road report zero traffic and no sign of you."

"Give me that," George said, pulling it from Mac's hand. He mashed the button. "Yeah, you'll find us at Psalm 94:1."

Chang fixed himself some tea, adding a strange concoction that included instant coffee with the highest concentration of caffeine he could find. He would crash when this ordeal was over, but he couldn't risk dozing now. It was clear the Greek GC had a bead on his people, and it wouldn't be long before they figured out Mac must have a plane at the abandoned strip not twenty minutes more up the road. He certainly wasn't going to escape into Albania. How long would it take Mac and his people to board, and how far could they get before needing to refuel?

Meanwhile, from what Chang could hear, Carpathia was at least entertained — if not totally distracted — by feeds from his regions where it was still daytime. The potentate for Region 0, the United South American States, announced an event he said his wife, "the first lady," was personally attending right then.

"And where are you while she is doing your work?" Carpathia asked.

"Oh, my revered risen one, you may rest assured that I am doing the greater work. We have taken you at your word regarding the effort to root out infidels here, and I am working closely with our Peacekeepers and Morale Monitors, as well as with civilian undercover groups. We expect to have dozens more face the guillotine or take your mark within twenty-four hours."

"Dozens? My dear friend, we are hearing from your compatriots around the world that some are finding hundreds, even thousands, who will suffer for their disloyalty. Some are stepping up efforts even in our part of the world, in the dark of night."

The South American sighed. "Sir, sadly, we are so dependent on the seas that our forces have been dramatically reduced."

"But surely so have your dissidents, have they not?"

"That is true. But please, allow me to take you live to Uruguay, where my wife attends the public ceremony culminating in loyalty enforcement."

Chang switched quickly to Mac and his crew — nothing new — then tapped into the video feed from the United South American States. The first lady was receiving enthusiastic applause. She had her arm around a shy-looking middle-aged man. "This gentleman is finally getting his mark of loyalty to our risen potentate!"

More cheering.

"And tell us, Andrés, what took you so long?"

"I was afraid," he said, smiling.

"Afraid of what?"

"The needle."

Many laughed and cheered.

"But you will do it today?"

"A very small 0, yes," he said.

"You are no longer afraid of the needle?"

"Yes, I am still. But I fear the blade much more."

The crowd cheered and continued to applaud as Andrés sat stiffly for the application of the mark. His forehead was swabbed, someone held his hand, the machine was applied, and he looked genuinely relieved and happy.

The first lady said, "You may now return to what you were doing when you were discovered without the mark."

The camera followed Andrés as he ran back to the image of Carpathia and fell to his knees before it. The first lady told the crowd, "Andrés avoided detection for so long because he obeyed the decree to worship the image, and no one suspected."

Carpathia did not seem impressed. "He worships me and yet he is afraid of a little pinprick. Agh!"

"But you will be most pleased, Potentate," the South American leader said. "Following the leads of several loyal citizens, we have uncovered a den of opposition. Six were killed when they resisted arrest, but thirteen have been brought to this worship and enforcement center."

"How many will take the mark now?" Carpathia said. "How many have had their attitudes adjusted by the very presence of the loyalty enforcement facilitator?"

"Well, uh, actually none so far, sir."

Chang heard a fist slam. "Stubborn!" Carpathia said. "So stubborn. Why are these people so resolute? so stupid? so shortsighted?"

"Today they will pay, Highness."

"Right now, even as we speak?" Carpathia's voice evidenced his excitement.

"Yes, right now."

"What is the music?"

"The condemned ones hum and sing, my lord. It is not uncommon."

"Shut them up!"

"One moment. Excuse me, sir." He called to someone in the background, "Jorge! Communicate to the officers at the site that the supreme potentate does not allow the music. Yes, now! Your Highness, it will be stopped."

"These have definitely chosen the blade?"

"They have, sir. They are in line."

"What are we waiting for?"

"Only to carry out your wish to stop the music, sir."

"Get on with it! The blade will silence them."

Chang recoiled when he saw a guard with a huge rifle and bayonet nudging the first person in line, a woman who appeared to be in her late twenties. She was singing, her face turned toward heaven. The guard yelled at her, but she did not acknowledge. He bumped her and she stumbled, but still she sang, eyes upward.

He jabbed her in the ribs with the butt of the rifle, and she dropped to one knee, then rose and continued singing. Now he set himself to her side, planted his feet, and drove the bayonet through her arm and into her side. She cried out as the bayonet was removed, and she reached with her other hand to press it over the wound. Her singing now came in sobs as the people behind her fell to their knees.

"What is she singing?" Carpathia demanded.

The sound was enhanced, and Chang found himself breathless as he listened to the woman's pitiful, labored singing. She could no longer hold up her head, but she stood wobbling, clearly woozy, struggling to sing, ". . . did e'er such love and sorrow meet, or thorns compose so rich a crown?"

The guard was joined by others, swinging the stocks of their rifles at the heads of those who bowed.

"Tell the guards to stop making a spectacle of it!" Carpathia raged. "They are playing right into these people's hands. Let the crowd see that no matter what they do or say or sing, still their heads belong to us!"

The guillotine was readied as the woman continued to force out the lyrics, though she had long since lost the tune. As she was grabbed by guards on each side and wrestled into place, she cried out, ". . . demands my soul, my life, my all!"

The blade dropped and the crowd erupted.

"Aah!" Carpathia sighed. "Can we not see from the other side?"

"The other side, sir?" the South American potentate repeated.

"Of the blade! Of the blade! Get a camera around there! The body does not drop! It merely collapses. I want to see the head drop!"

The next several in line approached the killing machine with their palms raised. The guards kept grabbing their elbows and pulling down their arms, but the condemned kept raising them. The guards slashed at their hands with bayonets, but the people instinctively moved and mostly avoided being cut.

The guards moved in behind them and prodded them with bayonet points in the lower back. Now the camera moved around behind a man who held a safety lever with one hand and used the other to grab the hair of the victim and pull the head into place. He lowered the restraining bar onto the neck, let go of the lever, and nodded to a matronly woman. She yanked at the release cord.

The blade squealed against the guides as it dropped in a flash, and the head fell out of sight, blood erupting from the neck.

"That is more like it!" Carpathia whispered.

"We're home free, aren't we?" Hannah said.

Mac turned to look at her. "My plane has about enough fuel to get us to Rome. There's a small airstrip south of there manned by Co-op people who stockpile fuel. I'm not going to feel safe until we take off from there."

"But these people, I mean," she said. "They'll never reach this airport before we do, will they?"

"Not in cars."

"What're you saying?" George said.

"It won't take 'em long to guess where we're going. They won't think we're trying to beat 'em to the border by car."

"Your plane hidden?"

"From auto traffic, sure. From the air? No."

"How long would it take them to fly here?"

"Out of Kozani, in a fighter? They could beat us there."

"Could they destroy your plane?"

"Only if they get there first."

"How much personnel could they bring?"

"Not many if they use a small, quick plane."

George sounded irritated. "This has been too much work to see it fail now, Mac. Let's get it all on the table. You hoping we just show up, climb aboard, and take off?"

"That's the only plan I've got," Mac said.

"We've got to figure they'll beat us there," George said, "and decide what to do about that."

"You want to assume the worst?"

"Of course! We have to. You think I got away from those idiots by hoping they'd let me go? Tell me about this airstrip."

"Runs east and west. I'm at the east end, facing west."

"If they can get a plane in there before we take off, all they have to do is get in our way."

"Let's get in their way first," Mac said. "I'll dump you guys at the plane; you get the engines warm while I drive out onto the runway and sit directly in our path. They're going to have to be pretty crafty and flexible to avoid hitting me on landing. When we take off, we angle enough to miss the car and them, and we're gone."

George shook his head. "And when do you board? You're leaving a lot to chance."

"Leaving it to God, George. I don't know what else to do."

Mac's phone buzzed. "Go, Chang."

"They're in a jet ten minutes from touchdown. Stefanich, the three philosophers, and a pilot. Plane does not appear to be offensively equipped, but they are heavily armed."

"We're closer than that," Mac said. "We just have to beat 'em, that's all."

He asked Chloe if she could get any more out of the little car, but it was whining as it was, speeding along on a bad road. "When we get there, get off the road and come in on the east end."

Mac was giving Sebastian instructions about the plane when he thought he heard the scream of jet engines in the distance. He and George rolled down their windows to listen. "That's our clearing, Chloe! Easy!"

She whipped off the road, down into a ravine, and up the other side. The car bounced and jerked, and Mac's head hit the ceiling. "Use your brights! I have no idea what's out here."

"Am I going to be able to get through those trees?" she said.

"Assume you will. Just get us there."

Chloe hit a rocky patch that threw the car into the air. When it landed, the left rear tire blew. "Great!" she said.

"At least it's in the back," George said. "Stand on it!"

With the brights on, Chloe saw only uneven, rocky terrain up to a thick grove of trees. She couldn't imagine a way through, but there was no turning back now. The left rear side was dragging from the flat as if someone had dropped an anchor. It didn't help that Sebastian, the biggest person in the car, sat back there.

With the jet looming, Chloe wished she could kill the lights and just plow on through. But it had all come down to timing. And determination. These were the people who had killed her comrades and who would now snuff out this little surviving band of Trib Forcers without a thought.

Chloe had wanted action, to be in the thick of it. And though she would do whatever it took to get back to Buck and Kenny, she was already long past any option but recklessness. Caution, diplomacy, trickery — that was all out the window now. She had to get to that plane and they had to take off, or none of them would see the sun rise again.

She picked her way through the trees, only occasionally lifting her foot from the accelerator. The little car had front-wheel drive, a small blessing in a bad situation. Making her own path, she smacked the car against a tree first on one side, then the other, and kept going.

Now she could see Mac's plane, but a three-wire fence was in the way. Slowing even a bit could make the car get tangled in it. She glanced at Mac, who braced himself with a palm on the ceiling. He merely nodded at the fence as if she had no choice. Chloe kept the accelerator down, and the car caught the lower wire, made the top two slip over the hood, pulled a wood post from the ground, and snapped its way through to the edge of the runway, forty feet from the plane.

Banking at the other end came the GC jet, landing lights illuminating the strip all the way to the car.

Twelve

For the first time since he had been running the point for the Tribulation Force at the palace complex, Chang wondered if he had been found out. His computer screen was suddenly ringed with a red border, meaning an outside source was testing his firewall.

He immediately switched to a screen saver that scrolled the date and time and temperature, cut all the lights in his apartment, disrobed, and jumped into bed — prepared to look as if he had been sleeping, should Figueroa or one of his minions come knocking. There was really no way of knowing what the warning meant, but David Hassid had told him he had built the security in just to alert the operator that someone was nosing around.

Maybe someone was checking to see

every computer that was turned on. Who knew whether the search was capable of hacking in and finding out who the mole was?

The latter didn't seem possible, if David could be believed. He had rigged the system so elaborately that it seemed there wouldn't be enough years left before the Glorious Appearing before someone could decode it. Chang's mind began playing games. Perhaps Akbar had instructed Figueroa to sense every computer running, eliminate the mainframe that ran the whole place, isolate the laptops and personal computers, and do a fast door-to-door search to see what people were up to.

Chang's computer would show no record of what he had been doing during the hours since he got back from his office. For that reason, he hoped someone would show up and check.

As he lay there in the darkness, heart galloping, Chang was frustrated at having to quit monitoring Greece. Ironic, he thought, that with all the technology God had allowed them to adapt for the cause of Christ around the world, he was suddenly left with nothing to do to help, except old-fashioned praying. He wished he could check the bugs in Carpathia's and Akbar's offices once more to see if the computer recording showed them giving a directive. It wouldn't be long before someone at the highest level ran out of patience with all the hacking going on.

Chang eased out of bed and onto the cold floor, kneeling to pray for Mac and Chloe and Hannah and George. "Lord, I don't see how they can escape now, outside your direct help. I don't know if it's their time to join you, and I have never assumed our thoughts were your thoughts. Everything happens in your time for your pleasure, but I pray for them and the people who love them. Whatever you do I know will prove your greatness, and I ask that I be able to know soon what it was. Also, please be with Ming as she searches for our parents, and may they be able to communicate with me somehow."

Chang felt the urge to let Rayford know what was going on. He looked at his watch. It was well after midnight, but would the people in Petra be sleeping after all that had gone on there that day? Nothing indicated that his phone was not still secure, so he dialed.

"Out! Out!" Mac hollered as the doors flew open. "Let me over there, Chloe. I've got to get in the way of that jet."

"I'll crank 'er up," Sebastian told Mac, "but I'm not inclined to leave without you."

"Listen, George. You do what you have to do. Worrying about me might distract 'em long enough for you to get in the air. If that's what it takes, I'll see you at the Eastern Gate."

"Don't talk like that!"

"Don't get emotional on me now. Get yourselves on home!"

Mac waited a beat for George to back away from the car, and when he didn't, Mac just floored it and wobbled down the runway, in line with the jet that was just about to touch down.

Rayford was not asleep, but he had finally settled and was breathing easier, gazing at the stars through a slit in the tent. His phone indicated Chang was calling.

"Give me good news," he said.

"I wish I could," Chang said, "but I think the Lord just wanted me to let you know so you could pray."

Rayford didn't feel as glib as he sounded, but when he heard the story, he said, "God protected a million people in a fiery furnace; he can get four out of Greece."

He slipped on his sandals and hurried to

where Tsion and Chaim were to bed down. If they were sleeping, he would not wake them. It didn't surprise him to find them awake and huddled around a computer with some of the other elders. At the keyboard was the young woman, Naomi, who had summoned him earlier.

"Tsion, a word," Rayford said.

Dr. Ben-Judah turned, surprised. "I thought you were sleeping, as we all should be. Big day tomorrow."

Rayford brought him up to date.

"We will pray, of course, right now. But get back to Chang and tell him the computer warning was a false alarm. Naomi has been exulting in the hundreds of pages of instructions David built into the system here, including one that allows us to check the palace computers. That is what she has been doing, and that sent Chang's computer a warning."

Tsion hurried back to the elders and asked them all to pray for the safety of the Tribulation Force contingent in Greece. To see a dozen and a half people immediately go to their knees for his people warmed Rayford, and he couldn't wait to get back to Chang.

When George Sebastian's foot hit the first

step up to the plane, he heard the engines whine and then scream to life. He had not realized either of the women knew how to fly. So much the better. He squatted to pull the door up behind him, but when he turned toward the cockpit, he noticed both Chloe and Hannah strapping themselves into the back two seats. They looked as surprised as he felt.

George set his Uzi and pressed his back up against the bulkhead that separated the cabin from the cockpit. He slowly edged around to where he could peer up front to see who was there. The surprise pilot, in brown and beige Bedouin-type robes, was working from the copilot's chair. Without turning, the man raised a hand and motioned George toward the pilot's chair.

George pulled back and faced the women. "Who is that?"

"We thought it was you," Chloe said.

"We've got to get him off here or we won't have room for Mac. Cover me."

Chloe unstrapped and knelt behind George with her Uzi ready. Hannah raised her weapon and stood on the arm of her seat so she could peer over George's head into the cockpit.

Sebastian hopped into view of the copilot's chair. Empty. "All righty then,"

George said, exhaling loudly and climbing over the back of the seat to take the controls. He jammed on the earphones. "Why doesn't God just let these guys do the flying?"

"I can do that too," a voice said.

George jumped and saw the reflection of the man in the windshield. But when he looked to his right, the copilot's chair was still empty. "Quit that!" George said, his pulse racing.

"Sorry."

"Michael, I suppose."

"Roger."

George saw Mac and the rattling GC car struggling down the runway in the face of the oncoming jet. He wanted to ask Michael if he wouldn't be more help riding next to Mac.

"Illuminate landing lights," he heard.

"For takeoff?"

"Roger."

Sebastian wasn't about to argue. He flipped on the landing lights, which merely shone into Mac's back window. "Should I start the taxi, angling away from Mac, like he said?"

"Stand by."

"No?"

"Hold."

For an instant, Mac thought the GC jet didn't see him. He slammed on the brakes and stayed in line between the two craft. When the jet finally stopped, about fifty feet in front of him, he realized it could easily go around him. Why wasn't Sebastian rolling? With the right angle, he could get past Mac and the GC and be in the air in seconds.

Not wanting to give the GC a chance to cut George off, Mac hit the accelerator and pulled to within ten feet of the jet. He realized someone could open the door and have a clear shot at him, but they couldn't do much to his plane if he sabotaged their aircraft. Not wanting to give them time to think, he raced forward and lodged the front of the car under the nose of the jet, banging into the landing gear. He had raised the plane off the ground a few inches but couldn't tell if he had done any damage.

Mac rolled down his window and leaned his torso all the way out, firing his Uzi at the tires. He was amazed how resilient they were, and he heard bullets bouncing off and hitting the fuselage and the car. Reaching farther and experimenting with angles, he finally got one of the tires to blow. But where was George? Why weren't they advancing? Was something wrong with the plane?

Sebastian just sat at the end of the runway with those lights on.

Mac expected the GC to come bounding out any second, weapons blazing. Could they not see he was the only person in the car? What were they afraid of? He was a sitting duck, lodged under their jet.

Mac tried to open the door, found it hopelessly stuck, and tried getting out the other side. It too was out of shape and not moving, but he thought he sensed a little more give on that side. He lay on the front seat and pushed with his hands on the driver's side door while pressing against the passenger door with his feet. It finally broke free and he scrambled out.

He crouched beneath the jet, Uzi trained on the door. He would take them as they came out, if they dared. Maybe they were waiting for him to make a break for his own plane or for Sebastian to come and pick him up. But opening the door for him would slow George too, and all of them would be in danger.

As he waited, locked in a bewildering standoff, Mac didn't know what to do. Should he try to shoot through the skin of the jet and take them all out? If it was armor plated, which was likely, he would waste ammunition. Why weren't they coming after him? And why was George still waiting?

The GC jet shut down. Now what? Nothing. No movement inside or out.

Frustrated, Mac grabbed his walkie-talkie. "Chloe or Hannah," he whispered desperately, "come in, please."

"Chloe here, Mac."

"What's going on?"

"Got me. George is at the controls."

"What's he doing?"

"You wanna talk to him? Here."

"Kinda busy here, Mac. What's up?"

"You can see what's up! What're you doing?"

"Waiting for clearance."

"You're clear! Go! Go now! Angle to your right! These guys are hung up and I've got one of their tires blown. They've shut down their engines."

"Waiting for you, partner."

"Don't be silly. I'd run right into their line of fire. Go to the other end of the runway, and I'll meet you there. But if they come after me, just keep going."

"Yeah, I know, and you'll see me in heaven."

"Exactly — now quit being stupid and go!"

"I'm not being stupid, Mac. I'm obeying."

"You're supposed to obey *me,* so do as I say."

"Sorry. You've been superseded."

"What?"

"You're supposed to put down your weapon and walk this way."

"You got GC on that plane!?"

"Negative. Come unarmed, and you will be safe."

"Have you lost your mind?"

"God is telling you to come."

Mac shook his head. "Ah, stand by."

"Come now."

Mac sighed, his eyes darting back and forth between the jet door and his own plane. He pushed the transmit button. "Lord, if it is you, command me to come that way."

"Come."

The voice had not been George's.

"Unarmed?"

"Come."

Mac waited a beat, then unstrapped the Uzi and laid it on the ground. He turned off the walkie-talkie and jammed it into his pocket. He walked past the car and stood directly under the cockpit. He felt exposed, vulnerable, indefensible. If that jet door opened now, he was a dead man.

He heard nothing above him, saw nothing beside him. Mac stepped out from under the plane and headed directly in front of it.

He kept imagining he heard movement behind him — the engines roaring to life, footsteps from the cabin to the door, the door opening, weapons firing.

He prayed urgently as he strode along, "Lord, save me!"

Immediately he felt as if God's hands were upon him, and he barely felt his feet on the ground. "O you of little faith, why do you doubt?"

The voice was clear as crystal, but the walkie-talkie was off and George had his engines roaring. Mac broke into a trot, then a run. Every step sounded like a gunshot. Hannah was lowering the door when he got there, and he leaped in.

"Flyin' or backseat drivin'?" George said, unstrapping as if ready to take the copilot's chair.

"Here is fine," Mac said. "I don't think I could ride a bike right now."

Chang was relieved to hear from Rayford and eager to meet Naomi even if only online. He was tempted to scold her for scaring him, and so decided to wait until the next day to try to make contact. Meanwhile, he checked in on Mac and his team, fearing the worst despite all the praying that had been going on.

Mac answered his phone, sounding exhausted.

"I need to meet this Michael someday," Chang said, after hearing the story. "You guys get all the fun."

"I could use a little less fun, frankly," Mac said. "And you might as well know, Sebastian here doesn't call him Michael anymore. Calls him Roger."

"Roger?"

"Says he told him he assumed he was Michael, and the guy said, 'Roger.'"

"So Stefanich and those guys are just sitting on the runway with a wounded plane?"

"Yeah, and they're gonna need some repair work before they can take off again."

"Why didn't they shoot you?"

"I thought you could find out. What was going on in that cockpit when I strolled out from underneath, unarmed?"

"I'll let you know."

Within half an hour the rest of the Tribulation Force had heard the good news out of Greece, and Chang had paved the way for George to land south of Rome for the refuel. They were on their own for getting back to the safe house without going through Kankakee, Illinois, and without arousing more suspicion. That should be the easiest part of their ordeal.

When Chang was finally able to hack back into the Ptolemaïs GC system and find transmissions between the plane and the Kozani tower, he could only shake his head. The pilot had reported seeing the plane at the end of the runway, putting down, and seeing a car approaching. But at the same time Chang figured Michael had instructed George to turn on his landing lights, the pilot reported a light so blinding that "we have lost visual contact with the plane and the auto."

A few minutes later the pilot reported being struck — by what, he did not know. His jet was being jostled and the front end lifted, but no one aboard could take his hands from his eyes because of the intense light. They heard shooting and feared for their lives, heard one of their tires blow, and shut down the engines. In essence they sat in fear, unable to peek out of the cockpit for the next several minutes, until they heard the plane thunder past them and rise.

Chang listened as they finally ventured out, shoulder radios left on, weapons ordered at the ready, only to find their damaged plane, wounded landing gear, flat tire, beat-up squad car, and an Uzi on the runway. Only now they were being rescued by a fleet of GC in cars, who reported that others had picked up the injured officers at the side of the road on the way. They were being treated for severe burns they claimed were caused by a ray gun.

It was still a couple of hours before Ming was to leave San Diego for the Far East. Chang was finally finished with his night's work. He dropped into bed, spent. How strange, he thought, to feel so pivotal and indispensable and then discover that the entire success of an operation was out of his hands. In fact, he had been out of commission when God worked his miracles.

There were victims to grieve, martyrs to praise, and much work ahead. Chang didn't know how long he could evade detection. He was willing to hang in and work in the office during the day, doing his real work after hours, for as long as God chose to protect him.

Rayford stirred at dawn's first light, amazed he had been able to sleep at all. Petra was already humming, families gathering the morning's manna and filling any container they could find with the pure springwater God provided.

Thousands were working on the caves, thousands of others erecting more tents. On everyone's lips were stories of the miracle from the day before and the promise of live teaching from Dr. Tsion Ben-Judah himself later in the day.

From the elders and organizers came word that building materials were on their way and that the people should pray for the safety of pilots and truckers who would begin delivering materials. Volunteers were sought with expertise in various crafts. Rayford knew the current spirit could not last forever. The memory of the miracle would fade, inevitably, though he could not imagine it. And people, regardless of their shared faith, would find living elbow to elbow taxing after a while. But for now he would enjoy this.

Rayford would have to get back to the Tribulation Force at some point, but Carpathia's people would target anyone coming or going from Petra. Perhaps if the supplies were able to get in, that would be a clue it was prudent to try to get out.

Naomi and her team of computer gurus already reported that *The Truth* cyberzine had been transmitted from Buck Williams, recounting stories from around the world. The whole episode of what had gone on in Greece the day before was played out in detail, as was the truth about what had happened at Petra.

A team of computer experts from Israel said they had the technology to project *The Truth* onto a giant screen, if one could be fashioned. And among the various supplies already in the camp was enough white canvas to be stretched several stories high. Thousands gathered to read the stories.

Rayford loved the idea that it was not just believers, not just the so-called Judah-ites, who read *The Truth*. Many undecideds and even some who had taken the mark of Antichrist risked their lives by downloading Buck's magazine from the Tribulation Force site. All over the world the believers' underground and Co-op personnel translated it and printed it and distributed it. Carpathia could get away with nothing.

Sadly, Rayford knew, there were hundreds, if not thousands, of uncommitted people right there in Petra. Tsion had already promised to address them too, going so far as to say many of them would *still* be deceived and eventually spirited away by liars and charlatans. It was hard to understand or believe. How could someone have survived what Rayford had lived through and even question the one true God of the universe? It was beyond him.

Late in the morning, nearly twenty-four hours since the bombing, the people began to gather. Word spread that Dr. Ben-Judah would begin his teaching on the mercy of God. Throughout the crowd, however, stories also spread from around the world that persecution had intensified against believers and particularly against Jews.

Chang had tapped into the feeds to Akbar's and Fortunato's and Carpathia's offices and had set on automatic the utility that sent to Buck Williams's computer the reports from the sub-potentates around the world. As the sun rose in various countries, news of the bloodshed and mayhem of the night before and the relentless daytime raids was transmitted not just to New Babylon, but also from Chang to Buck and from Buck to the world through *The Truth*.

As the crowds gathered to hear Dr. Ben-Judah, they were riveted to the giant screen, set on a wall away from the sun for best viewing. Buck had transmitted the visuals Chang had sent him from the United South American States, and the masses booed and hissed as the shy man accepted the mark of loyalty. They cheered, then wept, then sang and praised God for the testimony of the brave martyrs who faced the blade with such peace and courage.

The remnant at Petra seemed outraged en masse at the reports from Greece about a midnight raid that had destroyed what was left of the small contingent of underground believers. Buck had added audio to that video report, reminding his readers and listeners and watchers that it had fallen to Greek believers to be among the first to give their lives rather than accept the mark of the beast.

Now, it seemed, on every continent the Morale Monitors and the Peacekeepers had been revitalized, financed, equipped, and motivated to more than turn up the heat. From every corner of the globe came reports of the end of the patience of the Global Community for dissenters or even the undecided. It was either accept the mark now or face the consequences immediately. Even many who had already taken the mark of Carpathia were punished for not bowing to worship his image three times a day.

Leon Fortunato came on — in full regalia and introduced by every title and pedigree he had ever enjoyed — to warn that "those of Jewish descent who are as stubborn as the Judah-ites and insist on worshiping a god other than our father and risen lord, Nicolae Carpathia, shall find themselves receiving their just reward. Yea, death is too good for them. Oh, they shall surely die, but it is hereby decreed that no Jew should be allowed the mercy of a quick end by the blade. Graphic and reproachful as that is, it is virtually painless. No, these shall suffer day and night in their dens of iniquity, and by the time they expire due to natural causes — brought about by their own rejection of Carpathianism — they will be praying, crying out, for a death so expedient as the loyalty enforcement facilitator."

Those in Petra appeared to Rayford shocked by the lengths New Babylon would go to, to take revenge on its enemies and humiliate Jews. But their greatest wrath and derision were saved for the report from GCNN about what had happened the day before, right there in the red rock city.

An anchorman intoned that the attack on Petra — two incendiary bombs and a land-based launch missile — had missed their target and that the enemy encamped there had swiftly struck back and downed the two fighter-bombers, killing the pilots. The laughter began with that report and turned to waving fists and hisses and boos as Carpathia came on to mourn the deaths of the martyred airmen.

"While there is no denying that it was pilot error, still the Global Community, I am sure, joins me in extending its deepest sympathy to the surviving families. We decided not to risk any more personnel in trying to destroy this stronghold of the enemy, but we will starve them out by cutting off supply lines. Within days, this will be the largest Jewish concentration camp in history, and their foolish stubbornness will have caught up with them.

"Fellow citizens of the new world order, my compatriots in the Global Community, we have these people and their leaders to thank for the tragedy that besets our seas and oceans. I have been repeatedly urged by my closest advisers to negotiate with these international terrorists, these purveyors of black magic who have used their wicked spells to cause such devastation.

"I am sure you agree with me that there is no future in such diplomacy. I have nothing to offer in exchange for the millions of human lives lost, not to mention the beauty and the richness of the plant and animal life.

"You may rest assured that my top people are at work to devise a remedy to this tragedy, but it will not include deals, concessions, or any acknowledgment that these people had the right to foist on the world such an unspeakable act."

In the middle of that newscast, from Chang through Buck, came a reproduction of the conversation between Suhail Akbar and the two pilots from the Petra bombing raid. Though the GCNN tried to speak over it and stream words in front of it saying it was false, a hoax, anyone listening heard the pilots defending themselves to Akbar, and his order for their executions.

Rayford could not fathom how Carpathia could have a supporter left in the world, and yet it was clear that Scripture foretold he would. At Petra the crowd grew restless and murmured among themselves about both the lies and the truth they had just been exposed to. But the rumor was that Micah, the one who had led them out of Israel to this safe place, was about to emerge and introduce Dr. Ben-Judah.

Spontaneously, the entire crowd fell silent.

Thirteen

Chaim Rosenzweig held both hands aloft and addressed the assembled in a huge voice that could be heard everywhere.

"It is my great pleasure and personal joy to once again introduce to you my former student, my personal friend, now my mentor, and your rabbi, shepherd, pastor, and teacher, Dr. Tsion Ben-Judah!"

The only reason Rayford did not applaud and cheer was that he knew Tsion hated personal adulation. Yet he hoped the rabbi would appreciate that these people were merely trying to express their love for him.

When Dr. Ben-Judah was finally able to quiet the crowd, he said, "Thank you for the warmth of your welcome, but I ask that in the future, when I am introduced, you do me the honor of merely silently thanking

God for his love and mercy. That is what I will be talking about primarily, and whether you pray, raise your hands, or just point to the sky in acknowledgment of him, your adoration will be properly directed.

"In the fourteenth chapter of the Gospel of John, our Lord, Jesus the Messiah, makes a promise we can take to the bank of eternity. He says, 'Let not your heart be troubled; you believe in God, believe also in me. In my father's house are many mansions; if it were not so, I would have told you. I go to prepare a place for you. And if I go and prepare a place for you, I will come again and receive you to myself; that where I am, there you may be also.'

"Notice the urgency. That was Jesus' guarantee that though he was leaving his disciples, one day he would return. The world had not seen the last of Jesus the Christ, and as many of you know, it still has not seen the last of him.

"Think with me now of the five paramount, pivotal events of history. From Eden until this present moment, God has given us in the Bible an accurate history of the world, much of it written in advance. It is the only truly accurate history ever written.

"The first pivotal event was the creation of the world by the direct act of God.

"Next comes the worldwide flood. This flood had a catastrophic effect on the world and still boggles the minds of scientists who find fish bones at altitudes as high as fifteen thousand feet.

"The third pivotal event in history was the first coming of Jesus the Messiah. That event made possible our salvation from sin. Jesus lived a perfect life and died as a sacrifice for our sin. He died for the sins of the world, for all those who would call upon him.

"But that is not the end of the story, as we all know, because none of us here called upon him to forgive our sins until after the fourth pivotal event in history — when he came back.

"Most of us have since rectified that situation, and it is a good thing. Both the Old and the New Testaments of the Bible point to his coming one last time — the fifth pivotal event in world history. This glorious appearing will signal the beginning of the millennial kingdom, true utopia.

"Imagine paradise on earth with Messiah in control. Many believe that during his thousand-year reign, which will begin less than three and a half years from now, the population will grow to greater than the number of all the people who have already lived and died up to now. How can that be? Because ours will be a world without war. Imagine a globe in which government will not be responsible for killing the nearly 200 million it has slain to this day.

"Serving God has never been the choice of mankind. But when Messiah returns, he will establish his kingdom and people will live at peace. We will live in righteousness. We will have plenty. It is difficult to describe what an incredible time it will be. Everyone will have enough.

"God wants this kind of a world, and he wants it for us for one reason: He is gracious. In the Bible, Joel 2:13 says he is merciful, slow to anger, and abundant in loving-kindness. He relents from doing harm. Jonah, 125 years after Joel was born, described God in the same words. And Moses, fifteen hundred years before these men lived, said the Lord is merciful and gracious, long-suffering, and abundant in goodness and truth.

"Those are the prophets' views of God. Where do you get your view of God? What better picture of him could we have gotten than what we lived through yesterday? When you kneel to pray, remember that event and what the prophets have said. Yes, we have an august God — the only supreme,

286

omnipotent potentate. But if the Bible teaches one thing about God, it is that he is for us. He is not against us. He wants to bless our lives, and the key to the door of blessing is to give your life to him and ask him to do with it as he will. How could you not love the God the prophets describe? How could you not love the God Jesus the Messiah refers to as our Father who is in heaven?

"How wonderful it is that we can come as children into the presence of God himself, the creator of everything, and call him our Father.

"We find ourselves enduring the worst period in human history. Sixteen of the prophesied judgments of God have already rained down upon the earth, each worse than the last, with five yet to go. The Antichrist has been revealed, as has the False Prophet. That is why Messiah referred to this period as the Tribulation, and the second half of it — in which we now find ourselves — as the Great Tribulation.

"How can I say this judging, avenging God is loving and merciful? Remember that during this period he is working in people to get them to make a decision. Why? The millennium is coming. When Jesus makes his final glorious appearing, he will come in power and great glory. He will set up his kingdom exclusively for those who have made the right decision. That decision? To call on the name of the Lord.

"Does that sound exclusivistic? Understand this: The Bible makes clear that the will of God is that all men be saved. Second Peter 3:9 says, 'The Lord is not slack concerning his promise . . . but is long-suffering toward us, not willing that any should perish but that all should come to repentance.'

"God promised in Joel 2 that he would 'show wonders in the heavens and in the earth: blood and fire and pillars of smoke. The sun shall be turned into darkness, and the moon into blood, before the coming of the great and awesome day of the Lord. And it shall come to pass that whoever calls on the name of the Lord shall be saved. For in Mount Zion and in Jerusalem there shall be deliverance, as the Lord has said, among the remnant whom the Lord calls.'

"Dear people, *you* are that remnant! Do you see what God is saying? He is still calling men to faith in Christ. He has raised up 144,000 evangelists, from the twelve tribes, to plead with men and women all over the world to decide for Christ. Who but a loving, gracious, merciful, long-suffering God could plan in advance that during this time of chaos he would send so many out in power to preach his message?

"Remember the two supernatural witnesses who preached the Word of God in Jerusalem and on global television? After three and a half years they were murdered in full view of the whole world. And then after their bodies lay in the streets for three days, God called them to heaven. Why? Because as a loving and merciful God he wanted to manifest his power and glory so men and women could see and make the right decision about him.

"Here we have the supernatural God of heaven fulfilling his promises of ages past, preserving the children of Israel while Antichrist tries to persecute you.

"Whom will you serve? Will you obey the ruler of this world, or will you call on the name of the Lord?

"God has done all these great and mighty things because he wants to save mankind. Many will still rebel, even here, even after all they have seen and experienced. Do not let it be you, my friend. Our God is merciful. Our God is gracious. He is long-suffering and wants all to be saved.

"If you agree that God is using the period we now live in to get people ready for the millennial kingdom and for eternity, what will you do with your life? Turn it over to Messiah. Worship Jesus, the Christ. Receive him as the one and only Lamb of God that takes away the sins of the world. Receive him into your life and then live in obedience to him. He wants you. And a God who will go to such lengths to save to the uttermost anyone who will call on him is one worth trusting. *Will* you trust a God like that? *Can* you love a God like that?

"Messiah was born in human flesh. He came again. And he is coming one more time. I want you to be ready. We were left behind at the Rapture. Let us be ready for the Glorious Appearing. The Holy Spirit of God is moving all over the world. Jesus is building his church during this darkest period in history because he is gracious, loving, long-suffering, and merciful."

All around Rayford, people had bowed their heads, and many began praying. They prayed for friends and loved ones in Petra and in other places in the world. They had to have heard, as Rayford did, the emotion in Tsion's voice as he pleaded once again for all to make the decision to follow Christ.

"The time is short," Tsion cried out, "and salvation is a personal decision. Admit to God that you are a sinner. Acknowledge that you cannot save yourself. Throw yourself on the mercy of God and receive the gift of his Son, who died on the cross for your sin. Receive him and thank him for the gift of your salvation."

"Major, major problem," Aurelio Figueroa said, steepling his fingers as he leaned back in his chair. Chang sat across the desk from him, praying silently. "It's not just the bogus entries in the palace database, the phony personnel and checks and balances that have allowed the enemies of the GC to fool local leaders. Now we clearly have bugs in offices as high as the director of Security and Intelligence. Do you know that earlier today, while the potentate was trying to properly mourn our dead pilots, someone superseded the feed with a bogus conversation Director Akbar was supposed to have had with the pilots?"

"Bet you're glad it was bogus."

"I don't follow, Wong."

"If it was real, it could have been catastrophic. We all heard it, sir. Akbar lecturing the pilots, their disagreeing, and his having them executed."

The tall, bony Mexican studied Chang. "Where would someone have gotten that kind of a recording?"

"You're asking me?"

"I don't see anyone else in the room."

"I'm sorry. I should have said, '*Why* are you asking me?' "

This was zero hour. If Figueroa accused him, Chang might have to be out of New Babylon within hours to avoid execution.

"I'm asking everyone, of course. Don't take it personally. You wouldn't believe what's been planted on the main database."

"Tell me."

Figueroa stood. "I'm not telling everyone this, but Akbar himself began to suspect something shaky in Chicago. You know the place was hit more than once during the war. The city was evacuated and declared off-limits, and we have virtually ignored it for months. Years."

Chang nodded.

"We didn't fly reconnaissance planes over it, didn't take pictures, didn't check heat sensors, anything."

"Because?"

"Because someone planted on the computer that the place had been nuked and would be radioactive for years. Akbar didn't remember it that way. He thought the city had been virtually destroyed, but not by nukes. Every time he had somebody check, they went straight to the database, checked the current levels, and said, 'Yup, it's radioactive all right.' Not until recently did anybody check the archives to find out if the readings could be right. Of course, they can't. The place is clean."

"Wow."

"Wow is right. You know as well as I do that there is only one reason someone would plant such information: to have the city to themselves. We've been able to bypass the phony readings, finally, and have tried to get a bead on what's happening there. Precious little, of course, because everyone else was getting the same info we were. But there has been activity. Water and power usage. Planes, choppers, coming and going. Jets from an airstrip on the lake. That would be Lake Michigan."

"Really?"

"Yes. There is evidence of both vehicular and pedestrian traffic. Very little, of course, but there could be up to three dozen people in the city."

"Hardly enough to worry about," Chang said.

"Oh, on the contrary," Figueroa said. "These people are going to wish they'd never been born."

Chang was dying to ask but desperate to appear remote. He waited.

"You'd think we'd just send a team of Peacekeepers sweeping in there and round them up, wouldn't you?"

Chang shrugged. "Something like that, sure."

"Akbar has a better idea. He says if somebody wants it to appear radioactive, let's nuke it."

"You can't be serious."

"Totally."

"Waste technology like that at a time like this?"

"It's brilliant, Chang."

"It's a solution, I'll say that. But has he thought of the freshwater that flows through there?"

"We're harvesting Lake Michigan from northern Wisconsin. We don't have to worry about the Chicago River."

"People living downstream from it do."

"Well, anyway, word is the big boss loves the idea."

"Really."

"You kidding? Carpath— uh, the potentate loves stuff like this."

"We've got an atomic bomb we can spare?"

"Come on, Wong! Whoever these people are, they're up to no good. If they were loyal citizens, wouldn't they say, 'Hey, we didn't know this place was off-limits and we mistakenly settled here, and you know what, we're okay'?"

Chang shrugged, wanting to know how much time he had to warn the Trib Force but not daring to ask. "I guess."

"You guess? There's no record of a loyalty mark application site there, of course. And nobody who's registered with us would live there without telling us."

"You're right."

" 'Course I'm right. Hey, Chang, you don't look so good."

Chang had been surreptitiously holding his breath and not blinking. His face had reddened and his eyes watered. "Just tired," he said, exhaling finally. "And I think I'm coming down with something."

"You all right?"

Chang coughed, then pretended he couldn't stop. He held up a hand as if to apologize and say he was okay. "Didn't sleep that well last night," he managed. "I'll be fine. I'll go to bed early tonight."

"You need a nap?"

"Nah. Too much to do."

"We're okay. Take a break."

"I couldn't."

"Why not?"

"Want to do my share, pull my weight, all

that." He disintegrated into a coughing spell again.

"Just knock off early. You've got sick time left, don't you?"

"Just used some during the, you know, plague thing."

"Boils? Yeah, didn't we all? Take the rest of the day off, and if you're not in tomorrow, I'll understand."

"No, now really, Mr. Figueroa, I'll be fine. See? I feel better already."

"What is it with you, Wong? I mean, I'm all for gung-ho, but —"

"Just don't like being a wimp."

"You're anything but that."

"Thanks," Chang said, covering his mouth and coughing longer than he had before.

"Stop by Medical and get something."

Chang waved Figueroa off. "I'm going back to my desk," he wheezed.

"No, you're not. Now that's a directive."

"You're *making* me leave work early?"

"Come on! You think I'm thinking only of you? Get over yourself. I don't want a department full of coughers, and I think you've contaminated my office enough too. Get going."

"I really —"

"Chang! Go!"

It was the crack of dawn in Colorado, and Steve Plank, aka Pinkerton Stephens, was asleep in his quarters. He had spent until midnight firing off warnings to his friends in the Tribulation Force that something big was coming for Chicago and that if they knew what was good for them, they would escape, and fast. He had reached Rayford Steele by phone in Petra and urged him to stay there and not let Abdullah Smith or anyone else go back to Chicago either.

When the insistent banging on his door woke him, his first thought was that in his haste he had not used a secure phone or that his computer had been bugged. If they caught him, they caught him. Warning the Trib Force was the most productive thing he'd done since becoming a believer — or at least since helping them get Hattie Durham out of his custody and to a place where she became a believer.

Plank tried to call out to see who it was and what they wanted, but his facial appliance was next to the bed, and without it, he could not make himself heard. The best he could do was grunt, and he felt for the plastic pieces in the dark.

"Mr. Stephens, sir, no need to open the door." It was Vasily Medvedev, Steve's second in command. "I just wanted to give you fair warning. New Babylon is cracking down on the handful of employees around the world who have not yet received the loyalty mark. You're expected to have yours applied by noon mountain time at Carpathia Resurrection Field. Just acknowledge that you got that."

Steve slung himself into his motorized wheelchair and rolled to the door, then tapped twice on it.

"Thank you, sir. This puts me in an awkward spot, but I've been ordered to accompany you and see to it."

Steve rolled back to the bed stand and quickly snapped on his appliances. "Hold on a second, Vasily!" He opened the door and waved him in.

"I'm sorry, sir," the Russian said. "What could I do or say?"

"Tell them I already have it."

"There's no record of it."

"You know it cannot be applied to synthetic. You want to see it?" Plank began to unsnap the forehead piece.

"No! Please! Now, sir, I'm sorry, but I tried looking once, and that was more than enough. Forgive me."

"Well, I'm going to see if the administrator of the marks wants a look," Steve said.

"Come, sir, there'd be a record, wouldn't there?"

"I should be exempted. Can you imagine the pain of having it applied to the membrane —"

"Please! I was told to inform you and to —"

"See to it, yeah, I know."

"Sir? Why don't you just have it applied to your hand?"

"My hand? My hand, you say? You forget my hand was also donated to the cause?"

Steve held up the stub, and Vasily recoiled. "I am so stupid," he said. "Can you forget I —"

Steve waved him off. "Don't worry about it."

"When would you like to leave, sir? They open at eight and we're about an hour away."

"I know how far away we are, Vasily."

"Of course."

"I'll let you know."

When Medvedev left, Steve bowed his head, weeping. "God, what should I do? Bluff them? See if I can get a waiver? Is this it? Is it over? Can I be of no more service to the believers around the world?"

Steve spent the morning communicating with Chang in New Babylon, where it was late afternoon. They worked frantically to come up with suggestions as to where the Chicago-based Trib Force might go. No one anywhere could take them all. The Strong Building had been perfect, if only briefly.

Neither Chang nor Steve had yet been able to ascertain when the bombing of Chicago might commence, but clearly speed was of the essence. Only after they had informed everyone and made their recommendations did Steve tell Chang what was happening with him.

"I knew they were cracking down," Chang said, "but I had no idea how soon. Let me put in the database that you've had the mark applied. I can copy you on the documentation."

"Can't let you do that, brother."

"Why? I just did it for a Co-op flier the other day. He didn't even know till it was done."

"With the way they're watching at the palace right now? I go from no documentation one day to totally clear the next?"

"It doesn't have to be at Resurrection. I could say it came from anywhere."

Steve paused. It was intriguing, enticing even. But it didn't resonate. "Maybe if you'd thought of it before — if it had just showed up, like an accident, like you did with the other guy. But this would be like my choosing the mark. I couldn't do that."

"Then you're getting out of there, right? Where will you go and how will you get there? Should I send someone for you? appropriate a ride?"

"It's not going to work, Chang. That'll make you vulnerable. And you know they've got to be watching me."

"No one's on to me yet," Chang said. "I don't think they're even suspicious."

"You need to keep it that way."

"Can you get to Petra? There's a Co-op flight out of Montana today. I could have him —"

"I'll let you know, Chang. I appreciate it, but it may be time to take my stand."

"What are you saying?"

"You know."

"Oh, Steve, at least make them catch you. We need you, man."

"On the lam? What good would I be?"

"We need everybody we can get."

Buck debated waking the Greek contingent and decided against it, though it meant more work for everyone else. Chloe, Mac, Hannah, and Sebastian had staggered in during the wee hours.

Buck could tell Kenny was fascinated by

all the activity. People scurried everywhere, deciding what they absolutely had to have, packing small boxes, ignoring printouts, notes — anything that was in a computer anyway. The person allowed to take more than anyone else was Zeke. There were things he simply could not do without: his files, his wardrobes, the tools of his trade.

Leah spent most of her time on a secure phone to Co-op people all over the country. She told Buck, "Everyone is resigned to the fact that they may have to take a few people in, and they honestly seem honored, but no one is excited about it. They are stretched to the limit for space and necessities as it is."

"We have no choice, Leah. It's time to call in the chips. I hate to say it, but a lot of these people owe us nothing less. We have run the Co-op from here and provided them with stuff that keeps them alive."

Albie seemed glum. And why not? Buck wondered. The only place Albie could think of to go — and wanted to go — was back to Al Basrah. "But I don't want to take a plane when so many of you have places to go."

"Do what you have to, Albie," Buck said. "See if Leah can get you a ride with someone delivering supplies to Petra. You know we'll be calling on you frequently."

"You'd better," Albie said.

Enoch's people were under the building, checking vehicles, seeing how many were in running condition. He had traded the privilege of choosing cars and SUVs as a concession against trying to get all thirty of the others from The Place onto planes. Leah had already lined up for them several underground centers within driving distance, Enoch himself in Palos Hills, Illinois.

"You know the danger of a caravan pulling out of here in broad daylight," Buck said.

"I sure do. But we also know the danger of being here when the GC hits."

Steve Plank had communicated to Vasily that he wanted to leave the GC compound at 11 a.m. He spent much of the rest of the morning behind closed doors, agonizing in prayer. Finally he called Buck. *What a strange turn,* he thought. Seeking solace and counsel from a young man who had once been his best — and most challenging — employee. The glory days of *Global Weekly* were long gone.

Steve's news was met with silence. Then a subdued Buck: "Steve, don't do it. Please."

"You think I want to? C'mon, man! Don't get personal with me now, Buck. I just wanted to say good-bye."

"Well, I don't want to, all right? I've said enough good-byes for one lifetime. Anyway, we need you. This is no time to be giving up."

"Don't insult me."

"I'll do what I have to, to keep you from this, Steve."

"I had hoped for more from you."

"I could say the same," Buck said.

"You think I'm taking the easy way out? Don't do this to me."

"What're you saying, Steve? That I'm supposed to just support you, wish you the best, say I'll see you on the flip side?"

"That would help. Tell me you trust my judgment."

"When I think you've lost your mind?"

Steve sighed. "Buck, I've got no one else to call. If I tell you that you can't talk me out of it and that's why I'm calling, will you just tell me you're with me?"

"Of course I'm with you, but —"

"I'm not a coward, Buck. You've seen me. You know I should have died. I was buried underground for almost a week. I live in pain every hour of every day, but I've misled, I've conspired, I've finagled, I've double-crossed the enemy every way I know how. Well, there's something I won't do. I won't run like a child and I won't deny Christ."

"I know you won't."

"Well, that's something. That wasn't so hard, was it?"

"Don't tell me I have to like this, Steve."

"Will you pray for me?"

"Of course, but I'd pray you come to your senses."

"I'm going through with this, Buck. And I won't pretend I'm not scared. The GC considers this an oversight, a timing thing, something to do with my limitations. But when they make it official, make me make my decision and take my stand, I don't want to fail God."

"You won't. He promises grace beyond measure and a peace that passes understanding."

"I gotta tell ya, Buck, I'm not feeling any of that yet."

"God," Buck began, but Steve could tell he had to compose himself before he could continue, "please be with your child. Give him your grace, your peace. I confess I don't want him to do this. I hate it. I'm tired of losing people I love. But if this is what you're calling him to do, give him courage, give him words, give him power over the enemy. I pray that people who see this will be so moved that they will make the same choice."

Buck was so shaken that his comrades seemed to gather round him spontaneously. When they learned what was going on, they knelt and prayed for Steve. Buck called Chang.

"He'll be going to the center at Resurrection south of the Springs," Buck said. "Any chance they monitor that visually?"

"They do."

"Could that be transmitted here?"

"I can do it."

"I don't know why I want to see it, but I'll feel like I'm there with him."

Steve was aware of Vasily's double take when Steve rolled up in the parking lot in casual clothes. In fact, less than casual. He wore slip-on shoes, khaki pants, and a white undershirt.

"You're wondering about protocol," Steve said as Vasily lifted him into the car.

Vasily nodded. "I've learned not to question you, Chief."

"Are you armed, my friend?"

"Of course."

"I'm not."

"I can see that."

Steve reached out a hand to Vasily, who looked at it. "Shake," he said. "Sorry the hand isn't what it used to be." Vasily touched it gingerly. "The name's Steve Plank."

"Excuse me?"

"You heard me."

"Steve Plank?"

"So, you *were* listening, as usual. You know *Global Weekly*?"

Vasily appeared to have trouble concentrating. "What? The magazine? Sure. We get it from New Babylon."

"You remember when it was independent, before the disappearances?"

"Of course."

"I was on the masthead."

"The — ?"

"Masthead. That list of the staff. I was the boss — the editorial boss, anyway." And Steve told Vasily his story. They were fifteen minutes from their destination when he finished.

Medvedev shook his head. "What am I supposed to do with that?"

"Well, you don't need to arrest me. You already have me in custody, and you're following orders. You're taking me to the center."

"And you will take the mark, continue to live as a secret enemy of the Global Community, and I am to look the other way because we have become friends?"

"Have we, Vasily?"

"I thought we had, but of course you have not trusted me with the truth until now."

"If we are friends, you could do me a favor."

"Let you go? Let you make a run for it? Where would you go?"

"No. I was thinking you might rather shoot me."

"You're joking."

"I'm not. It would look good on your record. Say what you want. You found me out, worried I would escape, whatever."

"I could not."

"Well, I couldn't either. Do myself in, I mean. Not that I didn't give it some thought."

"What are you asking me to do, short of shooting you? I am supposed to watch you die?"

"You are to 'see to it,' aren't you? Isn't that your assignment?"

Vasily sighed shakily and nodded. "You are not really going to go through with this, are you?"

Steve nodded. "I am. Running would only put off the inevitable. And you have to admit, I'm fairly recognizable."

"That is not humorous to me."

"Nor to me. Vasily, I regret only that when you came to me it was already too late for you. You had taken the mark, and proudly."

"I'm not so proud of it anymore."

"That is the tragedy of where we find ourselves."

"I know."

"You do?"

"You think I do not sneak a look occasionally at the Ben-Judah Web site? I know my decision is irreversible."

"You wish it wasn't?"

"I don't know. I am not blind, not deaf. I can see what's happening. If I had to say right now, I would say I envy you."

Fourteen

It was time to wake Chloe, at least. And once she was up, the others soon followed.

Chang had called. The Trib Force needed to be packed and prepared to relocate at a moment's notice.

Chloe worked quickly, though bleary-eyed, with Kenny wrapped around her neck most of the time. George and Mac collected large quantities of canned and boxed foods, then started loading cars. Hannah, who helped Leah get the Co-op stuff in order, looked like she could use several more hours of sleep.

George told Buck he had arranged for someone to come and get him in Chicago but agreed he should reroute them, possibly through Long Grove, and meet them there. "We've got room for you and Chloe and the baby in San Diego, and I'd love to be your pilot."

Buck had to think about that one. He could think of worse scenarios. Leah had tentatively arranged for him and his family to move in with Lionel Whalum and his wife. Buck didn't know the man — but he wouldn't likely have personally known anyone they might stay with. Whalum had agreed to the setup, telling Leah he had a large suburban home but that he was planning to be gone frequently with runs to and from Petra.

"Leah," Buck said, "maybe you and Hannah ought to move in with the Whalums and let us take this opportunity George is offering. That way, you'd have a pilot, and so would we."

"Why don't you just take over and do this job, Buck, if you're going to make all my work a waste of time anyway."

"Chloe's up now anyway, Leah. Why don't you just get yourself ready to go."

She looked stricken and hurried away. Buck intercepted her. "Listen, let's forgive each other under the circumstances. Think about this: Whalum is transporting stuff to Petra all the time."

"I know, Buck. Chloe and I have been helping coordinate that."

"Are you thinking?"

"Are you insulting?" she said.

"You're not thinking."

"What?!"

"Catch a ride over there with him sometime, Leah. Anybody in Petra you want to see?"

That stopped her, briefly. "Oh, Buck, you can't be serious. I don't deny I'm enamored of Tsion. Who isn't? But he's not going to have the time for a friend with all he has going over there."

"So, what, are you afraid Long Grove is going to be too close to Chicago when the bomb hits? It may be."

"No. I —"

"You want to go with George to San Diego? They might need medical help out there. And there are private quarters. Nobody's sharing a house. They're in underground shelters, like Quonset huts."

"No, that sounds perfect for you and your family. I'll talk to Hannah about Long Grove."

"Did I hear my name?" Hannah said. "I prefer the Southwest."

"Got a contact?" Leah said. "Need one?"

Within a few minutes Hannah had agreed to stick with Leah. Zeke and Mac were the only two left without arrangements. "I got to be somewhere where people can get to me to take advantage of my services," Zeke said. "Someplace safe but central."

"Workin' on it," Chloe called out.

"I want to be where I can make runs to Petra," Mac said on one of his trips in for more boxes. "Maybe get Rayford out."

"Rayford ought to stay there," Buck said. "Might drive him crazy after a while, but he's got everything he needs to safely keep track of everybody."

By the time they were set to pull out if and when the word came, Albie had invited Mac to Al Basrah, and Zeke was set up with an underground unit in western Wisconsin, a city called Avery, not far from the Minnesota border. Buck called Chang. "We're gonna be noisy parading out of here," he said, "but I don't guess we have any choice."

"Go in the wee hours," Chang said, "only a few at a time over the next few days. I'll be able to tell if anyone's on to you. It's a risk, but you know the odds if you wait."

The entire group — all forty of them, including the thirty-one from The Place — met in a huge circle. They wrapped their arms around each other and prayed for each other and wept. All of them. Even George and Mac. And seeing all those tears made Kenny cry, which made the others laugh.

"It seems as if we just got here," Buck said. "And now we don't know when we might see each other again. I have a list here of what order we'll go in, and my family and I will be the last ones out."

The Strong Building had been safe for only so long. And now it would disgorge a few of them at a time into a hostile world that belonged to Antichrist and the False Prophet, the Global Community, and millions of searching eyes that demanded a sign of loyalty none of these had.

"I could lose you," Vasily said. "Misplace you. What can I say? You escaped."

Steve sat with him in the parking lot at Resurrection Airport. "What, I raced away in my chair, and you couldn't keep up? Too late. Let's go."

It wasn't easy, and Steve wasn't going to pretend it was. He had often wondered, when reading or seeing a movie about a condemned man, what it must have felt like to make that last long walk. It wasn't long enough, he felt, especially in a chair.

As they approached the loyalty mark application site in the north wing of the airport, Steve noticed the line was longer than he had seen it in ages. The crackdown, the intensifying — whatever New Babylon wanted to call it — was working. Hundreds milled around the statue of Carpathia, bowing, praying, singing, worshiping. For the moment, the guillotine was silent. In fact, Steve didn't know if it had ever been used in this part of the state. Some had been martyred near Denver. Others in Boulder. Maybe he would be the first here. Perhaps no one was trained to use the facilitator. But there it stood, gleaming and menacing, and those in line for the mark laughed nervously and kept glancing at it.

Steve was still in the part of the line that snaked its way to the decision-making point. No one was expected to make the "wrong" choice, of course. The stocky, sixtyish, red-haired woman with the documents and the files and the keyboard barely looked up as people identified themselves and chose what they wanted tattooed and where they wanted it. As they were administered the mark, they raised their fists or whooped and hollered. Then they made straight for the image, where they paid homage.

Steve had lived for his daily encouragement and education from Tsion Ben-Judah. It had been his only form of church. There was interaction between him and Rayford and him and Chang, and occasionally him and Buck or one of the others. But he was starved for live contact with other believers. That would be quickly remedied.

Steve debated whether to use his real name, to finally come clean and tell the GC he had been undercover for a long time. But his name would easily be linked with Buck Williams from their days at the *Weekly*, and how long would it take to progress from there to the link with Rayford, then Chloe, then the Co-op, and — who knew? — maybe even Chang?

He couldn't risk that kind of exposure, especially for people who didn't know it was coming. When it was finally Steve's turn, the woman noticed Vasily in his dress uniform and said brightly, "We've been expecting you two. This must be Pinkerton Stephens."

"In the flesh, Ginger," Steve said, studying her badge.

"How about a nice –6 and a tasteful image of the supreme potentate?" she said, looking him up and down, clearly puzzled by his garb.

"And where would you put it?" Steve said.

"Your choice."

"Well, this won't work," he said, showing his stump. Ginger's smile froze, and she searched his eyes. She had not found that amusing and looked as if she wanted to say so. He had put her in an uncomfortable position, and she clearly didn't like it. "And I understand it doesn't work on plastic."

"That is true," Ginger said, appearing relieved to move on.

"Then we can't put it here, can we?" he said, knocking on his fake forehead.

Snap, snap, snap. He popped off his combination nose and forehead appliance, exposing his eyeballs and brain sac. "Guess this would be the only option, Ginger," he said in the nasal voice resulting from no covering on the nose.

"Oh! Oh, my — ! Mr. Stephens, I —"

"Who wants to put it there?" Steve said. "Who'll volunteer for that chore? And when I wanted to display it, would I just pop my face off?"

She turned away. "I'm sure that will work. It's totally hygienic and should cause no problem."

"I could take my mouthpiece off too, Ginger, if you want the full effect."

"Please, no."

"Well, anyway, I'm in the wrong line."

"Pardon me?"

"I'm not accepting the mark of loyalty."

"You're not? Well, that's not really an option."

"Oh, sure it is, Ginger. I mean, the other is

317

a much shorter line — in fact, I'll be the only one in it. But it's most definitely an option, isn't it?"

"You're choosing the, uh, the loyalty enforce —"

"I'm choosing the guillotine, Ginger. I'm choosing death over pretending that Nicolae Carpathia is divine or ruler over anything."

She looked to Vasily. "Is he putting me on?"

"Sadly, he's not, ma'am."

Ginger studied Steve, then reached for her walkie-talkie. "Ferdinand, we need someone to run the facilitator."

"The what?"

"You know!" she whispered. "The *facilitator.*"

"The blade? You serious?"

"Yes, sir."

"Be right there." A tall, balding man with red cheeks hurried over. "You're not taking the mark?" he said.

"Yes," Steve said, "but I thought I would try the blade first. Please, can we just get on with this? Do I have to go through the whole ordeal again?"

"This is no joking matter."

"It's no redundant matter either, so could you just do what you have to do and get me processed?"

"There is no processing. You just sign, stipulating that you made this choice of your own free will, and we, ah, you —"

"Die."

"Yes."

"Do I get some last words?"

"Anything you want."

Cheeks found the proper form, Steve signed "Pinkerton Stephens," and the man said, "You realize this is your last chance to change your mind."

"About Carpathia being Antichrist, evil personified? About Leon Fortunato being the False Prophet? Yes, I know. No changing my mind."

"Dyed-in-the-wool, aren't we?"

"Let's just say I've thought it through."

"Clearly."

Steve glanced at Vasily, who had paled and held a hand over his mouth. Others in the line murmured and pointed, and now all eyes were on the strange-looking wounded man in the undershirt.

Ferdinand slipped between a couple of chairs and went to study the guillotine. "They say it can be run by one person," he said. He looked up. "Over here, Mr. Stephens."

Steve rolled to a line four feet in front of the contraption. His belly began to tighten and his breath came in short puffs. "God, be with me," he said silently. "Give me the grace. Give me the courage."

The grace came. The courage he wasn't so sure about. He wished he were at a facility with more experience. Ferdinand had raised the blade to its full height, but as he worked with the elements at the business end of the shaft, he looked tentative and kept peeking up and pulling his fingers back.

"I think if that safety lever is set, you're okay," Steve said.

"Oh, sure enough. Thank you."

"Don't mention it. You can owe me."

It took Ferdinand a second, but that elicited a wry look. He set the restraining bar in place, none too easily, then found the release cord and surveyed the whole scene once more.

Kenny was asleep. Buck sat hunched before the TV, to which he had hooked his phone. Chang had devised some digital marvel to transmit the images from Colorado. A TV camera in a corner showed the entire area, and Chloe pointed. "That's him, Buck. He's right there."

Buck's chest felt heavy and he was short of breath. Steve was the only one before the guillotine, and a man seemed to be fiddling with it.

"Do you have a basket of some sort?" Steve said.

"Excuse me?" Ferdinand said.

"A container? Unless you wanted to just chase after my —"

"Yes! Thank you. One moment."

Steve wanted to say, "Happy to be of service."

Ferdinand found a corrugated box that for some reason had been lined with tinfoil. Steve didn't even want to think about why. "Now," the man said, looking up, "if I can get you to come here."

Steve rolled close.

"Can you get down, or —"

"I can get myself in there," Steve said, "though it seems a little lacking in customer service that I should be expected to —"

"I will get assistance."

"No! I will get situated, once I've had my say."

"Oh yes, your say. Now is the time. Feel free."

"Will this be recorded?"

The man nodded.

"Well, then . . ."

Steve spun halfway around to face those

in line for the mark of loyalty. Their eyes would not meet his, but he sensed a hunger on their faces for what they clearly felt privileged to soon see.

"I don't expect you to believe me or to agree or to change your minds," he began. "But I want to go on record for my own sake anyway. I have chosen the guillotine today so that I can be with God. I am a believer in Jesus Christ, the Son of God, the maker of heaven and earth. I renounce Nicolae Carpathia, the evil one, Satan incarnate. When you take his mark today, you once and for all forfeit your chance for eternal life in heaven. You will be bound for hell, and even if you want to change your mind, you will not be able to.

"I wish more of my life had been dedicated to the one who gave his for me, and into his hands I commit myself, for the glory of God."

Steve spun back around, launched himself out of the chair and into the guillotine. "Please just do it quickly, Ferdinand," he said.

Buck could not take his eyes from the screen. Chloe sat next to him, her face buried in her hands. The picture disappeared, but Buck sat there for almost an hour. Finally his phone chirped. It was Chang, who also sounded shaken.

"A confidential note was added to the report from personnel at the loyalty center," he said. "It tells Suhail Akbar, 'You will no doubt be hearing from the Global Community command center in Colorado, which will need not only a replacement for the deceased Pinkerton Stephens, but also for his second in command, Vasily Medvedev. The latter was just found in his GC automobile. Medvedev died of a self-inflicted gunshot to the head.'"

Of course, neither death was reported on the Global Community News Network.

By the time Ming Toy landed in Shanghai after flying all night, she was more than exhausted. She had made the seemingly interminable flight many times before, but she could not sleep this time because she was getting to know the pilot. He was an acquaintance, if not a friend, of George Sebastian's. And while she had not met George, they had many mutual friends by now. Her pilot, a South Korean named Ree Woo, had been a naturalized American citizen at the time of the Rapture and was stationed at the same base as Sebastian.

"Everyone knew George," Woo said. "He

323

was the biggest man most of us had ever seen, let alone the biggest on the base. There was nothing George couldn't do."

Woo had been a pilot trainer specializing in small, fast, maneuverable craft with high-fuel capacity and thus long-distance capability. "I was unusual for a Korean-American, Mr. Chow, because I acted more American than Asian, even though I did not move to America until after I was a teenager. I had no religion. I would have made a good Chinese. You grew up atheist, I bet."

"I did," Ming said, "but Korea, especially South Korea, is about half Christian, half Buddhist, isn't it?"

"Yes! But I was neither. I wasn't really an atheist either. I was just nothing. I didn't think about religion. My feeling was, there might be a God; I didn't know and didn't care, as long as if there *was* one, he left me alone. I worshiped me, you know what I mean?"

"Of course. Didn't we all?"

"All my friends, we all worshiped ourselves. We wanted fun, girls, cars, things, money. You too?"

"I want to hear the rest of your story, Ree," Ming said, "but it's time for me to use my real voice and tell you the truth."

He leaned toward her and squinted in the

darkness at the change in her tone.

"No," she said. "I never wanted girls. I wanted boys."

He recoiled, smiling. "Really?"

"It's not like that," she said. "I am a girl. In fact, I am a grown woman. I have been married. I am a widow."

"Now you are putting me on!"

"I'm telling you the truth." And she told her own story for the next hour or so.

"Would you believe I have heard of your brother?" Woo said.

"No!"

"It's true! No one mentions his name, but many in our underground group in San Diego know he is there, inside the palace."

Woo then finished his own story of how scared he was when the disappearances occurred. "I did not know such fear existed. Nothing ever bothered me before. I was a daredevil. That's why I wanted to fly, and not big commercial jets or helicopters or props. I wanted to fly the fastest, most dangerous. I had many close calls, but they only thrilled me and never made me cautious or careful. I couldn't wait to live on the edge of danger again.

"But when so many people disappeared, I was so scared I could not sleep. I went to bed with the light on. Don't laugh! I did! I knew something terrible and supernatural had happened. It was as if only an event that huge could have slowed me down and made me think about anything. Why did these people vanish? Where did they go? Would I be next?

"I asked everybody I knew, and even many people who were just like me and had never even been inside a church started saying that it was something God did. If that was true, I had to know. I began asking more people, reading, looking for books in the chaplain's office. I even found a Bible, but I couldn't understand it. Then someone gave me one that was written in simple language. I didn't even know for sure there was a God, but I prayed just in case. This Bible called itself the Word of God, so I said, 'God, if you are out there somewhere, help me understand this and find you.'

"Ming — now that *is* your real name, right? No more surprises?"

She nodded. "No more."

"Ming, I read that Bible the way a starving man eats bread. I devoured it! I read it all the time. I read it over and over, and if I found books and chapters that were too puzzling, I skipped and found ones I could follow. When I found the Gospels and the letters from Paul, I read and read until I collapsed from exhaustion.

"In the back of the Bible, it listed verses that showed how a person could become a Christian, a follower of Christ, and have their sins forgiven. It said you could know you were saved from your sins and would go to heaven when you died or be taken to be with Christ at the Rapture. I was heartbroken! I was too late! I believed with all my heart that this was what the disappearances were all about, and I cried and cried, regretting having missed it.

"But I followed the verses the salvation guide listed, and I prayed to God and pleaded for him to forgive me. I told him I believed he died for me and would receive me to himself. I felt so clean and free and refreshed, it was as if I had not missed anything at all. I mean, I wish I had been a believer in time to have been raptured, but I have no doubt that I am saved anyway and that I will be in heaven someday."

Hours later it seemed to Ming that she and Ree had been lifetime friends. Exhausted as she was, she would rather hear him talk and watch him respond to her than sleep. As the sun rose on the Yellow Sea, Ming was sickened by the vast expanse of blood that extended all the way into the harbors. The lower they flew, the more she could see the devastation, the rotting wild-life. When they landed they were issued face masks that did little to filter the stench.

Ree was delivering goods for the Co-op in Shanghai, but he agreed to take her on to Nanjing, two hundred more miles west. Chang had told his parents of an underground church there, and though it was a big city, Ming prayed God would lead her to them.

Ree stayed with her as she carefully sought out secret believers. It was not easy. They would sit in small eateries, and she would carefully tip back her cap occasion-ally so a fellow believer might see her mark. It was not until Ree did this at a small gro-cery that an old woman approached and did the same to him. The three of them met in an alley and quickly shared stories. Ming understood the woman's dialect and trans-lated for Ree.

The old woman said that the under-ground church was almost nonexistent now in Nanjing and had largely relocated to Zhengzhou, yet another three hundred-plus miles northwest. Ming finally slept on the last leg of the journey, but even uncon-scious, she worried Ree might doze at the controls. In the days of tighter aviation rules, he would never have been allowed to fly on so little rest.

The GC seemed on the rampage in Zhengzhou, hauling the unmarked to loyalty mark centers, rounding up Jews to take to concentration camps, and shouting through bullhorns every time a new session of worshiping the image of Carpathia came due. Even the thousands who already boasted his mark appeared weary of the constant requirements and the treatment of the undecided.

Ming and Ree found a cheap hostel that asked no questions and rented them tiny individual rooms, not much bigger than cots, where they paid too much to sleep too little. But the rest took the edge off, and when they met up again they set off to find the underground believers.

Ming finally connected with a small band of Christ followers who hid in the basement of an abandoned school. Ree had to get back to the airport and eventually to San Diego, and parting with him — though they had just met — felt to Ming like an amputation. He promised to come back and to be sure that the little church in Zhengzhou was added to the Co-op list, though they had little with which to barter.

Ming had been able to connect with Chang in New Babylon and learned of the gradual dispersion of the Tribulation Force from Chicago and the soon relocation of the Williams family to San Diego. "You must get to know them, Ree," she said, "and become more than acquaintances with Sebastian. My dream is to find my parents and take them back there with me one day."

It was more than a week before Ming found anyone who had heard of any Wongs, despite the popularity of the name in that area. It was a weary old man with liquid eyes who sadly told her, "We know Wongs. Late middle-aged couple. He very loyal to potentate but never took mark."

"That's him!" Ming said.

"I so sorry, young one. He was found out."

"No!"

"He die with honor."

"Please, no!"

"He was believer. Your mother grieving but okay. She with small group about fifty miles west in mountains."

"And she is a believer too?" Ming asked through tears.

"Oh yes. Yes. I take you to her when time is right."

Fifteen

Chang never felt so isolated, so alone, as over the next five months. He grieved for his father but rejoiced that he was in heaven. He prayed for his mother and his sister, urging Ming to stay there and not try to bring the old woman out. It was, he knew, a horrible time to be in China, but escaping was more precarious.

Chang was intrigued by Ree Woo and helped Chloe arrange Co-op flights and connections for him. But for the most part, Chang lay low, especially on the computers. Suhail Akbar had made it a personal quest to ferret out the mole in the palace. All employees were interrogated again and again, but Chang was certain he had aroused no more suspicion than anyone else. He longed for the day when he could be as free to keep up with the Trib Force as he once had.

The day was likely over when he could pave the way for them with phony credentials. And he had to ask Buck to go easy with what he provided him from the palace for *The Truth*. It was one thing for Buck to write what he knew, but quite another to prove it with recordings and video feeds that could have come only from bugs in New Babylon itself.

Chang was thrilled that the dark-of-night relocations of the Trib Force had gone smoothly. So far they had lost no one since Steve Plank, who had never officially been part of the Force but was mourned as if he were.

Leah and Hannah were staying close to their new home in Long Grove. Their occasional missives about Lionel Whalum and his wife proved them to be the type of couple the Trib Force, and the Co-op, needed.

Albie and Mac flew recklessly all over the world in aircraft Albie seemed to trade on a new black market. Chang worried that they didn't have solid phony credentials anymore, but Mac, at least, seemed to feel invincible after the triumph in Greece.

Zeke, from what Chang could tell, flourished in a country environment the GC seemed to have forgotten. Many secret believers traveled for miles to be transformed by the young man with the master's touch.

Word from Enoch and his charges from The Place was less encouraging. The group had been split up and parceled out to various underground homes, individuals, and families. Most of them were still active in trading via the Co-op, but many despaired of ever having the kind of camaraderie they had enjoyed in Chicago.

That city had been devastated again, this time by the real thing — a nuclear bomb that hit three days after Buck and Chloe and Kenny had rendezvoused with Sebastian and flown to San Diego. GCNN reported a thousand casualties, all Judah-ites, but viewers realized that confirming the deaths or numbers would have jeopardized the very people who claimed the count.

Most thrilling to Chang was keeping up with Buck and Chloe and Kenny, who now lived literally underground in a bunker near San Diego. Sebastian and his family had smoothed the transition, and the secret church there seemed one of the most vibrant Chang knew of. There Kenny was just one of several babies born since the Rapture.

With the military technology still mostly intact, Buck was able to re-create the setup he had enjoyed in Chicago, and he broadcast his cyberzine every few days. He had been careful to stay close to home but envied Rayford's getting to live at Petra.

Now there was where the real action was.

Four Years into the Tribulation;
Six Months into the Great Tribulation

While the atmosphere was still festive and the daily messages from both Tsion and Chaim inspiring, Rayford would not say Petra was entirely cocooned from the real world. The million there were reminded daily of the havoc wrought by Carpathia all over the globe. From everywhere came reports of miracles by thousands of deities who seemed loving, kind, inspiring, and dynamic. It was easy to watch them live on the Internet, reattaching severed limbs, raising the dead, taking blood from the sea and turning it into water so pure and clear that many stepped forward to drink it without harm.

"False!" Ben-Judah preached every day. "Charlatans. Fakers. Deceivers. Yes, it is real power, but it is not the power of God! It is the power of the enemy, the evil one. Do not be misled!" But many were, it was plain.

Jews were mistreated, persecuted, tortured, and killed on every continent. They were paraded across the screen of the Global Community News Network and trumped-up charges leveled. They were traitors, commentators said, enemies of the risen potentate, would-be usurpers of the throne of the living god.

Over the months, New Babylon's policy on those found without the mark of loyalty changed from one that gave violators one last chance to have it applied immediately to one of zero tolerance. There was no longer any excuse to have neglected one's duty. Most barbaric to Rayford was the vigilante law that now allowed a loyal citizen with a valid mark to kill an unmarked resident on sight. The act was the opposite of a crime. It was lauded and rewarded, and all that was required was to deliver to a local GC facility the body of a victim who clearly bore no mark on forehead or hand.

Pity the citizen who was mistaken, however. The murder of a loyal Carpathianite was itself punishable by death, and trials were unheard of. If you could not produce an alibi against a charge of murdering a marked loyalist, you were dead within twenty-four hours.

Rayford terribly missed his family and the other Trib Force members, but what was good for one was good for all. They had re-located and were staying put for a time. He knew it would not, could not, always be that way. He wanted so badly to get to San Diego, he could taste it.

The highlight of his day, beyond hearing the teaching and keeping up with the scattered Force, was the evangelistic message delivered every day by one of the two preachers. Had he been asked if he would enjoy a daily diet of preaching that laid out the plan of salvation and gave unbelievers the chance to receive Christ, he might have predicted it would wear thin.

But every day, day after day, Tsion insisted on either Chaim or himself delivering just such a message — following the normal teaching for the majority who were already believers. And every day, Rayford found himself thrilled to hear it.

It wasn't only because someone was saved every day — and usually more than one. But also, the defiant ones and the undecideds often fell in anguish, battling, fighting God. Rayford marveled to watch the spiritual warfare as selfish, sinful men and women couldn't evade the preaching and yet would not give in, even for their own benefit.

Every evening Chaim would ask new believers to identify themselves and talk about their old lives and their newfound faith. This gathering always culminated in singing, praying, and celebrating.

One night, still high from the meeting that spotlighted the new believers, Rayford was enjoying a lesson taught by Naomi, the young computer whiz. She was teaching anyone who wanted to learn how to access the various databases and get news from around the world.

Rayford was just one of several gathered to learn what they could, but he was summoned from the session by none other than Chaim himself, who wanted to introduce a new friend.

Rayford followed Chaim a couple of hundred yards, and all along the way, people reached out to "Micah," blessing him, thanking him, telling him they were praying for him and appreciated his leadership. "Thank you, thank you, thank you," Chaim said, gripping hands and shoulders as he went. "Praise God. Bless the Lord. Blessings on you."

Finally they reached a clearing where several young people of different races and cultures sat chatting. They appeared to be in their late twenties or early thirties. "Ms. Rice?" Chaim said quietly, and when the short black woman excused herself, the others watched with interest as she joined Chaim and Rayford.

"I know you, don't I?" Rayford said, bending to shake her hand. "Don't tell me. You're a friend of — no, you've been on television."

"Bernadette Rice," she said, with a clipped British accent and a gleaming smile. "Reporting from Petra, but no longer for the GCNN."

Rayford didn't know what to say. So she was here on assignment — or not? — or what? He smiled at her and glanced at Chaim. "I'll let her tell you," Chaim said.

The three sat on rocks. "I was at the Temple Mount for GCNN the day that Micah, well, Dr. Rosenzweig, first emerged. I didn't recognize him. None of us did. I don't know what I would have thought had I known who he was. It was well known, of course, that he was the one who had assassinated Carpathia.

"But I was not even thinking of that when I was called to the scene. A woman, a GC Peacekeeping corporal named Riehl — forgive me, but I remember everything and talk this way as a means of organizing my thoughts — pulled me away from a story I was doing about families visiting the Temple Mount that day. To tell you the truth, I was none too pleased when she insisted that Rashid — that was my cameraman — and I wrap it up and come with her. I demanded to know what was going on.

"As she dragged me across the plaza, she said Rashid and I were about to get a rare privilege. A high-ranking Morale Monitor was about to carry out an order from the potentate himself. When we got there, the tall young man, dressed as the MM do — dressy casual, you know — was standing with what looked to me like a frail, little old man. Forgive me, Dr. Rosenzweig, but that is my recollection.

"Well, sometimes non-journalists have different ideas of how exciting a particular story is. I didn't even know if they expected this to show live or if we were to record it. This MM gentleman just wanted to get on with it, so I asked central control — who was producing the broadcast — what I should do. They wanted to know who the MM guy was, and before I knew it, he was insisting that we roll.

"He said he was Loren Hut, new *head* of the Morale Monitors, and that he had been ordered by Carpathia to execute this Micah person for refusing to take the mark and for resisting arrest. I do a fast lead-in, Rashid focuses on the pair, and it goes live over GCNN.

"You'll recall that everyone was starting to get the boils around this time, and Hut was suffering. He was wriggling and scratching and making me do the same just watching. Did you happen to see it, Captain Steele?"

"No, but I heard about it from my —"

"Then you know what happened. Hut shot Micah several times from point-blank range, and except for the deafening sound, the bullets had no impact. The crowd laughed and accused Hut of using blanks. He shot a man through the heart for saying that, proving he was using real bullets. The crowd dived for cover and I fell right to the ground, scared to death. Then Carpathia himself showed up. When I could compose myself at all, I crawled away — toward the loyalty mark application lines, in case anyone was looking.

"But from there I went straight to my hotel. I was so glad I had not gotten around to accepting the mark yet. This man was an enemy of Carpathia's, and he had some sort of supernatural protection I wanted. My superiors thought I was suffering from the boils like everyone else, but nothing was going to keep me from following Micah. I watched from my hotel room, learned about the meeting at Masada, disguised myself, went there, and came here as part of the airlift. Only recently did I finally pray for salvation."

"Praise God," Rayford said. "May I ask what took you so long? You were here when the bombs were dropped. You were protected by God though —"

"Set afire."

"Yes! I'm really curious. What could give you pause after that? Surely you did not still doubt God."

"No, that is true. I don't know how to explain it, Captain Steele. All I can say is that the enemy has a stronghold over the mind until one surrenders it to God. I was a pragmatist, proud, a journalist. I wanted control over my own destiny. Things had to be proved to me."

"But what more proof — ?"

"I know. It mystifies me still. I suppose what comes closest to explaining the lunacy is the verse that both Dr. Rosenzweig and Dr. Ben-Judah have often quoted — how does it go, Doctor? Something about wrestling not with flesh?"

Chaim nodded. "We do not wrestle against flesh and blood, but against principalities, against powers, against the rulers of darkness of this age, against spiritual hosts of wickedness in the heavenly places."

"Yes, that's it! And that's why we have to wear the armor of God, right?"

"That you may be able to withstand the evil day, having done all, to stand. Amen."

"I appreciate very much hearing your story, Ms. Rice," Rayford said. "You know my son-in-law was —"

"There, yes. Dr. Rosenzweig told me. That's why he thought you might like to hear it."

Rayford looked to Chaim and back at Bernadette. "Please tell me Buck hasn't heard this yet," he said.

"Not from me," Chaim said.

She shook her head.

"Then, if you'll excuse me . . ."

Rayford hurried back past where Naomi was finishing her computer class, down through the tent area where many of the younger people preferred to sleep, and finally to a small encampment of prefabricated modular homes. They were tiny but well built, had been provided almost wholly by Lionel Whalum, the new Co-op member, and had been assembled by a team of volunteers who seemed to reshape the landscape of Petra nearly overnight.

Rayford, hoping and planning that his

stay in the rock city would be only temporary, chose one of the smallest — but for him, efficient — units not far from where Abdullah stayed. Smitty liked an open fire and had opted for a tent, not much smaller than Rayford's enclosure, on the edge of one of the bivouac villages.

Before Rayford ducked into his place, which was barely big enough for his bed and an area for his computer and transmitting equipment, he peered down the way to see if Abdullah was still awake. The Jordanian, silhouetted behind a smoky fire, waved at him, then beckoned him.

"I will join you in an hour or so, my friend!" Rayford called.

He sat before his computer with two glass jars, one containing water, the other manna. No preservative or storage was necessary for the manna. It would spoil overnight, but there was always a fresh supply every morning anyway — so saving it was considered a lack of faith, and forbidden.

Rayford entered his code, keyed in the coordinates that allowed him to interact securely with San Diego — some ten hours earlier on the clock — and typed, "Praise God for David Hassid and Chang Wong."

He waited. Buck and Chloe's machine would signal them that he was trying to communicate, and when one of them typed in their code, the units could talk to each other. Not only that, but they also had video capability. Sensors around the edges of the respective screens stored and interpreted digital images and transmitted them back and forth, so — unless the sender turned off that feature — both parties could see each other on the screen.

A minute later Chloe came on with twenty-month-old Kenny squirming on her lap. She had to block the boy from reaching for the keys. Seeing them both made it even harder for Rayford to wait to get to San Diego.

"Hi, Dad," Chloe said. "Say hi to Grandpa, sweetheart."

Kenny said, "Gampa!" and stared at the screen. Rayford tried to situate himself for the best light and transmission and waved.

Kenny smiled and opened and closed his hand before the screen.

"I miss you, Kenny!"

"Miss! Big boy!" Kenny threw his hands over his head and arched his back, forcing Chloe to hold him tighter to keep him from slipping off her lap.

"Are you a big boy?" Rayford said.

But Kenny had already lost interest. He wriggled until Chloe let him down. "You need to come see him," Chloe said.

"Maybe soon," Rayford said. "I miss you all so much."

They brought each other up to date. Buck was somewhere with Sebastian and Ree Woo, so Rayford told Chloe Bernadette Rice's story.

"Buck will be thrilled," she said. "You know Ree is headed back to China. Ming's still not aroused any suspicion. She comes and goes as she pleases, but she sure wants to get out of there and bring her mother with her. Maybe this time."

"They would come to San Diego?"

"Yes. I think she's sweet on Ree."

"Doesn't surprise me. I got to meet him, you know, on one of his runs here."

"Nobody told me that!"

"Yeah, he talks about her. Seems preoccupied with her. I thought I told you."

"No. 'Course I'm buried with Co-op stuff most of the day. It's getting harder and harder, Dad. Has Tsion said anything about the lifting of the plague? Or are these things permanent?"

"The previous ones haven't been. But this has held the longest. Tsion thinks the Bowl Judgment on the lakes and rivers is imminent. That one is for sure not permanent."

"It's not? How does he know?"

"He says there's a later judgment, one of those that ushers in the Battle of Armageddon and the Glorious Appearing, that calls for the drying up of the Euphrates River. And it clearly says it dries up its waters."

"That's a relief, but if the rivers and lakes turn to blood soon and don't happen to turn back to water until almost Armageddon, I don't know. Should the seas clear up before the rivers and lakes turn, or does that even make sense?"

"No one knows, Chloe. And what happens if the seas do turn back to salt water? How long would it take to replenish them?"

"And what would we do with everything that's dead now? The cleanup alone would take a hundred years. At least we might be able to treat salt water and make it potable, because if the lakes and rivers turn too — and if the seas are still affected — I don't know how anybody or anything stays alive."

"Tsion says God will winnow out many who have the mark of the beast so they can't continue to evangelize for the evil side. I guess he wants to even the odds a little for the last battle."

"As if he needs to do that, Dad."

"How are you holding up, honey?"

"Exhausted, that's all. But we love the Sebastians and the body of believers here. If you have to live through this time, this is the place to be."

It was well after midnight in Zhengzhou, and Ming was homesick. For where, she was uncertain. She had no home anymore. She wanted to be with Ree Woo, though they had never so much as held hands. He had visited her — more than once — as he had promised, and they had become dear friends, a brother and sister in Christ.

Ming didn't know whether it made sense to think of him in romantic terms anyway, with only three years left before the Glorious Appearing. Besides, Ree had a ridiculously dangerous job, and who wanted to risk being widowed twice within a few years? On the other hand, what might it be like if they both survived? She would have to study what Dr. Ben-Judah had to say about married couples entering into the millennial kingdom.

Though Ming was with her mother, still she did not feel at home. Sure, she understood the language, even some of the more obscure dialects, because she had grown up in China. But the believers lived in constant fear, slept in communal rooms with little privacy, and never knew who might come knocking in the dead of night.

Her mother seemed remarkably at peace

in spite of the recent loss of her husband, though she told Ming she wished she could have died with him. Though Mrs. Wong was a new believer, she was a worrier by nature, and she had grown fatalistic over the past several weeks. Ming tried to talk her into sneaking out of China and going to live in San Diego, but her mother would not hear of it. This was her home — such as it was — and California sounded like a different planet. She worried about Chang, and she worried about Ming, both playacting as employees of the Global Community.

Ming, still masquerading as Chang Chow and living essentially as a man when away from the underground shelter, was constantly on edge. Her brother offered to set it up in the computer that she was a full-fledged employee, entitled to a paycheck and benefits. She refused for his sake, knowing how intense the scrutiny had to be in New Babylon. A little money would allow her to complete the ruse and live in her own small place, but it would not be worth it if it left Chang vulnerable at the palace. And so she scraped by on the meager pool of resources among the believers.

Ming tried to keep her distance from other Peacekeepers, though some wanted to be chums and invited her to various places with them. She always found excuses. Hardest for her was being randomly assigned duties by anyone superior to her in rank. She herself had been a top official at the Belgium Facility for Female Rehabilitation (BFFR), a women's prison better known among the GC as Buffer. But now, in her male Peacekeeper uniform, Ming was just a grunt, someone for most of the others to boss around.

At least this gave her some access to information, and she was able to warn fellow believers about raids and surprise canvasses.

At two o'clock one morning the local GC had planned a raid not of Christ followers but of a small Muslim contingent who lived in the northeast corner of the city in caverns where the subway once ran. Ming was surprised to hear of this group, as she had been largely unaware of holdouts against Carpathianism besides the so-called Judah-ites and the mostly Orthodox Jews. At a meeting rallying the GC troops to root out the dissidents, Ming learned that these "zealots" still read the Koran, wore their turbans, almost totally covered their female popula- tion, and practiced the five pillars of Islam.

She had not seen anyone bowing toward Mecca five times a day, but Intelligence had determined that this group still followed that dictum in private. They also contributed alms — a communal giving and sharing of resources that would have been necessary anyway, given the current political climate. It was not known whether these adherents — more prevalent in western China — still fasted during Ramadan. It seemed everyone was fasting in one way or another since the seas had turned to blood. There was no getting to Mecca at least once in a lifetime anymore either, not since the Global Community and Carpathianism had leveled the Muslims' sacred city.

The pillar of their faith that so enraged the potentate and thus the Global Community Peacekeepers and Morale Monitors was the first and foremost tenet of the Islamic religion. Their profession of faith declared a monotheistic god — "There is but one God, Allah . . ." — and the high status of the founder of the religion — ". . . and Muhammad is his prophet."

Of course, that flew in the face of Carpathianism, which was also monotheistic. Neither were the Muslims idol worshipers, so not only were there no statues associated with their practice of faith, but they were also loathe to pay homage to the image of Carpathia.

"That will be their choice in about half an

hour," the local leader, a thick man named Tung, told the GC troops. "We'll storm their little enclave, fully armed and prepared to shoot unmarked people on sight. But our wish and our hope are that they do not resist. I have it on good authority from high levels in the Global Community Palace that a certain someone at *the* highest level wants these people used as living examples.

"We will march them to the loyalty mark application site about six blocks from their hideout, and there they will spend the night deciding what they will do in the morning. As the sun rises on the beautiful, jade, life-size image of Supreme Potentate Carpathia, these infidels will either bow the knee to him — prepared to accept his mark of loyalty — or they will be executed in full view of the public. Little do they know that regardless of their decision, they will be executed anyway. GCNN plans to air this live."

The GC all around Ming burst into cheers and applause. They then lined up to be issued weapons; hers turned out to be a grenade launcher she would not use, no matter what. If that meant the end of her life too, so be it.

Rayford found Abdullah Smith warming himself by his fire. Smitty, who had become much more expressive and emotional over the past few months, rose quickly and embraced Rayford. "It is as if I am already in heaven, my friend," he said. "I miss the flying, but I love all this teaching. And the food! Who would have guessed that the same meal three times a day would be something I so looked forward to?"

Rayford didn't know how Abdullah could sit so flat and comfortably cross-legged. He made it look normal and easy, yet Rayford seemed to creak and groan going down, and cramped up as he sat. He always gave way to unfolding himself and leaning on one hand with his legs out to the side. This amused Abdullah to no end.

"You westerners brag so much about working out, and yet it has not made you limber."

"I think you sit on a magic carpet," Rayford said.

Abdullah laughed. "I wish Mac were here. He inspires me to think of earthy . . . of earthy what? Comebacks? Is that what he calls them?"

"Probably. With Mac, you never know. Did you see him today?"

"Of course. He and Albie always look me up when they get here, tease me about getting fat on the manna, and want to know when I will join their little band of fliers.

The day will come soon, I hope. For now, the elders think it is too dangerous, but my guess is that you too are eager to get going."

"More than you know," Rayford said. "And while I am content to submit to the authority here, still I wonder."

"So do I! God is clearly supernaturally protecting those who fly in and out of here, despite all the efforts of the enemy. You would think that would give the GC an idea to stop wasting bullets and missiles. Have they hit anyone or anything?"

Rayford shook his head. "Not yet. And the stories. Have you heard the stories?"

Abdullah let his head fall back and gazed at the stars. "I have heard them, Captain. I want to be part of one. I want the Lord to once again protect me from harm and death by sending one of his special visitors. The flight here, when the GC were shooting right through our craft? That was like living in the Bible days. I felt like Daniel in the den of the lions. I could see the missiles coming and I knew we were in the way, yet they passed right through.

"Captain, what must the GC think when they see this happen in the light of the sun almost every day?"

Sixteen

Ming marched through the streets with the other local GC to the northeast corner of Zhengzhou. Few citizens were out and about, but the Muslims were known to have one of their worship and lecture periods at this time of the morning.

The GC leader, Tung, fanned out the armed group of around thirty Peacekeepers and sent them to four entrances to the old subway that marked the borders of the area the Muslims occupied. Apparently the group had never been bothered after midnight, because it was guarded merely by a lone man at each entrance at the bottom of the stairs. The guards were quickly and quietly overtaken, and none could produce a mark of loyalty to show the GC. They were taken to the surface by a couple of GC who would walk them to the mark application site. The rest of the Peacekeepers silently moved in on the meeting of about four dozen men and women. The Muslims immediately realized their security had been breached and no resistance was possible.

So they simply stayed where they were, listening to a speaker, one of their own. Tung had foreseen this possibility and had instructed his people to merely wait and listen themselves, gathering evidence of treason and disloyalty to Carpathianism.

The speaker seemed to quickly assess the situation and began to close his remarks. But often looking directly at his captors, he was devout and defiant to the end. "And so," he said, "we view god as more than the creator of all things, but also all-knowing, full of justice, loving and forgiving, and all-powerful. We believe he revealed the Koran to our prophet so he could guide us to justice and truth. We are his highest creation, but we are weak and selfish and too easily tempted by Satan to forget our purpose in life."

He paused to gaze at the GC once again. "We know that the very word *Islam* means to submit. And those of us who submit to god, repenting of our sins, gain paradise in the end. Those who do not will suffer in hell."

The Muslims then bowed toward Mecca and began to pray — all but three. These sat together at the back of the assemblage, and when Tung stepped forward to call a halt to the proceedings, one of the three stood and pointed at him and held a finger to his lips. "Wait," he said quietly, but with such strength of character and — Ming couldn't put her finger on it — conviction, perhaps, that Tung stopped. His people looked at him and back at the standing man.

The Muslims looked up from their prayers and turned to sit again. The three men carefully stepped through the crowd and made their way to the front where the speaker had been. "This meeting is not over yet," one of them said.

Ming was puzzled. The three were not armed. Though they wore garb somewhat similar to the Muslims, it was not the same. They wore sandals and robes, no turbans. Their beards and hair were relatively short. They did not look Asian or Eastern. In fact, Ming realized, she would not have been able to guess their nationalities from their look or the speaker's accent. He spoke just loudly enough to be heard, but again, with a certain quality everyone found riveting.

"My name is Christopher. My coworkers are Nahum and Caleb. We visit you on behalf of the one and only true God of Abraham, Isaac, and Jacob, the Holy One of Israel and the Father of our Lord and Savior, Jesus the Messiah. We come not to discuss religion, but to preach Christ and him crucified, dead, buried, and resurrected after three days, now sitting at the right hand of God the Father."

Suddenly Christopher spoke with a voice so loud that many covered their ears, yet Ming believed they could still hear every syllable. "Fear God and give glory to him, for the hour of his judgment has come! Worship him who made heaven and earth, the sea and springs of water!"

Christopher seemed to let that settle with everyone, then in more muted tones said, "Christ died for our sins according to the Scriptures; he was buried, and he rose again the third day according to the Scriptures. Now if Christ be preached that he rose from the dead, how say some among you that there is no resurrection of the dead?

"If there be no resurrection of the dead, then is Christ not risen. And if Christ be not risen, then is our preaching vain, and faith in Christ is also vain. We testify of God that he raised up Christ. If Christ be not raised, men and women are yet dead in their sins."

Ming searched the faces of the Muslims,

whom she expected to rise in protest. Perhaps it was because their captors were at hand, or because they realized that this preaching also defied Carpathianism, but they did not object. They appeared mesmerized, if only at the audacity of an outsider disregarding their beliefs and preaching his own.

Christopher stepped back and Nahum stepped forward. "Babylon shall fall," he said. "That great city, because she has made all nations drink the wrath of her fornication, shall surely fall. Hers has been a system of false hope not only religiously, but also economically and governmentally.

"God is jealous, and the Lord will have his revenge. He will take vengeance on his adversaries, and he reserves his wrath for his enemies.

"The Lord is slow to anger and great in power. He will have his way in the whirlwind and in the storm. The clouds are the dust of his feet."

The GC seemed to tremble, and Ming looked to Tung, whose lips quivered. He gripped his weapon tighter, but he did not move.

Nahum continued: "God rebukes the sea and makes it blood. He can dry up all the rivers. The mountains quake at him, and the hills melt, and the earth is burned at his presence, yes, the world, and all that dwell in it.

"Who can stand before his indignation? Who can abide the fierceness of his anger? His fury will be poured out like fire, and the rocks shall be thrown down by him.

"The Lord is good, a stronghold in the day of trouble. He knows them that trust in him. But with an overrunning flood he will make an utter end of the place that opposes him, and darkness shall pursue his enemies."

Everyone in the underground sat or stood unmoving, arms close to their sides. It was as if they were folded in upon themselves, made fearful by Nahum's pronouncement. When he stepped back, Caleb moved up, but rather than address everyone, he turned and stared directly at Tung.

"If any man worships the beast and his image, and receives his mark on his forehead or on his hand, that one shall drink of the wine of the wrath of God, which is poured out into the cup of his indignation. The one with the mark shall be tormented with fire and brimstone in the presence of the holy angels and in the presence of the Lamb, who is Christ the Messiah.

"The smoke of his torment ascends forever and ever, and he will have no rest day or night, he who worships the beast and his image and receives the mark of his name."

At first no one moved. Then one GC and another, then one more, raced from the underground, taking the steps to the street two at a time. Tung shouted after them, called them by name, threatened them. But two and then three more followed.

The Muslims had not moved. Finally some stood, but the GC who watched Tung did not know what to do. He raised his weapon toward the three outsiders but appeared unable to speak. Finally finding his voice, he said, "To the center!"

The GC began surrounding the Muslims, who, except for a half-dozen, allowed themselves to be led out and up the stairs. Tung nodded to two of his men and signaled that they should join him to round up the final six. But as they approached, Christopher merely leaned toward the GC and said, "It is not yet their time."

Ming stalled and maneuvered in such a way that she was the last one out, trailing the main group. It was clear that Christopher, Nahum, and Caleb were talking with and praying with the six stragglers. Christopher told Tung, "These will come when it is their time." And to Ming's astonishment, the GC leader beckoned the last two guards, and they left.

Ming had been so moved, she realized she had not noticed whether the three strangers had the mark of the believer on their foreheads. They had to, didn't they? She wanted to know, but she did not expect to see them again.

As the petrified group of Muslims was led through the streets to the loyalty mark application site, Ming allowed herself to hang back far enough that, despite her small stature, she could see past them for several blocks.

Huge klieg lights lit up the center, but no one in the area knew of the raid, and few spectators were there — only the GC who had first rousted the four Muslim guards. But unless her eyes deceived her, Ming believed she saw three more strangers in robes with short hair and beards and no turbans. They could have been a matched set with the other trio!

But as the GC and the Muslims drew closer, they all began to point and talk among themselves. It was the same three! They stood at the head of the line, ignoring the vociferous GC clerical workers who told them to move aside.

As the Muslims were herded into line, Ming got a closer look at the three. They did not have the mark of the believer on their foreheads! She didn't know what to make of it. Were they underground rebels, charlatans, what?

Tung rushed them, brandishing his rifle. "Where are the others? We will hunt them down, and you will be responsible —"

"They will come when it is their time," Christopher said again. And somehow that shut Tung up.

The Muslims were instructed on how to be processed. When Tung asked how many would be taking the mark of loyalty to Carpathia, about half raised their hands. The others groaned and argued with them.

Tung laughed. "It makes no difference! Don't you see? You waited too long. You were discovered this very morning, months past the deadline for taking the mark. You will die at dawn with the rest."

He turned to the others. "And how many of you are *choosing* the guillotine, as if there was a choice?"

The rest of the Muslims raised their hands, and yet Ming noticed that none of them had the mark of the believer either. Christopher addressed them. "Resist the temptation to choose the guillotine without choosing Christ the Messiah. You will die in vain."

"We will die for Allah!" one shouted, and the others raised fists of defiance.

"You will die all the same," Tung said.

His attention was diverted to the street, and everyone turned to see the last six Muslims striding purposefully toward the site. Ming could tell Tung had not expected to see them again. When they arrived, they seemed to assess the layout, then headed directly for the area that led to the guillotines.

"I am glad you are so decisive," Tung said. "But we are closed until daybreak. Then you will be television stars, and a live audience will enjoy the show as well."

Christopher and Nahum and Caleb sat before the undecideds, each talking to a small group, pleading, explaining, urging them to receive Christ before it was too late. Finally Tung had had it. "Enough!" he shrieked. "You are finished here! These people made their choices long ago, and punishment will be meted out in the morning. Now, begone!"

The three ignored him. But he would not be put off.

"In five seconds I will open fire on you and instruct my people to do the same."

Ming panicked. She would not fire on these men of God! Could she pretend, hide, somehow go unnoticed?

Tung waited a few beats and raised his weapon. He was six feet from Christopher's head when he released the safety and squeezed the trigger, calling out, "Peacekeepers, open fire!"

Ming moved into position and made a show of readying her grenade launcher. Surely Tung did not expect her to deposit an explosive in the middle of everyone, Muslims, GC, and all. But she quickly realized she was the only one moving. Everyone else appeared frozen. Tung's face was set in the grimace of a man about to blow another's head off.

Ming tried to stop moving but was off balance and tripped on the foot of the man next to her, having to catch herself on yet another on her other side. She feared she had been exposed now, the only one not under the spell of the holy men.

But Christopher addressed her directly. "Do not fear, dear sister."

So she had been given away! Now all would know she was not even a man!

"God is with you," Christopher said. "None of these can hear us, and none will remember what happened here, except that their offensive against the spokesmen of the Lord was futile. Be encouraged. Be of good cheer. Your Father in heaven looks upon you with pleasure, and you will not see death before his Son returns again."

Ming felt a glow as if she were flushed from head to toe. A warmth rode through her that enlivened her, gave her strength and courage. She was curious. If Christopher knew the mind of God, could he tell her more? Ming could not open her mouth, yet she had so many questions.

Christopher answered even the unasked. "Neither will your mother see death before the glorious appearing of the King of kings. But you will be separated soon. You will return to your friends, not all of whom will remain on this earth to the end."

Ming wanted to ask who, but still she could not make herself speak. Her limbs, warm and liquid, felt heavy and immobile. All she could do was stare at Christopher. She felt as if she were smiling, in fact as if her entire body was.

Christopher stood, and Nahum and Caleb joined him. As she watched, they seemed to grow larger until they towered over the area. Christopher reached out an open hand to her, but she could not move to take it and feared anyway that her body would be enveloped by it.

"And now," he said, "may the God of peace who brought again from the dead our

Lord Jesus, that great Shepherd of the sheep, through the blood of the everlasting covenant, make you perfect in every good work to do his will, working in you that which is well pleasing in his sight, through Jesus Christ, to whom be glory for ever and ever."

The three were gone, and suddenly it was morning. The sun was bright and warm. Tung and his people acted as if they knew they were on the air, serious looks plastered on their faces. They strode about through the crowd of onlookers and Muslims.

All the victims of the raid were in line for the blade, and to Ming's surprise and great joy, at least twenty-five of them bore not only the mark of the believer, but also a look of assurance and deep peace that said they would have the grace to accept the consequences of their decision.

It was nearly half a year later before Chang began to feel the pressure had lightened, if only a bit, at the palace compound. He tried a little something new every day, tapping in here and there, checking the memory disk David Hassid had buried deep within the system. It was all there, everything that had gone on in the place since Chang began to lie low. He had not listened in to anything live, but he could check his calendar for specific events and go back to hear what had gone on behind closed doors on those days.

His sister had finally escaped China, their mother insisting that Ming go back to the United North American States "with your young man. I will be fine here." Ming told Chang she had not told their mother of Christopher's promise that neither of them would see death before the Glorious Appearing, but that "Mother seems to get along as if that is her intention anyway — to make it to the end."

Ming rhapsodized to Chang about how wonderful it had felt to finally get on board with Ree, to fly all day, to get past easier checkpoints and wind up in San Diego, finally able to get rid of her male GC Peacekeeper's uniform and let her hair grow out . . . to be a woman again.

"For Ree?" Chang had asked via secure phone.

"For me!" she said. "Well, maybe a little for him."

"How's that going?"

"None of your business."

"Of course it is."

"It's safe to say we're an item," she said, "but it's awfully hard to concentrate on that with him gone almost all the time. The people here tease me about it, even Captain Steele. But Ree and I are not really romantic yet."

"He hasn't kissed you?"

"I didn't say that."

"That sounds romantic."

"It was a kiss good-bye before his last run and a kiss of greeting when he returned. It was in front of people, so no, romantic it was not."

Chang was curious about how Rayford was getting along, relocating once again.

"It's been hard for him, Chang. He's thrilled to be back with his family, of course, and you should see him with that grandson! But he still feels isolated from much of the Tribulation Force, even though Sebastian has had a techie in here giving him — all of us — whatever we need to carry on as before. Living literally beneath the ground can get depressing. And I know he misses many of the advantages he had at Petra."

To Chang's mind, the one who had benefited most at Petra was Abdullah Smith. He was flying again, making regular runs in and out of the place, many of them with his old friends Mac and Albie. But he had chosen, and they had agreed, that he should continue to live in Petra. He had become expert on the computer and frequently regaled the rest of the Trib Force with his latest escapades, many of which happened right there at Petra. He had just filed a long account with Rayford and copied everyone else. He wrote in English for everyone's benefit, and was still learning. It read:

Late yesterday after the noon we had a very special time here as Dr. Ben-Judah instructed us on living in the Spirit. That is the Holy Spirit, which I knew some about from his previous teachings, but not nearly enough.

Captain Steele, you will recall that just before you left, there had been some trouble here. Nothing too major, but people getting on each other's nervousness and complaining to the elders about this and that. Well, do you know who straightened all that out and got people to get along better? No, not Dr. Ben-Judah, but Chaim. Yes, it's true. He has become quite a wise leader and very belovered by everyone here. My spell checker is making *belovered* blink madly, but that is what he is, most certainly.

Anyway, today Dr. Ben-Judah talked about Chaim, who many here still like to call Micah. His Bible passage was Ephesians 5:18–21, which talks about being filled with the Spirit, having a song in your heart (I liked that especially), having an attitude of thankfulness, and submitting to one another. He said those were characteristics of Chaim, and from the reaction of the people, I would have to say they agreed enthusiastically.

He also referred to Galatians 5:22–23, which list the nine fruits of the Spirit. I know you know this, Captain Steele, but as my messages to you also go into my personal journal, let me list them here: love, joy, peace, patience, gentleness, goodness, faith, humility, and self-control. I don't know about you, but many of these were not part of my nature, culture, or background. But again, they have become part of the personality of Chaim, making him a great leader here.

It was such good teaching, Captain Steele. I took many notes. Dr. Ben-Judah told everyone that if we could all learn to walk in the Spirit, we would have an easier time getting along for two and a half more years. He told us that besides the nine characteristics and the joyful, thankful, submissive heart, we will know we have the Spirit when we have the power to tell other people about Christ. He took that from

Acts 1:8, where Jesus told his disciples that they would have power after the Holy Spirit came upon them and that they would be witnesses to him to the ends of the earth.

Believe it or not, we have to be witnesses even here. There are still some among us who have not chosen Christ. The trouble now is that there are rumors of miracle workers in the Negev, not far from here. Many have said they heard about this from friends outside. Some even said they read of it in Mr. Williams's *The Truth.* Well, I know they could have, because it was in there, but he made it very clear that these people were fakes, pretenders. Even if they can perform some magic tricks, they were put in place by Carpathia and are not to be trusted.

But can you believe it? There are groups here who plan to venture out and hear these people! I must have the Spirit, Captain Steele, because I myself — and you know how shy I am — am preaching against this, pleading with people not to go.

Have you heard the rumors that the head of Carpathianism, the one we know to be the False Prophet, is himself challenging Dr. Ben-Judah to a televised debate? I cannot believe his foolishness! Does he not remember that it was Dr. Ben-Judah's television message about Jesus being the Messiah that first brought him to the attention of the world? Why does he think Dr. Ben-Judah has such a big following yet today?

No thinking person would allow Leon Fortunato inside Petra, of course, and neither would any of us advise Dr. Ben-Judah to venture out to some Global Community–approved site. So if this is to happen, Tsion will probably be on camera from here, and Leon from who knows where? Frankly, I hope the GC is foolish enough to follow through with this and that they have the courage to air it live and not censored.

I continue to be thrilled to be able to serve God under his divine protection. And though it happens nearly every time I fly, I never get tired of seeing the GC threaten and warn and even try to blast us out of the sky and then waste their missiles and bullets, missing us from point-blank range. Many of them must be among those who would change their minds about God and about Nicolae Carpathia, if only it wasn't too late for them.

Rayford always loved hearing from Smitty. There was a youth and innocence about him that had nothing to do with his age. In fact, he was still in his early thirties, but Rayford loved him like a son.

He was shutting down his computer when Chloe came knocking. She was alone. "Got a minute?" she said.

"For you, are you kidding? Where are your men?"

"Doing Kenny's favorite thing."

"Wrestling on the floor," Rayford said.

"Exactly. I'm telling you, Dad, since a little before his birthday, we've been finding out what the Terrible Twos are all about."

"It's not that bad, is it? He's naturally going to be a little rambunctious, having to play inside all the time."

"We'll survive. Roughhousing with his dad takes a little of the steam out of him. He's all boy, I can tell you that. But, hey, this is a business call."

"Really?"

"I need to call in a favor. Do you owe me anything?"

"Let's pretend I owe you everything. Give me an assignment. Co-op, I assume."

"Oh yeah. One of our biggest trades ever could happen in about three months, but it has to be done by air, and we need a larger than normal crew. I'd like you to head it up on the western side. Mac's going to run things from the east."

"That big, huh? I'm all ears."

"I've been sitting on this awhile, trading off bits of it here and there, but both parties have too much inventory. They don't need what they've got, but they're ready to trade with each other. You know how water has become as valuable as wheat?"

"Sure."

"Our Argentine friends are willing to prove it. We've got a contingent, run by a Luís Arturo, at Gobernador Gregores on the Chico River. They've harvested thousands of bushels of wheat. Naturally they are worried they're on borrowed time, with the size of the operation. And they're worried about water. The Chico is getting more polluted all the time, and they are suspecting it's intentional on the part of the GC."

"They've got wheat and need water. Who's got water?"

"The most unlikely place. Well, maybe not as unlikely as the middle of the desert, but this isn't a place you normally think of for bottled water. Probably the biggest underground church outside of America. Bihari's group at the Rihand Dam."

"You're not saying . . ."

"I am."

"India?"

"That's the place. They've got about as much volume of water as the Argentineans have wheat, and they're willing to trade straight up."

"You need more than a big crew, hon."

"Tell me about it. We need big planes. Albie got something lined up out of Turkey, of all places, and he's having it retrofitted to hold the skids of water."

"Regardless, it should work fine for the wheat."

"Thing is, Dad, we can't wait. We've got to do this almost simultaneously. The wheat's got to be heading toward India while the water's on its way. Albie and Mac are going to pick up Abdullah and bring Bihari with them. I'd like you to choose three other guys from the States —"

"Well, Buck and George —"

"Not including Buck this time, if you don't mind. Don't look at me that way. It's just a feeling."

"That this is a doomed mission? Thanks for sending me!"

"Not at all. I just think Kenny needs him right now, and frankly — I may be self-serving or prejudiced or whatever — I don't think he has the time to take away from *The Truth*."

Rayford leaned back and looked at the

ceiling. "George and Ree from here, if you can spare 'em."

"We've got time to work around their schedules, sure."

"And I'd look first to Whalum for a plane that big. And if he's got one, he ought to bring it here to pick us up and serve as our fourth."

"I'm for that," Chloe said. "That'll get Leah off my back."

"Still wants a ride to Petra?"

"Yeah. Which is not all bad, except we haven't been able to work it out yet, and I think she's taking it personally."

"What a shock, eh?"

"Well, we both know what she's up to, and I'd almost like to get Tsion's permission before I send her over there to start stalking — that's overstated — shadowing him."

When the time came for the project, Lionel Whalum was en route to San Diego, sans Leah, who was none too happy.

Seventeen

"If your wizards can do all these tricks, Leon, why can they not turn a whole sea back into salt water?"

Chang sat listening through headphones.

"Excellency, that is a lot to ask. You must admit that they have done wonders for the Global Community."

"They have not done as much good as the Judah-ites have done bad, and that is the only scorecard that counts!"

"Your Worship, not to be contrary, but you are aware that Carpathian disciples all over the world have raised the dead, are you not?"

"I raised *myself* from the dead, Leon. These little tricks, bringing smelly corpses from graves just to amaze people and thrill the relatives, do not really compete with the Judah-ites', do they?"

"Turning wooden sticks into snakes? Impressive. Turning water to blood and then back again, then the water to wine? I thought you would particularly enjoy that one."

"I want converts, man! I want changed minds! When is your television debate with Ben-Judah?"

"Next week."

"And you are prepared?"

"Never more so, Highness."

"This man is clever, Leon."

"More than you, Risen One?"

"Well, of course not. But you must carry the ball. You must carry the day! And while you are at it, be sure to suggest to the cowardly sheep in Petra that an afternoon of miracles is planned, almost in their backyard, for later that same day."

"Sir, I had hoped we could test the area first."

"Test the area? Test the *area?*"

"Forgive me, Excellency, but where you have directed me to have a disciple stage that spectacle is so close to where we lost ground troops and weapons and where we have been unsuccessful in every attempt to interrupt their flying missions, not to mention where, my goodness, we dropped two bombs and a —"

"All right, I *know* what has gone on there, Leon! Who does not?! Test it if you must, but I want it convenient to those people. I want them filing out of that Siq and gathering for *our* event for a change. And when they see what my creature can do, we will start seeing wholesale moves from one camp to the other. You know who I want for that show, do you not?"

"Your best? I mean, one of your —"

"No less. Our goal should be to leave Petra a ghost town!"

"Oh, sir, I —"

"When did you become such a pessimist, Leon? We call you the Most High Reverend Father of Carpathianism, and I have offered myself as a living god, risen from the dead, with powers from on high. Yours is merely a sales job, Leon. Remind the people what their potentate has to offer, and watch them line up. And we have a special, you know."

"A special, sir?"

"Yes! We are running a special! This week only, anyone from Petra will be allowed to take the mark of loyalty with no punishment for having missed the deadline, now long since past. Think of the influence they can have on others just like them."

"The fear factor has worked fairly well, Potentate."

"Well, it *is* sort of a no-more-Mr.-Nice-Guy campaign, one would have to admit. But the time is past for worrying about my image. By now if people do not know who I am and what I am capable of, it is too late for them. But some blow to the other side, some victory over the curse of the bloody seas — that can only help. And I want you to do well against Ben-Judah, Leon. You are learned and devout, and you ask for worship of a living, breathing god who is here and who is not silent. It takes no faith to believe in the deity of one you can see on television every day. I should be the easy, convenient, logical choice."

"Of course, Majesty, and I shall portray you that way."

Lionel Whalum turned out to be a compact black man, a tick under six feet and about two hundred pounds. He wore glasses and had salt-and-pepper hair, and was a skilled pilot of almost any size craft. He brought a transport lumbering into the clandestine strip in San Diego, and within an hour was airborne again with George and Ree in the back and Rayford in the copilot's seat.

"Chloe has told me so much about you," Rayford said, "but it's all been business. I think I know the basics of that story, but how did you become a believer?"

"I love when people ask," Whalum said. "A big reason I was left behind had to do with how I lived. I know there's nothing wrong with being successful and making money, but in my case, speaking just for me now, it made me deaf and blind somehow. I had tunnel vision. Don't get me wrong. I was a nice guy. My wife, she was a nice lady. Still is. We ran in our circles, had nice things, a beautiful home. Life was good.

"We were even church people. I had grown up going to church, but I was a little embarrassed about it, to tell you the truth. I thought my mama and my aunties were a little too emotional and showy. And about the time I should have figured out what the whole church thing was about, I was old enough to not want people knowing I even went. When Felicia and I got married, we didn't go to church in Chicago regularly. And when we did, it was to a higher sort, if you know what I mean. Very proper, subdued, not demonstrative. If my people had visited that church, they would have said it was dead and that Jesus wouldn't even go there. I would have said it was sophisticated and proper.

"That's the kind of church Felicia and I found in the suburbs too. It fit our lifestyle to a T. We could dress the way we did for work or socializing. We saw people we knew and cared about. And we definitely were never hollered at or insulted from the pulpit. Nobody called us sinners or hinted that we might need to get something right in our lives.

"Now our kids, on the other hand — two girls with a boy in between — they went the other direction. They got off to college and wound up, every *one* of them, in the kind of church I grew up in. Wrote us. Pleaded with us to get saved. Asked why we hadn't exposed them to this when they were kids. Flabbergasted me, I have to tell you.

"But did it reach me, change my mind? Not on your life. But then somebody in our neighborhood invited us to a Bible study. If it hadn't been for who it was, we never would have gone. But this was a cool guy. This was a guy who had made it, and big, in real estate development. He made this deal sound as casual as a golf game. No pressure. No hassle. They just read the Bible and talked about it, and they traded off meeting in about six different homes. We said sure, put our house on the list, and never missed.

"I was kind of bemused by it. After a while they started adding prayer to the thing. Nobody got called on or had to pray, and so

Felicia and I didn't. But people starting telling prayer requests, asking for prayer for their families and themselves, their ailments, even their businesses. I mentioned a couple of prayer requests now and then, but still I never prayed.

"One time the guy who invited us the first time asked if he could talk to us afterward. When it was just the four of us — his wife didn't say anything — he kind of put it to us. Wanted to know where we were spiritually. I thought he meant where did we go to church, so I told him. He told me that wasn't what he meant. He laid out how to become a born-again Christian. I had heard it. I knew. It was just a little overboard for me, that's all. I told him I appreciated his concern and asked if he would pray for us. That always got 'em, was my experience. But he thought I meant right then, and so he did.

"He wasn't pushy. Just a little intrusive. I forgave him. That's sort of what it felt like. I thought it was good to feel so strongly about something and feel so deeply that you felt you should tell your friends and neighbors about it. That was it for me, end of story. No big deal.

"Two days later, millions of people all over the world disappeared. Including —

are you ready? — every last person in that Bible study except us. And all three of our kids were gone.

"Saved? We got saved in, like, ten minutes."

Abdullah was so excited about the operation with his old friends that he had been packed and ready for several days. He didn't know or care how much of the actual piloting he would get to do. It would be enough to be together with Mac and Albie. To him the idea that the International Commodity Co-op could pull off such a huge trade, given the stepped-up persecution of believers around the globe, was just one more proof of the sovereignty of God.

When he knew Rayford and the other three from San Diego were in the air, he could barely contain himself. They would head directly to Argentina to load the wheat, which meant Mac and Albie would soon be on their way to pick up Abdullah. They were often spied upon and followed, so the plan was that they would bring some supplies into Petra and stay the night, not leaving for India until the next day. That way, if everything worked according to plan, the three of them plus their Indian fourth, Bihari, would be in the air toward Argentina at the same time the Americans were on their way from Argentina to India.

Abdullah felt a spring in his step as he moved about Petra, singing more loudly with the mass congregation, trying to pay attention and listen as Tsion and Chaim taught the Scriptures. This was the day that the computer and television technology center in the city would beam a signal of Tsion to Global Community headquarters at the palace in New Babylon, and a large monitor in Petra would receive the GC's transmission of Leon Fortunato. Abdullah, for one, believed Leon didn't have a clue what he was up against in a man as scholarly as Tsion — especially considering Tsion was a man of honor and truth.

Early in the afternoon Abdullah scaled the heights and peeked down from one of the high places onto the airstrip that had been built just for runs in and out of Petra. When Mac and Albie arrived, Abdullah would pilot a chopper to the end of the runway and bring them into the city.

As he scrambled back down, looking for something to occupy him until the great debate, he was surprised to see yet another gathering of thousands, with Chaim and Tsion trying to quiet them. Were they early for the telecast, or was something amiss? As he drew closer, he could see that several hundred of these did not bear the mark of the believer on their foreheads. They were jostling for front position for the debate because, one of them hollered, as soon as it was over, they were leaving Petra for a few hours to hear another speaker. "He will be right close by, and many believe he is the Christ. Jesus come back to earth to perform miracles and explain the future!"

"Please!" Chaim called out. "You must not do this! Do you not know you are being deceived? You know of this only through the evil ruler of this world and his False Prophet. Stay here in safety. Put your trust in the Lord!"

"Who are you but the second in command?" someone demanded. "If the leader will not beseech us to stay, why should we stay?"

"I *do* beseech you," Tsion began, but Chaim interrupted.

"Why would you trouble the mind of this man of God on the very day he has been anointed and called to counter the False Prophet? You are being used by the evil one to wreak havoc in the camp."

To Abdullah's dismay, he noticed that some of the dissidents rose up before Tsion and gathered themselves together against him and against Chaim, and said, "You take too much upon you. Why do you put yourselves above the congregation?"

Tsion slowly covered his face with his hands, fell to his knees, and pitched forward onto the ground. Then he raised his head and said, "The Lord knows who are his and who is holy. For what cause do you and all those gathered here speak against the Lord? And why would you murmur against Chaim?" Tsion called on two among the assembled and said, "Please, come to your senses and stand with me against this shortsightedness!"

But they said, "We will not stand with you. Is it a small thing that you have taken us from our motherland, our homes where we had plenty, and brought us to this rocky place where all we have to eat is bread and water, and you set yourself up as a prince over us?"

Abdullah had never seen Tsion look so stricken. Tsion cried out to God, "Lord, forgive them, for they know not what they do. I have neither set myself over them nor demanded anything from them except respect for you."

Tsion continued, "God is telling Chaim and me to separate ourselves from you to save ourselves from his wrath."

Many fell on their faces and cried out, "O God, the God of all flesh, must we die because of the sins of a few? Would you take it out on all of us?"

Tsion spoke to all the assembled and said, "Unless you agree with these, it would do well for you to depart from the presence of these wicked men, lest you be consumed in all their sins. From this point on, let it be known that the Lord has sent me to do all these works; I do not do them in my own interest. If these men do what is in their minds to do and God visits a plague of death on them, then all shall understand that these men have provoked the Lord."

As soon as he finished speaking, the ground under hundreds of the rebels opened and swallowed them. They went down into the pit, screaming and wailing as the earth closed upon them, and they perished from among the congregation.

Thousands around them fled as they heard the mournful cries from beneath the earth. "Run!" they said. "Run or the earth will swallow us also!"

But Abdullah heard many grumbling and saying, "Tsion and Micah have killed these people. We will stay with our plan of leaving from this place to hear the man who would be Christ."

Abdullah went to comfort Tsion and Chaim, but as he drew near them, he heard them. "Lord," Tsion said, "we pray an atonement for those left. Spare them your wrath so that we may yet reach them with your truth."

By now Chang was bold. Not only was he tapped in to GCNN to monitor the great debate between Tsion and Leon, but he was also prepared to override New Babylon control. He was so tired of hearing the advertisements for Leon's special envoys and their "Miracle Fairs" that when he noticed Tsion was speaking to the assembled at Petra just before the debate was to begin, he patched him through and put him on the air early.

Tsion was telling the several hundred closest to him that they should repent of their plan to leave Petra and go into the wilderness to hear the charlatan who claimed to be Christ. Once Chang had Tsion on the air, he switched to Carpathia's office for the expected outrage.

Tsion was saying, "I would ask that all pray during the broadcast that the Lord give me his wisdom and his words. And as for you who still plan to venture away from this safe place, let me plead with you one more time not to do it, not to make yourself vulnerable to the evil one. Let the Global Community and their Antichrist and his False Prophet make ridiculous claims about fake miracle workers. Do not fall into their trap."

Carpathia shrieked, "What are we doing? We *want* these people to come and to hear and to be persuaded! Get him off the air!"

Tsion said, "Messiah himself warned his disciples of this very thing. He told them, 'Many false prophets shall rise, and shall deceive many. And because iniquity shall abound, the love of many shall wax cold. But he who endures to the end, he shall be saved. And this gospel of the kingdom shall be preached in all the world for a witness unto all nations.

" 'If any man says to you, "Lo, here is Christ," believe it not. For there shall arise false Christs and false prophets, and they shall show great signs and wonders — so much so that if it were possible, they would deceive even you. If they say to you, "Behold, he is in the desert," do not go. "Behold, he is in the secret chambers," believe it not.' "

Abdullah stood in the midst of the million or so in Petra, thrilled to see that Tsion was already on the air and that he was speaking against the thousands of false Christs springing up everywhere. They claimed power from Carpathia himself and from the leader of Carpathianism, the Reverend Fortunato. They taught heresy, and yet multitudes were taken in by them.

Resounding off the rock walls, a woman's voice came from New Babylon GCNN control. "Dr. Ben-Judah, please stand by as we switch to our studios, where the Most High Reverend Father Fortunato waits to engage you in respectful debate."

"Thank you, ma'am," Tsion said, "but rather than stand by, as you flip your switches and do whatever it is you have to do to make this work, let me begin by saying that I do not recognize Mr. Fortunato as most high anything, let alone reverend or father."

Fortunato appeared on the split screen in one of his elaborate outfits, all robed and hatted and vested in velvet and piping. He was behind an ornately carved pulpit, but it was clear he was seated. His smile looked starkly genuine.

"Greetings, Dr. Ben-Judah, my esteemed opponent. I heard some of that and may I say I regret that you have characteristically chosen to begin what has been intended as a cordial debate with a vicious character attack. I shall not lower myself to this and wish only to pass along my welcome and best wishes."

He paused, and Tsion did not respond. After a few seconds' silence, Tsion said, "Is it my turn, then? Shall I open by stating the case for Jesus as the Christ, the Messiah, the Son of the living —"

"No!" It was the moderator, the woman from central. "That was merely a welcome, and if you choose to ignore it, we shall begin."

"May I ask a question, then," Tsion said, "if we choose to be so formal? Is one of the ground rules that the moderator is permitted to editorialize about the statements from this end of the argument? Such as concluding that my ignoring a greeting from an enemy was rude?"

"May we begin, sir?" she said. "The Reverend Fortunato has the floor."

"My premise is simple," Leon began, looking directly into the lens. Abdullah was rattled. He had always considered Fortunato a bit of a buffoon. But the man on the screen, though Abdullah knew better, seemed so warm and kind and loving that it had to give him credibility among the uninformed.

"I proclaim Nicolae Carpathia, risen from

the dead, as the one true god, worthy of worship, and the savior of mankind," Leon said. "He is the one who surfaced at the time of the greatest calamity in the history of the world and has pulled together the global community in peace and harmony and love. You claim Jesus of Nazareth as both the Son of God and one with God, which makes no sense and cannot be proven. This leaves you and your followers worshiping a man who was no doubt very spiritual, very bright, perhaps enlightened, but who is now dead. If he were alive and as all-powerful as you say, I challenge him to strike me dead where I sit."

"Do it, Lord," Abdullah prayed. "Oh, God, show yourself right now."

"Hail, Carpathia," Leon said, still smiling, "our lord and risen king."

Leon looked as if he were about to continue, but Tsion took over. "I trust you will spare us the rest of the hymn written by and about the egomaniac who murders those who disagree with him. I raise up Jesus the Christ, the Messiah, fully God and fully man, born of a virgin, the perfect lamb who was worthy to be slain for the sins of the whole world. If he is but a man, his sacrificial death was only human and we who believe in him would be lost.

"But Scripture proves him to be all that he claimed to be. His birth was foretold hundreds, yea, thousands of years before it was fulfilled in every minute detail. He himself fulfills at least 109 separate and distinct prophecies that prove he is the Messiah.

"The uniqueness and genius of Christianity is that the Virgin Birth allowed for the only begotten son of God to identify with human beings without surrendering his godly, holy nature. Thus he could die for the sins of the whole world. His Father's resurrecting him from the dead three days later proves that God was satisfied with his sacrifice for our sins.

"Not only that, but I have discovered, in my exhaustive study of the Scriptures, more than 170 prophecies by Jesus himself in the four Gospels alone. Many have already been literally fulfilled, guaranteeing that those that relate to still future events will also be literally fulfilled. Only God himself could write history in advance — incredible evidence of the deity of Jesus Christ and the supernatural nature of God."

Fortunato countered, "But we *know* our king and potentate arose from the dead, because we saw it with our own eyes. If there is one anywhere on this earth who saw Jesus resurrected, let him speak now or forever hold his peace. Where is he? Where is this Son of God, this man of miracles, this king, this Savior of mankind? If your Jesus is who you say he is, why are you hiding in the desert and living on bread and water?

"The god of this world lives in a palace and provides good gifts to all those who worship him."

Tsion challenged Leon to admit to the number of deaths by guillotine, that ground troops and weapons of war were swallowed up by the earth outside Petra, that two incendiary bombs and a deadly missile had struck Petra with full force, yet no one had been injured and no structure jeopardized. "Will you not also admit that Global Community Security and Intelligence Peacekeeping forces have spent millions of Nicks on attacking all traffic in and out of this place, and not one plane, flier, or volunteer has been scratched?"

Leon lauded Carpathia for the rebuilding effort around the world and added, "Those who die by the blade choose this for themselves. Nicolae is not willing that any should perish but that all should be loyal and committed to him."

"But, sir, the population has been cut to half what it once was, the seas are dead from the curse of blood — prophesied in the

Bible and sent by God. Yet the believers — his children, at least the ones who have survived the murderous persecution of the man you would enthrone as god — are provided water and food from heaven, not just here, but in many areas around the world."

Leon remained calm and persuasive, soldiering on, praising Nicolae. At one point he disparaged "disloyal Jews, of whom you are one, Dr. Ben-Judah."

"You say it pejoratively, Mr. Fortunato, and yet I wear the title as a badge of honor. I am humbled beyond measure to be one of God's chosen people. Indeed, the entire Bible is testament to his plan for us for the ages, and it is being played out for the whole world to see even as we speak."

"But are you not the ones who killed Jesus?" Fortunato said, grinning as if he had parried the killing dagger.

"On the contrary," Tsion said. "Jesus himself was a Jew, as you well know. And the fact is that the actual killing of Christ was at the hands of Gentiles. He stood before a Gentile judge, and Gentile soldiers put him on the cross.

"Oh, there was an offense against him on the part of Israel that the nation and her people must bear. In the Old Testament book of Zechariah, chapter 12, verse 10 prophesies that God will 'pour upon the house of David, and upon the inhabitants of Jerusalem, the spirit of grace and of supplications; and they shall look unto me whom they have pierced, and they shall mourn for him.'

"Israel must confess a specific national sin against the Messiah before we will be blessed. In Hosea 5:15, God says he will 'go and return to my place, till they acknowledge their offense, and seek my face; in their affliction they will seek me earnestly.'

"The offense? Rejecting the messiahship of Jesus. We repent of that by pleading for his return. He will come yet again and set up his earthly kingdom, and not only I but also the Word of God itself predicts the doom of the evil ruler of this world when that kingdom is established."

"Well," Leon said, "thank you for that fascinating history lesson. But I rejoice that *my* lord and king is alive and well, and I see him and speak with him every day. Thank you for being a quick and worthy opponent."

"You call me that and yet never answer the claims and charges I have made," Tsion said.

"And," Leon continued, "I would like to greet the many citizens of the Global Community who reside with you temporarily and invite them to enjoy the benefits and privileges of the outside world. I trust many will join one of our prophets and teachers and workers of miracles when he ministers in your area less than an hour from now. He will —"

Tsion interrupted, "The Scriptures tell us that many deceivers are entered into the world, who confess not that Jesus Christ is come in the flesh. Such a one is a deceiver and an antichrist."

"If you'll allow me to finish, sir —"

"Whoever abides not in the doctrine of Christ, has not God. He who abides in the doctrine of Christ, he has both the Father and the Son. If any come to you and bring not this doctrine, do not receive him into your house, neither bid him Godspeed, for he who bids Godspeed partakes of his evil deeds."

"All right then, you've worked in all your tiresome Bible verses. I shall be content to merely thank you and —"

"For as long as you have me on international television, Mr. Fortunato, I feel obligated to preach the gospel of Christ and to speak forth the words of Scripture. The Bible says the Word shall not return void, and so I would like to quote —"

But he was cut off the air, and much of the

multitude at Petra cheered and applauded his presentation. A remaining rebellious faction, however, even after hearing all that Dr. Ben-Judah said, began its exit. "We shall return," many of them shouted when confronted by the majority, who chanted and pleaded with them not to go.

Tsion cried out, " 'Be sober, be vigilant; because your adversary the devil walks about like a roaring lion, seeking whom he may devour.' "

"There is amnesty for us!" one said. "No one pays for missing the mark of loyalty deadline, now so long past!"

Abdullah could not make it compute. Surely these had to be among those who waited too long to consider the claims of Christ. Their hearts had to have been hardened, because there was no logic in their behavior.

He hurried back to his quarters and took binoculars that had been delivered with the last shipment from the Co-op. He climbed again to a high place to watch for their emergence from the Siq and their two-mile walk to where the Global Community had already erected a platform.

Eighteen

Mac had learned to ignore the warnings of the GC when he flew into restricted airspace over the Negev. They came on the radio, they sent reconnaissance planes, they even tried to crowd him out of the sky. Often the threatening GC planes flew close enough to reveal the pilots' faces. The first few times, Mac recalled, they looked determined. Later, when their mounted rifles missed their targets without explanation, they looked scared. When their heat-seeking missiles found their targets but seemed to pass through, the GC had backed off so as not to become targets themselves.

Today they went through all their typical machinations: the radio warning, the fly alongside, the shooting, the missiles. When Mac could see the pilots, they looked bored or at best resigned. They seemed as puzzled as the Co-op pilots why the GC continued to waste such expensive equipment, munitions, and warheads.

Mac looked at Albie and they shook their heads. "Another day, another deliverance," Albie said.

"I'll never take it for granted," Mac said. "I'm glad it doesn't hinge on clean living."

"You live clean enough," Albie said.

"Not by any virtue of my own, friend."

As they went screaming over the desert to the Petra landing strip, Mac looked for the oversize plane Chang had appropriated from New Babylon. It sat at the end of the runway, big and plain as day. "How do you figure that?" Mac said. "God must be blinding these guys. You can see it from a mile away, maybe more."

"Look there," Albie said.

Almost directly below them was a serpentine line of several hundred exiting the mile-long Siq that led into and out of Petra. They were headed for the concertlike setup in the middle of the desert. As Mac focused on the airstrip and began his descent, he saw the chopper hopping from inside Petra to the end of the runway from where Abdullah would ferry them in.

"You think Smitty would want to get a

closer look at this deal?" Albie said.

"Why? Would you?"

"Sure."

"I'm game. We protected that far out?"

"In the air we are. Might be takin' a chance on foot."

"Let's go in the copter."

"This is an answer to prayer," Abdullah said a few minutes later. "I so want to see what is going on out there."

"It's a risk though, Smitty," Mac said. "You've got a pretty good cover, lookin' like you belong out here. Albie and I have had our covers blown, and we got no disguises, no aliases, no fake marks, no nothin'. You'd better decide if we're worth being seen with."

Abdullah could not hide a smile.

"You rascal," Mac said, grinning. "I set myself up for a shot there, didn't I? And you almost took it."

"I was not about to shoot you, Mac."

"Verbally you were. You sure were."

"I guess I have decided I would rather not be seen with you when we get back to Petra."

"Cute. But seriously now . . ."

"I believe God will protect us. We should stick together, look official, but not make it plain that we do not have marks."

"Your turban covers you, and we've got caps. You think that's enough? Should we be armed?"

"I have no idea how many GC will be there," Albie said, "but I'm guessing once we get there we're going to be vulnerable. Guns won't help is what I guess I'm saying."

Abdullah rubbed his forehead. "We should stay in the chopper. If we can see and hear from there."

"And if we're approached?"

"You speak Texan at them and they will be puzzled long enough for me to lift off."

"Oh, you're hot today, Smitty."

"Who would want to come close to a helicopter when the blades are turning?"

Abdullah studied his friends. It was clear they were as curious as he was.

"Should we check in with someone?" Mac said.

"Who?" Abdullah said. "Your mommy?"

Mac nodded, conceding that Abdullah was developing a sense of humor, but not rewarding him with more than that. "Rayford's in the air somewhere. It's on us. What're we gonna do?"

"I'm in," Albie said.

Abdullah nodded.

Mac climbed in the back of the chopper.

Abdullah slid in behind the controls. Albie sat next to him.

When they were in the air, Abdullah shouted over the din, "We could check with Chang. Have him put something in the computer."

Neither responded, so Abdullah abandoned the idea. He wondered if they were being foolish. Down deep he knew they were. But he could not stop himself from going.

It was clear to Mac that this show was set up exclusively for the rebels from Petra. He tried to get out of Abdullah why anybody would want to leave the safety of that city, but it was an unanswerable rhetorical question.

Abdullah was clearly taking his time, but the chopper quickly overtook the walking masses and set down about a hundred feet from the stage, whipping up a cloud of dust that a light breeze carried directly to the people on the platform. They stared at the chopper.

Mac saw several armed GC looking and talking among themselves. One approached, a young, thick-chested man who would have been stocky even without the bulletproof vest that became apparent as he drew near. Abdullah had shut down and the blade had just stopped.

"Just sit here and look at him," Mac said. "Make him make the first move."

Vest Chest stood with his weapon dangling, totally nonthreatening, but he looked expectantly at Albie, who sat in the second seat by the door. "You going to open up?" the young man said.

"Not if we don't have to," Albie said. "The AC still has this thing cooled."

"You have to," the Peacekeeper said.

Albie looked back at Mac. Mac nodded. Albie opened the door.

Mac leaned forward and spoke in a gruff voice, "You don't want to be too close to this machine, son! Engine's still hot, and she's been known to spit some oil. And we might want to fire her up again, just for a little air."

"What's your business here?"

"Same as yours. Security. Monitoring. Now I'm going to have to ask you to back away from the craft."

It was gutsy, but after what Mac had been through the last year, to him it was like a walk in the park. If the guy wanted to get into a contest of wills, Mac would stall him long enough for Smitty to get the engine roaring again, and they would be out of there. Of course, even small-weapons fire could bring down a chopper from close range, but maybe planting in his mind about the spitting of hot oil would give the GC pause.

Mac's ruse worked. The man just nodded and backed off.

"Start 'er up, Smitty," Mac said. "Got to give him a reason to concede."

The dust blew again. Abdullah shut down quickly. The GC returned. Mac took the offensive. He leaned past Albie and opened the door himself. "Don't worry," he said, "that's the last time we do that till we leave. We don't want to get people dusty or keep 'em from hearin' or anything, okay?"

"Just what I was going to say, sir."

Mac gave him an index-finger salute, and the people began showing up, already looking exhausted.

It took only a few minutes for the crowd to gather, and it appeared that an otherwise normal-looking guy, whom Mac thought looked like a younger version of Leon Fortunato, grabbed the microphone. He wore white shoes, white slacks, a white shirt, and sounded like a motivational speaker, all peppy and crisp. He said he was the whole show — announcer, performer, everything.

"But I'm not typical. No, folks. People have called me a type of Christ. Well, you be the judge. All I can tell you is that I am not from here. That was not a joke. I am not even from this world. There's no music today, no dancing girls, just me, a wonder-worker. I come under the authority of the risen lord, Nicolae Carpathia, and I have been imbued with power from him.

"If you are skeptical, let me ask you to look at the sky. I know the sun is still high and hot and bright, but would you agree with me that there are no clouds? None. Not one. Anyone see one anywhere? On the distant horizon? Forming somewhere in the great beyond? Shade your eyes, that's all right. But do me the favor of removing your sunglasses, those of you who have them. You're squinting, and that's all right. Some of you are frowning, but you won't be in a moment.

"Would you like a nice cloud? Something to block the sun for just an instant? I can provide one. You're skeptical, I can tell. Don't look at me; you'll miss it. You'll think it was a trick. But what do you call that?"

A shadow fell over the crowd. Even the GC gawked at the sky. Abdullah leaned over. Albie bent forward. Mac turned his body between them and looked up. A thick, white cloud blotted out the sun. The people oohed and aahed.

"How does he do that?" Abdullah said.

"He already told you," Mac said. "Power from Nicolae."

"Too quick?" the miracle worker said. "Did the sudden change in temperature chill you, even out here in the desert? Maybe that's enough shade for the moment, hmm?"

The cloud disappeared. It didn't move, fade, or dissipate. It was there, and then it was gone.

"How about half shade, but still enough of the sun coming through to keep you warm?" It was instantaneous.

A woman near the stage dropped to her knees and began worshiping the man.

"Oh, ma'am, thank you ever so kindly. But what is the cliché? You have seen nothing yet. How about this microphone stand? A solid steel base, long two-piece shaft, separate microphone and cord, attached at the top. Anyone want to come up and prove it is what I say it is?"

An older man limped up the steps to the platform. He felt the mike and stand and then rapped on the upper shaft, causing thudding noises through the sound system. "Oops, look at that!" Miracle Man said. And the mike stand and mike had been replaced by a snake that led from his hand all the way to the transformer box.

The people recoiled and some cried out, but as quickly as it had appeared, the snake disappeared and the mike and stand were as before.

"Magic tricks? You know better. Had trouble getting enough water lately? Or shall we believe the stories coming from inside Petra? Think a spring in there was an act of God? Then what does that make me?"

He pointed into the middle of the crowd, and a spring gushed from the ground, splashing over their heads. "Cool, crisp, and refreshing, no?" he said. "Enjoy! Go ahead!" And they did.

"Hungry? Tired of the fare in your new home? How about a basket of real bread, warm and chewy and more than enough for all?"

He reached behind him and brought out a wicker basket with a linen napkin in it. Five popover-sized chunks of bread, warm and golden brown, were piled in it. "Start that around. Here you go. Sure, take one. No, a whole one! Take two if you'd like. There's more where that came from."

The basket passed from hand to hand and everyone took at least one piece, several two, and yet the basket was never depleted.

"Who am I? Who do you say that I am? I

am a disciple of the living lord, Potentate Carpathia. Have I persuaded you that he is all-powerful? His patience has run out with you people, however. He would like me to administer the mark of loyalty to you, which I can do without technology. You don't doubt me anymore, do you?"

People shook their heads. "Who will be first? I will do four simultaneously. You, you, you, and you. Ask your friends what they see."

Even Mac could see that they had Carpathia's mark on their foreheads.

"More? Yes, raise your hands. Now those of you who have your hands raised right now, hear me. No, no new ones. Hands down if you did not have them up when I said that. Why have you waited so long? What was the holdup? The one I serve wants me to slay you, and so, you're dead."

More than a hundred dropped to the desert floor, causing the rest to shriek and cry out.

"Silence! You do not think I could slay the lot of you? If I can slay them, can I not also raise them? These six, right up here, arise!"

The six stood as if they had just awakened. They looked embarrassed, as if they didn't know why they had been on the ground.

"Think they were merely sleeping? in a trance? All right, they're dead again." They dropped again. "Now if you know them, check their vital signs."

He waited. "No breath, no pulse, correct? Let that be a lesson to those who remain. You see that, in the distance? Yes, there. The little cloud of dust, what appears to be tumbleweed rolling this way? Those are vipers of the deadliest sort. They are coming for you."

Some turned and began to run, but they froze in place.

"No, no. Surely you do not think escape is possible from one who can create a cloud to cover the sun? If you want the mark of loyalty, raise your hand now and receive it."

The rest of the crowd raised their hands, frantic. "But more of you should die before the vipers get here." About three dozen keeled over.

"Why do the vipers keep coming?" a woman cried. "We have all obeyed! We have all taken the mark!"

"The vipers are wise, that is all," he said. "They know who was serious and loyal and who acted only out of fear for their lives."

The spring turned to blood, and the people near it backed away.

"Fools!" he said. "You're all fools! Do you think a god like Nicolae Carpathia wants you as his subjects? No! He wants you dead and away from the clutches of his enemies. You are free to run now, and it is entertaining to me to see you run as fast and as frantically as you can. But let me warn you. You will not outrun the vipers. You will not reach Petra in time to save yourselves. Your bodies will lie bloated and baking in the sun until the birds have their way with your flesh. For as I leave, I take with me the shade I provided."

The people burst from the scene, screaming and staggering madly in the sand toward Petra. The GC guards seemed apoplectic and stared as the vipers changed course to chase down the people. The spring dried up, the cloud disappeared, and dozens of chunks of bread lay in the sand.

Mac looked at Albie and Smitty and they all shook their heads, trembling. Suddenly the wonder-worker stood directly in front of the chopper. Though he did not open his mouth, Mac heard him as if he were inside the craft. "I know who you are. I know you by name. Your god is weak and your faith a sham, and your time is limited. You shall surely die."

Mac had difficulty finding his voice. "Let's go," he croaked, and Abdullah started the engines. The cloud of sand blew up and then away, and as Smitty lifted off, Mac looked down to see nothing but a long stretch of undisturbed sand, dotted only by the dead who had dropped at the site. No GC. No miracle man. No platform. No bread. No vehicles.

What about the snakes? He didn't see them either. But stretched for a quarter mile were the rest of the people, still and flat and grotesque on the desert floor, limbs splayed.

Tsion was troubled in his spirit by a deep sense of foreboding. He knew he would not be able to shepherd all the way to the Glorious Appearing every person who had arrived in Petra. And yet he believed that when they had seen the mighty and miraculous hand of God, many of the undecided would be persuaded.

Many had been; of that there was no doubt. That was what Chaim and the other elders were saying as Tsion despaired, deep in one of the caves. It was as if the Lord had told him that the rebels would not be returning — not any of them. But he didn't know if God would slay them, as he did in the Korah rebellion in the days of Moses, or whether Antichrist would kill them after luring them into the desert with his great deception.

He looked up when Naomi hurried in from the technology and communications center and went directly to her father. She stole a glance at Tsion as she whispered in her father's ear, and when Tsion saw the slump of his shoulders and the sad shaking of his head, he knew.

The young woman left, and her father made his way up to Chaim. Tsion leaned over. "Tell us both. I must know of this eventually anyway."

"But, sir," Naomi's father said, "could you not be spared the totality of this until even one day after your triumph over the False Prophet? Why must your rejoicing be tempered?"

"I am not rejoicing, my friend. I was unable to keep the False Prophet from enticing the rebels to go their own way, no matter what I did or said. Tell me the whole of it. Spare me nothing."

"Three of your friends from the Tribulation Force were eyewitnesses and are just now returning. They request a moment with you."

Tsion stood. "Of course! Where are they?"

"On their way from the helipad."

As he and Chaim neared the entrance to the cave, Mac, Albie, and Abdullah were coming in. They all embraced. The elders maintained a respectful distance as the five huddled and Mac told the story.

"You should not have attended," Tsion said sadly.

"If we'd known what we were gonna see, we wouldn't have," Mac said. "But you know, sometimes us pilot types are as curious as little boys. This just mighta cured us."

"That man was not even human," Tsion said. "Surely he was a demonic apparition. Revelation 12 says that when Satan, who will deceive the whole world, was cast down from heaven to earth, 'his angels were cast out with him.' And of course it is no surprise that these people were not even recruited for the Global Community. John 10:10 says Satan wants only to steal and to kill and to destroy."

"I have a question, Dr. Ben-Judah," Albie said. "Is it okay not to like this? I mean, everybody's outraged about what happened, but just when I think I have an idea what God might be up to, he lets something like this happen, and I don't understand him at all."

"Do not feel bad about that, my brother, unless your questioning of him makes you doubt him. He is in control. His ways are not our ways, and he sees a big picture we will not even be able to fathom this side of heaven. I too am distraught. I had so wished that some of these might run back to us, pleading that we intercede for them before God, the way the wayward children of Israel did in Old Testament times. I would have loved to pray for atonement for them or to hold up an image of a bronze snake so that those bitten could look upon it and be healed.

"But God is doing his winnowing work. He is cleansing the earth of his enemies, and he is allowing the undecided to face the consequences of their procrastination. You know as well as I do that no one in his right mind should choose against the God who can protect them against weapons of mass destruction. But here were these fools, venturing out into the desert, outside of God's blanket of protection, and there they lie. As the apostle Paul put it, 'O the depth of the riches both of the wisdom and knowledge of God! How unsearchable are his judgments, and his ways past finding out! For who hath known the mind of the Lord? Or who hath been his counselor? . . . For of him, and through him, and to him, are all things — to whom be glory for ever.' "

Mac was up before dawn, eager to get

going. But as he waited for Albie and Abdullah, he was aware of a buzz throughout Petra. An announcement was going out, through an elaborate word-of-mouth system, that Tsion and Chaim were calling for everyone to assemble after they had eaten their morning manna.

Abdullah and Albie ate quickly and packed, joining Mac with the million others before the three of them were to lift off.

Chaim addressed the crowd first. "Tsion believes the Lord has told him that no more indecision reigns in the camp. You may confirm that by looking about you. Is there anyone in this place without the mark of the believer? Anyone anywhere? We will not pressure or condemn you. This is just for our information."

Mac made a cursory pan of the people within his vision, but mostly he watched Tsion and Chaim, who waited more than ten minutes to be sure.

Then Tsion stepped forward. "The prophet Isaiah," he said, "predicted that 'it shall come to pass in that day that the remnant of Israel, and such as have escaped of the house of Jacob, will never again depend on him who defeated them, but will depend on the Lord, the Holy One of Israel, in truth.

" 'The remnant will return, the remnant of Jacob, to the Mighty God. For though your people, O Israel, be as the sand of the sea, a remnant of them will return. . . .' And of the evil ruler of this world who has tormented you, Isaiah says further, 'It shall come to pass in that day that his burden will be taken away from your shoulder, and his yoke from your neck, and the yoke will be destroyed.' Praise the God of Abraham, Isaac, and Jacob.

"The prophet Zechariah quoted our Lord God himself, speaking of the land of Israel, that 'two-thirds of it shall be cut off and die, but one-third shall be left in it. I will bring the one-third through the fire, will refine them as silver is refined, and test them as gold is tested. They will call on My name and I will answer them. I will say, "This is My people." And each one will say, "The Lord is my God." '

"My dear friends, you remnant of Israel, this is in accord with the clear teaching of Ezekiel, chapter 37, where our barren nation is seen in the last days to be a valley of dry bones, referred to by the Lord himself as 'the whole house of Israel. They indeed say, "Our bones are dry, our hope is lost, and we ourselves are cut off!" '

"But then, dear ones, God said to Ezekiel,

'Therefore prophesy and say to them, "Thus says the Lord God: 'Behold, O My people, I will open your graves and cause you to come up from your graves, and bring you into the land of Israel. . . . I will put My Spirit in you, and you shall live, and I will place you in your own land. Then you shall know that I, the Lord, have spoken it and performed it.' " ' "

It had been a long time since Rayford had done such hard physical labor. Even at Mizpe Ramon, the building of the airstrip for Operation Eagle had largely been done under his supervision but by others with heavy equipment. He was in charge of this operation too, but there was no getting around that every pair of hands was crucial.

Lionel Whalum had landed almost without incident at Gobernador Gregores. The only trouble was that the main runway had been destroyed during the war, and the Co-op had rebuilt it by duplicating it a hundred feet parallel to the original. The GC were unaware of the rebuilding or of the huge encampment of underground believers who had been harvesting wheat and trading through the Co-op ever since.

But when the destroyed runway was discarded, which Rayford's main contact there

— Luís Arturo — later told him had taken weeks to haul away, what was left was a smooth, dark depression in the ground. From the air, it looked as if the runway was still there.

Luís had spent his high school and college years in the United States and spoke fluent, though heavily accented, English. He had had enough exposure to campus ministry groups that when he returned to Argentina and suffered through the disappearances, he knew exactly what had happened. He and some friends from childhood raced to their little Catholic church, where hardly anyone was left. Their favorite priest and catechism teacher were gone too. But from literature they found in the library, they learned how to trust Christ personally. Soon they were the nucleus of the new body of believers in that area.

Luís proved to be an earnest, fast-talking man, and while he took especially to Ree Woo and was friendly and cordial to everyone, his top priority was getting the plane loaded and these men on their way again. "All we hear are rumors that the GC is polluting the Chico and that they are onto us," he said. "I have many reasons to believe that is only the talk of the paranoid, but we cannot take chances. The time grows short anyway, so let's move."

He seemed to like Ree so much because, though the South Korean was the youngest and smallest member of Rayford's crew, with the exception of George Sebastian he proved to be in the best shape of everyone — Americans and Argentineans combined.

Big George's reputation preceded him, and while he worked, lifting heavy sacks of wheat aboard the plane by himself, many of the South Americans tried to get him to talk about his imprisonment in Greece and his escape.

Rayford noticed that George tried to downplay it. "I overpowered a woman half my size."

"But she was armed, no? And she had killed people?"

"Well, we couldn't let her keep doing that, could we?"

Rayford worked mostly alongside Lionel, each of them able to handle one sack of wheat at a time. Ree helped too, but he was young and fast and wouldn't feel it in the morning like Ray and Lionel would.

After two solid days' work, thanks to hydraulic-lift loaders and six aluminum pallets that held up to thirty thousand pounds each, the wheat was nearly loaded and the plane partially full when Luís came running. "Señor Steele, to the tower with me, quick. I have field glasses."

Rayford followed the young man to a new, wooden, two-story tower that had been designed to blend into the landscape. Aircraft had to watch for it, but nosy types unaware of it might not see it at all.

Rayford had to catch his breath at the top of the stairs, but when he was ready, Luís passed him the binocs and pointed into the distance. It took Rayford a few seconds to adjust the lenses, but what he saw made him wonder if they were already too late and their work had been wasted.

Nineteen

Though it wasn't a long flight from Petra to India, Mac was sound asleep when Albie put the cargo plane down at Babatpur. With the delay at Petra, losing a couple of hours to time zones, and the cumbersome plane, it was the middle of the night when they arrived.

It took Mac a moment to get his bearings, but within seconds he and Abdullah and Albie were rushed from the plane by the man known only as Bihari. Serious and no-nonsense, he said, "Hurry, please. We remain about a hundred miles north of the Rihand Dam."

"A hundred miles?" Mac said. "How we gettin' this water back to the plane?"

"Trucks!"

"The GC asleep over here, or what?"

"The GC, my friend, enjoy the drinking water."

Bihari averaged more than seventy miles an hour in a minivan that had no business going that fast on roads that may never have seen that speed before — especially in the dead of night. Ninety minutes later, in a swirling cloud of dust, he swung into a clearing near a small processing plant and showed Mac and the others towering skids of bottled water that looked as if they would fill two large trucks.

"Where's the rest of it?" Mac said. "We got us a big, big plane."

"I wondered if you would notice," Bihari said. "Did you not hear me honk at passing traffic on the way?"

"Occasionally, I guess."

"All but two trucks are already on their way to the plane. When we heard you were in the air, we got started. The prospect of real wheat to eat has motivated all of us. With you gentlemen and forklifts, we can load the last two trucks by dawn and be on our way."

A few minutes later, as Mac backed a forklift toward a stack of skids, he passed Albie. "These people make me feel like a lazy old fool," he said. "Our job is cushy compared to theirs."

"They wouldn't want to worry about the missiles and bullets," Albie said. "They get away with this by supplying the GC with a little water?"

Bihari interrupted the last of the loading by waving his hands over his head at Mac. "Will your people be discouraged by a setback?" he said.

"Depends," Mac said. "We still gonna be able to take off and get outta here?"

"Yes, but I believe *we* are doomed."

"That wouldn't make our day. What's the trouble?"

"We will drive by the dam on our way back to the airport. It is a little out of the way, but you must see it."

"I've seen dams before. Somethin' wrong with yours?"

"My people tell me the next curse from the Lord has fallen."

"Uh-oh."

"I cannot imagine what blood looks like, being forced through the control doors of a dam."

"Me neither," Mac said. "How's your water inventory, minus what we're takin'?"

"Maybe six months. But the GC will surely raid us when they discover we no longer have sources either."

"They know where you are?"

"They have to have an idea. It will not take them long."

"Hidin' this place oughta be your top priority."

The sun was going down, and yet heat still shimmered off the plains of Argentina. Rayford tried to hold the binoculars still enough to make out what all the commotion was about. It could have been anything, but none of the options hit him as positive. There were an awful lot of people out there, that was sure. But he couldn't quite tell if they were military, GC, Morale Monitors, peasants, people from the city, or what.

He handed the glasses back to Luís. "Do we just get in the air? Or had we better check this out?"

"You know what I think."

"Do we go armed? How many go with us?"

Luís shook his head. "How about I supply the vehicle, and you supply the ideas?"

"Fair enough," Rayford said. "Sebastian and I will go. And we will be armed but not on the offensive. We're just seeing what's going on and keeping you and yours out of it."

As they descended from the tower, Luís said, "Oh, dear Lord, I pray it hasn't already happened."

"What's that?"

"Do you smell that, Captain Steele?"

Rayford sniffed the air. Blood.

Mac was preoccupied on the drive from the processing plant. Would the huge shipment of wheat have to be trucked all the way down here too? Did they have enough trucks? And where would they store it?

On the one hand he worried about it, and on the other he was glad it wasn't his problem. Better thinkers than he had put this deal together. It was their concern.

When Bihari stopped at the dam, the other loaded truck pulled up behind. At first no one disembarked. Then all four of them did.

They just stood and watched for a minute. Two of the great doors in the wall of the dam were open, both disgorging huge arcs of liquid, splashing into a ravine and sweeping past them. Blood was so much thicker than water that it sounded and acted differently. It smelled awful, and Mac found it frightening somehow. It reminded him of a nightmare and chilled him.

A man stood several hundred yards from the dam, downstream from the rushing blood. He looked familiar. "Who is that?" Mac said, pointing.

"Who is who?" Albie said.

Mac turned him the right direction and pointed.

"I don't see so well this time of the morning, Mac. Who do you see?"

"No one sees that man by the rock down there? He's close to the river."

No one said anything.

"I'm going to check him out. He's looking right at us! Waving us down there!"

"I don't see him, Mac. Maybe this is one of your cowboy marriages."

Mac cocked his head at Abdullah. "One of my *what?*"

"One of those things you cowpokes see in the desert when you're thirsty. It looks like water but it's just a cactus or something. A marriage."

Albie threw back his head and laughed. "I grew up ten thousand miles from Texas and I know that one! It's a *mirage,* Smitty. A mirage."

"Well, this ain't a marriage or a mirage," Mac said. "I'll be right back."

He drew within a hundred yards of the man, who watched him all the way. "If you're going to come," the man said, "why not bring an empty bottle?"

"What do I want a bottle of blood for? Anyway, I don't think I have an empty one."

"Empty one and bring it."

Mac turned around, as if it was the most normal request and he had no choice.

As he hurried back, Abdullah said, "So what was it, pod'ner? A marriage?"

"Very funny, camel jockey."

Mac pulled a bottle from one of the skids, drank half of it on his way back, then poured out the rest.

"Hey!" Bihari called, "that stuff's as valuable as wheat, you know."

Mac watched his footing as he reached the rushing crimson tide. "You get around, don't you, Michael?" he said. "You omnipresent or something?"

"You know better than that, Cleburn," Michael said. "Like you, I am on assignment."

"And coincidentally in the same part of the world as me. I never got to thank you for —"

Michael held up a hand to silence him, then reached for the bottle. He sighed and looked to the sky. He spoke softly but with great passion. "Great and marvellous are thy works, Lord God Almighty; just and true are thy ways, thou King of saints. Who shall not fear thee, O Lord, and glorify thy name? for thou only art holy: for all nations shall come and worship before thee; for thy judgments are made manifest."

Michael carefully walked among the rocks, down to the edge of the rushing river. The surging blood was so loud that Mac worried he would not be able to hear Michael if he spoke again. And as if he knew Mac's fear, Michael turned and beckoned him closer. Mac hesitated. Michael was being spotted with blood. His brown robes were speckled, as were his beard and face and hair.

"Come," he said.

And Mac went.

Michael stood with one foot on a rock and the other just inches from the river. He said, "Thou art righteous, O Lord, which art, and wast, and shalt be, because thou hast judged thus. For they have shed the blood of saints and prophets, and thou hast given them blood to drink; for they are worthy."

Then another voice, Mac did not know from where: "Even so, Lord God Almighty, true and righteous are thy judgments."

Michael bent low and thrust the bottle into the current. The rushing blood pushed against his arm and soaked his sleeve and filled the bottle. And when he drew it from the river and turned toward Mac, there was no blood on him. His robe was dry. His face was clean. His arm was clean. The bottle was full of pure, clean water.

Michael handed it to Mac. "Drink," he said. Mac put the cold bottle to his lips and tipped it straight up. As Mac closed his eyes and drank it all, Michael said, "Jesus said, 'Whosoever drinketh of the water that I shall give him shall never thirst; but the water that I shall give him shall be in him a well of water springing up into everlasting life.' "

Mac opened his eyes and exhaled loudly. Michael was gone.

"All due respect, sir," Sebastian said, "but you realize it's just you and me, a couple of guns, and a few rounds of ammunition, and we don't have a clue what we're driving into?"

"I was hoping you'd protect me," Rayford said. "This military stuff is fairly new to me."

"We're not really going to take these people on, are we?"

"I hope not, George. We're hopelessly outnumbered."

"Sorta what I was getting at, sir."

"Let's just play this out and see what we find."

"Uh, hold on. Could you stop a second?"

"You serious?"

"Yes, sir."

Rayford stopped and put the vehicle in park.

"You didn't read that in some military strategy book, did you?"

"What's that?"

"The see-what-we-find gambit?"

"George, listen. Nothing is as it used to be. We improvise every day. You're a living example of that. We have no choice here. We've got a whole bunch of our brothers and sisters trying to survive out here, and now something could be threatening them. If I went back and got all of them and armed them all, they would be no match for the GC if they decided to advance. So let's see what this is. We shouldn't have to get right into the middle of it before we know we should turn back. Use the binocs. You see armed GC, say the word, and we turn around. Fair enough?"

George looked like he was thinking. "Consider this," he said. "See over there? Over your other shoulder. There's a big group of somebody heading toward the gathering place. Let's go wide around the back way and get into that group. They aren't military and they aren't threatening."

"Makes sense."

"Always does. Make use of your resources."

"Like your mind, you mean?" Rayford said.

"Well, I wasn't going to say that."

Mac looked around, his heart stampeding as if he'd run up a mountainside. He scampered down to the rushing river of blood and plunged the bottle into the current. Blood splashed all over him, but when he pulled the bottle out, it was pure freshwater again.

He laughed and shouted and charged back toward Albie and Abdullah and Bihari. But they had apparently never seen Michael and quickly tired of Mac's antics. "You didn't see him! You didn't, did you?"

They looked at him gravely from the trucks.

"Did you see me pour the water out? Well, did you? Bihari, you did, 'cause you told me it was worth its weight in wheat. Remember? Well, then where did I get this?"

Bihari got out of the truck. "Where *did* you get that?" he said.

"From that river right there! And do you see any blood on me?"

"I don't!"

"Still think you're doomed? The GC is going to leave you alone when they see what's happened to your water source. But you send your people and your equipment down here like usual. God takes care of the ones he's sealed, amen?"

By now Albie and Abdullah had come to see as well.

"Try a taste of this, gentlemen. You'll want to drink it all, but it's for sharing."

Rayford and George found themselves in the middle of a pilgrimage of some sort. Almost everyone else was on foot. From their clothes they appeared to be both town and country folk, and some peasants. "English, anyone?" George said.

Two more times he said it, and finally a man — who appeared to be with his wife and perhaps a couple of other family members — came alongside the vehicle. "English? Yes," he said.

"Where are we going?" George said.

"We are going where we have been invited," the man said.

"All of you? Invited?"

"I do not know about the others. We were invited."

"Who invited you?"

"Three men. They came to the door and told us to meet them out here and they would tell us good news."

"But you are not Carpathia loyalists,"

434

George said. "I see no mark."

"On you either, sir," the man said. "And yet you seem no more afraid than we do."

"You don't even seem concerned," George said.

"The men told us not to fear."

"Why did you believe them? What gave you such confidence?"

"They were believable. What can I say?"

"Ask some others why they are here."

The man spoke to another group in Spanish. Then to another.

"We were all invited by the same men," he said.

"And who are they?"

"No one knows."

"And yet you all risk your lives to be here."

"It is as if we have no choice, sir."

Rayford stopped and the crowd surged past him. "What does this sound like to you, George?"

"The same thing it sounds like to you: Ming's story."

"Exactly. And we'll know for sure from the first words that come from their mouths. If the one . . . Christopher — ?"

"Right."

"— starts out with the gospel, and the

next one predicts what's going to happen to Babylon . . ."

"Nahum."

"Right. And Caleb warns about taking the mark, well, that's all we need to know."

"But where's the GC, Rayford? These guys got people saved in China, but the Peacekeepers still killed 'em."

Both men turned in their seats to watch for the enemy.

"Maybe God and these guys work differently in different parts of the world."

Leah Rose worked in the basement of Lionel Whalum's huge home in Long Grove, Illinois. She and Hannah were making an inventory of medical supplies and a list of what was needed at various Co-op locations. They were working with print-outs from Chloe Williams.

"I'm looking for a place that needs more than supplies, frankly," Leah said.

"I hear you. Is anything more exhausting than being idle? I don't know if I want to be in the middle of combat again, but I've got to be somewhere I'm needed."

"Problem is," Leah said, "Petra doesn't need medicine *or* nurses. But I'd like to at least stop by there on the way to my next assignment."

"Hmm, really? Wonder who? I mean, wonder why?"

"Shut up, Hannah."

Suddenly, Leah's knees buckled and she almost fell.

"What was that?" Hannah said. "You all right?"

"Yeah. I don't know. I just went weak all of a sudden, but it passed."

But as soon as she had said that, she dropped to her knees.

"Leah!"

"I'm okay. It's just — it's just that I . . . oh, God, yes. I will, Lord. Of course."

"What? What is it?"

"Pray with me, Hannah. We're supposed to pray for Mr. Whalum."

"Should I get his wife?"

"We're supposed to do it right now. Lord," Leah said, "I don't know what you're impressing upon me except that Mr. Whalum needs prayer right now. We trust you, we love you, we believe in you, and we know you are sovereign. Do whatever you have to do to keep him safe, and all those who are with him. He and Rayford and George and Ree should be leaving soon, so give them whatever they need, protect them in whatever way they need protection, and go before them into India."

★ ★ ★

"Here they come," Rayford said, pointing past the west end of the crowd to show George the GC. They pulled up in Jeeps and vans, maybe a hundred troops, uniformed and armed. They had bullhorns.

While Rayford drove to the other side of the crowd and parked where he could see the people, the GC, and the front of the assembly, a GC officer announced, "This is an unlawful assembly. You are violating the law. There is no facility here for administering the mark of loyalty, and you are so many months past now that you will not be allowed to rectify that oversight. Appearing in public without the mark of loyalty is punishable by death at the hands of any law-abiding citizen, but if you will disperse now and go directly back to your homes, we will offer a brief extension and allow you to take the mark within twenty-four hours. An application site is available as close as Tamel Aike or Laguna Grande, both within sixty miles of here."

The people did not stop, did not look, did not appear troubled. The GC began again. "This is your last warn—"

"Silence!"

The commanding voice came from the front, from one of the three, and without amplification.

"My name is Christopher, and I speak under the authority of Jesus Christ the Messiah and Son of the living God. He has determined that those of this company who receive his everlasting gospel today shall enter into his millennial kingdom at his glorious appearing, just over two years from now."

The people began to murmur, and the GC were on their bullhorns again, but the horns malfunctioned and no one could hear them.

"My coworkers Nahum and Caleb are here with me only to proclaim that which the Lord has assigned us to proclaim. And then God's message of salvation as found in his only begotten Son will be presented by one of the 144,000 witnesses he has raised up from the tribes of the children of Israel.

"And now begone, you workers of iniquity, you servants of the evil ruler of this world. You shall come nigh unto these people and this place never again. Begone lest the God and Father of our Lord Jesus Christ strike you dead where you stand!"

The GC ran for their vehicles and for their lives. Christopher said, "Fear God and give glory to Him, for the hour of His judgment has come; and worship Him who made heaven and earth, the sea and springs of water."

Nahum followed with his curse on Babylon, and Caleb warned of the consequences of accepting the mark of the beast. Then a white-robed evangelist strode to the front and said, "There shall be signs in the sun, and in the moon, and in the stars; and upon the earth distress of nations, with perplexity; the sea and the waves roaring; men's hearts failing them for fear, and for looking after those things which are coming on the earth: for the powers of heaven shall be shaken.

"And then shall they see the Son of man coming in a cloud with power and great glory. And when these things begin to come to pass, then look up, and lift up your heads; for your redemption draweth nigh."

"Wheat's a-comin' and you've got water galore, Bihari. 'Scuse me while I make a phone call." Mac punched in Rayford's number. "Ray? Where you at, man? When you guys headin' this way? Good! Listen, you've seen the rivers? That's right, you're *on* the Chico. Let me tell you, it doesn't affect the believers. At least it doesn't here." He told him of his encounter with Michael and what had happened to the blood. "We're about an hour from takin' off, so tell those brothers and sisters the water is comin'! Well, that's right, they don't need it that bad now, do they? Bihari here's lookin' at me like I've just lost it. Well, hey, you tell 'em a deal's a deal."

"Can I tell him, Captain Steele?" George said.

"Tell who what?"

"Luís. About the GC having to leave this area alone. And about the water."

"Like to share good news, do you?"

"You bet!"

"Knock yourself out."

When they got back, Luís jogged up to the car. "Well?"

"George wants the privilege," Rayford said. "We roll in ten minutes."

Lionel would take the first four hours, then Ree would take over, but Rayford would land the craft. Ray was strapping into the copilot's chair when Lionel fired up the engines, but as he put his headphones on he sensed something wrong. "You okay?" Rayford said.

Lionel pressed his lips together. "Did all my preflight."

"Me too. So?"

"Doesn't feel right."

"Long flight, big plane, lots of cargo, friend. We don't go till you're happy, hear?"

"I appreciate that, but I can't put my finger on it."

"Wanna do preflight again, check every box from top to bottom, just to be sure?"

"Nah, just let me think a minute."

Rayford turned in his seat. "How you doing, Ree?"

Ree gave him a thumbs-up and laid his head back, as if ready to sleep.

"Here comes your last crew member, Mr. Pilot. Should he shut the door, or are we holding?"

"Aw, nuts. Hold a second. I'm checking the cargo."

"Need help?"

"Nah, I got it."

"Cold back there."

"Don't I know it!"

Rayford waited just past ten minutes. Ree and George were strapped in and dozing already. Ray unstrapped and started back to the cargo hold when he met Lionel coming the other way. "All set?"

Lionel gave him a look. "Tell the tower we're ready."

As they strapped back in, Lionel looked at Rayford again. "Praise God, is all I've got to say."

"No, it isn't. Tell me."

"Had a whole pallet that never got secured. First bank, it would have shifted."

"Could have put us down."

" 'Course."

"Surely you'd checked the cargo on preflight."

"I did. I always do. Hardly anything's more important than keeping that load centered and secure."

"What made you think of it?"

"I have no idea. I double-checked every lock. All were up. I just got a feeling I should check again."

"Well, buddy," Rayford said, "if we land in India, that feeling will be the reason."

Twenty

Five Years into the Tribulation

Chang spent hours monitoring the palace, his ears always pricking up when he heard Carpathia.

"Something in the atmosphere of that ancient Edom region interferes with our missiles, our flights, our artillery," Nicolae said one evening. "The entire area has become a Bermuda Triangle. Ensure the peace but do not waste another Nick on armory that does no more than what we can accomplish diplomatically."

Chang knew Global Community diplomacy was an oxymoron. Standard operating procedure no longer included any semblance of public relations for the potentate. Someone was trying to protect the potentate from it, but from all over the globe came evidence that even the millions of citizens who bore marks of loyalty to him now knew that the risen god of the world had become a despot king. Hundreds of thousands were dying everywhere for want of drinkable water.

One report from Region 7, the United African States, showed a woman railing in public before a small, obviously fearful crowd: "Justice, fair play, even juries are relics from another time! We obey the GC and bow to the image of the supreme ruler only because we all know someone who has been put to death for failing to!" She was shot to death where she stood, and the crowd scattered for its life.

From the same area came a sham of a recording depicting a programmed parade for the benefit of the Global Community News Network. The people marched listlessly, their faces blank, as they held aloft placards and chanted, "Hail, Carpathia" in monotones.

Chang both suffered and benefited from the chaos at the palace. In many ways New Babylon had become a ghost town. Citizens could no longer afford pilgrimages to the gleaming edifices. He knew from the real figures — not the cooked books whose sum-

maries were announced to the populace —
that half the world's population at the time
of the Rapture had now died.

The capital city of the world didn't work
very well anymore. Factions and mini-
kingdoms sprang up, even around
Carpathia — top people threatening, ca-
joling, surrounding themselves with syco-
phants. Everyone was suspicious of
everyone else, while all were obsequious and
cloying around the big boss. Revolt was out
of the question. Theirs was a ruler who had
proved himself impervious to death. What
was the point of killing him again? You
could take power for three days, but you had
better loot the place and be gone when he
resurrected.

The sad state of services in New Babylon
was nothing compared to everywhere else in
the world but Petra. Trib Force and Co-op
fliers reported that everywhere they went,
they saw that things simply wore out and
were not replaced. The huge depletion of
the population cost society half the people
once employed in service jobs. Few were left
to transport fuel, fix cars, keep streetlamps
and traffic lights working, maintain order,
protect businesses. Buck recounted in *The
Truth* that the GC, especially at the local
level, used their uniforms, badges, and

weapons to get more for themselves. "Pity the shop owner who doesn't grease the palm of his friendly neighborhood insurer of security."

Chang watched all this from his spot as a journeyman techie in Aurelio Figueroa's computer department — but mostly from the system so expertly designed and installed by his predecessor, David Hassid. Ironic, Chang thought, that it was the one thing still humming along perfectly.

Carpathia himself was a madman, and no one around him even pretended otherwise — except to his face. Everyone seemed to cater to his craziness, competing to see who could be first to curry his favor by carrying out his latest directive — which usually came in a fit of fury.

"Insubordination!" he shrieked late one night as Chang listened to his weary lieutenants trying to stay awake with him. "My sub-potentate in Region 7 must wake up tomorrow to find that the heads of both Libya and Ethiopia and their entire senior cabinets have been assassinated!"

Suhail Akbar said, "I'll talk with him, Excellency. I'm sure he will realize that —"

"Did you not understand that to be a directive, Suhail?"

"Sir?"

"Did you not understand my order?"

"You literally want those leaders and their cabinets dead by morning?"

"If you cannot accomplish it, I will find —"

"It can be done, sir, but there would not be time to send our strike force from here —"

"You are director of Security and Intelligence! You have no contacts in Africa who can —"

"I'm on it, sir."

"I should hope you are!"

The deed was accomplished by an S & I force of African Peacekeepers and Morale Monitors. Akbar was lauded the next day, then suffered in Carpathia's doghouse for more than three weeks because the boss was having trouble "getting useful information out of Region 7."

Rayford lived in an underground hut, like everyone else who worked out of the former military base in San Diego. And like Mac and Albie out of Al Basrah, Rayford flew missions directly between San Diego and other International Co-op centers — places so remote and well hidden that if the fliers could elude GC radar — and even that was crumbling with the loss of personnel all over the world — there were no pesky airport details they had to bluff their way past. The head of the Tribulation Force worried that he and his people might lower their guard and see their whole network come crashing down. He actually had felt more in control and careful when the GC had been at full strength. The world had become a cauldron of individual free-market systems.

When he was "home" in San Diego, Rayford studied the reports that came to Chloe from Co-op workers all over the globe. Hardly anywhere in the world escaped the evil influence of the GC-sponsored deceivers. Magicians, sorcerers, wizards, demonic apparitions, and deputies of Leon Fortunato preached a false gospel. They set themselves up as Christ figures, messiahs, soothsayers. They lauded the deity of Carpathia. They performed wonders and miracles and deceived countless thousands. These were lured away from considering the claims of Christ himself, usually by the promise of drinkable water, but once they had made their decisions for the evil ruler, either he snuffed them out as he had done in the Negev or God slew them. Tsion Ben-Judah continued to maintain that God was continually evening the score, removing from the earth those with the sign of the beast, because a great war was coming.

"It is not as if the God of gods could not defeat any foe he chooses," Dr. Ben-Judah taught, "but the stench of the other side evangelizing for evil has offended him and kindled his wrath. Yet the wrath of God remains balanced by his great mercy and love. There has been not one report of death or injury to any of the 144,000 evangelists God has raised up to spread the truth about his Son."

Though weary of the battle and longing for heaven or the Glorious Appearing — sometimes Rayford didn't care which came first for him — still he thrilled to the reports from all over the world. The Tribulation Force saw many of these 144,000 brave men venture into public, calling the undecided from their homes to confront them with the claims of Christ. The men were powerful preachers, anointed of God with the gift of evangelism. Often they were accompanied by angels, guardians to protect them and their listeners. GC forces were incapable of stopping them.

"The archangels Gabriel and Michael have been seen in various parts of the world, making pronouncements for God and standing in defense of his people," Tsion and Chaim told the people of Petra and thus the world via the Internet. Rayford thanked God silently as he read that the angel with the everlasting gospel, Christopher, often appeared in remote regions where Christ had never been preached. Nahum continued to warn of the coming fall of Babylon, sometimes with Christopher, sometimes by himself. And Caleb was reported somewhere else almost every day, warning of the consequences for anyone accepting the mark of the beast and worshiping his image.

Besides these, it was not uncommon for the Tribulation Force to see or feel the presence of angels protecting them wherever they went. Often, even outside of the routes to Petra, GC planes would intercept theirs, warn them, try to force them down, then shoot at them. Never knowing when and where they might be protected outside of the Negev, Tribulation Force pilots took evasive action. But thus far God had chosen to insulate them, to the frustration and astonishment of the GC.

With less than two years to go before the Glorious Appearing, Rayford met with Buck and Chloe to assess the current state of the Tribulation Force. "Where are we," he said, "and where do we need to be for maximum benefit to the entire body of believers around the world?"

Chloe reported that Lionel Whalum and

his wife had somehow been able to keep their home in Illinois, "though Leah and Hannah have developed serious cases of cabin fever. I mean, I think they're encouraged by God's work in their lives. Lionel was, of course, thrilled by Leah's story of having been compelled to pray for him before he ran the final check on the cargo out of Argentina. You know, Dad, he's one of our busiest pilots now, delivering supplies all over the world."

"How bad is it with Leah and Hannah?" Buck said. "I don't know either of them that well, but Leah would get on anybody's nerves. She still pining for Tsion?"

"They keep low profiles," Chloe said, "and say they feel as if they live only at night. They don't dare venture out during the day. GC activity is spotty in that area of the suburbs, but all it would take is one report of someone without the mark, and one of our major thrusts would be jeopardized."

"I hardly ever hear from Z anymore," Rayford said.

Chloe shook her head. "Of all people, Zeke has probably changed the most. There's almost zero call for his services there in western Wisconsin. No uniforms to tailor, no disguises to invent, no undercover agents to transform."

"Could we better use him out here?" Rayford said.

"Not when you hear this," Chloe said. "Zeke has sort of settled into a new persona. He's taken such an interest in studying the Bible that he's become the de facto assistant to the spiritual leader of the underground church there."

"Zeke an assistant pastor?" Rayford said. "Push me over with a feather."

"Chloe's been keeping up with Enoch and some of his people," Buck said.

"Yeah, I apologized for intruding on their lives and their community, because I felt responsible for the split-up of much of The Place congregation. But Enoch reminded me that if I hadn't discovered them, they never would have known of the coming destruction.

"On the other hand, Dad, I know that if I had not been traipsing around Chicago in the middle of the night, there might never have been that secondary destruction."

One morning in Petra, the assemblage awoke to the news that all the seas of the world had spontaneously turned from blood to salt water again. "God has given me no special knowledge about this," Tsion announced. "But it makes me wonder if something worse isn't coming. And soon."

Little changed except that Carpathia tried to take the credit for the cleansing of the seas. He announced, "My people created a formula that has healed the waters. The plant and animal life of the oceans will surge back to life before long. And now that the oceans are clear again, all our beautiful lake and river waterways will soon be restored as well."

He was wrong, of course, and the blunder of his bluster cost him even more credibility. God had chosen, in his own time, to lift the plague from the seas, but the lakes and rivers remained blood.

Just before being executed, a Swedish insurgent announced, "What our so-called potentate ignored in exulting over the revived seas is that there is still an international mess. Dead, rotting, smelly fish still blanket the shores around the world and still carry the diseases that have driven most of the coastline populations inland. And where are the refining plants to turn the seas into potable water? We die of thirst while the king hoards the resources."

Sixty-Eight Months into the Tribulation

Chang was intrigued to hear of an unscheduled meeting in Carpathia's conference room.

Leon had actually called the meeting, much to Carpathia's frustration, but Suhail Akbar, Viv Ivins, and Nicolae's secretary Krystall all quickly came to Leon's defense. "This is about water, Excellency," Leon began. "Because you no longer need nourishment, including water, perhaps you don't underst—"

"Listen to me, Leon. There is water in food. Are you people not eating enough food?"

"Potentate, the situation is dire. We try to harvest water from the seas and convert it. But even getting new ships out there is a chore."

"It is true, unfortunately," Akbar said, "and our troops everywhere are suffering."

"*I'm* suffering," Viv said. "Personally, I mean. There are times I think I should die if I don't find a swallow of water."

"Ms. Ivins," Carpathia said, "we shall not allow the administration of the Global Community to grind to a halt because you are thirsty. Do you understand?"

"Yes, Highness. Forgive that selfish expression. I don't know what I —"

"In fact, do you have a whit of expertise in this area?"

"Sir?"

"In the matter before us! Do you bring anything to the table that helps get us to a solution? Are you an expert? a scientist? a hydrologist? There is no need to shake your head. I know the answers. If you do not have pressing business in your office, why do you not just sit and listen and be grateful that you draw a paycheck here?"

"Would you prefer I leave?"

"Of course!"

Chang heard her chair push back from the table.

"A little tie with my family," Nicolae said, "and you ride that horse as if it is your own! Do not turn from me when I address you!"

"I thought you wanted me to leave!" she whimpered.

"I do not cater to subjects, employees, friends, or otherwise who disrespect their sovereign. This same attitude made you think you could sit on *MY THRONE* in *MY TEMPLE!*"

"Your Lordship, I have apologized over and over for that indiscretion! I am humiliated, repentant, and —"

"Excellency," Leon said softly, "that *was* more than two years ago. . . ."

"You!" Carpathia roared. "You call this meeting and now you counter me as well?"

"No, sir. I apologize if it sounds as if I am c—"

"What would you call it? Would you like

to join *Aunt Viv* and return to your office to work on what you have been assigned? You are head of the church, man! What happens to Carpathianism while you worry about water? Where are the scientists, the technologists who have something to offer here?"

Leon did not respond.

"Ms. Ivins, *why* are you still here?"

"I — but I thought you —"

"Go! For the love of all —"

"Sir," Suhail began, as if the voice of reason, "I did consult the experts before coming, and —"

"Finally! Someone who uses the brain I gave him! What do you have?"

"If you'll notice here, Your Highness . . ."

Chang heard the rattle of paper, as if Akbar was spreading a document.

"Satellite photography has detected a spring in the middle of Petra that has apparently been producing freshwater since the day of the bombings."

"So we are back to Petra, are we, Director Akbar? The site of so many billions of Nicks poured into the desert sands?"

"It has been a boondoggle, sir, but notice what the aerial photography shows. Apparently the missile struck an aquifer that supplies thousands of gallons of pure water every day. It only stands to reason that the

457

source of this spring extends far outside the city of Petra, and our people see no reason why we could not access it as well."

"Where do they believe it extends?"

"To the east."

"And how deep?"

"They are not able to tell from this kind of technology, but if a missile could tap into it in Petra, surely we could drill — or even use another missile — east of there."

"Use a missile to tap into a spring? Suhail, have you heard of using too much equipment for a job?"

"Begging your pardon, sir, but two daisy cutter bombs and a Lance missile produced only drinking water for a million of our enemies."

Mac had called Abdullah to tell him of the news of the finishing of a new Co-op airstrip, "beautifully hidden" just east of Ta'izz, north of the Gulf of Aden in southern Yemen. "Albie's got a shipment he'd like to deliver to Petra, if you could run it down there sometime in the next day or so."

"Me?" Abdullah said. "By myself?"

"Need me to hold your hand there, Smitty?"

"No. It is not that. It is just that such errands are so much more fun with company."

"Yeah, I'm a barrel o' laughs, but that's a quick one-man run you can do with one of the lighter planes."

"One of Mr. Whalum's people left a Lear here. Can the new strip take a Lear?"

"Sure. A 30 or smaller. Anyway, watch for us around noon. When do you think you'd do this?"

"Probably today. If I finish with my hair and nail appointments in time. I was going to have my face done too, but —"

"What in heaven's name are you goin' on about?"

Abdullah laughed. "I finally got you, Mr. Mac! I was doing a joke on you!"

"Very funny, Smitty."

"I got you, didn't I, cowboy?"

Abdullah was checking the weather at the communications center when Naomi called out to him. "Mr. Smith, could you tell me what you make of this?"

He hurried over.

"What does that look like to you?" she said.

Abdullah's stomach dropped. Dare he say it? Dare he not? "That looks like incoming."

"That's what I thought! What do I do?"

"Get Tsion and Chaim. Code red."

"May I tell them you said that, sir?"

"Tell them whatever you need to, but quickly."

She pushed a button and spoke into a microphone. "Communications central to leadership."

"Leadership here. Morning, Naomi."

"I need Drs. Ben-Judah and Rosenzweig here ASAP on a code red, authorized by Mr. Smith."

"I will not ask you to repeat that if you can confirm what I thought you said."

"That's affirmative, Leadership. Code red."

Abdullah met Tsion and Chaim at the entrance. Several grave-looking elders accompanied them. "Abdullah," Chaim said, "code reds are reserved for threats to the well-being of the whole."

"Follow me."

He took them to Naomi, where they formed a half circle behind her and stared at the screen.

"A missile?"

"Looks like it," Abdullah said.

"Headed for the city?"

"Actually no, but close."

"From?"

"Probably Amman."

"Time?"

"Minutes."

"Target?"

"Looks east."

"Where they have been drilling?"

Abdullah nodded.

Tsion said, "They have been drilling for weeks, and we have seen nothing. No oil, no water, no blood. Now they are going to bomb the place? It is not like Carpathia to take up arms against his own forces, depleted as they are. Do we have time to watch? Would it be prudent?"

Abdullah studied the screen. "I was at ground zero for two bombs and a missile two years ago. I would not fear another missile at least a mile from here. We have field glasses on tripods at the high place north of the Siq."

"Shall I warn the people?" Naomi said.

Tsion thought a moment. "Just tell them," he said, "to not be alarmed by an explosion within — when would you say, Abdullah?"

"Fifteen minutes."

"This is not a surprise to the drilling crew," Abdullah said a few minutes later, bent to look through high-powered binoculars.

"They have moved," Tsion said.

"Quite a ways, actually. More than a mile. Maybe two. And the drill rigging has been disassembled. That tells me that they don't want it destroyed by the missile. It is probably programmed internally for a specific coordinate."

Chaim sat on a rock, breathing heavily. "Is it just my age or is it particularly warm today?"

"I am perspiring more than usual myself, my friend," Tsion said.

Abdullah pulled up from the binocs and shaded his eyes with his hand. "Now that you mention it, look at the sun."

It seemed larger, brighter, higher than it should have been.

"What time is it?" Tsion said.

"About ten."

"Why, that could be a noonday sun! You don't suppose . . ."

Abdullah heard a whistling sound in the distance. He looked north. A white plume appeared on the horizon. "Missile," he said. "It will be hard to follow with the glasses, but you could try."

"I can see it with the naked eye," Tsion said.

"I am warm," Chaim said.

They watched as the winding missile streaked into view and began to descend. It appeared aimed for the original drilling site. It soared past the disassembled drilling rig on the desert floor, then slammed a hundred yards south of it, raising a huge cloud of sand and soil and digging a deep, wide crater.

The rumble of the explosion reached them in seconds, and the cloud slowly dissipated. Abdullah readjusted the binoculars to study the crater. "I cannot imagine it went nearly as deep as the hole they had already been drilling," he said. "Regardless, so far it has produced nothing."

"I am amused," Tsion said, "but I wonder what they thought they might accomplish. If they were hoping to strike water, would they not have simply produced a geyser of blood anyway?"

Twenty-one

Chang took an unusual risk and surreptitiously followed the missile-for-water effort from his desk at work. He listened through headphones but kept an eye out for anyone walking by.

Nicolae swore. "What did that little project cost, Suhail?"

"It wasn't cheap, Excellency, but let's not assume failure just yet."

"Assume? The Lance we sent to Petra immediately produced a gusher that flows to this day! This is a disaster plain as day!"

"You may be right."

"I am always right! Face it. You are going to have to attack this water thing another way."

Chang heard a knock and Krystall's voice. "Begging your pardon, sir, but we are getting strange reports."

"What kind of reports?"

"Some kind of a heat wave. The lines are jammed. People are —"

Chang heard shouting and realized it came from his office and not from the surveillance. He quickly exed out and removed his earphones. He followed his coworkers to the windows, where they crowded to look outside.

"Get back!" Mr. Figueroa screamed as he burst from his office. "Get away from the windows!"

But like toddlers, these people wanted to do whatever they were told not to, and anyway, they were curious. What was causing all the explosions outside? Fortunately for the crowd around the window Chang peered out from, it wasn't the first to go. But two of their coworkers — the cocky, condescending Lars and a young woman — were impaled with shards of glass when the window before them gave way.

As they lay writhing, pale and panicked, the steamy desert air blew in. The first woman who knelt to aid the injured immediately reddened from the heat, and as she surrendered and tried to evade it, her hair curled, produced sparks, burst into flames, and was singed off.

Others tried to drag the first two to safety, but they too had to scamper from the heat.

"What *is* this?" someone shrieked. "What's happening?"

Those in front of Chang quickly backed away from the window, and he saw what was going on below. Car tires exploded. People leaped from their cars, then tried to get back in, burning their hands on the door handles. Windshields melted, greenery turned brown, withered, then became torches. A dog yanked loose from its leash, raced in circles, then dropped, panting, before being incinerated.

"To the basement!" Figueroa shouted, and to people who seemed reluctant to leave the fallen injured, "It's too late to help them!"

People watched over their shoulders as they hurried away, and by the time they reached the door, they saw Lars and the young woman flailing at flames that would soon consume them.

Chang was one of the last out of the room, because he was only faking the effects of the heat. He saw the results, but aside from being aware that the temperature outside seemed higher than normal, he was impervious to the killing force.

He was glad to reach the elevator just as

the doors were closing. "I'll catch the next one," he said and ran to his quarters instead.

At midnight in San Diego, Rayford was awakened by insistent tones from his computer. He dragged himself out of bed and turned on the monitor. Tsion was informing his cyberaudience around the world that the terrible fourth Bowl Judgment had struck, as prophesied in the Bible, and would affect every time zone on the earth as the sun rose. "Here in Petra," he wrote, "by ten in the morning, people out in the sun without the seal of God were burned alive. This may seem an unparalleled opportunity to plead once again for the souls of men and women, because millions will lose loved ones. But the Scriptures also indicate that this may come so late in the hearts of the undecided that they will have already been hardened.

"Revelation 16:8–9 says, 'Then the fourth angel poured out his bowl on the sun, and power was given to him to scorch men with fire. And men were scorched with great heat, and they blasphemed the name of God who has power over these plagues; and they did not repent and give Him glory.' "

Rayford keyed in a request to interact privately with Tsion or Chaim; he did not care which. "I know both of you will be terribly busy just now, but if either can spare a moment for the sake of the Tribulation Force, I would appreciate it."

Three Quonset huts away, Ming Toy had been awakened by a call from Ree Woo. Ree had promised to look up her mother, so maybe this was his update, but Ming was alarmed at the hour. She rested in the promise Christopher had given about her and her mother surviving until the Glorious Appearing, but that — she knew — was no guarantee that her mother might not live out her days imprisoned.

"Is everyone all right?" she said.

"Better than all right," Ree said. "Although I was not so sure when I arrived. I was warned to stay away from the underground shelter, because rumor had it that the GC had found them out and were planning a raid. The believers were busy packing and were going to sneak away in the night. They were praying the GC would raid them later — as is the custom — when they were supposed to be sleeping.

"But as the sun rose, they realized they heard very little noise from the street. Some ventured out and saw the damage from the sun. Everything is scorched, dried up, burned, melted, wasted. No one was on the street, though charred remains were scattered. The believers are protected, but the GC and the Carpathian loyalists cannot face the sun. The underground moved by the light of day, and if the GC come for them in the night, they will be disappointed. The believers did not move far away, but it is a better hiding place.

"Something they saw along the way would have been amusing, had it not been so sad. A small faction of GC had apparently tried to use fireproof suits and boots and helmets to protect themselves from the enormous heat. They lasted long enough to travel about a hundred yards; then they split up as their suits caught fire. Piles of burning material are dotted here and there in the streets."

"Will you hurry back, Ree? I miss you terribly."

"I miss you too, Ming, and I love you. This will allow me to leave during the daytime, so I should be back early."

"Be safe, love," she said.

Rayford sat on the edge of his bed, head in his hands, enveloped in the unmatched darkness provided by an underground shelter. Rayford was tired and knew he should get more sleep. But he would not sleep. This plague, perhaps unlike any leading to it, might provide unique opportunities for him and his team.

Finally the signal came, and Tsion was on the other end of the private messaging system. "Forgive me for not turning on the video," Rayford said, "but it's the middle of our night here."

"Quite all right, Captain. Let me ask, need this be a private conversation? I am in the tech center and others may overhear."

"No problem, Tsion. Is everyone all right there?"

"We are fine. We feel some extra warmth and some are fatigued, but we are apparently protected against the real effects of this plague."

"I know you're busy, but I need confirmation. Do you believe those of us with the mark of the seal of God are immune to the heat?"

"Yes."

"Do you see what this could mean for the Tribulation Force, Tsion? We could do what we wanted during the daylight hours. As long as we are hidden again by the time the heat of the day subsides and the GC venture out again, they would be powerless to interfere."

"I see. I would caution that God has never

been predictable with these things. We know the sequence, and we used to think that one plague began and ended before another started. But the curse on the oceans lasted well past when the same curse hit the lakes and rivers, and the oceans turned back not too long before this one hit. I would not want to see you some bright day when the curse ends. You would be most vulnerable."

"Point taken. I'd like to think this would last long enough to allow us some elbowroom. I've never seen the world in worse shape or more people in need of help."

"Oh, Rayford, the world is a spent cartridge. Even before God unleashed this curse, the globe was in the worst condition imaginable. It makes me wonder how the Lord can tarry until the end of the seven years. Really, what will be left? Poverty is rampant. Law and order are relics. Even Global Community loyalists have lost faith in their government and their Peacekeepers. The Morale Monitors are all on the take, it seems. The people who are to be out and about do not even dare venture into the streets without being armed.

"Cameron tells me he does not know one common citizen who does not own and carry a weapon. I hardly hear from countries where there are not marauding bands of thieves and rapists, not to mention vandals and terrorists. The best things we have out there are the 144,000 evangelists and the increase in angelic activity the Lord has so graciously allowed.

"Remember, Rayford, we are down to three kinds of people now: those of us with the mark of God, those who bear the mark of Antichrist, and the undecided. There are fewer and fewer of these, but they are the ones we must reach out to. They are suffering now, but oh, how they will suffer as the sun rises each day. Imagine the turmoil, the devastation. Power shortages, air conditioning overloads, breakdowns. And all this coming with half the population already gone.

"We are not far from anarchy, my friend. The GC does not care to crack down because they benefit. I am amazed there remain any loyal to Carpathia. Look what he has wrought."

"Dr. Ben-Judah, how does this square with your contention that these judgments are as much about God's mercy and compassion as they are about his wrath? The angel that announced the rivers and lakes turning to blood said it was to avenge the blood of the prophets."

"God is just and God is holy, Rayford, but

I do not believe he would send any more judgments on the world now if he weren't still jealous that some repent. No doubt some will. I know the majority will not, because of what the Scripture says about their blaspheming the name of God. Obviously, by now everyone knows these judgments are from God, yet many refuse to repent of their sins."

"I agree with you, Tsion. No one could possibly argue that God doesn't exist. There's overwhelming evidence of his presence and power — yet most still reject him. Why?"

"Captain Steele, that is the question of the ages. You remember the Old Testament story of when Moses grew up and refused to be called the son of Pharaoh's daughter, even though he could have? The Bible says he chose 'rather to suffer affliction with the people of God, than to enjoy the pleasures of sin for a season.'

"Well, these people certainly are not Moses. They will suffer torment and lose their souls, all to enjoy the pleasures of sin for a season — and what a short season. I applaud your thinking that this may be the time for the Tribulation Force to step up its efforts, to help struggling believers, to find the remaining undecided and help the evangelists and the angels bring them in before it is too late. I wish you Godspeed with whatever you decide."

Buck hurried to George Sebastian's underground quarters, where George's wife played on the floor with their child.

"I've got to get out and see this," Buck said.

"Got to be careful of radar," Sebastian said. "The GC would be astounded to see anybody in the air during the day."

"What do you recommend?"

"Chopper."

"You up for it, George?"

"You don't have to ask twice."

Buck had seen vapor appear above the water inlets on cool mornings, but he had never seen the Pacific emit steam as far as the eye could see. "Do you believe this?" he said.

"I'll believe anything now," George said.

Buck was reduced to silence as fires broke out all over what was left of San Diego. The closer it got to midday, the brighter the sky became. Houses and buildings no longer began smoking and smoldering and finally kindling. Now they shimmered and shook, windows bursting, roofs curling, then whole structures exploding and sending flames and sparks showering about.

George cruised back over the ocean, where Buck saw the sand change colors before creeping carpets of flame began dancing about. The waves brought the bubbling water in, and it hissed and boiled as it touched the blistering shore. Without warning, the entire ocean reached the boiling point and became a roiling cistern of giant bubbles, sending a fog of steam that blocked Buck's view of the sky and sun. The chopper was engulfed in white so pure and thick that Buck feared Sebastian would lose control.

"Totally on instruments now, friend," George said.

The helicopter bounced and shook in the soup as they *thwock thwock thwock*ed toward the shore. Sebastian was half a mile inland before they escaped the steam cloud and peered down on the burning grasses and neighborhoods.

"What's the boiling temperature of blood?" Buck asked.

"Not a clue," George said, but he immediately banked and headed toward the San Diego River.

"Whatever it is," Buck said, "we've reached it." He gawked at the huge crimson bubbles that formed and burst, emitting a fine spray that rose with the steam. "Agh!" he said, grimacing and holding his nose. "Let's get out of here."

The Tribulation Force was free to come and go, as long as they were careful to plan their travel into time zones that kept them in daylight as long as possible. The only relief for the Global Community forces and citizens with the mark of loyalty was to stay inside below ground level and invent ways to take the edge off the suffocating heat. Even then, hundreds of thousands died when their dwellings burned and fell in on them. Homes and buildings were largely allowed to burn themselves out, as firefighters could not venture out until well after dark.

Gardens, crops, grasses died. The polar ice caps melted faster than at any other time in history, and tsunamis threatened every port city. Shores and coastlines were buried under floods, and the dump of dead sea creatures washed miles onto land. Had it not been for people having moved inland to avoid the stench and bacteria in the first place, more lives would have been lost.

In the midst of such turmoil and grief, Rayford and Chloe worked harder than ever to rearrange their storehouses of goods and products traded through the International Commodity Co-op. Knowing their time was limited, they took advantage of everyone's obsession with finding shelter and relief from the sun. They strategized with Chang to move equipment and aircraft around and created new warehousing and distribution centers, preparing for the last year of existence on a wounded planet.

In New Babylon, Carpathia himself insisted the heat did not bother him. Chang overheard people in maintenance repeatedly ask whether he wanted draperies over the second story of his penthouse office. Even the ceiling was transparent. The sun was magnified through the glass and roasted his office for hours every day, making the entire rest of the floor uninhabitable. Krystall was relocated deep in the bowels under Building D and had to communicate with him via intercom all day. No meetings could be held in his conference room or office, but he spent most of the day there, ordering people about via telephone or intercom.

Executives on lower floors had their windows replaced, then taped and coated and even painted black, and most other employee offices were moved to the basement of the vast complex. Chang's department worked only at night, so he was often able to listen in as Nicolae hummed or sang softly as he worked in his office all day.

"I will sunbathe in the courtyard while the mortals eat," he told Krystall one day at noon. Chang snuck to a corner window where he scraped a hole in the coating. He was appalled to see the potentate strip to his trousers and undershirt and lie on a concrete bench, hands behind his head, soaking in the killer rays.

After an hour, as flames licked at the concrete, Carpathia seemed to think of something and pulled his phone from his pocket. Chang sprinted back to his quarters and listened in as Nicolae told Leon he was on his way to Fortunato's temporary underground shelter.

Later, Chang recorded Leon's call to Suhail.

"I'm telling you, the man is inhuman! He had been outside, sunbathing!"

"Leon . . ."

"It's true! He was so hot I could not stand within twenty feet of him! The soles of his shoes were smoking! I saw sparks in his hair, which was bleached white — even his eyebrows. His shirt collar and cuffs and tie had been singed as if the dry cleaner had over-ironed them, and the buttons on his suit and shirt had melted.

"The man is a god, impervious to pain. It's as if he prefers being outside in this!"

One day Chang overheard Carpathia call Technical Services. "I would like a telescope set up that would point directly at the sun at noonday."

"I can do that, Your Highness," a man said. "But of course I would have to do it after dark."

"And might it have recording capability?"

"Of course, sir. What would you like to record?"

"Whether the sun has grown and if bursts of flame from its surface would be visible."

The instrument was set up and calibrated that night, and Chang watched the next day as Carpathia hurried outside at noon. He actually peered at the sun through the lens for several minutes. An hour later the lens had melted, and the entire telescope stood warped and sagging in the heat.

The technician called Carpathia that evening to report that the recording disc had also melted.

"That is all right. I saw what I wanted to see."

"Sir?"

"That was a very nice piece of equipment. It provided me a crystal-clear image of the noonday sun, and indeed, I could see the flares dancing from the surface."

The techie laughed.

"You find that humorous?" Carpathia said.

"Well, you're joking, of course."

"I am not."

"Sir, forgive me, but your eyeball would be gone. In fact, your brain would have been fried."

"Do you realize to whom you are speaking?"

Chang was chilled at his tone.

"Yes, sir, Potentate," the techie said, his voice shaky.

"The sun, moon, and stars bow to me."

"Yes, sir."

"Understand?"

"Yes, sir."

"Do you doubt my account?"

"No, sir. Forgive me."

Seventeen Weeks Later

Chang was idly monitoring various levels and temperature records at his desk one evening when he realized that the third Bowl Judgment had been lifted. He called Figueroa. "You'll want to see this," he said.

Aurelio hurried from his office and stood

480

behind Chang. "Look at this reading."

" 'Boiling water overflowing the Chicago River,' " his boss read quietly. " 'Overheated and radiation contaminated.' Nothing new, is it?"

"You missed it, Chief."

"Tell me."

"It doesn't say blood. It says water."

Figueroa was trembling as he used Chang's phone to call Akbar. "Guess what I just discovered?" he said.

"The waterways will now heal themselves over time," Chang heard Suhail Akbar tell Carpathia the next day.

Maybe, Chang thought, *if there were decades left.*

It seemed to Chang that Carpathia was less concerned about water and heat because neither plague had affected him personally. What occupied most of his time was the failure, particularly in Israel, of his master plan for taking care of the Jewish "problem." In many other countries, the persecutions had had relative success. But of the 144,000 evangelists, those assigned to the Holy Land had had tremendous success seeing the undecided become believers. And then, for some reason, they had been able to evade detection. Just when

Carpathia and Akbar thought they had devised a sweep to rid the area of Messianic Jews, the sun plague had hit and the GC were incapacitated.

Now, though Carpathia rarely saw Suhail Akbar face-to-face during the day, they were constantly in touch. Chang was amazed at how much firepower was still available to Global Community forces after all they had lost and had wasted in many skirmishes with the protected Judah-ites.

The United African States threatened secession because of what Carpathia had done to their ruling elite, while a rebel group there was secretly scheming with the palace about taking over for the disenfranchised government.

"Suhail," Chang recorded one day from Carpathia's phone, "these plagues have always had their seasons. This one has to end sometime. And when it does, that may be the time for us to pull out the half of our munitions and equipment that we have in reserve. Would you estimate that the confidentiality level on that stockpile remains secure?"

"To the best of my knowledge, Excellency."

"When the sun curse lifts, Director, when you can stand being out in the light of day again, let us be ready to mount the most massive offensive in the history of mankind. I have not yet conceded even Petra, but I want the Jews wherever they are. I want them from Israel, particularly Jerusalem. And I will not be distracted or dissuaded by our whining friends in northern Africa. Suhail, if you have ever wanted to please me, ever wanted to impress me, ever wanted to make yourself indispensable to me, give yourself to this task. The planning, the strategy, the use of resources should make every other war strategist in history hang his head in shame. I want you to knock me out, Suhail, and I am telling you that resources — monetary and military — are limitless."

"Thank you, sir. I won't let you down."

"Did you get that, Suhail? Lim-it-less."

Six Years into the Tribulation

Chang arose at dawn, as usual, but he realized immediately that things had changed. He had not been vulnerable to the damage of the sun, but he had been aware of the difference in temperature and humidity. This morning, the air felt different.

He hurried to his computer and checked the weather. *Uh-oh. Show's over.* The temperature in New Babylon was normal.

Chang ate, showered, dressed, and hurried out. The palace was abuzz. Windows were open. People streamed in and out. He even saw smiles, though most of the depleted employee population was overworked, undernourished, and looked pale and sickly.

The brass announced that the noonday meal would be served picnic-style, outside. Little was accomplished that morning as everyone anticipated lunchtime. Then the mood was festive and the food plentiful. Many got a peek at Carpathia, striding purposefully about as if he had a new lease on life.

Chang hurried back to his quarters after work that day, eager to check on the rest of the world. The Tribulation Force had trimmed its sails and pulled in its cannons. They were back in hiding, picking their spots, strategizing for returning to an after-dark schedule.

Carpathia remained tireless and expected the same of others. He held another high-level meeting with the brass that had spent much of the day moving back to his floor. Even Viv Ivins was invited, and from what Chang could hear, all had been forgiven.

"For the first time in a long time," Nicolae

said, "we play on an even field. The water-ways are healing themselves, and we have rebuilding to do in the infrastructure. Let us work at getting all our loyal citizens back onto the same page with us. Director Akbar and I have some special surprises in store for dissidents on various levels. We are back in business, people. It is time to recoup our losses and start delivering a few."

The new mood lasted three days. Then the lights went out. Literally. Everything went dark. Not just the sun, but the moon also, the stars, streetlamps, electric lights, car lights. Anything anywhere that ever emitted light was now dark. No keypads on telephones, no flashlights, nothing irides-cent, nothing glow-in-the-dark. Emergency lights, exit signs, fire signs, alarm signs — everything. Pitch-black.

The cliché of not being able to see one's hand in front of one's face? Now true. It mattered not what time of day it was; people could see nothing. Not their clocks, watches, not even fire, matches, gas grills, electric grills. It was as if the light had done worse than go out; any vestige of it had been sucked from the universe.

People screamed in terror, finding this the worst nightmare of their lives — and they had many to choose from. They were blind — completely, utterly, totally, wholly unable to see anything but blackness twenty-four hours a day.

They felt their way around the palace; they pushed their way outdoors. They tried every light and every switch they could remember. They called out to each other to see if it was just them, or if everyone had the same problem. Find a candle! Rub two sticks together! Shuffle on the carpet and create static electricity. Do anything. Anything! Something to allow some vestige of a shadow, a hint, a sliver.

All to no avail.

Chang wanted to laugh. He wanted to howl from his gut. He wished he could tell everyone everywhere that once again God had meted out a curse, a judgment upon the earth that affected only those who bore the mark of the beast. Chang could see. It was different. He didn't see lights either. He simply saw everything in sepia tone, as if someone had turned down the wattage on a chandelier.

He saw whatever he needed to, including his computer and screen and watch and quarters. His food, his sink, his stove — everything. Best of all, he could tiptoe around the palace in his rubber-soled shoes, weaving between his coworkers as they felt their way along.

Within hours, though, something even stranger happened. People were not starving or dying of thirst. They were able to feel their way to food and drink. But they could not work. There was nothing to discuss, nothing to talk about but the cursed darkness. And for some reason, they also began to feel pain.

They itched and so they scratched. They ached and so they rubbed. They cried out and scratched and rubbed some more. For many the pain grew so intense that all they could do was bend down and feel the ground to make sure there was no hole or stairwell to fall into and then collapse in a heap, writhing, scratching, seeking relief.

The longer it went, the worse it got, and now people swore and cursed God and chewed their tongues. They crawled about the corridors, looking for weapons, pleading with friends or even strangers to kill them. Many killed themselves. The entire complex became an asylum of screams and moans and guttural wails, as these people became convinced that this, finally, was it — the end of the world.

But no such luck. Unless they had the wherewithal, the guts, to do themselves in, they merely suffered. Worse by the hour. Increasingly bad by the day. This went on and on and on. And in the middle of it, Chang came up with the most brilliant idea of his life.

If ever there was a perfect time for him to escape, it was now. He would contact Rayford or Mac, anyone willing and able and available to come and get him. It had to be that the rest of the Tribulation Force — in fact, all of the sealed and marked believers in the world — had the same benefit he did.

Someone would be able to fly a jet and land it right there in New Babylon, and GC personnel would have to run for cover, having no idea who could do such a thing in the utter darkness. As long as no one spoke, they could not be identified. The Force could commandeer planes and weapons, whatever they wanted.

If anyone accosted them or challenged them, what better advantage could the Trib Force have than that they could see? They would have the drop on everyone and everybody. With but a year to go until the Glorious Appearing, Chang thought, the good guys finally had even a better deal than they had when the daylight hours belonged solely to them.

Now, for as long as God tarried, for as long as he saw fit to keep the shades pulled down and the lights off, everything was in the believers' favor.

"God," Chang said, "just give me a couple more days of this."

Epilogue

Then the fifth angel poured out his bowl on the throne of the beast, and his kingdom became full of darkness; and they gnawed their tongues because of the pain. They blasphemed the God of heaven because of their pains and their sores, and did not repent of their deeds.

Revelation 16:10–11

About the Authors

Jerry B. Jenkins (www.jerryjenkins.com) is the writer of the Left Behind series. He owns the Jerry B. Jenkins Christian Writers Guild, an organization dedicated to mentoring aspiring authors. Former vice president for publishing for the Moody Bible Institute of Chicago, he also served many years as editor of *Moody* magazine and is now Moody's writer-at-large.

His writing has appeared in publications as varied as *Reader's Digest, Parade, Guideposts*, in-flight magazines, and dozens of other periodicals. Jenkins's biographies include books with Billy Graham, Hank Aaron, Bill Gaither, Luis Palau, Walter Payton, Orel Hershiser, and Nolan Ryan, among many others. His books appear regularly on the *New York Times, USA Today,*

Wall Street Journal, and *Publishers Weekly* best-seller lists.

Jerry is also the writer of the nationally syndicated sports story comic strip *Gil Thorp,* distributed to newspapers across the United States by Tribune Media Services.

Jerry and his wife, Dianna, live in Colorado and have three grown sons.

Dr. Tim LaHaye (www.timlahaye.com), who conceived the idea of fictionalizing an account of the Rapture and the Tribulation, is a noted author, minister, and nationally recognized speaker on Bible prophecy. Dr. LaHaye was chosen the "Most Influential Evangelical of the Last Twenty-Five Years" by the Institute for the Study of American Evangelicals at Wheaton College. He is the founder of both Tim LaHaye Ministries and The Pre-Trib Research Center.

He also recently cofounded the Tim LaHaye School of Prophecy at Liberty University. Presently Dr. LaHaye speaks at many of the major Bible prophecy conferences in the U.S. and Canada, where his current prophecy books are very popular.

Dr. LaHaye holds a doctor of ministry degree from Western Theological Seminary and a doctor of literature degree from Liberty University. For twenty-five years he pastored one of the nation's outstanding churches in San Diego, which grew to three locations. It was during that time that he founded two accredited Christian high schools, a Christian school system of ten schools, and Christian Heritage College.

Dr. LaHaye has written over forty books that have been published in more than thirty languages. He has written books on a wide variety of subjects, such as family life, temperaments, and Bible prophecy. His current fiction works, the Left Behind series, written with Jerry B. Jenkins, continue to appear on the best-seller lists of the Christian Booksellers Association, *Publishers Weekly*, *Wall Street Journal*, *USA Today*, and the *New York Times*.

He is the father of four grown children and grandfather of nine. Snow skiing, waterskiing, motorcycling, golfing, vacationing with family, and jogging are among his leisure activities.